SWIMMING BACKWARDS

Swimming Backwards

Jack Reardon

Evolutesix Publishing

Paperback ISBN: 978-1-913629-15-1

e-book ISBN: 978-1-913629-16-8

A CIP catalogue record will be available from the British Library.

Typeset using LaTeX (PDF) and pandoc (EPUB).

Cover design and illustrations by Nikyta Guleria.

For my wonderful children
Elizabeth and Patrick

INTRODUCTION

Joanna Turnus

I could have confessed to Alexander in the North End, Faneuil Hall, the Seaport District, or even Carson Beach, despite the cool, chilly night; but I chose the Old Post Inn, my grandfather's favorite, where he and I went once a week; our dinners lasting three or four hours, always talking, usually about me, about my struggles, my gender confusion, the latest boys of interest.

Of course my meeting ran late. I texted Alexander several times, but he wasn't answering. Perhaps he was stuck in traffic or forgot about our dinner or had a premonition about my confession and decided to skip out altogether? (And who would blame him if he did?)

I asked the maître d' to look for someone 6'3"; strong, adorable, with sparkling green eyes; a deep tan that would linger well into the winter, and soft, playful brown hair that most women would consider a tad too long, combed straight back, pillowed against his ears, loose strands sometimes taking a life of their own. She immediately replied that Alexander was indeed at the bar, nursing a beer. She complimented my choice in men, which would have thrilled any woman, but knowing how things were and how things might pan out, only increased my despair.

The Inn was just outside Boston, on the Old Post Road, which in colonial times connected Boston and New York. Inside, its cozy, oak-paneled walls were interspersed with tall, stained-glass windows, beautifully etched with colonial travelers: some tired and weary, some smiling, boastful of their travels; most too poor to stop, too embarrassed to glance inside; some sad, as if traveling to a funeral; others exuberant, anxious to celebrate a birthday, an anniversary, the birth of a child.

Alexander was stunning in a black, faintly pinstriped suit that showed off his broad, muscular shoulders. His beautiful green eyes sparkled as he handed me a dozen roses, hinting a smile at my lacy black dress, my shiny red nails, my diamond stud earrings. He wrapped his arm around me; my head softly on his shoulder—kissing my forehead, whispering that I looked absolutely beautiful.

I wanted this moment to last forever.

As the maître d' escorted us to our booth (the same booth that my grandfather and I sat in for our weekly dinners), complimenting how nice we looked together, I remembered my psychiatrist warning that people like me (his words) should never expect to get married or even have a long-term relationship with someone from the opposite sex, that we should look for happiness elsewhere.

I brushed away a tear, fearful that he was right.

I ordered champagne, wondering if any of the colonial travelers etched in glass were pretending to be someone else to please others, unsure and confused about their gender. But despite a little sadness and apprehension, I saw no doubt, despair, or ambiguity.

The waitress uncorked the champagne bottle, presenting it to Alexander. I watched her meticulously fill each glass, jealous of her confident femininity, jealous that every morning she'd choose something to wear, do her makeup, her hair, never thinking twice about being a woman; no questions asked.

For an appetizer, I ordered clams and linguine (my favorite dish as a little girl), even though it wasn't on the menu; while Alexander ordered the grilled beef medallions peppered with Gonzaga cheese. I also suggested the mushroom soup, the best around.

Alexander agreed, asking our waitress to bring it with the appetizers. He smiled at me, raising his glass. "To a nice dinner!"

We clinked glasses, small-talking about a predicted early frost, the Red Sox missing the playoffs, the upcoming Patriots game against the Jets. As Alexander talked about his work, and I mine, I sipped my champagne, imagining us walking in the rain, on the beach, my head softly on his shoulder.

The waitress delivered our appetizers.

Alexander sliced his bite-size medallions into even smaller bite-size medallions, praising the soup as the best he's ever had. I straightened my silverware, wondering his reaction to what I was about to say, wondering how quickly he would leave, wondering if I'd ever meet someone like him again.

I brushed away a tear, innocently feigning something in my eye.

"You OK?" Alexander asked.

I said I had to pee. Yes, I was nervous and yes, the champagne had made me lightheaded, but I really had to pee. Feeling nauseous, like I was pregnant—how could I be?— I excused myself. I rushed to the restroom, opened the stall and sat down. Alexander and I seemed to be getting back on track and if I confessed, I'd never see him again. But then again, why should I define myself by someone else, and who I'm with?

At the sink I let the water run cold, dabbing my forehead with a cool paper towel, surprised at how pretty and feminine I looked, surprised at how confident I appeared.

"This is the men's room," interrupted a stern masculine voice.

I lightly screamed, turning to find a young man, kind of cute, his baritone voice not matching his youthful appearance, silently inspecting every inch of my body, silently inquiring why I was in the men's room.

"This is the men's room? Oh my God! How embarrassing." I turned off the water, snatched a paper towel and dried my hands. "I'm so sorry. I felt nauseous and rushed in, not even looking."

The young man smiled at my feminine voice, relieved that I was a woman (at least superficially). But despite my breasts, my body curves, my lacy black dress, my pretty legs; despite my lip gloss, mascara, and shiny red nails, I'm sure he knew that something was dreadfully wrong.

"No problem," he said. "Can I get you something? An aspirin?"

Admiring his self-possession, I apologized and shuffled back to Alexander, back to the same booth where my grandfather and I ate dinner once a week; feeling like an escaped convict after years on the run, finally caught and forced to confess. For those of us who as Ovid said, 'Hover between the sexes,' we live our lives fearing that we'll be found out—before we're ready to confess—no matter how hard we cover up —not that we deceive or lie, but it's just too visceral—too overwhelming to confess all at once.

"You OK?" Alexander asked as I nestled into the booth.

"I guess I'm not used to the champagne." I dabbed my eyes with a napkin, imagining us walking in the rain, holding hands, my head softly on his shoulder. But a jarring inner voice warned that I must confess; a threatening, ominous, persistent voice warning that I couldn't keep putting this off. Indeed, I couldn't live this lie any longer. "Alexander, there's something I have to say."

The waitress asked for our order.

"We'll have the roasted spit for two," I blurted, without realizing that I could never eat all that boar, steak, venison, and sausage. "I'm sorry, Alexander, I should have asked you."

"That sounds perfect. I was just looking at that."

I pushed my barely eaten clams and linguini aside, wishing someone else would say what I had to say, wishing I could fast-forward to the end of my confession already said without hearing a word. I took a sip of champagne, imagining us walking in the rain, my head softly on his shoulder. "Alexander...I have a female *and* a male identity." I carefully avoided his contorted look of unsure superiority that something was wrong, that something was amiss. "Perhaps in an ideal world I could be both, affirming each, accepted by my husband for who I am. But that's not the world I live in." I was relieved to have finally mentioned 'it,' relieved that I had finally broached the subject with a 'normal' person; surprised at how easy the words formed. "It took me a long time to realize...and an even longer time to accept it...I didn't choose this—nobody in their right mind would."

"I don't understand. Separate identities? Female *and* male? What are you saying?"

"I'm glad you don't understand, Alexander. I'm glad that you never awoke in the middle of the night unsure and confused, never witnessed your friends commit suicide because they couldn't pretend to be someone else, never struggled to stay alive while your *own* family disparaged you and your so-called friends disowned you."

For a split second I thought I saw a modicum of understanding.

"Why didn't you say something when we first met?"

"I'm telling you now."

"So does this mean you dress as a man?"

"Sometimes."

"In public?"

"Yes."

"What exactly do you wear?"

Couples around us were smiling, talking, eating, celebrating. I felt like I was going to throw up. I slouched forward, fidgeting my knife; my voice subdued. "Everything... jackets, jeans... underwear... even a Fu Manchu."

"A Fu Manchu? Why?"

I shrugged.

"And *underwear* you said? Men's underwear?"

"Yes."

"Why?"

"I just do."

The waitress rearranged our glasses and utensils, making room for the roasted spit of boar, steak, venison, and sausage. I wanted to finish my confession and leave, for I realized that confessing was tiring and debilitating. "I've spent a lifetime trying to understand who I am and why I was born like this. I've spent a lifetime blaming others. I've spent a lifetime trying to survive. I'm transgender, Alexander. There—I said it. Now you can leave and find someone else, someone halfway normal." I dabbed at my plate, not sure if I was eating sausage, venison, steak, or boar.

"My world's black and white," Alexander said. "Male *and* female. I'm hard-wired to like a certain type of woman."

"I'm also hardwired, Alexander. Something I can't help, something I've no choice, something I have to accept and live with." I rose to leave, my eyes watering, avoiding his look of complacent contempt. "I hope you find someone normal, someone safe and secure, someone you can listen to, someone you can share your life with—you deserve that."

I bid Alexander good-bye, softly kissing his forehead, and hurriedly left.

I remembered my grandfather comforting me during our first dinner at the Old Post Inn, that someday I'd meet someone who will love me for who I am. Yeah right. I'm sure that stuff happens. Somewhere. Perhaps in the movies. I stopped at the register informing the maître d' that it wasn't the food, the service or the ambience, but that I had been feeling nauseous all day (anticipating my confession) and perhaps shouldn't have come for dinner. The maître d' offered to call a cab. I paid the bill, leaving a generous tip for the waitress, promising to return soon, thanking him, saying my car was in the parking lot. As I bid the maître d' goodnight, I noticed Alexander rising, straightening his jacket, brushing his hair back; the waitress talking, as if reprimanding, handing him the dozen roses, the stems wrapped in foil.

Outside in the chilly evening air, I hurriedly passed a young couple entering the Old Post Inn, exuberant, anxious to celebrate a birthday, an anniversary, the birth of a child; her head softly on his shoulder, his arm wrapped around her, whispering how beautiful she was.

BOOK ONE

Chapter 1

Joanna Turnus

My parents were happiest when my mother was pregnant with me, at least that's what my grandfather had said—except for one minor and short-lived argument early during her pregnancy; the major ones would come later: My mother wanted to name me Joseph Michael Turnus after my two deceased brothers, but my father adamantly objected—thank God. And I'm not giving anything away to say that they were never so happy again.

In anticipation of my birth (twenty-nine years ago this month) my parents had painted my bedroom blue and gold with a white trim, and stenciled Red Sox and Patriots' logos on the walls. They stocked my room with soldiers, footballs, baseballs, a horse rocker. On the walls, an autographed portrait of Carlton Fisk, photos of Knute Rockne, Ara Parseghian, and Joe Montana; an aerial view of Fenway Park.

It was a fun time for my parents, sharing their dreams for me. My father saw me in the family construction business, after college of course; while my mother insisted that her young husky (her nickname for me during her pregnancy) would play football, eventually getting a scholarship to Notre Dame, following her father's footsteps. While my father saw me as a tight end, maybe a defensive end, my mother saw me as a quarterback, just like her father. In their dreams there was plenty of room for compromise.

Sounds ideal, right? Off to a great start while still in my mother's womb?

Except that I was born a girl.

At the hospital, my parents had either forgotten, didn't want to, or were too upset to give me a middle name, but my grandfather insisted. He said that not having one would complicate my life (as if my complicated life could've been any more complicated). Adamant, he expected an argument with my father—after all, they had argued about everything else—but surprisingly my father quietly deferred, no doubt distracted by my mother's grief.

I was named Joanna Meredith Turnus.

Sometimes I wonder if I initially was a boy in my mother's womb, then somehow became a girl. Sometimes I wonder what it would've been like to be happy in my gender, never imagining anything but. Sometimes I wonder if my parents had done everything right—even if they had treated me like a girl from the beginning and were happy for me—if I still would have been screwed up. I mean, look at my best friend Rachel: from a happy and 'normal' family, but she always knew that something was wrong: that she was a woman trapped in a man's body.

If my mother had known that she was pregnant with a girl, she would have aborted me. I know that. I overheard her tell my aunt when I was eight years old, before I even knew what the word meant.

Chapter 2

Alexander Morgan

"Morgan!" Phil yelled. "Help the welder watch the sparks so the roof don't go up in flames, you goddamned son-of-a-bitch."

"After I finish," I said, centering a wickedly large concrete shard into my wheelbarrow; careful so it wouldn't tip.

"Now!"

Sure as hell, Phil had forgotten that Zella Asphalt was about to pave the bank's newly expanded parking lot, and that we—make that I—had to pick up all the accumulated bricks, bottles, cans, nails, spikes, sawed-off planks, concrete shards, pieces of strapping, and other crap; assuming, of course, that pick-up duty was ever on his schedule.

"Send Paul," I said, nudging my wheelbarrow forward to the left, compensating its slight tilt to the right. "Zella will be pissed as hell—"

"If you ain't on the roof in two minutes, you can start working for Zella."

I threw my hands up in disgust and headed toward the backside of the bank.

"Are you deaf?" Phil yelled, waving his arms up and down. "I just asked you to grab a goddamned extinguisher."

If I insisted that he had said no such thing, he would've ranted and raved even more, but I had better things to do than to bear witness, so I slipped away and did as asked.

To be honest I don't know where they got this bastard. Zachary should have started him on an easy one-story addition rather than this bank which was challenging even for a semi-competent supervisor: Originally two stories, the bank was expanding 200 feet in back and five floors up in the middle of a busy city block, while remaining open for business,

The extinguisher wasn't where it was supposed to be—but when is shit ever rightfully returned? I snatched a yellowed invoice from the desktop and wrote in bold, black letters:

Please return the extinguisher to where it friggin' belongs!

I double-underlined the sentence, highlighted it, then hooked the yellowed invoice on the wall above the desk, exactly where the extinguisher should have been.

At the back of the trailer, I plowed through square shovels, round shovels, picks, bars, rakes, water hoses, boots, water pumps, stepladders, sledgehammers, chipping hammers, buckets, paint cans, cement bags, asphalt shingles, compressor hoses—everything was heaped in an organized mess. Finally, I found an extinguisher wedged between a compactor and a flat-tired, one-armed wheelbarrow.

With a half-broken shingle, I scraped off the dirt and grime caked on the extinguisher from years of non-use. Then I monkeyed up the long aluminum ladder leaning against the bank's backside, shouldering the extinguisher like a Christmas tree. On the roof, I tapped the welder's shoulder, letting him know that his all-important spark-watcher was ready for duty.

He tipped up his Darth Vader mask just above his nose, bracing it with his index finger, barking instructions like I was an idiot, like I didn't know that the sun-baked insulation was dry as a bastard.

The welder slipped off his mask, rubbing its Plexiglas eye cover. "Give me a minute."

I meandered to the roof's front edge. A delicious aroma of baking bread knitted the stale smells of gasoline, lumber, fresh dirt, diesel, and sawdust.

"Don't disappear, I'll be—"

The welder was snuffed by the whining and screeching of screw guns—metal against metal—whirring from the newly-built partitions below. A constant, day-long, seductively irritating rhythm: One gun. A second. A third. A brief silence. Then the first, second, third.

Directly below the roof's edge, Nick, Abe, and Walter were framing a wooden form for the new sidewalk on what used to be a broad expanse of grass studded with tall oak trees: a peaceful buffer between the bank and the busy street traffic. But the bank president had ordered the trees cut down, claiming that they obstructed the view. Really? A traffic-clogged rotary fed by three, traffic-clogged streets, and that's a friggin' view?

The welder signaled that he was ready; ready to strengthen the steel beams across the old roof that would soon support the new floors. The steel skeleton of the upper addition was already in place.

I kicked a few pebbles over the roof's edge, then scooted back.

"Cut the shit!" I heard Nick yell above the whining and screeching.

At the roof's far end a crane operator was unloading steel beams. A huge American flag draped motionless from his cab. As fast as he unloaded, guys aligned and welded, showering sparks in every direction. I gave the crane operator the finger, like I did every morning, and he ignored me, like he did every morning. Sure, he makes triple my salary, but does that entitle him to be a prick?

Watching sparks ain't as easy as it seems. Yeah, you wait for nothing to happen, but no matter how hard you try, you can't help glance at the welding arc. It won't blind like you a friggin' eclipse, but even a casual glance hurts your eyes, and then you suffer like a bastard that night.

Below us was an old computer billing room. Everything flammable had long been removed; polyethylene covered the still-remaining metal filing cabinets. Guess who was chomping on an unlit cigar, looking up at me, armed with a water hose? Gary. I'm sure he had reserved this job days ago before anyone else even knew about it. Everyone says that he used to be a good laborer but that must have been years before his triple chin and large, protruding stomach.

Why have two guys standing around waiting for nothing to happen? I clicked on my cell phone to call Phil and was surprised as hell to find three text messages from Lisa, and it wasn't even eight o'clock.

I stepped back from the welder, away from view, reading the first message, "Derek's working overtime tonight. I'm making a nice dinner, why don't you stop by?" Then the second: "He won't be home until nine!!!" And the third: "Call Me!"

Maybe, just maybe, if she wasn't married to my brother. "Call you later," I texted. "I'm working." My message didn't send. I tried resending. Finally, after three tries.

Suddenly the insulation began crackling and sizzling. Shit! The welder whipped off his mask, stomping and swearing like a bastard. I sprayed the extinguisher, but nothing came out. Gary threw us the hose and the welder extinguished the flames, and not a second too soon.

"What the hell were you doing?" demanded the welder. "Why'd you bring an empty extinguisher? Get another one that works! And no more fuckin' screwups."

Chapter 3

Joanna Turnus

It was an unusually warm day during an unusually warm spring. Trees had budded early, the grass was green, and everyone was mowing their lawns. It was Thursday, March 30, 1997—my grandfather's birthday—that's how I remember. I was in the sixth grade.

At school I had made my grandfather a nice birthday card out of yellow construction paper, and with a red marker had sprawled in my neatest script,

> HAPPY BIRTHDAY TO THE BEST GRANDFATHER IN
> THE WHOLE WORLD!!

I had crossed out 'WORLD' and replaced it with 'UNIVERSE.' But instead of gluing a photograph, I drew a picture of us; I knew that he'd appreciate that more.

My parents said that I was his clone, never nicely of course, but I didn't realize how true it was until I began drawing. We both have small ears, which I never minded (as if I had a choice). We both have large foreheads, which looked good on my grandfather, especially with his receding hairline, but not on me, although he always said so just to assuage me. We both have wide, brown eyes. Mine are soft—that's what everyone says—but soft is just a nicer word for too big. My grandfather's eyes were definitely not soft, and if they were any bigger, you'd swear he was a frog.

Thank God I didn't have his beak nose. A large forehead is bad enough, but I couldn't imagine having a beak nose *and* a large forehead—I'd never go out in public. My nose is small, too small (if there's such a thing) but at least it matches my small ears (as if that matters). But I worry that my kids will have super big noses (things like that usually skip a generation), although my father has my grandfather's nose.

My grandfather always wore a full moustache to distract attention from his nose (at least that's what he said) but it didn't work: You saw the moustache you saw the nose.

I drew my mouth a little smaller. Everyone says I have my mother's wide-open mouth. My grandfather said it was from her constant laughing, at least before her two miscarriages. He also said that my mother was the prettiest girl in the senior class at Walpole High, when she met my father, who was, by the way, no slouch himself.

I didn't have the heart to draw all those deep lines across my grandfather's temple making him look older. However, I did draw him a little taller and me a little shorter, so that we were almost the same height. He always boasted being average height, although he was actually shorter than average; and I was taller than average—I still am—in fact, I was the tallest girl in sixth grade.

When school ended my grandfather was waiting for me. I was wearing olive-green shorts with an over-sized white shirt. (Just before school ended that afternoon, I had changed from long pants to shorts.) I wore shorts a lot, even in winter. I liked feeling the hair on my legs and how it made my legs look stronger, as if I had muscles.

He opened the passenger door of his new Silverado truck and extended his helping hand—a big step even for me. He smiled and I smiled back.

"Bubbling Brook just opened for the season," my grandfather said. "How does that sound?"

I nodded enthusiastically—he didn't even have to ask.

For a split second my grandfather had that perplexed stare, that contorted look of unsure superiority that something was wrong, that something was amiss; a conscripted stare that I would become so inured to from so many people that even now when I'm introduced to someone I look to the ground, the sky, anywhere but their eyes.

I carefully removed my grandfather's birthday card from my backpack. Noticing an edge was bent just a little, I smoothed it before handing it to him. "I made you something," I said, with a hint of apprehension.

He smiled. "It's absolutely beautiful." He blew his nose with a Kleenex.

I never knew anyone so emotional. Too bad none of that rubbed off on my father.

Bubbling Brook had already opened its seasonal shed behind the main restaurant; a pleasant area with lots of picnic tables and shady pine trees. We decided to eat there on such a warm, sunny afternoon.

The line to the shed was long, but it moved quickly; lots of mothers with their kids, talking and laughing. Two boys stood behind us with their mother. One, short with red hair, the other, my height with black hair. They didn't look related—the mother had blond hair—but she talked as if she was their mother. The tall boy was really cute, a little older than me, like in junior high school. I kept glancing at the back of the line pretending to look for someone just to sneak a peak.

A brook meandered between the tables, and sometimes if quiet enough—although it never was—you could hear it swooshing over deep sinkholes, like someone gargling mouthwash. I never heard it, but my grandfather swore he had, once when he took me here in my stroller.

On the other side of the brook, beyond the tables, were blueberry bushes. During the summer, Bubbling Brook makes the best blueberry ice cream, but you really have to like blueberries because it's like eating a blueberry pie. They also grow their own strawberries, raspberries, peaches, watermelons, and apples, making them into ice cream, but blueberry is their best. My grandfather agreed.

The ground was wet and mucky, suggesting that the brook had recently overflowed. The wonderful smell of grilled hamburgers made me hungry. My grandfather read my mind, as always. I nodded enthusiastically when he asked if I wanted a hamburger (if I had said no, he would've ordered one anyway).

When it was our turn to order my grandfather stepped to the

window. "Do you have any blueberry ice cream?"

I heard the boys laughing.

"No," replied the waitress. "We sold the last of the summer lot just yesterday with the warm weather, but we still have peach ice cream?"

"No. Give me two vanilla cones and two hamburgers: one with everything and one with just extra ketchup." My grandfather winked at me.

The boys continued laughing.

Curious, I was about to turn to see why, when I realized that they were laughing about me.

"That's disgusting," said one, loud enough for me to hear. "I'd never go out with someone like that."

I'm sure my grandfather heard, although out of the corner of my eye, he was still talking to the waitress.

"I bet she doesn't shave her armpits," said the other.

"Why would someone that pretty not shave her legs?" asked the mother. "Why would her mother allow it?"

"Disgusting," the boys said.

I knew my grandfather heard, although he pretended not. His smile disappeared, that's how I knew. I wished the brook was deeper and carried to the ocean. I imagined swimming backwards, my ears submerged, listening to the water, arms slicing, legs kicking, immersed in my hidden world.

My grandfather asked for extra napkins. He said something to the mother. I snuck behind him, hidden from view. He wrapped his arm around me, guiding me away. He was talking. I wasn't listening.

The engine was running. We were sitting in his truck. My grandfather had finished his ice cream and his hamburger. I must have finished mine because my hands were gooey, although I didn't remember eating.

"Sometimes boys say things they don't really mean," my grandfather said, handing me a napkin. "Sometimes they say things without thinking, especially when together. Sometimes they say things that they'd never say alone, just to please their friends. It's natural for boys to..."

I saw my mother peeking from behind our living room curtain, smiling, watching me play touch football with the neighborhood boys. I was the only girl ever asked to play, although everyone considered me a boy because I dressed like one and was better at every sport. My mother smiled when I scored a touchdown, smiled when I ran faster than anyone else, smiled when I made a nice block; so I ran faster, blocked harder, and scored more touchdowns. More touchdowns than anyone.

Chapter 4

Alexander Morgan

I tapped the welder's shoulder, asking if he wanted anything for coffee break. He propped up his mask just above his nose, bracing it with his forefinger. "Just a small coffee." He handed me a ten-dollar bill. "Black. And an English muffin. Buttered."

"Both sides?"

"Yes."

"Why don't you join us?"

"By the time I climb down, shut the machine off, coffee break will be over. Just bring it up you with you. And the change."

"Who's going to watch for sparks while I'm gone?"

The welder shook his head, lowering his mask.

I descended the ladder and headed to the front of the bank sidestepping two-by-fours, pipes, planks, bricks, spikes, and unannounced holes.

"Leaving for the day?" Nick dropped his hammer in his holster. "I wish I had your goddamn hours." Admiring his almost-finished wooden form for the concrete sidewalk, he fished deep in his overall pockets pulling out a pack of cigarettes.

"What you want for coffee?" I asked.

Nick lit a cigarette, then handed me a five-dollar bill. "Take a wild guess. And make sure there's four goddamn sugars. Yesterday—"

"I put them four in myself."

Nick removed his hard hat, brushing back his blond hair—what was left of it—then hurriedly put it back on, as if shying away from baldness. But there ain't nothing you can do about it. And I'm sorry, but blonde dudes shouldn't try to grow a beard. A moustache perhaps, even a friggin' Fu Manchu, but definitely not a beard.

Nick exhaled smoke in my face, "Make sure there's four god-damned sugars."

"One large coffee with four goddamned sugars." I typed his order into my cell phone—you have to with these bastards. "Hey, if they're out of *goddamned* sugars—they sell out pretty quickly—"

"Four goddamned sugars. And don't disappear after coffee. You have to put the wire down for the sidewalk."

Yeah, no shit.

This was damn fine weather. Just like an August day but without the humidity. If I didn't have my truck payment hanging over me, I'd call in sick and head to the beach, but with my luck some reporter would do a story on construction guys playing hooky and then everyone in the city of Boston would know that I wasn't sick.

"Well, well, well," Abe said. "Look who's coming to work." He stood at the other end of the wooden sidewalk form, steadying a plank lengthwise, while Walter braced it with a piece of strapping. Abe removed his thick black glasses, wiping them with a handkerchief before putting them back on. "Give us a hand."

"We're good," said Walter. A short man with a perfectly round face and an always-red left eye, like he was suffering a perpetual hangover. "The kid's goin' for coffee."

"First work he's done all day," said Abe.

Despite Walter being white and Abe black, at first glance you'd swear these two bastards were related: Same height, same stout build, same upturned, pudgy nose, but Abe's stomach is flat and his eye ain't always red, although sometimes it's hard to tell with them heavy glasses. Everyone says Abe is a youthful 59, but if you ask me, he looks exactly 59; whereas Walter's leathery, weather-beaten skin makes him look even older. So much for first glances.

Walter handed me a twenty-dollar bill, then said to Abe: "I'm buyin'."

"You win the lottery or something?" asked Abe.

"Haven't bought in a while."

"The friggin' understatement of the year." Abe picked up another plank, eyeballing it for straightness. "Make sure them both sides of my English muffin are buttered."

"You should be double-checkin' everyone's order," Walter said to me. "And take Gary's out of my twenty."

"I'll need a lot more that," I said, extending my hand.

"Just get him one coffee. And one goddammed muffin."

"English?"

"Bran," said Walter. "He's on a new diet."

"Every week he says he's on a new diet," snickered Abe.

"If he exercised every now and then," I said. "He wouldn't need no diet. So, he don't want his muffin slabbed with butter as usual?"

Walter frowned. "Didn't say, but yesterday he was full of piss and vinegar that his muffins were marmaladed."

"*Marmaladed?*" asked Abe.

"His words."

"Then *he* should've said something if he was so pissed."

"He did," Abe said. "He raised quite a stink during coffee. Don't you remember?"

"Dozin' off again?" Walter said. "You should be payin' attention during coffee break."

"Hey, the kid put in a good fifteen minutes of work and needed to rest."

Walter fondled a piece of strapping, then, at a forty-five-degree angle, nailed it to the plank. "Gary wants a small black coffee, no cream and *no* sugar. And one friggin' bran muffin. Get goin' kid, it's almost time for lunch."

"Where's Paul?" I asked, typing in Gary's order. Of course, everyone knew that he was still snapping off them rods sticking out from the newly poured foundation, and probably will for the rest of his life.

"He's found a new home," Walter said.

"If he'd listened to me, he'd be done by now," I said.

"Why would anyone listen to you?" asked Abe.

"He better not get too comfortable," added Walter. "When they start gradin' he might be backfilled along with the dirt."

"Not the worst thing to happen," I muttered.

"Get goin' kid, it's almost time for lunch."

At the rear of the bank, I straddled a six-foot mound of fresh black dirt, paralleling the newly poured foundation, carefully side-stepping the aluminum ladder. Not that I'm superstitious about shit, but I have enough bad luck without inviting more. Sure enough, Paul was leaning against the foundation clasping an open-ended pipe around a two-inch, exposed reinforcing rod, pushing it to the right, left, right, left, right, left.

"Hey Paul. Time for coffee."

"*Time for coffee!*" I repeated. "I ain't got all friggin' day."

The rod snapped, throwing Paul to the ground. He pushed himself up with his long, bony hands, wiping his forehead with his sweaty tee-shirt.

"Look at you: Sweating like a bastard and it ain't even nine o'clock. If you had torched them rods like I suggested, you'd be done by now."

"You know I get the *same* thing every day," Paul said, searching for his open-ended pipe.

"Because the one day I don't ask, you'd want something different and then I'd never hear the friggin' end of it—and besides I need money."

"Use the change you *still* owe me from yesterday."

"Change? You owe me twenty cents, you cheap bastard."

Paul handed me a sweaty five-dollar bill. "Twenty cents? And I'm the cheap bastard?"

"Twenty cents one day, forty cents another; it adds up."

Just then a large flatbed truck hauling a bulldozer and a grader rumbled into the bank's newly expanded parking lot.

"I thought they weren't grading until Friday?" Paul said.

"Friday? Who said that?"

"Phil."

"And you believed him?" I pointed to the far end of the foundation. "What about them two rods still sticking out?"

"Two rods? Big deal."

"*Big deal?* Why not leave them all in?"

"Don't tell me how to do my job." Paul shuffled down the dirt mound, giving me an over-the-shoulder the finger. Like I really gave a shit.

Chapter 5

Joanna Turnus

I wasn't going to mention underwear—after all it's no one's business—but since you'll soon find out, I'll tell you now so that at least you'll understand. I wear male boxers, except, of course, when I have to wear a dress or a skirt for work, then I wear male briefs, which aren't nearly as comfortable. When I get married next spring (yes, I will wear a wedding dress—a friend of mine is designing it) I will wear boxers. I've already informed my fiancé and he's fine with that—he's such a wonderful man.

I'm not blaming anyone, and I don't have an axe to grind. I'm also old enough to make my own decisions, but like every aspect of my life this decision was made for me, by others; more specifically, by my mother.

It was a cold December afternoon. I was nine years old. After snowing all morning, it abruptly stopped, giving way to a clear blue sky. It was the first snowfall of the season, and quite unexpected since the forecast had called for rain and then freezing rain. I wanted to play in the backyard but needed my winter clothes that were stored in the basement, which I hated, partly because of the ubiquitous smell of heating oil—so bitter you could taste it. (We still used an old-fashioned oil furnace, only because my father was supporting his friend's oil business.) And partly because of our furnace, and for good reason: Just one month earlier, I was in the basement getting something—I don't remember what—when I heard the furnace clicking. Curious, I noticed that the small, circular glass window on the furnace front was broken. I could see the dull orange flame in the center. Suddenly, the furnace made a low hammering noise, spitting out sparks; one brushed my leg, and another landed on the rug. I ran upstairs, screaming, scared that it was about to explode. Of course, my father didn't believe me, laughing that I had made the whole thing up. But I didn't lie (I've never lied to anyone; well actually only once—I had to, which I'll tell you in due time) and I know what I saw.

My winter clothes were thankfully shelved underneath the wooden staircase, easily retrievable without nearing the furnace. Nevertheless, I patiently waited until it shut off, then quietly descended, fearful that any noise might trigger it. I was putting my snowsuit on, leaning against a glass cabinet filled with never-used wedding dishes. I had one leg in when I noticed my mother methodically descending the stairs clutching a small package. Reaching the bottom, she tersely handed it to me. It was underwear. Boys' underwear. Her cold, empty eyes were far away in a distant past, a past which I knew nothing; a past which I'll never know.

I shoved the underwear back into my mother's chest. I'm not sure why; I had never before disobeyed her. Maybe because of how callously she presented it, like presenting the head of John the Baptist to Salome; maybe because she didn't even ask, presuming that I'd do whatever she wanted; maybe because even for me—only nine years old—I knew something was dreadfully wrong: Girls aren't supposed to wear boys' underwear and their mothers aren't supposed to make them.

She stumbled backwards, steadying herself on the railing. She brushed her short hair back, revealing streaks of grey. She glanced at me, then opening the door to the glass cabinet, placed the underwear on a shelf next to a stack of dusty dishes. Relieved, I assumed she had changed her mind. Then she took a dish, blew off the dust, methodically examining it. She raised it high as if offering a sacrifice, then let it crash to the floor. A small piece nicked my bare leg. I winced. She removed another dish; examined it, blowing off the dust. She held it high, then let it crash to the ground, shattering it. Another dish. Another. And another.

I screamed, fearing what she might do next. I took the underwear from the shelf and slowly removed my snow pants. I tried balancing myself but couldn't see through my watered eyes and fell. My mother closed the cabinet door, then snatched my panty just as I had slipped it off. I inched the underwear up my leg, shivering, crying, ashamed; wondering if any other mother in the world made her daughter wear boys' underwear.

Chapter 6

Alexander Morgan

"Where've you been?" demanded Walter.

Snapping turtles—all of them—crouched in a circle waiting to snap. You'd think they'd be relaxed, basking in the shade, waiting for their hand-delivered morning coffee.

"We thought you took the rest of the day off," Walter said. He was sitting on an overturned plastic bucket, underneath a lone, yellow-leaved oak tree.

"How can he take the rest of the day off when he ain't even worked the first part?" said Abe, squeezed next to Walter on a stack of old newspapers; his back against the water barrel.

"He's got a point, kid," Nick said to me, lighting a cigarette. He sat on a stack of two-by-fours, opposite Walter.

"Where's my coffee, kid?" Walter asked. "It's almost time for lunch."

"Did you get my hot water?" asked Gary, squished next to Abe.

"Hot water?" I said. "You didn't ask for no hot water."

"I most certainly did. I told Walter to—"

"You didn't mention nothing about no hot water," I said to Walter, who seemed to be busying himself with his coffee.

"I did kid, you wasn't listenin'."

I handed Gary his coffee, then showed everyone Gary's order from my cell phone, while reading Walter's words: "Gary wants a small black coffee, no cream and *no* sugar. And one friggin' bran muffin. Get goin' kid, it's almost time for lunch."

"Sounds like something you'd say," said Nick.

"Hot water?" Abe asked Gary.

"With my new diet I'm drinking nothing but tea."

"New diet?" asked Walter.

"It's a new week," I noted.

"All the tea in goddamned China won't help you lose a goddamned ounce," said Abe.

Gary, unwrapping his muffin, turned toward me: "I supposed you had both sides buttered?"

"I figured that with starting a *new* diet you'd only want one."

"See, the kid's always thinkin'," said Walter.

"It's called anticipation." I was sitting on the bare ground on Nick's left, against a stack of two-by-fours still wet with morning dew. Closing my eyes, I inhaled its sweet, apple cider perfume. The fifteen minutes for coffee break seemed like an eternity.

Nick tugged my shoulder. "You'll get worms sitting on the goddamned ground."

"Paul out sick again?" asked Gary.

"Jealous?" Abe asked.

"Well, well, well; speaking of the goddamned devil," Nick said, as Paul slumbered in, his tall skinny frame hunched like a camel.

"You're the slowest fuckin' rod-snapper I've ever seen," Abe said.

"My change?" Paul demanded, sitting on Nick's right.

"I'll get it after coffee."

"You should see him dab cement on them holes," Gary said. "Like he was Picasso or someone."

"You're jealous because you didn't get that job," Walter said.

"Christ, if he did," added Nick, "he'd ask Phil for a goddamned addition just to keep workin' on them goddamned holes."

Gary wiped his face with a handkerchief. "I thought about it, but with my back there ain't no way I could work like that for eight friggin' hours."

"Since when you ever worked eight friggin' hours?" Walter said. "Maybe if you did some work now and then you wouldn't have no back problems. I'm your age but you don't hear me complainin' about my friggin' back every wakin' hour."

"Hey Walter," Nick suggested. "Give Alex some newspapers to sit on."

"He can get his own."

Nick tugged my shoulder. "With Zella here, you'll have to move our trailers so they can start grading."

Walter cleared his throat, smiling; a smile that boasted of advanced, privileged knowledge. "Just this mornin' Zachary said this tree's stayin'."

"Talking to Zachary again?" Gary asked.

"In fact, this little section right here ain't bein' hot-topped at all. They're keepin' the tree and makin' a little oasis so the bank employees can eat their friggin' lunch outside."

"What about the rest of the parking lot?" I asked.

"From here to the bank, asphalt," Walter replied, beaming as if it was his own idea. "And from here to the back alley, grass."

"I was thinking—" said Paul.

"A fuckin' first," Nick said, a cigarette dangling from his lower lip, as if held tight by a groove. I tried that once, but sucked the cigarette into my mouth, practically singeing my tongue.

"I was thinking why no one's invented nothing for snapping them rods off. It wouldn't take much: take a six-inch, open-ended pipe, smooth it, paint it; then attach a compressor to the sucker, just like a chipping hammer."

"No one would buy it," Gary snorted. "Them open-ended pipes are a dime-a-dozen."

Walter balanced his half-eaten bran muffin on the rim of his coffee cup. Either his muscular hands were too big for his small body, or his body too small for his fast-moving hands as if they had a life of their own, as if they were pushing and pulling and coaxing the slow-forming words out of his mouth—and sometimes they would intimate a completely different line of thought before words could follow. "Ever since foundations have been poured, them rods have been taken out the same friggin' way. I did it, you're doin' it, and—"

"He's right," added Nick. "You can't sell nothin' no one wants to buy."

"It takes me two days to snap off them rods," Paul said.

"Only two hours with a friggin' torch," I noted.

"And my invention can do it in *one hour*," said Paul with newfound confidence. "Think of the savings."

I could tell Paul was itching to say something like, *'I'll be rich someday and then I'll show all you bastards.'* Every week he dreams up a new invention, but to be honest, they all suck. Like last week's retractable, pocket-sized cat's paw, especially made for women. Can you imagine! I've dated lots of women and I've yet to meet one who knew—or even wanted to know—how to use a cat's paw.

Walter blew his nose on a napkin. "So, what you call this friggin' invention of yours?"

He inspected the napkin as if searching for lost change, crumpled it, and tossed it in the water barrel.

Paul frowned.

"How can you invent something without first naming it?" I asked. "Anyone can *think* of shit to invent. No wonder all your ideas suck."

"How about the all-purpose snapper?" offered Gary.

Everyone laughed, except Paul, of course.

"How about a video?" I suggested. "Paul busting his skinny ass, manually snapping off each rod, taking all day just for one, then Gary snapping, not even breaking a sweat."

"We don't want it too realistic," said Abe.

"I'll call it *The Cabrini*."

"You don't name something after yourself, you dipshit," I said. "Call it what it does, so everyone knows what the hell it is."

Lisa texted me, "Hello???"

"It's that time," Walter said, rising from his bucket.

That's how he ends every break, like we're about to march off a cliff or something.

"Time for what?" I asked.

"What'd you think?" Nick flicked his cigarette butt at me.

"You can't sit on your ass all mornin'."

"Why don't you ask Zella to join us for afternoon coffee," Nick suggested.

Walter nodded. "Not a bad idea kid."

"They can get their own."

Walter took my arm. "Listen kid, you want people rememberin' you as the prick who never bought coffee? Asphalt guys remember shit like this: here just for a few days, then onto the next job, spreadin' news like friggin' wildfire." He tightened his grip. "If you want to get elected AFL-CIO president, you have to make people remember you."

"I'll vote for you just to get your ass out of here," Nick said, lighting a cigarette.

Walter removed a wad of bills from his wallet, handing me a twenty. "Every bastard you meet is a friggin' vote."

"Christ Almighty!" exclaimed Nick. "How'd you get so loaded?"

"So, doing shit jobs and scrounging everyone's coffee will get me elected?"

Walter waved me away. "Get goin' kid, it's almost time for lunch."

Chapter 7

Joanna Turnus

Our first vacation—if you want to call it that—was the summer before sixth grade. Even deciding *where* to go was a major ordeal. My mother insisted on North Falmouth—she had vacationed there as a teenager and craved the salt air, the morning fog, the seafood. My father adamantly objected, insisting on camping in the Green Mountains. I had no idea why, other than Vermont was the one place my mother didn't want to go. (My father hated the ocean, hated being near it, and hated being in it—at least that's what he had told me.)

I was surprised when they asked for my vote, surprised that for the first time they had asked my opinion about anything. Perhaps in a normal family I would have abstained rather than automatically offend one person, but ours was not a normal family. I sided with my mother.

We rented a cottage one block from the beach. It rained the first two days, relentless and torrential, with fierce winds blowing the rain sideways against the house, against the windows. A record-breaking tropical depression had stalled right over the Cape. Seventeen inches of rain in two days. Nothing worse than vacationing at the beach in the rain with your parents. Nothing to do but watch movies, sleep, read, play solitaire. Of course, it was sunny and warm in Vermont, as my father constantly reminded us; I don't know why he even stayed.

On the afternoon of the third day the rain had stopped, the sky brightened with broken patches of blue. Everyone went to the beach. Water had pooled on the road, on the rain-drenched lawns, but no one cared—the rain had finally stopped.

The salt air mixed with sweet-smelling seaweed intoxicated me.

Two distant fog horns alternated pitches: one low, one high. Dark thundery clouds lingered on the horizon. Boiling waves spat up broken lobster traps, logs, soda bottles, plastic bags, and oily-brown seaweed that glistened in the misty sunlight. I never knew the sea contained so much waste yet was so eager to give it up.

My father took off his shirt and handed it to my mother. As he dove into one wave then another, I wondered how a normal daughter in a normal family would feel watching her father battle the waves. Would she be scared? Would she scream? If a wave knocked him unconscious, submerging him, how would she react? What would she do?

My father treaded water, catching his breath. Beyond, about fifty feet or so, was an anchored raft tossed about by the heavy surf. He glanced at it, then at me. Through the mist-brightened sunlight, he had that same hateful look as he had that recent warm spring morning.

I was in our bathroom, the window open, readying myself for school; happy, giddy even, breathing deep the sweet perfume of the outside lilacs. I was in a girly mood. Such moods were becoming more frequent and more unpredictable (I didn't understand it then, but my "natural" hormones were slowly changing me into a woman, surreptitiously usurping my body) and would often, like a riptide, channel me far away. I never fought them—how could I when I didn't understand (then) what was happening?

I liked best weaving my hair slightly up and to the right, but of course I didn't have any barrettes, so I asked my mother, nicely, of course, to borrow some—the first time I had ever asked for any girly things. I mean, it wasn't like I was asking for mascara or lip gloss, just two stupid barrettes. Silly me thinking it was an OK question to ask, silly me for thinking it was a normal daughter-mother question.

I heard commotion on the stairs. I expected my mother, excited, rushing to help me. Did she finally realize that I was a girl, and was pleased that I finally wanted to dress like one? I hurried to the landing, my hair falling over my eyes; then tossing it back I was surprised to see my father charging the steps, alone. Did my mother faint or have a heart attack and he was rushing us to the hospital?

I swear he flew off the last two steps. Maybe he did. In that eternity-long, split-second before his hand hit my forehead with such ferocity that I stumbled backwards, I covered my face so I couldn't see his elongated disgust, his crazed, twisted revulsion. I don't remember what happened next, not that I blacked out (I don't think I did) but I was numb, so numb that even if he had lacerated my arms, I wouldn't have felt anything.

My father selected a large wave and body-surfed, perfectly extending his arms and legs. As the wave ebbed, he pushed himself up, peeling strips of oily-brown seaweed from his shoulders, basking in the attention. Just behind, a huge brown wave was rolling, churning, surging. My mother faintly smiled as the wave engulfed him, thrashing him in the brown surf before spitting him up on the beach like a wayward lobster trap. He laid face down, motionless. My mother watched as one man rolled him over and another gave him mouth-to-mouth forcing him to cough water.

We approached tepidly, trying to feign emotion—we had to: everyone was watching.

My father sat upright, gripping his chest. My mother tossed him his shirt, muttering about his stupidity. He stood up; wiping his face, he tilted his head, shaking water from his ears. He threw his shirt over his shoulder, glared at me, then staggered toward the cottage.

That night I couldn't sleep, harassed by my father's snoring. I don't remember leaving the cottage, or walking to the beach, or why I was wearing only one shoe, or if the water was calm, or warmer than the air, or if the wind had subsided, or if the surf was still rough. At the beach, I dove deep, skimming the sandy bottom; then surfacing, I flipped over, swimming backwards toward the raft, imagining being far away. The water caressed and soothed me, not caring if I was male or female, not noticing that my breasts were growing—changing me into someone I didn't want to become—that my body was curving, that I never wore makeup, that my hair was short, that I was the only girl in sixth grade without pierced ears; that deep down inside I wanted to be a boy.

I treaded water for a bit, catching my breath; then alligator-like, skimmed the surface towards the raft. I pulled myself up, washed away the seagull turds and sat down on the gristly surface. An enveloping peace infused me. I curled up and drifted asleep, seduced by the distant foghorns: one loud, one soft... one loud, one soft.

Chapter 8

Alexander Morgan

The next morning the drywall guys joined us for coffee, looking like vampires with their pasty-white skin. Paul was unusually talkative, chatting as if they were long-lost friends: "I was half-way up the ladder, when this big bastard demands that I come down immediately."

"You? On the ladder?" I asked. "Actually working?"

"A much-needed break." said Abe.

"He probably had no idea who you were, that you even worked here," added Nick, lighting a cigarette.

"Who'd you piss off now?" asked Gary. "The Carpenters' BA?"

"Our guys use more sophisticated tactics," Nick said, exhaling smoke in my face. "Like cutting your ladder in half with a Skil-Saw."

"He was from the mafia," Paul replied, "asking me to work for him."

"You?" I asked, joining the laughter. "In the mafia?"

"They must be really scraping the bottom of the barrel," said Abe.

"In a year I'd triple my salary," said Paul. "Although I'd have to start at the bottom."

"And end up at the bottom of the harbor," added Abe.

"At least you won't have to worry about no goddamned pension or health benefits," Nick said.

"It's the only goddamned job in the world where you can say no to your boss and get away with it," Abe said, pretending to talk into a phone: " 'Hey Vinny, I need you to take care of someone Tuesday.' 'Tuesday? No, sorry boss; I got plans.' 'Oh, OK. How about Wednesday?' 'My nephew's visiting and we're going to the ballgame.' 'Hmm. Thursday?' 'Sorry boss: in the morning I got a dentist appointment, then I'm playing golf if the weather's good.' 'Friday?' 'Yeah, Friday works.' "

"I should try that with Phil," I said, mimicking Abe. "Hey Alex, I need you to dig a trench this morning. Sorry boss, I got plans."

"So, how'd you say no and friggin' live to tell it?" Walter asked.

"I told him about my inventions, and that I'll be striking it rich."

I spat out my coffee, joining the laughter. "You actually said that?"

"That's almost as funny as Morgan wanting to be AFL-CIO president," Abe said, trying to contain his laughter. "Christ, I'll bet my last paycheck that five years from now you two clowns will still be here, slaving away like the rest us."

I rose, slurped what was left of my coffee and tossed the empty cup at Abe. "Five years from now I *will* be District president and five years later I *will* be ALF-CIO president. Then I'll make your sorry asses miserable."

"Five years from now we'll all be retired," said Abe, pointing to Walter and Gary.

"Then, I'll just have to make it in four." I headed toward the aluminum ladder, giving everyone an over-the-shoulder finger.

Chapter 9

Joanna Turnus

Sometimes I tried reading with my mother, wondering if her morning readings could ever calm me, perhaps even bring us closer. But she always read coldly, methodically, fogged in by an elusive serenity, fumbling her cross necklace, staring past me as if veiled, her face obscured—and in a way I wished it were, for at least she would have appeared more consoling and more humane.

One morning I asked my mother for readings for a confused and depressed eighth-grade girl—not confused over which lip gloss to wear, what skirt to wear with what blouse, what not to say to a boy she liked—but confused over her own identity, not knowing if she was a boy or a girl, not knowing who she was or who she was supposed to be, or even who she wanted to be. My mother exploded. I was used to my father hitting me but not my mother, although her cold, callous looks were far worse.

That was the last time I sat with her.

Chapter 10

Alexander Morgan

I jabbed the welder's shoulder, reminding him that it was almost lunchtime.

"It's only ten to," he said, waving me away.

He was done, clear as day, just pissing around the edges. I waited five more minutes, then tapped his shoulder goodbye. If he wanted to be a prick and work until precisely noon, then he'll have to find another spark watcher or slip off his mask and watch for sparks himself.

"I need you to get a compactor from the shop, you lazy son-of-a-bitch," Phil demanded as I was scampering down the ladder.

"In the middle of the day?"

I stood face-to-face, or more accurately, face-to-chest with him. Another reason why that bastard hates me, like it's my fault that I'm six-foot-three, like there's anything anyone can do about it. Some things in life you can't change, so just accept your God-given body and live with it. But even if Phil was my height, he'd still be a prick.

"Let me get this straight," I said, my anger escalating. "You want me to go to the shop, get a compactor, then drive all the way back? Why didn't you say something at the shop this morning? There's three of them there; I could've brought them *all* with me. It don't make sense to waste the whole afternoon stuck in traffic—what about the compactor in the trailer?"

"It's on another job." Phil's neck veins pulsated; the left side of his face was sunburned, like he had fallen asleep at the beach. "Ain't the word 'yes' even in your fuckin' vocabulary?" A tidal wave of hatred roiled his flat nose into his black pindrop eyes.

"Because you're asking me to do something totally ridiculous!" *I almost added 'as usual' but held back.* "So what do I say if I run into Zachary at the shop?"

"He knows."

"You talked to him?"

"I left a message. You'll be back by 2.30. Compact for an hour. That's more work than you've done all day."

"Why not rent one instead of paying me to run all over town? Fifteen minutes to the rental center and fifteen minutes back. I'll be back by 1.00."

Phil tilted his head to the left and his neck veins stopped pulsing, so at least I knew the bastard was thinking. He can't simultaneously think *and* talk. "They're all out."

"You called?"

"I just *said* they're all out."

"Fine." I waved my hands in disgust and headed to the front of the bank. "You want me to drive all over town, I'll drive all over town."

"Where you going?" demanded Phil, as I headed toward the front of the bank, hoping to grab lunch. "Your truck's in the opposite direction!"

"My contract allows thirty minutes for lunch."

"Your contract also allows you to be fired. Get going! You need to be back in less than two hours to make up for the time you'll be stuck in traffic—and don't forget to tie it down."

"Tie it down? It's a fuckin' compactor, not a leaf blower."

Just as I thought, that prick: Rental Resources had three available compactors. Either he's too stupid to assume I'd check, or he assumes that I'm too stupid to question his own stupidity. But I didn't care how much he ranted: if I ran into Zachary at the shop or anyone else for that matter, I'd be immediately fired, no questions asked, and deservedly so.

I reserved a compactor for 1:06, then drove west out of the city along the river, surprised at the low water level revealing huge boulders where before there was nothing but water. But with no rain since August, we're lucky there's still a friggin' river.

"Can't wait to see you!" Lisa texted me.

If I answered immediately, she would've assumed that I was thinking of her all morning, but if I didn't answer, she'd keep bugging the shit out of me.

Exactly fifteen minutes later I passed Rental Resources. Perfect. I continued west following the narrowing, twisting, turning river. Maple trees with reddened leaves dotted the riverbank. As the river took a sharp bend to the south, I came across a windowless, red-stuccoed restaurant right on the river's edge.

I snagged the last spot in the gravel parking lot, half-parking on the grass, surprised that a windowless restaurant on the river's edge would be so busy.

Above the restaurant's front door hung a huge wooden sign: *The Edge*. Really? They get a friggin' A for originality.

Another text from Lisa: "Can't wait to see you!"

I knew what she wanted, and she knew that I knew what she wanted but then again, I never said yes; I only didn't say no, which ain't the same thing as saying yes.

I opened the door to *The Edge*, texting Lisa, "Working, talk later."

"Do you have a reservation?" inquired the hostess. She wore a dark blue shirt with a black tie.

"No. I don't."

"Then you'll have to sit at the bar."

"Fine." I took the last spot at the long mahogany bar, next to a young woman and man, both around my age—about thirty or so, sharing a heaping dish of pulled pork and sweet potato fries.

Two more texts from Lisa. I shut my phone off.

"Can I get you something?" the bartender asked, pointing behind him to an impressive array of tap beers. Nineteen, I counted: not bad for a windowless restaurant on the river's edge. Tempting, but Zachary has zero tolerance for drinking on the job and just my luck he'd find out. It's amazing how some people think they're irreplaceable. Like Brett, who used to work with us, that is, until this one

Saturday when he had already made fishing plans, and then was told to work the weekend along with the rest of us bastards. But instead of morning coffee, he and another laborer opted for a local bar's two beers and a shot special. Guess who was walking by just as they were walking out? Nothing they could've done or said to save their asses.

"We just tapped the Oktoberfest yesterday," the bartender said, like there was any friggin' way of changing my mind.

I asked for a Diet Pepsi, no ice.

"House special," said the woman next to me, pointing to her plate. "Pulled pork and sweet potato fries."

Yeah, no shit.

Her long blond hair was streaked black. Either she originally had blond hair, then dyed it black, or had black hair then dyed it blond. But her eyebrows were black, so I assumed that was her original color. But if she took all that trouble, why not dye her eyebrows? Maybe she was blonde and dyed her hair black to convince everyone that it was originally blond? Or maybe her original hair was brown, and she just wanted to confuse the hell out of everyone?

"They give you way too much," she said, pushing the plate to the dude. She had a nose ring and her left eyebrow was pierced. She wore a loose-fitting tank-top, white with blue horizontal stripes. The dude's head was shaved, his muscular arms tattooed with fighting serpents, and his black T-shirt was a half-size too small.

The bartender delivered my Diet Pepsi. I drained it; glancing at the tap beers, before ordering another Diet Pepsi and the house special.

"Ask for corn bread," the woman suggested; "it's delicious. They add maple syrup and jalapenos making it really sweet and really hot."

"It's addicting," agreed the dude.

I ordered the cornbread.

"You work for the DFG?" the dude asked. He had three small hoops in his left ear.

"No," I snickered. "Why do you ask?"

"Upriver they're setting brush fires and you smell of smoke, so I assumed you're DFG."

I had forgotten the fire, and the dude was right: I smelled of smoke.

"Good wages and benefits," said the woman. "We can't get near them."

I looked at her, not sure what the hell she was talking about.

"The DFG," she explained.

The dude looked at her and she at him, then both at me. They whispered to each other extending their hands: "I'm Lily... And I'm Brian. We're organizers from the Teamsters."

We shook hands.

"Here for a month," Lily said. "Organizing cops."

"Cops? Really?"

"Why so surprised?" Brain asked.

"Cops are pretty conservative, at least the ones I know, and you don't—"

"Look conservative?"

"Organizing is about relationships," Lily said, "building trust and commitment."

"And trust is about honesty," added Brian. "Wearing a suit and tie wouldn't be honest, and people appreciate honesty more than anything else."

"Our message really resonates with cops," Lily said. "So, what do you do, Alexander?"

"Let me guess," Brian immediately answered. "President of the Young Republicans. Lives in Wellesley. Went to a private high school. Dating your high school girlfriend, also a Republican. Some friction between you two: she feels better qualified to be President and you know she's right, so you compensate by going to the gym."

"I live in Roslindale," I snorted. "I went to Roslindale High and I'm not dating anyone right now."

"So, I guess first impressions matter," Brian said with a smirk.

The bartender delivered my corn bread. I buttered all sides, crumbling the bread.

"You like a lot of butter?" Lily asked.

I grunted.

"So what do you do, Alexander?" Lily asked.

"I'm a laborer at General Construction."

"General?" They both said, glancing at each other.

"You've heard of it?"

"Ahh, yes." Lily answered in a sing-song voice.

Maybe they're Zachary's spies? But how could he have possibly known that I was here? Or maybe they're spying for Phil? But that moron wouldn't know a spy if he tripped over one.

The bartender delivered my lunch. I took a bite of pulled pork, explaining with my mouth half-full that we're headquartered in the Seaport district, with our shop in Milton.

"Seaport district?" Brian said, more of a statement than a question, glancing at Lily. "Must be doing well."

Lily dabbed away a smudge of ketchup on Brian's upper lip, then turning to me, said, "General's family held, right?"

"Yes. Zachary, the son, took over after his father unexpectedly passed away."

"I heard he's a prick," Brian said.

I had taken a bigger bite of pulled pork than expected, apologetically pointing to my full mouth. "Haven't met the bastard," I finally said.

"Really? The guy signs your paycheck, and you haven't met him?" Brian asked.

I swirled a sweet potato fry in ketchup.

"One reason I'm running for local union president... I think I have a good shot." I'm not sure why I said that; it just came out.

"So, no one's running against you?" Brian started to laugh but stopped when he noticed Lily wasn't.

"How do you know so much about General?" I asked.

Lily turned to me, leaning on her elbow. "It's no state secret: General's at the top of our list."

"General? We're non-union. We've always been."

"Why you think it's at the top of our list?" Brian asked. "The largest construction company in New England and still non-union?"

"We've received some complaints about management," added Lily.

"From us?" I finished my cornbread, swishing my knife in the still-warm butter.

"You're running for local president and you didn't know that?" Brian asked.

I shoved my plate away.

"Hey, ease up," Lily reprimanded Brian, apologetically rolling her eyes at me.

"Looks like we will be paying General a visit," Brian said. "Soon."

"Don't mention my name," I said.

"Just what like I," Brian mocked; "A man of conviction."

If Lily wasn't sitting between us, I would've smacked that arrogant cocksucker. I'm sure that's why the Teamsters sent her along: to prevent his ass from being kicked whenever he opened his mouth.

Brain looked at his watch, rising with Lily. "We don't want to be late."

Lily handed me her business card. "You have a number we can reach you?"

I scribbled my number on a napkin and handed it to her. Not sure why, I just did.

"You'll need a business card if you're running for office," Lily said.

"Yeah right."

"We'll be in touch." Lily smiled; a smile that lingered long after she left.

Chapter 11

Joanna Turnus

One day in sixth grade science class we learned about sedimentary, igneous, and metamorphic rocks. Due to the Earth's inner heat and pressure, my teacher explained, sedimentary or igneous rocks could, under the right conditions, metamorphize into something else. While my friends dutifully took notes, feigning interest, I realized that the same thing was happening to me, that I was metamorphosing into something else, that my body was changing against my will. But was I a girl changing into a boy, or a boy changing into a girl? Or into both at once? Or into something completely different?

Later that afternoon at the school library, I looked up everything about metamorphosis, eventually stumbling upon Ovid's *Metamorphoses*. The librarian recommended something else, claiming that a sixth-grade girl would never understand it. But I insisted, asking why the book was even at the library if a sixth-grade girl could not understand it.

It was one of many books that I would read, not to escape (as my father callously insisted) but because I was terribly alone when I wasn't reading, terribly alone at school, in my house, in my room, terribly confused about who I was, about who I was becoming, about who I was supposed to be, terribly confused about why this was happening to me and no one else.

In Ovid's day, the gods monitored your every move and if you stepped out of line—whammo, you were changed into a bird or a tree, but they also listened and answered your prayers. Of course I took Ovid literally: that gods actually cared, that they heard your anguish, your cries, your pleas, and intervened; but as I got older, I realized that we make our own gods, that they are within us, that only *we* have the power to change. But this understanding came later, after several suicide attempts, and well—I'm getting ahead of my story.

I especially identified with Ovid's Iphis, a thirteen-year-old girl living as a boy; in fact, I had read this story so many times that I thought I was Iphis.

When Ligdus (the soon-to-be father of Iphis) had learned that his wife was pregnant, he prayed for a male child, warning his wife that if the child was born a girl, she must be put to death—as if the mother could control her child's gender (although I'm sure he assumed his wife would somehow heed his warning). The infant, still in the womb, hearing this crap, became screwed up before she was born. I know. The same had happened to me.

A goddess instructed Telethusa (the mother) that if the child was born a girl, she must deceive her husband and raise her as a boy. Of course, Iphis was born a girl and of course to appease the father, she was raised a boy. Then at thirteen, the father arranged a marriage for Iphis to the most beautiful girl. Of course.

Iphis lamented, "How I wish I had never been born."

How many times have I cried the same words?

Of course, the deceit couldn't continue and of course mother and daughter wouldn't challenge the father's wishes and of course the beautiful girl had no knowledge that the boy she was marrying was actually a girl. After interminable postponements, mother and daughter begged the goddess to intervene. She finally obliged, changing Iphis into a boy, making everyone happy. Of course.

But didn't Ovid send the wrong message? That a child is only instrumental to her parents' wishes? Wouldn't it had been better for Iphis, if the father, learning that the child was actually a girl, immediately put her to death as promised? Isn't physical death preferable to mental and psychological anguish? If quality of life is measured by one's cumulative happiness or misery, perhaps the child should have been put to death? And if the gods really were gods, why didn't they castrate the father, before he could do any damage?

Like Iphis, I begged to be changed into a boy. So many nights I cried myself to sleep, hoping that when I awoke, I would be a boy, but the gods didn't listen, even though my cries were just as real and just as visceral as those of Iphis.

Perhaps one book that I shouldn't have read, especially in the seventh grade when I first began having suicidal thoughts, was *The Sorrows of Young Werther*, a story about this guy who becomes distraught over not winning the beautiful girl (Lott), and methodically plans his suicide—a conscious and deliberate act no different than planning a wedding.

I hated Lott's arrogant self-confidence, clamoring for an author who "shows me my own world, conditions such as I live in myself with a story that can engage my interest and heart as much as my own domestic life does, which is certainly no paradise but is still on the whole a source of inexpressible happiness."

Inexpressible happiness? With guys fighting over her? Are you kidding?

But I also envied Lott wanting "to sit in some corner on a Sunday and share with my whole heart in Miss Jenny's happiness and sorrows." And then to be entertained by another fictional character informing her life's banality so that she can smile and feel satisfied, smugly congratulating herself and her boyfriend that she understands the world.

How would have Lott treated me if we had met? I pictured her in her kitchen with her boyfriend cursing me for challenging God's will, for disturbing her peacefully banal Sunday afternoon, for not accepting my God-given gender like everyone else. I felt her wrath, her ruthlessness, all in the name of God.

Chapter 12

Alexander Morgan

I dillydallied back to the bank, stopping along the river, checking my watch, determined to return exactly at two-thirty: thirty minutes ahead of schedule, but deliberately missing afternoon coffee so I wouldn't have to explain where the hell I was and where the hell I was supposed to have gone.

I parked my truck in my usual spot next to the dumpster behind the two trailers, unhitched my tailgate, laid two planks diagonally to the ground and dragged the hundred-pound compactor down—you have to, since if you start the sucker on a decline, it might unexpectedly swerve, taking you with it.

"Back so early?" Phil barked, racing from his trailer.

I was halfway down the planks and couldn't have stopped even if I wanted. On the ground, I tossed the planks into my flatbed and slammed the tailgate.

"There ain't no way in hell you could've gone to the shop and back," Phil said, gagging me with his stale breath.

I summoned all my strength not to smack him, but one day I will, and everyone will thank me. "Christ all-mighty: You asked me to get a compactor; I did. You asked me to bring it back this fuckin' afternoon; I did. You asked me to return by two-fucking-thirty and it's exactly two-fucking-thirty. So why are you so fuckin' pissed?"

He stepped back and in a slightly calmer voice told me to start compacting on the far side of the bank, where they had just removed two tall, graceful oak trees—a peaceful buffer between the bank and the lone house in this commercial zone. Yeah, I know Massachusetts zoning laws are crazy, but I never understood why this all-wood house was ever built: a sore thumb in a neighborhood of blood-red, brick commercial buildings.

"They were just here yesterday?"

"Christ if you spent some time actually working, you'd know what was going on."

"Just yesterday you said them two trees were staying, so what happened between today and yesterday?"

"The bank wants to add a side driveway from the street to the alley."

"What about the friggin' house?"

"The bank's suing the residents to leave."

Before I could ask about the state-of-the-art tree fort that I had built for Alex, the eight-year-old kid living in the house with his brothers, mother, and a shit-load of relatives—and yeah his name is Alex; he couldn't believe that someone as important as me—his words—had the same name, although everyone else, even his mother calls him A-hole—with asphalt shingles, carpeting, toilet seat, and even an Anderson window, Phil had retreated inside to the bank.

The one-hundred-pound compactor looks like a lawn mower, and once started, its weight does the work, so you only have to push and turn the sucker. Compacting is the only job where you can go around in circles, yet everyone thinks you're working. I could compact all afternoon, and no one would give a shit, although you do have to pay attention. Like this one time I sank the compactor in a foot of muck and needed the backhoe to extricate it; another time I hit a boulder and it ricocheted off my foot, knocking me backwards.

Alex suddenly raced out of his house clutching a backpack. His rolled-up sleeve revealed an American flag tattoo, with two cobra snakes intertwined into a mast.

I shut the compactor off. "Is that a tattoo?"

"Yep."

"A wash-off, right?"

"Nope."

"You got a real tattoo? Why?"

He took out a small scooper from his backpack and started digging.

"You can use one of our shovels," I said. "I'm sure Phil won't mind."

"Why'd you let them cut down the fort?"

"I had nothing to do with it. So, is that why you got a tattoo?"

He continued digging.

"If God wanted you tattooed," I said, "you would've been born with one."

"If God *didn't* want me to have no tattoos, he wouldn't have invented tattoo parlors."

Wise-ass.

"So why didn't you get a fake one?" I asked.

Alex dumped a small plastic bag filled with seeds into the hole. "Fakes run. Everyone knows that." He uncapped a water bottle from his backpack, drenching the seeds with a brown, syrupy liquid.

"What's that?"

"It'll make the tree grow a million miles tall."

"Hmmmm. Not with these zoning laws. Maybe a hundred thousand miles, but certainly not a million."

"Huh?"

"They'll be hot-topping later this week."

Alex dug deeper, furiously covering the seeds with dirt. His mother raced out of the house yelling at him in Spanish and then at me, shaking her fist. He retrieved his scooper and scurried home. His mother slammed the door behind him.

Why would anyone want to tattoo themselves? And why would his mother allow it?

"Loafing again?" Phil yelled. "Just once I'd like to see you actually working."

And just once I'd like to see you actually supervising. "I'm getting a prick and shovel from the trailer," I said, grinning at my accidental slip-up.

"So staring at the sky will get the job done? And if I see you once more praying to fuckin' Buddha—." Phil scurried like a weasel back to the bank. But he'll be back; you can count on it.

Back compacting, someone jerked my shoulder from behind. Expecting Phil, pissed that I was going too slow or too fast, or too much in a circle or not enough in a straight line, I was surprised to see Paul, who never leaves his job, except for coffee and lunch—although maybe he should: it might give him an idea how slow he really is.

"No need to be compacting with all them heavy trucks," Paul said, "just a waste of time."

"The trucks can't get close to the foundation, you dipshit; that's where it's most needed."

"Walter wants to see you."

"He knows where I am."

"Now he said."

"Why?"

"How the hell do I know?"

I shut the compactor off and headed toward the front of the bank, wondering why Walter wanted to see me half an hour before quitting time and why it couldn't wait until four o'clock.

"You really went back to the shop?" Walter half-smiled when he saw me. "I would've rented a compactor from Rental Resources and signed Paul's name."

OK, so how did he find out so quickly?

"Relax kid, your secret's safe with me. But next time stand up to Phil; he thinks he can walk right over you." Walter took my arm, clearing his throat. I instinctively stepped back, not wanting a long-winded speech, especially with only half an hour left until quitting time. "Phil's first week here, I was layin' bricks for this here back wall. I stopped to wipe my brow just for a second, and he's in my face barkin' that I was slower than whale shit."

"Whale shit?"

"I climbed down from the stagin', sayin' if you've a problem with how I lay bricks, let's go straight to Zachary's office.' He stood there stone silent. I picked up my tools and he ain't said boo to me since." Walter handed me his trowel and scraper. "Clean them off and wash them tubs out good; I don't want cement stuck in 'em in the mornin'.

And throw one of 'em in my truck. I'm workin' on my patio tonight—want to help, kid? You're always needin' cash."

"Tonight?" I suddenly remembered Lisa. "No, I can't. Not tonight." I started toward my compactor, then returned. "You need to talk to Zachary about Phil. Before an accident happens. He'll listen to you—you're the *only* one he'll listen to—you worked with his old man, and Jesus, you don't have to make nothing up."

Walter laughed. "How you think Phil got this friggin' job?"

"So he keeps screwing up until there's a major accident?"

Walter frowned, as if remembering something. "Ok, kid, if you want. I'll talk to him."

I washed out his cement tubs, cleaned his tools, and organized his tool chest—the most disorganized mess I had ever seen. "Do you think them beams are going up too fast?" I asked when finished.

"What?"

"Them steel beams? You think they're going up too fast?"

"No. Not at all."

I was too tired to argue, especially with only fifteen minutes left, so I said goodbye, hurriedly returned to my compactor, then guided it toward my truck, hoping to make it by 4.00 but the friggin' compactor has only one speed—too friggin' slow.

I arrived with two minutes to spare, opened my tailgate, laid the planks diagonally to the ground and dragged the sucker up from behind. It's a lot easier dragging it up than down. I slammed shut the tailgate, and climbed into my brand-new, black Silverado.

It was four o'clock. I closed my eyes and breathed deep. Done for the day. Finally.

Chapter 13

Joanna Turnus

Were my friends really happy or was their happiness, like mine, a façade? I would often search their faces for frustration, questioning, annoyance, aggravation, a wrinkled forehead, an upturned mouth, an angry eye—anything suggesting that something wasn't right, anything suggesting that they were confused just like me. But nothing. Never. Not even a trace.

Once I had asked a friend if she ever wanted to wear boys' clothes, to cut her hair short—to be a boy. I might as well had asked if she wanted to go to Mars for lunch. I thought I had noticed a confused look, a gestating anger, but she looked at me like I was a confessed axe murderer. It was then that I realized I was different.

Why did God select me to participate in his evil experiment? Wouldn't it had been more equitable to designate every family's first-born, or perhaps one person from every neighborhood, or every city, or every state, as *gender-confused*, rather than randomly select me? (Maybe in a former life I had sinned against God and he was now exacting his revenge?) I mean God made both genders but if he really wanted us to be both he would have made it palatable and more tolerable so that others—and especially ourselves—could accept it.

Why did God make me an aberration, a weirdo; my prison-body trapping and suffocating me, announcing to the world that I'm a girl, that I'm expected to wear girl clothes and do girly things? It would've been easier if I was also attracted to girls but as my body was changing all I could think about was boys, but what boy would ever be attracted to a girl who also wanted to be a boy?

My friends at school relished their changing bodies with excited apprehension, envying those who had progressed the most, and chastising those who had progressed least. That's all we talked about, when, of course, we weren't talking about boys. My friends (and everyone I knew, for that matter) accepted their gender, although looking back, I don't think 'accept' was the right word, since that implied a choice and, at least as far as I knew, no one ever gave it any thought.

Outwardly I shared their excitement but inside I was becoming more depressed and more alone. My prison-body announced to the world that I was a girl changing into a woman, but the inner me wanted something completely different and actively rejected all the girly things I was obligated to do. I felt like a convicted felon receiving a life sentence with no possibility of escape or parole. The only interest shared by my prison-body and the inner me was liking boys—that's all I could think about.

My mother had planted a faulty compass inside me that I couldn't extirpate or even deny. It was there, every day, so that no matter what girly things I was forced to do to my body, no matter how much I liked boys, I was on course to be one myself.

Chapter 14

Alexander Morgan

At two minutes past four, my phone rang. I assumed it was Walter reaming me out for forgetting to put something away or for putting something away in the wrong spot. But it was Phil. Fuck him. This was my time. I shifted into reverse and backing up I heard a loud bang, like I hit a wall or something, but there was nothing there.

Suddenly Phil thrust his head into my window, scaring the shit out of me, with only my seatbelt preventing my head from going through the roof of my cab. "Why didn't you answer the phone, you goddamned son-of-bitch?" His foul breath reeked of stale coffee.

Would you, knowing who it was? "It's recharging."

"I need you to stop at Hudson Brothers for a half pallet of brick, you goddamned son-of-a-bitch."

"I'll get it first thing in the morning."

Phil thrust his face even closer, his neck veins pulsating, displaying coffee-stained teeth and a capped front tooth. "We *need* it first thing in the morning."

I was tempted to raise the window lever right then and there and chop his head off and be done with him. A quite convincing accident: I could say that his finger got wrapped up in my shoulder strap, and everything happened so quickly that neither of us could react in time. Who wouldn't believe me?

Phil scribbled something on an index card, then tossed it to me, "Half a pallet of blood-red brick, you goddamned, lazy son-of-a-bitch. Do you think you can handle that?"

I was about to say no—and would've otherwise—that I would get it first thing in the morning, that I had a basketball game or something, but thinking for a minute, I realized that Hudson Brothers was only ten minutes out of my way and a ready-made excuse for not arriving too early at Lisa's. I slowly released my fingers from the window lever but was not about to let him off so easy. "This is my time, you know."

"If you don't get going, you'll have plenty of time on your hands."

"I have a dentist appointment. Right after work. That's when I schedule such things."

"Reschedule it."

"I just did." I squealed onto the road, like a high school kid roaring out of the school parking lot. Cars honked. I gave them the finger, crumpled Phil's index card and tossed it out the window.

Lisa was texting me, "Can't wait to see you! Everything's ready!"

Stuck in the usual stop-and-go mess on Route 128, my mind drifted to first meeting Lisa, or perhaps more accurately, when Derek and I had first met Lisa. We were returning from a Canadian fishing trip—my first and last trip with that bastard—when an hour or so into New Hampshire, I suggested stopping for lunch, but Derek wanted to keep driving until at least Manchester, and maybe even Nashua. But since it was my truck, and I was starving I pulled into the first decent-looking restaurant: A turkey farm restaurant just south of Center Harbor on a large lake. The restaurant was literally right on the water with a shitload of expensive-looking boats all tied up to a shitload of docks.

Lisa waited on us. I thought she was absolutely beautiful, but then again, after spending four days with Derek in the Canadian woods, I would've said that about anyone. But she *was* beautiful and still is: Pesky, with lively blond hair that bounced to her shoulders and musical blue eyes that seemed to widen as she talked.

If I live to be 100—highly unlikely at the rate I'm going—I'll never understand why Lisa was so infatuated with Derek. No looks, no money, and he's an asshole. And I'm not just saying that because he's my brother—ask anyone. Perhaps if Lisa was using Derek to get to me, I would have understood. Perhaps if she was any taller—she's barely 5'2" on a good day—I would've been more aggressive, but I'm hard-wired to like really tall women, I guess like some guys are hard-wired to like blonds or brunettes or women with freckles or dimples or long hair or short hair or big boobs—none of that really matters—well, maybe just the last. Maybe she thought I was just another good-looking guy looking for sex, which I was, but that's beside the point.

Then the next day she calls Derek inviting herself to visit. They were married exactly one year later. I still don't get it. Go figure.

At Hudson Brothers the line stretched a quarter mile or so out to the friggin' service road. I waited fifteen minutes without budging an inch. Although I didn't want to arrive too early at Lisa's, I also didn't want to spend the entire night waiting in line at Hudson Brothers. Then, just ahead, I spotted what looked like a side-entrance with no line. Perfect. As I pulled ahead, truck drivers honked, giving me the finger, assuming I was cutting the line. Fuck them.

Pallets of bricks—every type and color—were stacked twelve-foot high on either side, but there was no traditional red? Perhaps they were sold out? Or perhaps they had reserved a special place for the most popular brick?

Yikes! What I thought was a road quickly became a narrowing fork-lift path, wedging my truck between pallets. I backed up, knocked one pallet over; then pulling forward, knocked over another, scattering bricks everywhere.

A forklift approached from behind, the driver laughing like a bastard. "Can't even keep your pecker in your pocket!"

A tall, thin man, balding, with a heavy grey moustache, ran from the office. "What the hell's going on?" he asked, loosening his tie and rolling up the sleeves of his white button-down shirt.

The forklift driver, trying to compose himself: "Mr. Hudson...Mr. Hudson...this peckerhead...this peckerhead—"

"I thought *this* was the entrance," I confessed, immediately realizing that I sounded like an idiot.

"*You thought this was the entrance!*" Mr. Hudson tried to approach but loose bricks were everywhere. "How can anyone be so stupid? Who do you work for?"

"General," answered the driver. "I've seen this clown before."

"Your name?" Mr. Hudson asked, holding pen and paper.

"Cabrini. Paul Cabrini."

"Clean up this mess," Mr. Hudson ordered the forklift driver. "Charge your time and the bricks to General. Then get this idiot out of here. If he ever comes in again, run him over!"

Chapter 15

Joanna Turnus

During our North Falmouth vacation—five dreary days that seemed like an eternity—I plucked *The Godfather* from a small, built-in bookcase; the book was sandwiched between *A History of Shipwrecks off Nova Scotia*, and *A Guidebook to Southern New England Birds*—it was either that or play solitaire with my parents. I was intrigued by the author name's—Mario Puzo, thinking that Joanna Meredith Puzo would be wickedly cool. I noticed that one of the book's characters was named Michael, just like my older brother. (Even though he had died at birth, my mother always referred to Michael as her eldest son and insisted that I call him my older brother.)

I couldn't put the book down, finishing in three days (I read slow). I was captivated by Sonny's temper, almost as explosive and unpredictable and uncontrollable as mine (my father's only trait that I inherited). I had tried everything to ameliorate it: counting to fifty, holding my breath, staring at the sky, tying my hands behind my back. Nothing worked except immediately walking away.

Whereas Sonny would fly off the handle in a rage, muscles tightening, face reddening, my anger would lie dormant for days, weeks—months even—never dissipating, always gestating; my calm veneer never betraying the inner turmoil, until one day I would unexpectedly explode like an overdue pressure cooker.

When I first realized that something was wrong, that I was different, I blamed myself (like there was anything I could have done) and God (as if God really cared), my parents, and even my friends (more envy than blame); and like Madame Defarge I kept a lot inside, silently knitting my anger, until this one day in junior high I exploded after reading in *The Globe* about this twelve-year-old girl (Savannah), born a boy, who always knew that she was a girl. (I've always admired people—especially young kids—who unambiguously know who they are, despite being born in the wrong body, despite countless people admonishing them to wait until they're older so that they can understand God's plan, whatever it was, as if *they* knew best, as if *they* and they alone were somehow privy to God's plan; despite countless people saying that they're too young to know better—even though they listen to their bodies when no one else does. But many of us are cursed with ambiguity and uncertainty and guilt, and some of us, like my best friend and soul sister Rachel, could never accept it, never mind live with it.)

Savannah wanted to try out as a cheerleader—everyone said that she was just as good and just as pretty as everyone else, except, of course, her parents who refused to accept her as a girl. They got a town ordinance passed that only born-females could be cheerleaders. Can you imagine? Her own parents? She pleaded with them but to no avail. Savannah hated being forced to be someone else. Of course her parents were shocked when she took her own life, but if you ask me, they were just as guilty as if they themselves twisted the knife deep into her heart.

I went to her wake and her funeral—yes, I know what you're thinking: that I shouldn't have gone (like Madame Defarge attending a royal costume ball), that I should have sent flowers, or a sympathy card (to whom?) or start my own foundation to help young people like Savannah (which I eventually did). But I had to attend, for even though I had never met Savannah, I felt like I had known her my entire life.

I hate to claim anyone's misfortune as a turning point, but Savannah's funeral was just that for me, an epiphany if you will (although more visible in the rearview mirror), setting me on a very different path with an interest in the law and how it can affect people, enabling (or sometimes not enabling) each of us to reach our full potential. For I began to realize (slowly) that only law can temper raw emotion, only law can attenuate the ubiquitous harassment and violence against people like us, and only law can help nudge values in the right direction. But at the same time, the wrong law or the lack of any law can have devastating effects. No one chooses gender confusion—who in their right mind would? But law can change society's values so that we can accept, tolerate, and even live with it. And, just as important, and more personal, by becoming a lawyer I could transmute my anger into something socially useful, for I refused to be like my father and to end up like Sonny Corleone and to sit idle while other Savannahs took their own life.

Chapter 16

Alexander Morgan

East Bay Drive.

I'd like to meet the bastard who named this street. Don't look for no water, except the nearby Neponset River, which ain't exactly swimmable, never mind drinkable, although just the other day I thought I saw a school of fish swimming upstream.

East Bay Drive overlooks a sprawling roofing mill, a linoleum plant, and a paper mill, draping the neighborhood in a milky white, ammonia and asphalt-stinking semi-fog that stings your friggin' eyes, forcing you to wear sunglasses even on a cloudy day.

The light had turned red. Lisa was standing curbside in front of her apartment, wearing brown shorts and a white tank top. She tossed her blonde hair back over her shoulders. I took a swig of my just-bought mouthwash. The light turned green. Someone honked. I gave the bastard the finger. I lowered my window. Assaulted by the stinging stench, I slowly pulled alongside her.

Lisa ran over to my window, resting her hands on my windowsill. "It's nice to see you Alexander!" Her chewed fingernails made her small fingers seem even smaller.

She hugged me immediately when I stepped down from my truck. "I'm so glad you could come."

I nudged her away, shaking dust from my jeans.

"What's the matter?" she asked.

"Everyone knows I'm your brother-in-law. They might get suspicious."

She led me toward her apartment: the top floor of a dull-grey triple-decker in a neighborhood of dull-grey triple-deckers. "You know how many rumors there are about who *I'm* dating, who *I was* dating, when *I'm* getting divorced?"

"You're getting divorced?"

"That's still a rumor."

I opened her front door, following her up a long flight of creaky, wooden stairs. "Does Derek still keep track of his steps?"

"Why do you think we live on the top floor?"

I had actually invited Derek to room with me for six months—the six months from hell—about a year before he met Lisa, so he wouldn't have to worry about rent after he got laid off. But his obsessive list-making—and that was the least of his nagging habits—drove me absolutely nuts. Yeah, lots of people make lists—even I tried it for a while, thinking it might give us something to talk about, but I kept losing them, and then forgetting to write down half the shit I needed to do—but Derek took it one step further, detailing every friggin' detail of every hour of the day. Like taking a friggin' nap, say Sunday at 3.30 for thirty-five minutes. Who schedules a nap? They're totally unplanned and unexpected. That's what makes a nap a nap. Maybe that was his problem: forcing his life—the epitome of dullness—into a logical, sequential orchestra, when it was anything but.

And then, most people when finished checking and crossing everything off will toss the list away? Right? Or perhaps use any unchecked items to start a new list? But Derek filed all his lists in a cabinet in the basement. I found this out one Sunday afternoon, seeing him in a chair next to the furnace, reading what looked like a set of instructions. Assuming he was fixing it—a quite logical assumption, even though it didn't need fixing—I asked. Without glancing at me, in a voice as if it were the most natural thing in the world, said that he was studying his old lists in order to map the future by connecting the past to the present. Yeah, my fault for asking, but bizarre behavior merits an explanation.

That was the last time I asked.

If I'm sentenced to hell—which right now looks like a good possibility—no worse punishment than rooming with Derek for all eternity, reading his lists night and day in the basement of hell, with no friggin' windows. Lisa's lucky: she only has to live with that bastard 'til death does them part.'

On the second-floor landing Lisa abruptly turned, catching me staring at her pretty, slender legs. "I wish he was that obsessive about me," she said, brushing away a tear. "Hugs with Lisa, kisses with Lisa, sex with Lisa, but then there'd be a lot of zeroes."

"You OK?"

"Allergies. And this damn east wind...God I hate this place."

We resumed climbing.

At the top landing, Lisa opened the door and ushered me in. I had forgotten how depressingly small her apartment was. Centered in her tiny kitchen was an almost real-looking marble table, with four black, straight-back chairs. An asparagus fir in the corner added a nice touch. Since my last visit, she had painted the walls mustard yellow, and on the opposite wall a four-foot, red rooster.

"Derek was supposed to work overtime," she said in a voice tinged with anger. "But they cancelled it and he'll be home soon." Lisa took out a casserole from the refrigerator and slipped it into the oven. "Swedish meatballs. My mother's recipe. It's already made, I just have to heat it." She opened the refrigerator and from a not-so-small wine box filled a glass. Overfilling, she carefully sipped it, handed it to me, then poured a glass for herself. She led me to the table; we sat opposite.

"I'm sorry things aren't going well between you two," I said.

She took a long sip of wine. "We live in two separate worlds. Last Sunday we were driving home—if that's what you call this dump— listening to this song on the radio. I was smiling, thinking of someone else—and so was Derek. We were in the same car, listening to the same song, but we might as well had been on different planets." She sighed, looking straight into my eyes. "I quit my job; did Derek tell you?"

"We don't exactly talk much. Why?"

"People loitering two hours over a cup of coffee don't exactly tip a lot. I got a new job at an espresso bar in a bookstore, tripling my old tips—in Cambridge, not too far from you, near the Coop."

"Really? I'm just a couple of blocks away, over the river."

"I know."

"So why haven't you stopped by?"

"I work nights, six to closing and you work days, 7.30 to four; so when could I stop by?"

I glanced at my watch. It was ten minutes to six. "Aren't you late?"

"Tonight's my night off—of all the nights for him not to work late; he's been working overtime every night the last two weeks." Lisa reached across the table and clasped my hand. "Alexander, I've a favor to ask: Next weekend I'll be at the Lake celebrating my birthday with my family. I don't want to be alone with Derek. I just don't—so I was hoping that, perhaps, you could come along?"

"Me? *Come along?*"

"Yes, take him fishing; he's been anxious to go with you again."

"Are you friggin' serious? That was the worst week of my life."

"Please, Alexander." A buzzing oven timer prompted Lisa to rise. "The casserole's done!"

I wanted to say no, excusing myself that I had to work overtime or something, but instead found myself saying yes, probably because I was so relieved that's all she asked, that she didn't want to make love right then in her stifling, suffocating apartment.

"Thanks, Alexander, I'll make it up to you!"

Lisa opened the oven door. "What?" She looked at me, confused. "I *did* turn it on? What the hell happened?"

"Maybe the pilot's out?"

"It's electric."

"I can't stay," I said, standing up. "I don't want to see Derek. Not tonight."

"What? What about the casserole? I made it for you!"

"Freeze it and bring it to the Lake."

"So you will come?" She kissed me.

"Yes."

We kissed again, this time a little longer.

Chapter 17

Joanna Turnus

If my two brothers had lived, would my mother have played with them on the beach, building sandcastles, happily answering questions, playing with their trucks, wearing a baseball hat backwards, oblivious to anything else? Would she have respected who they were? Would she have created a world for them with no uncertainty, no ambiguity, a black and white world with no grey; mother and sons happy and content with each other? Or, would she have over-masculinized them, forcing each to become someone else, reduced to an elusive stereotype? Or perhaps, satiated with boys, she would have craved a girl, dressing the youngest (or perhaps the oldest, or both) in girls' clothes and girls' underwear? I shuddered at the thought. Maybe it was better that both my brothers had died?

Chapter 18

Alexander Morgan

The next morning, I was relaxing in my truck, savoring my coffee, enjoying the last peaceful moments before work. The sun had just risen. It was a delightfully cool, crisp, wind-breaker morning. Suddenly Phil raced into the parking lot shattering the last peaceful remnants of the delightfully cool, crisp morning. He pulled alongside me, beeping his horn like a bastard, "Where's that other prick?"

"Which other prick? You have to be more specific around here."

"Where's that goddamned son-of-a-bitch?"

Just then Paul, carrying his backpack, lost in his Beats, slumbered toward us like a wayward camel.

"Get over here you goddamned son-of-a-bitch."

"He can't hear you with them Beats," I said, stepping down from my truck, removing my windbreaker.

"Have I got a job for you two." Phil smiled, pulling Paul closer. "You're going to wish you'd called in sick."

I put my windbreaker back on. "Actually, I ain't feeling that well. I could use the day off. Thanks for the suggestion."

"Park the compressor next to the rear door and take enough hose to reach the vault," Phil barked. "Hook up one hose for the chipping hammer and another for the jackhammer."

"What about the graders?" I asked.

"They'll have to wait. This is urgent."

"Everything's friggin' urgent," I muttered. *OK, so what the hell's going on? Did Phil find out about Hudson Brothers and The Edge, and now he's dishing out this shit punishment?* Bracing for the inevitable accusations, Phil instead explained that the architect forgot the air conditioning duct in the vault and now the sheet metal guys are pissed because they can't finish.

"You *are* serious?" I asked.

"No, I'm just here for a fire-side chat."

"What about the dust?" asked Paul.

"And the noise?" I asked, relieved and confused. *Did the architect really screw up or was this a shit punishment in disguise? Either way, it sucks.*

"Wear masks and ear plugs. And water down the dust with a thermos."

"A thermos? Are you friggin' serious?"

"I already outlined and aligned each hole," Phil continued impatiently, like he had someone to go and was already late—which I'm sure he was. "Build one level of staging, run a couple of planks through the top rungs. Hold the jackhammer horizontally. One prick holds the front just above the point, while the other holds the back."

"We know how to jackhammer; we ain't dimwits," I said. "What about the dust? How we supposed to fuckin' breathe?"

A flatbed truck lugging a grader and a bulldozer thundered into the parking lot.

"You'll think of something. Now get going. I want this done so the sheet metal guys can finish," Phil said before scurrying off.

The vault was bigger—much bigger— than I had expected, not that I've ever been in one before. It was about 100 x 75, giving the impression that it was originally something else, like a windowless office or a janitor's room and Phil had just realized that he'd forgotten the bank's heart and soul—how can you build a bank without a friggin' vault? And if it *wasn't* on the plans—which I'm sure it was—then Phil should've spotted it and made amends—that's what supervisors are supposed to do: solve problems before they become problems.

After Paul and I built one level of staging with six planks running across the top, and before we started hammering, I suggested that we double-check that both holes were centered.

"Phil said that he aligned them," said Paul matter-of-factly.

"Ain't that good enough reason to check? And whose asses will be in a sling if they ain't?"

Paul eyeballed the holes. "They look good to me."

"Either you're too blind to see or too stupid to know what you're looking for." I handed Paul the end of my tape measure while I climbed to the top level of staging. "Take it to the base of the wall," I said, writing down the measurements as Paul read them; then doing the same for the opposite hole. "Just as I thought: Off by three inches." *But which hole was off? With that bastard, they both could be?* The only way to make sure was to check the holes in the adjoining room.

Next door the drywall guys were slabbing the first layer of plaster over the screw holes. I tapped the closest guy's shoulder, asking to borrow his step ladder. He looked at me confused; I'm sure deaf from being around screw guns day after day.

"He don't speak no fuckin' English," someone said.

Then why's he working in America?

I asked anyone within ear range if I could borrow the guy's step ladder to take a quick measure.

"Why don't you bring your own, like everyone else?" someone asked.

"I don't want to waste time trampsing to the trailer just to take one friggin' measurement, and hold you guys up even longer; then you'd really be pissed off."

The bastard nodded his approval. Christ almighty, you'd think I was asking for his first born.

Just as I thought: Each hole was perfectly centered, meaning both holes in the vault were off. There's a surprise.

Back in the vault I properly re-aligned the holes—it would've been easier had we aligned the holes ourselves, saving half an hour. Before we started jackhammering, I called Phil so he wouldn't be pissed that we hadn't yet started and to casually mention that he screwed up again.

"Double-checked? Didn't I say they were aligned?—And?"

"They were three inches off," I said smugly.

Silence.

"Hello?"

"Thanks for checking," he answered calmly, without his usual friggin' adjectives and adverbs. Just a three-word, unadorned, almost unrecognizable sentence, which I, nor anyone else, ever thought possible.

I scribbled on a piece of scrap paper, for myself and all of posterity:

'On this day, Wednesday October 7, in the Year of Our Lord 2018, Phil O'Sullivan complimented Alex Morgan.'

Chapter 19

Joanna Turnus

Before you meet Terry, I guess I should tell you why I tried out for the eighth-grade boys' football team; although no matter what I say or how I say it, you'll think that I'm just a simpleton brandishing hackneyed gender stereotypes. (Indeed, sometimes I wish I were.)

Even today some people criticize my playing football as superficial, that it had nothing to do with being or wanting to be a male. And some of my TG friends, whom you think would have understood, asked (half-facetiously) why I didn't play hockey, drive a truck, or some other supposedly macho thing.

So why *did* I play football? Three and a half reasons. None sufficient on their own, and taken together might not convince you at all, but football was, and is, an important part of who I am. And besides, I never would've met Terry, and probably wouldn't be here today if I didn't play football.

One, I liked it (and still do—although now I'd rather watch than play). Two, back then, I was good at it (better than most boys—everyone said so). Now don't get me wrong, I wasn't on a mission to prove that girls were just as good as boys. If there was a girls' team, I would have been quite content.

Three, and perhaps most importantly, football provided my war-zone body with a rudder, without which I was captive to the slightest breeze from any direction. Admittedly, playing football was a puerile grasp at self-affirmation, without exactly knowing what I was self-affirming (just like my friends getting their ears pierced didn't make them a girl, but merely expressed who they were). Looking back, I played football to survive, which was hard for an eighth-grade girl to fathom—or anyone else for that matter—reconciling who I was with the body I was given. My body was a war zone, and I wasn't sure who was going to win; something none of my so-called 'normal' (God, I hate that word) friends could possibly have known or understood, or even related to.

Oh, the half reason: I knew what pleased my mother, although it wasn't until much later that I understood why.

To lessen the shock of a pretty girl (everyone said I was) trying out for the eighth-grade boys' football team I decided to meet Coach in mid-June, just after classes were done, to feel him out, to explain my rationale so that at least he'd understand, and to hopefully show how good I was.

The morning of my appointment with Coach I was nervous, not over what to say, for there really wasn't much to say except asking for a try-out; rather, it was deciding what to wear and how to wear it. Obviously, everyone knew I was a girl, so if I dressed as a boy, Coach would think I was pretending to be a boy, so I had to dress like a girl.

Thankfully, I hadn't cut my hair in a while, so I decided to tie it in a high pony. With my mother's mascara, I laced my upper lashes, and her lip gloss prettied my thick, pouty lips; bare, they looked like inflated earthworms.

I was ready, finally, or so I thought, until I glanced at my legs. I didn't know any girl who didn't shave her legs. (I'm sure their mothers made them, even if they didn't want to.) I thought about wearing sweatpants, but it was too hot—I would have died. So I had no choice: a girl asking to try out for the boys' football team had to shave her legs.

As I walked the mile or so to school, I pulled my shorts low over my thighs. I was glad that I wore a somewhat loose-fitting T-shirt, for I swore my breasts grew a little that morning.

Inside the cavernous gym I asked the janitor for directions—I'm sure curious why an eighth-grade girl wanted to see Coach in mid-June. I dabbed on my mother's lip gloss, which I had stashed in my pocket and quickly rapped on Coach's door before I became too nervous, before I could change my mind.

"Yes?" inquired a male voice. "The door's unlocked."

Expecting someone much older, a curmudgeon; a conservative gatekeeper of the status quo, I was pleasantly surprised to see a young guy, kind of cute, with black hair cropped short and spiky. His full moustache complimented a strong jaw, and his perfectly fitting South High T-shirt showcased strong, muscular arms.

Coach was sitting behind an oversized metal desk cluttered with papers, newspaper clippings, and clipboards. Behind him, dozens of trophies lined a cinder block bookcase. A small electric fan buzzed on the windowsill, sucking out the stuffy, sweaty air.

"I'm looking for the football coach?" Of course, I knew he was but didn't know what else to say.

Noticing that I was a girl, Coach smiled. "I *am* the coach, how can I help you?"

"I'm Joanna Turnus. I'd called earlier about—"

"Oh yes, yes," he rose enthusiastically to shake my hand. "Please sit down. So, you want to try out for the football team, is that right? You *do* know that tryouts aren't until August?"

"Of course...but I'm a girl and I would like your permission."

"Are you related to Zachary Turnus?"

I squirmed. "He's my father."

"You don't look anything like him?"

"Everyone says I look like my mother."

Suddenly I couldn't remember if I had left mascara on or removed it. I felt my eyelashes: yes, but more than I thought?

"What does your father say about this?"

"About mascara?" I shrugged, fidgeting my eyelashes.

Coach laughed. "I mean playing football."

"He doesn't know."

"You're trying out for the boys' football team and your father doesn't know?"

"Neither does my mother. There's a lot they don't know about me."

I expected him to say something, but he leaned back in his chair staring at me.

"If I make the team, I *will* tell them," I obligingly said.

"You sound pretty sure of yourself. What position do you play?"

"Receiver."

"Let me see your hands."

I showed him, extending my long, strong fingers.

"I've never seen such hands on a girl?"

I flinched, unconsciously extending my chest.

"I mean," Coach straightened himself in his chair. "What I mean is that you have *really* strong hands for a receiver—in college I was a receiver; hands are so important—what about defense? What position do you play on defense?"

"I don't play defense."

"All our guys go both ways, except the quarterback."

Was there any hidden meaning in what Coach just said, or was he just talking as coaches usually do? "If I have to play defense, then... defensive end."

"Too small."

"I'm taller than most boys."

"I mean weight, strength; there's some big linemen out there, not to mention fullbacks."

"I can beat boys in arm wrestling."

"Football isn't arm wrestling."

"How about throwing me some passes?" I asked, surprised by my bluntness.

Coach shuffled some papers on his desk. "I can't now. I'm drafting players for the League all-star game." He looked at his watch. "Tell you what: TC is stopping by and I'll ask him to throw you some balls, er...I mean, passes."

"TC?"

"Our quarterback. You're a receiver and you haven't heard of him?"

I shrugged. "I'm just starting eighth grade."

"He should be here soon. You can wait here while I finish and—." The door suddenly opened. Coach smiled, "Morning TC."

"*That's the quarterback?*" I exclaimed a little louder than intended. Oh my God: Cut-off T-shirt, tall, strong arms, blond, washboard stomach.

Coach pulled him closer, "TC, this is Joanna Turnus; she wants to try out for the team."

I stood up, blushing, feeling my breasts rustle underneath my T-shirt.

TC smiled. "Yeah, I heard there's a girl wanting to try out, who says she's pretty good."

I smiled back. "TC?"

"Terrance Connor," Coach answered immediately. "Everyone calls him TC."

"Except my mother and sisters who call me Terry," he said, winking at me.

Oh my God! Catching passes from this guy is going to be more difficult than I had thought.

"What position do you play?" Terry asked.

"Joanna, show him your hands."

I did, quickly pulling them away, embarrassed at my unpolished, chewed-off nails.

"Placekicker." Terry laughed. "We could use a good one."

"Why don't you toss her some passes, TC? See how good she is?"

"Sure, Coach, but only for a few minutes; I want to watch a few films before I cut the grass." Terry held open Coach's door. I stepped out, quietly dashing on my mother's lip gloss.

"TC, Joanna should wear a helmet and so should you; just grab one from the bin."

Without waiting, I fished a helmet from an old water barrel over-stuffed with helmets. I grabbed a new one and tried it on. Perfect!

"First time wearing a helmet?" Terry asked.

My face flushed. "How'd you know?"

"You didn't look at the inside pads, just tried it on."

"I knew it'd fit."

Outside, Terry said he needed to warm up a bit. On the ground, he stretched his left leg, then his right. Oh my God, I couldn't look. Facing opposite, I did the same, then jumping jacks. After five minutes or so I glanced at Terry still stretching. Oh my God. I turned away, jogging in place until he was ready.

We began with soft, short passes; then longer passes with more zip.

"I like how you catch the ball with your fingertips," Terry said, stepping back about twenty yards.

I caught everything he threw at me. Everything. I really had to concentrate, forcing myself to focus on his hands—looking at the rest of his body, even for an instant, I would have fluttered.

He unleashed a high bullet. I jumped, catching it with both hands, briefly accelerated toward the end zone, then jogged back.

"Impressive," Terry said. "How about some down-and-outs?"

This guy was good. Timed the ball perfectly, throwing some passes directly into my hands, others high/low, obviously testing me. I noticed Coach had slipped outside with his clipboard, standing next to Terry, talking, jotting notes.

Then I ran posts. My favorite because I could use my speed to catch off-target balls; in fact, the more off-target, the quicker my acceleration. Terry threw one pass, low and to my right; I dove, caught the ball, juggling it as I rolled over, never letting it touch the ground. Terry lobbed the next pass high. I jumped, batted it with one hand and caught it.

Coach waved me in. "Impressive." He tossed me a water bottle. I caught it with my fingertips, tucked it into my chest and ran a few yards toward the end zone. They shared a laugh.

"Coach, can we consider her officially on the team? She's quicker and stronger than any receiver we've got, and I could break the school record."

"You already have the school record. No one gets special treatment. She can't officially join the team until tryouts—you know that—but

I am impressed." Turning to me, Coach said, "If you catch like that during tryouts, you'll easily make the team."

"Easily make the team? She's going to be my star receiver."

"Terry, did you know that you *slightly* telegraph your throwing shoulder when you pass?"

Coach glanced at Terry, writing in his notepad. "Very observant."

"Hey Coach? Can Jo and I—"

"Joanna," I said tersely.

"Sorry Joanna," Terry said, appearing genuine. "Can Joanna and I work out during the summer? Practice routes and work on our timing?"

"Sure. You can do whatever you want, as long as it isn't official and as long as I'm not involved or even around."

"Got it. How about it Joanna? A couple of times a week? Here? Working on routes?"

"Sure," my voice blushed. "That would be nice."

Chapter 20

Joanna Turnus

We practiced every Tuesday and Thursday night for two hours out-side, or if it rained, in the gym. But that summer it hardly rained, at least from what I could remember.

This guy was good. And I'm not just saying so because I was falling in love with him. Here's just one example: In one of our favorite drills, Terry, blindfolded at the line of scrimmage, would call a route, count to four and throw it to where he thought I should be. By the end of July, he was on target eight times out of ten—better than most quarterbacks without a blindfold. Then he would blindfold me, forcing me to sense my route by touch. These two drills—perhaps more than anything else—helped us understand each other by synchronizing our speed and timing. By the end of the summer, catching a pass blindfolded from Terry was almost second nature.

Before every Thursday practice we watched films of opposing teams, together, alone, in Coach's office. Sometimes it was too much: Terry, practically naked, sitting next to me; forcing me to take refuge behind Coach's clipboard, scribbling notes about every defensive back, defensive lineman—even other receivers—forcing my thoughts elsewhere. Sometimes I wouldn't shave my legs for days, then one day I would. Terry always noticed. Immediately. A faint glimmer, a half-smile; a turned upper lip.

That summer was exhilarating. Each practice flew by, while each off day laboriously dragged into the next. But as July melted into August and tryouts loomed, I became more restless. I wanted a lot more from this guy than just catching his passes all season. And I knew he did as well. I just knew.

As I showered the morning of football tryouts, I let the water run on my face. I closed my eyes, imagining Terry embracing me in the warm, soothing rain. Long, soft kisses. I felt him inside me; his warm body pressed against my breasts.

When I opened my eyes, his sweetness was on my skin, in the soap, in the shampoo. With my mother's razor I shaved my left leg. Slowly. Methodically. Then my right leg. Methodically. Slowly. My bare legs exuded his salty sweetness. I tingled when my breasts touched my cool, bare thigh.

An hour before tryouts, I called Coach to say that I wasn't trying out, that I just couldn't. "Girl problems," I said. He was upset. Understandably. I apologized. He was yelling. I wasn't listening. I knew what he was saying. Staring at my chewed-off, unpolished nails, I carried my phone into the bathroom. In my mother's drawer, I found a purple nail polish with a hint of brown. Perfect. I sat on the hopper and painted each nail. Coach ranted. Too much polish on my middle finger, dribbling onto my thigh; surprised that it didn't stain. I hung up without saying goodbye—maybe I did, I don't remember.

I closed my eyes and could still smell Terry's sweetness. The phone rang. It was Terry. Angry. Of course. Girl problems? He wanted to see me. Immediately. I couldn't. He yelled. I didn't respond. I smiled, knowing how he really felt about me. I just knew. I painted each nail again. Then each toenail. The same color. Purple, with a hint of brown. Careful not to smudge, careful not to drip, careful not to apply too much. I spilled polish on my mother's small rug where she stood every morning applying her makeup after her readings, coffee on the sink. I noticed a small burn mark on the rug, a cigarette burn, but neither my mother nor my father smokes. Perhaps a late afternoon rendezvous?

Terry was yelling. I smiled, knowing how he really felt about me—I just knew. I dusted on my mother's mascara. Just the upper lashes. Perfect. And my mother's lip gloss prettied my thick, pouty lips. Bare, they looked like inflated earthworms.

Chapter 21

Joanna Turnus

Ok, so why didn't I try out? Why did I back out at the last minute? Sure, I would've helped Terry break his own school record and undoubtedly set a few of my own on our way to consecutive championships. But if so, we would have remained quarterback and receiver forever; nothing more, nothing less. I wanted more. A lot more. And besides, I couldn't picture myself hugging Terry after a touchdown pass (there'd be a lot). How could I trust myself to stop? Or riding home on the bus after a game, in the dark, sitting next to him? Or being alone with him practically naked in Coach's office watching game films?

I'm sure you're laughing right now: what does an 8th grade girl know about love? But in the 8th grade, like a war-orphaned child, I was wise and mature way beyond my years. I knew what I wanted. And I knew I would get it. I just knew.

But for us to become a couple, Terry would have to notice me as a girl, and what better spotlight than being an 8th grade cheerleader? Now I know what you're thinking: It was bad enough to embrace a stale, hackneyed caricature of maleness, but why do the same for femaleness (as if either word has any meaning)? Of course, being a cheerleader didn't make me a girl or enable me to become a girl (just like playing football didn't make me a male or enable me to become a male) but back in junior high, I was unsure and confused and volatile and depressed; not like my friends whose self-esteem and entire day depended on whether a certain boy smiled at them. My problem was deeper—a lot deeper. I needed something to focus on, to grasp, to occupy myself, anything to suppress the 'other' gender—although I never really knew which was the other. I thought that by extirpating one I could nurture the other. But it wasn't until I was much older that I realized that I was both, and that in order to survive I had to nurture and shepherd both—not exactly clear, digestible, or even palatable stuff for an eighth-grade girl.

So forgive me for playing football (I was good at it) and for becoming a cheerleader (I was pretty and athletic and still am, and I was in love with Terry) and for trying to understand who I was and who I was becoming. The only certainty in my screwed-up life was that I really liked boys and that I had a major crush on Terry (as did all of my friends, and for that matter, just about every girl in 8th grade) which made me feel somewhat good about myself. No one told me how to deal with gender ambiguity, no one had offered a recipe. And no one even suspected me—at least not yet.

I made the cheerleading squad. No surprise there: I was strong and athletic (a perfect bottom-post pyramid); I had a warm and engaging smile (the cheerleading coach said so); I had the nicest legs (everyone said that); and I was prettier than anyone else (my grandfather insisted).

I eventually became squad captain. Yes, Terry had noticed me as a girl and we began dating: the star quarterback (who reluctantly found other receivers, although none as good as me, breaking his own school records) and the pretty cheerleading captain became high school sweethearts. A story book romance, right?

It was cheerleading policy to wear a sports bra no matter how flat-chested you were. I'm sure the other girls didn't think anything about it: no big deal, I'll just grab one from my drawer. But I had never worn a bra and thankfully didn't really need one—I was completely flat-chested—until coincidentally practicing with Terry, or was it coincidental?

I almost asked my mother to accompany me to the mall, but she would have exploded; then again, it would've been nice to have gone with someone, anyone—even my mother, pretending to be normal, doing normal mother/daughter things. (All of my friends went with their mother to buy their first bra, turning it into a nice mother-daughter outing, even getting their ears pierced, if they hadn't already.)

I went to the store myself.

I had no idea my size, only that my breasts were growing and that they hurt. I asked the first clerk that I could find to help me, surprised that she wasn't that much older than me.

"This isn't—is this your first bra?" she asked with a touch of arrogance. "Is your mother with you?"

Obviously, I was alone. "She's sick."

"What's your size?"

I shrugged. "Do you have sports bras? I need a sports bra."

"Of course we have sports bras." She nodded to a small, semi-enclosed room filled with sweatshirts and sweatpants. "What sport do you play?"

"I'm a cheerleader."

For an instant she stared at me confused, as if peering deep inside my soul and finding something terribly wrong. Then with a measuring tape, she asked me to raise my arms.

I scooted back. "I can do this myself."

"For your first bra, it's better for me to measure you, so you can see how it's done."

I insisted I could so myself.

"Fine." She snatched a black bra and a pink one from an adjoining table, handing me both. "These should fit... A sport bra's tighter than a regular one," she explained in a somewhat nicer tone. "But it breathes—see the mesh? This one [the black bra] has a hook, which sometimes can be tricky."

I left the pink bra with her and took the other into the fitting room.

OK, this should be easy, right? The front's obvious, as is the back, and the straps go over my shoulders. I slipped the bra on but couldn't hook the back, so I removed it, hooked it, then slipped it on but couldn't squeeze my breasts into the cups and the straps dug into my skin.

"Everything OK?" the clerk asked, snooped outside the door.

"Yes!"

She repeated in a few minutes.

"I think it's too small?"

"Too small? Can I come in?" she asked, opening the door. "Yes, it is too small."

I reluctantly let her tape-measure me.

"Are you sure you've never worn a bra before?"

I felt like I was going to throw up.

The clerk left, then quickly returned with a black sports bra, definitely bigger. "This should fit."

In the fitting room, I hooked the bra, raised my arms, then lowered it onto my breasts. I put my blouse on. Looking at myself in the mirror, I was wowed, scared, amazed, and confused by how pretty I was; even the snotty clerk said so.

"We're running a special," she offered. "Buy one bra, half off the second. You'll need one when school starts; I'm sure you know how boys are. And tell your mother we're having a bra-fitting session later this week."

I forced a smile, nodding.

Chapter 22

Alexander Morgan

Using the jackhammer vertically—normal usage—is a lot easier than it looks. Its weight does the work, so you just guide it as needed. But horizontally, that's a different story—no wonder that bastard was smiling—no handles and nothing to grab, so you need two guys, although the hammer ain't long enough for two, and you need gloves because it gets hot as a bastard.

With 120 decibels reverberating against the walls, earplugs were useless, and our masks filled quickly with fine grey dust, making it more difficult to breath with them on. And dabbing water from a friggin' thermos—who was he kidding?

After thirty minutes or so I suggested hosing down the dust so we could at least see what we're doing. "The floor's concrete," I said to Paul. "So water ain't going to damage it."

A faint grunt, which I took as a yes; not that I needed his approval. I headed to the trailer to fetch a water hose, hacking up all sorts of dust and shit; I also grabbed a couple of extension cords and a hanging torch light.

Returning to the vault, I ran into Lily—literally.

"Alexander?" she asked, peering closer. "Is that you? What have you been doing?"

"Don't ask." I shook the dust from my hair. "What brings you here so early in the morning?"

"We had an all-night organizing session a couple of blocks away. I needed coffee—it was good to get out and ...I was hoping to run into you." She handed me her business card. "This has my personal number. I was wondering—"

"You live in Worcester?" I asked, noticing the central Massachusetts area code.

"Born and raised."

"I thought you and Brian were—"

"Together?" She laughed. "Are you kidding? We have absolutely nothing in common."

A short silence.

"Look, I find you very attractive, but if you're not interested." She removed her heels and hurried to the bank with a determination that said she was comfortable at a construction site, unfazed by pinching nails, shards of glass, scraps of wood. And she knew I was watching, staring at her long, slender legs glistening in the morning sunlight. At the bank entrance, she bent down, scraped the dirt from her feet and slipped on her shoes.

I called her number. No answer. I called again.

"Who's this?" she asked, recognizing my voice.

"Alexander Morgan. I work at General Construction. How about dinner Saturday night?"

"Hmmm. Brian and I are leaving for Albany Saturday morning, for a week."

A week? Together? And there's nothing between them?

"How about Friday night?" she suggested.

"Sure."

"Should we say seven? Oh, let's make it eight: I've an all-day session in Woonsocket. Call me this week, I've some good suggestions."

Back in the vault, Paul and I outlined the first hole with the chipping hammer, so that when we began jackhammering, the surrounding concrete wouldn't accidentally crack. We worked like bastards, finishing the first hole by 9:10, just in time for coffee. At this rate, we'd finish well before noon. But something wasn't right: it was too easy.

"Did you notice how weak this shit is?" I asked Paul, resting my arms on the upper planks. The ash-like dust was already an eighth-inch deep. "What if the whole building's like this?"

"It ain't."

"You've checked? And what about the steel rods?"

"What about them?"

"There ain't none; that's the problem: They're supposed to be *in* the concrete."

Paul lifted the chipping hammer. "I'll finish outlining the second hole while you go for coffee."

I waved my hands in disgust, then grabbed three small pieces of concrete: one for Walter, one for my truck, and the other for safe keeping in the trailer.

Outside, I coughed, hacking up more dust and shit.

A Zella guy approached in his friggin' grader. I waved but no response. I waved again. No response. Fuck him—he can get his own coffee.

Paul and I entered the coffee circle simultaneously but from different directions

"Where've you two clowns been?" Walter asked. "And why so dusty?"

"You tell him," said Paul. "You're better at explaining stuff."

Nick lit a cigarette. "The master bullshitter."

"He was voted best bullshitter in high school," noted Paul.

"An award for best bullshitter?" asked Abe. "In school? No wonder our goddamn country's so screwed up."

"They just didn't hand out them awards," I said, taking my spot next to Nick. "I won it fair and square."

"By lying," Paul said. "Like senior year, you were voted the most tallest, lying to everyone that you were, when, in fact, five guys were taller. And that's just one example."

"Which everyone knew—it wasn't exactly something I could hide—so I bullshitted. And that's why I won best bullshitter."

"How do we know you ain't bullshittin' now?" Walter asked.

"Everything's in the yearbook," I replied. "Check it out online."

"Liars, bullshitters?" Nick asked. "What's the goddamned difference?"

I sipped my coffee. "There's nothing worse than lying—the ultimate deception. Lying deliberately deceives. No one suspects you're lying because you're serious, but everyone knows when you're bullshitting. The opposite of bullshitting is not bullshitting and the opposite of lying is not lying, so if you're bullshitting you ain't lying. How does someone five-foot-five dunk a basketball? By bullshitting. How did only a handful of bastards defend the friggin' Alamo? By bullshitting."

"What kind of logic is that?" Abe asked, trying hard not to laugh.

"The honest bullshitter," added Nick.

"So why are you two clowns so dusty?" Walter asked.

"You really want to know?" I asked.

Walter sighed. "Let's hear it."

Abe glanced at his watch. "The condensed version, lunch is in three hours."

"You guys have no idea what we do every day getting coffee. Like this morning, just as we were leaving, this blinding sandstorm came out of nowhere. Paul and I were inching along, guided by my compass—thank God I remembered to bring it."

"The goddamned blind leading the goddamned blind," said Nick, lighting a cigarette.

"Then Paul suggested renting a camel."

"He's always thinking," said Abe.

"And charging it to General?" Walter said.

"They ain't cheap now-a-days," Paul added.

"Lucky for us there was a camel stand this side of the street; usually there ain't one when you need it. But our camel wouldn't budge—must've been deaf or something, so we exchanged it for another. Then we got attacked by this roving band of bandits."

"Them's the worst kind," added Nick.

"We whipped out our swords and drove the bandits back, back into the quicksand where they all disappeared."

"You always have a sword gettin' coffee?" Walter asked.

"Absolutely," I said. "You never know when it might come in

handy."

"That's it?" Abe asked. "No snakes or crocodiles snappin' at you?"

"That was yesterday—thank God we don't have to deal with them bastards every day."

Nick flung his cigarette butt at me.

Walter rose from his bucket, stretching his arms. "So, what's the real reason you're so dusty?"

"The real reason?" I laughed to Paul, "He thinks we made this up!"

"*The real reason!*"

I finished my coffee and tossed the empty Styrofoam cup into the water barrel. "If one of us fucked up one-tenth as much as Phil, we'd be out of here on our ass so quickly. *He* made us cut two holes in the vault for the air conditioning duct, saying that the architect screwed up."

"What?" Walter asked. "The duct's on the plans, clear as day."

"You sure?" I asked.

"Of course I'm sure—why wouldn't I be?"

"An expensive mistake if you ask me—and something ain't right with the concrete. It's cutting too easy. It's supposed to be zero slump, you know that, but it's a helluva lot weaker. How'd this get by the inspector?"

"Where'd you put it?" Walter asked.

"In the dumpster—where else would I put it? I also stashed a piece in my truck."

"Why?"

I shrugged.

Walter glanced at his watch. "Hey kid, you wanted to speak with Zachary; I set up a meetin' this afternoon. At his office. Be at my truck at exactly three-thirty. He even said we can leave early to leave beat the traffic—I told him it was urgent. And make sure you clean up; you can't go to his office lookin' like that." Walter grabbed my arm. "And who was you talkin' to this mornin'?"

"I was in the vault all morning."

"When you was returnin' from the trailer."

"Her? Oh, a bank customer. She was lost."

"So, she gives you her card?"

"Why so friggin' nosy?"

Walter frowned. "Listen kid, if I see you screwin' around and I ain't even lookin', then so can Phil, who's watchin' your every move. And why didn't you ask Zella to join us for coffee?"

"They're pricks." I reached in my front pocket and returned Walter his twenty.

Cutting the second hole was even easier. We finished at 11:00, three hours ahead of our self-imposed schedule. Our holes were laser-cut perfect. We wheelbarrowed the concrete into the dumpster, then vacuumed the vault floor with the industrial vacuum.

"Let's have a cigarette," I suggested to Paul when finished; "it'll clean out our lungs."

He didn't laugh. He never laughs at my jokes, although this time I was half-serious.

I texted Phil that we had finished, assuming he'd be pissed that we had finished so early. No answer. It was 11:35. I called again. Fuck it. I decided to take an early lunch. If that bastard wants to fire me, then let him explain his expensive screw-up to Zachary.

At the Scarlet Pumpernickel, I snagged the last river-adjacent table, surprised that it was still available. I stretched my legs on an adjoining chair, savoring the warm breeze. My forty minutes for lunch seemed an eternity. I closed my eyes, soothed by the river cascading off the rocks. Half asleep, someone jerked me awake. Assuming it was the waitress asking for my order, I was surprised to see Lisa.

"Alexander? Is that you? I almost didn't recognize you?" She wore an unflattering oversized brown maxi-dress, her blonde hair tied back. She smiled as I straightened myself up, shaking dust from my hair. "I kind of like you in grey," she said. "Makes you look distinguished."

"How'd you know I was here? Even I didn't know I was coming until the last minute."

"Paul told me."

That bastard.

She sat opposite, handing me a large Styrofoam cup. "A Switch-blade. Made it myself. Five shots of Espresso mixed with house coffee. I thought you might need one."

I took a long sip, nodding my approval. "No naps for me this afternoon. Or the rest of the friggin' week. Do you guys deliver? What's the name of your shop?"

"The Comet. We're on the other side of the river, only one stop away on the Red Line, although from here you can practically walk. Stop by when you're working overtime or something."

A waitress approached, asking for Lisa's order.

"How's the grilled avocado salad?" Lisa asked, scanning the menu.

"One of my favorites. You have to try it with alfalfa sprouts."

Lisa nodded.

The waitress turned to me.

"Can I have three cheeseburgers, extra fries, and onion rings? And a Diet Pepsi."

"Really Alexander?" Lisa asked. "*Three* cheeseburgers? Extra fries *and* extra onion rings? No dessert? Won't you be starving by mid-afternoon?"

"I'll manage." I swatted a wasp darting at me.

"That just makes him angry. Sit still and he'll go away."

I unlaced my boots and stretched my legs on an adjoining chair. "I thought you worked nights?"

"I'm subbing today. It's good to get out of the house. Hmmmm, maybe I should sub more often?" she muttered. "So, why so dusty, Alexander?"

I took a sip of my Switchblade, then another. "Paul and I were jackhammering in the vault."

"How much money did you abscond with, Alexander Ocean?" she asked, laughing.

"Yeah, right. I wouldn't know what to do with it all."

"Me? First, I'd get a manicure *and* a pedicure, then a trip around the world. In a sailboat."

"With Derek?"

"Are you serious?"

"That's on his list."

"Maybe so, but not with me. Of course, I'd ask you along—I think that'd be fun."

I laughed, "Phil won't even let me go to Allston, never mind a trip around the world."

The waitress delivered Lisa's salad.

Lisa spooned several grilled avocados onto my plate, urging me to try one, as if they were God's greatest invention.

"Can't stand the bastards."

"I bet you never had them grilled?"

"When I was seven my mother made me eat a whole plate of them."

"Lie bag. Just try one. There's nothing like a grilled avocado!"

"An avocado's an avocado no matter if you bake it, boil it, steam it, baste it, sauté it, dice it, eat it raw, or even grill it."

"Not necessarily. A good cook can take a basic avocado and transform it into something magical, something beyond recognition."

"Then why bother with it in the first place?"

"Where's your sense of adventure Alexander?"

"With avocados? Are you kidding?"

"Did you know that these onion rings are actually avocado rings, and your cheeseburgers are avocado burgers?"

I threw my napkin down and stood up.

"Alexander Morgan! Don't be so ridiculous."

"Ain't it reasonable to assume that if I order something, I know exactly what I'm getting?"

"Yes; and no—who cares! I didn't come here to talk about avocados."

I sat down. The waitress delivered my lunch. The onion rings were steeped high, practically burying everything else.

"You should've ordered more, Alexander, I don't think you have enough. But I'm glad that you ordered extra fries."

"What the hell's all this?" I asked, noticing tomatoes, relish, lettuce, pickles and who knows what else in my burgers. "I specifically asked just for extra ketchup and nothing else."

"You didn't. I was right here."

"I did."

"No you didn't."

I diligently scraped off everything, saving the ketchup.

"Are you sure got everything? I think I still see some lettuce."

Finally satisfied I took a bite, "So, how was your romantic dinner last night with Derek?"

"Romantic? With Derek? I wouldn't use those two words together." She took an onion ring, raised it her mouth, then put it down. "Did I ever tell what happened last Valentine's Day?"

I shook my head, not sure I wanted to know.

"I made him breakfast in bed. Yeah, I know: what I was thinking? Maybe I'm a hopeless romantic, that even when things hit rock bottom, they'll get better? I was wearing nothing underneath my bathrobe. Then you know what he said? That I didn't deserve a Valentine's day present *this* year but maybe *next* year if I worked at it. I dumped the whole tray on him." She brushed away a tear. "I packed my suitcase and went home to New Hampshire. My Dad initially thought I was pregnant and came home to surprise him. But how can you be pregnant if you don't have sex? And how can you have sex when you don't sleep together? And how can you sleep together when you're not intimate? And how can you be intimate when you don't like each other?" Lisa scattered her avocadoes. "Last night, it was supposed to be just you and me. *He* was supposed to work overtime. And today, I was going to surprise you with leftovers—a nice picnic lunch, but he was so pissed that he threw everything in the trash. Now he's accusing me of having an affair with you." Lisa stood up, drying her eyes with a Kleenex. "I have to get back to work. I can't be late, we're short-staffed as it is."

I hugged her. "You OK?"
She nodded. "You still coming next weekend?"
"Yes."
She smiled and kissed me goodbye.

Chapter 23

Joanna Turnus

For homecoming, Coach bought us these purple ball earrings—a small token of appreciation for working so hard for the fans, for helping us stay unbeaten, and for 'making her look good.' Yeah, I know what you're thinking: purple; yuk, too gaudy. But they were pretty in a sophisticated way, stylish even; something my grandmother might wear if she was feeling funky on Mother's Day or her birthday or anniversary. Although Coach told us that the earrings were inexpensive, some of the Moms insisted otherwise, even suggesting they were Sapphires. But whether they were or not, they were pretty and quite noticeable from a distance; and purple was our team color.

I was the only girl on the squad without pierced ears. I'm sure Coach would have understood if I didn't want to get my ears pierced (I guess like a Quaker excused for military service); she would've bought me a nice pair of clip-ons, just as pretty, and no one would have been the wiser; that's just the type of person she is. But I didn't have a good reason, at least that I could afford to tell, other than that I was part of this stupid family (a word I hesitate to use) where such a simple thing as getting my ears pierced was so problematic.

Three weeks before homecoming I asked my mother (nicely) to let me get my ears pierced. It certainly wasn't the first time (I was really tired of asking) but now I was more determined. I asked my mother during her morning readings, when she was (usually) halfway nice, waiting until she had crossed herself finishing some worn-out prayer.

"No," she firmly said, fondling a tiny gold cross draped around her neck—a gift from her mother shortly after my mother's first miscarriage. "Absolutely not."

"But everyone on the squad has pierced ears!"

"I don't care! You are *not* getting your ears pierced."

"We have to. Coach wants us to wear these purple—"

"You'll just have to tell her no."

"You want me to be the only cheerleader without pierced ears?"

"Then you never should've joined the squad. You—" Suddenly, my mother looked at me calmly and quizzically, even somewhat pathetically, as if seeing me for the first time. But just as quickly she pulled back, returning to her readings. "When you're sixteen," she solemnly said. "When you're sixteen."

"*When I'm sixteen?* That's three years from now!"

"Your father will explode if—"

"I'm a girl and girls are supposed to get their ears pierced!"

I wished that she had let me pierce my ears. I wished that she had taken me right then to the mall, or even did it herself, like some mothers. I wished that she, like Telethusa, protected her daughter. It would have changed everything.

That same night, a gripping sensation woke me, the same urge that had overtaken me before, but this time I was stronger, calmer, and more determined. I scooped some ice cubes from the freezer. Squeezing both sides of each earlobe until numb, I grabbed a pair of studs from my mother's small earring saucer in the bathroom and a needle from her sewing kit. I pushed the needle (I didn't even think of sterilizing it) through my left earlobe—it was surprisingly easy. Then I did the same for the right ear. I clasped the studs in my ears, feeling wonderfully calm.

Inspecting myself in the mirror, I noticed the left earring was perfectly positioned, but the right was too low. I thought I had pierced them both in the same position? I tried re-piercing my right ear slightly above the first piercing, but it was harder this time, as if pushing through bone. At first, I couldn't; then I re-tried just to the right of the initial hole. Finally, with all my strength (honestly, it was that hard), I pushed the needle through. Blood spurted. I inserted the earring into my still bleeding ear, removed it, squeezed a wet paper towel over my ear, then pressed an ice cube against it. When the bleeding stopped, I re-inserted the earring.

My right ear was red, but at least the earrings were even.

Chapter 24

Alexander Morgan

3:25.

No sign of Walter.

I sat on the hood of his truck; my feet perched on his radiator grille. 3:26; 3.27; 3:28; 3:29. At precisely 3:30, the horn honked right underneath my ass.

Walter craned out the driver's window. "You dizzy prick! How long were you gonna just sit there?"

"Why didn't you say something?"

"I *said* 3:30. And where do you think you're goin' like that? Clean yourself up! Stick your head in the water barrel or something."

"In that friggin' cesspool?"

"Christ, when I was your age, first thing every mornin' I'd dunk my head in the water barrel and be 'rarin' to go."

"I'll wash inside."

"If you're not back before you leave, I'm leavin' without you."

"Christ, you sound like Phil," I muttered.

No sooner inside, Walter was honking like a bastard. If the door was any bigger or his truck any smaller, he would've driven right inside. I cupped my hands and poured cold water over my face, scrubbing clean my dust-caked face.

Sure enough he had backed to the door, revving the engine. Picture the starting gate of the Indy 500, with everyone's foot on gas, counting down the seconds. A young woman, with big brown eyes, wearing a baseball cap backwards, was leaning into Walter's open passenger window yapping away on her cell phone.

"Who's she?" I asked, climbing into the passenger seat.

"Joanna. Zachary's daughter, General's legal counsel."

"Dressed like that?"

Walter shrugged. "She can write her own rules, kid."

She continued talking as if she was the only one on the planet. Then she hung up, abruptly bidding Walter good-bye without even acknowledging me.

"Someone so busy she can't even say hello?"

"She got her hands full, kid, believe me."

"That don't justify rudeness."

Walter leaned on the steering wheel, glaring at me. "I asked you to wear a clean shirt."

"I've one in my truck."

"Where is it?"

"Where it always is."

"It wasn't there yesterday."

"I moved it for Zella."

"So where's it now?"

"Where it always is."

Walter stepped on the gas, and like a high school kid done for the day, raced across the parking lot. "Your truck's blockin' the dumpster, kid. What if the dumpster guy comes?"

"He never empties it unless it's full. And it ain't close to being full. And besides, he just emptied it Friday." I jumped out, grabbed my T-shirt and was back in Walter's truck before he had shifted into neutral.

"A Patriots T-shirt? We're going to the Seaport District, not the Black Rose."

"Mr. Tux is running a special all week—everything but the shoes. We can stop on the way. And maybe you can rent one; I heard they're also offering a two-for-one special."

Walter reached over to the glove compartment and pulled out an electric razor. He tilted the rear-view mirror toward him and started shaving as we roared out of the parking lot.

"At least pull over so you don't get us killed."

"When did you last shave, kid?"

"Me?" I smiled, stroking my stubbled chin. "Two days ago. Women like it."

He handed me the razor. "Well, Zachary ain't no woman. When I was workin' with Anthony, he insisted we shave *every* mornin' before work. If not, he'd send us home. Only happened once, kid."

"That was then and this is now," I replied, stroking my chin. "Unless it interferes with how I do my job—which it don't—or if there's some friggin' regulation forcing me to shave every hour on the hour—which there ain't—I'll keep it."

"It's a matter of respect, kid."

"Respect for whom?"

"Most men would kill for a jaw like yours. Why don't you shave all that crap off so women can actually see it."

I returned the razor to its rightful habitat, slamming shut the glove compartment. Apologizing, I reopened it, then gently shut it.

"What's eatin' you kid? You've been like this all day."

"Nothing's eating me." I tried stretching the seat back. "Don't your goddammed seat go back any further?"

"That's as far as it goes, kid. Anything else?"

"Order a pizza. I'm sure they deliver."

"If you were ready on time like I had asked you, we would've missed all this."

"What? You made me sit on my ass for an hour."

"It wasn't even five—."

"My truck? I forgot to lock it."

"You did. I saw *and* heard you. And besides Phil locks the gate every evenin'. The one friggin' thing he gets right."

"Can you call and check if he did?"

"Why so worried kid? You stashin' away gold bars?"

"My truck's brand new."

"No shit. If you bought a used one like I suggested, you—"

"Don't start that shit again." I closed my eyes and stretched back as far as I could in a seat that didn't go back all the way.

Walter flipped on his stupid talk radio program.

"Can you turn that crap down?"

"If you saved some money now and then you could sleep better at night and wouldn't need no naps in the middle of the afternoon. That's the difference between you and me kid: When I was your age, I bought a '67 Chevy pickup. Used. Paid cash. No wonder you ain't got a pot to piss in."

"What the hell has that got to do with taking a nap? You ain't making no sense. You never make no sense." I was tired and needed a quick nap and the only way to do so would be if I could get him to tell a story, something that I've heard at least a million times—that should be easy; then he'd lower the volume and his voice would monotone me to sleep. The perfect question came easy: "What was it like working for Zachary's old man?"

Walter immediately lowered the volume, and in a perfectly pitched monotone, began retelling the story that everyone has heard at least a million times. "No matter how early I arrived at the shop, Anthony was always there pourin' over plans. Wooden clipboards hangin' on the bare sheetrock. You couldn't see nothin' with all the goddamned cigarette smoke. No windows, so you never knew if it was day or night. Next to his desk was a globe. He knew every country and its friggin' capital. Not bad for a guy who never left New England— except once when he went to Albany for his niece's wedding. He was always braggin' that he lived just a mile from where he was born. When I arrived at the office—5.30 sharp—I filled my thermos—there was always a full pot of coffee waitin' for me. Peerin' above his plywood-angled desk, he would salute hello, wrap up quickly while chattin' about the day's job and we'd soon be on our way.

"If it weren't for the cigarettes, his drivin' would've killed us: tail-gatin' and beepin', and passin'—even on a one-way street; he never understood no-passin' signs—while writin' in his notebook. He was always thinkin' and talkin' about the job, especially drivin', while smokin' a cigarette and drinkin' coffee. If cell phones had been invented back then, he'd be smokin', writin', and yappin' away, with no hands on the friggin' wheel."

"You ain't much better."

"He was the most recklessly careful driver I knew."

"What the hell does that even mean?"

"You know, drivin' with the flow, doin' what everyone else expects with no surprises: speedin' up for a red light, not lettin' no one in, not yieldin' at a rotary—we never got into an accident."

"A friggin' miracle if there ever was one," I muttered, closing my eyes.

"He even died with a cigarette in his mouth. Right there next to me, on the stagin'. I thought he had slipped and lost his balance, but by the time I realized what happened, it was too late."

I sat up, opening me eyes. *This was new? But how could I have missed this?* "That must've been something? Have him keel over right in front of you?"

"I called 911, givin' him mouth-to mouth but he died instantly. Massive heart attack. Nothin' no one could've done."

"Zachary must've been devastated, losing his old man, especially on the job like that?"

"Are you kiddin'? That was the happiest day of his life."

I looked at Walter, confused.

"They hated each other, always fightin',—you knew that kid. The friction, the dislike was so intense. Sparks flew whenever they was together, fightin' about everythin' and especially General. Zachary wanted the largest construction company in New England, while Anthony preferred it small and family-run. The irony of friggin' ironies: they was family in name only—just a collection of individuals who happened to be related. That's what killed him, if you ask me: none of his goddamned offspring gettin' along.

"Maybe that's why father and son never got along: two peas in a friggin' pod, with the same awful temper, although Zachary's was worse, like somethin' was always festerin' deep inside. His first day workin' with me, the day after Christmas his sophomore year in high school—are you listenin', kid?"

Unfortunately.

"He was pissed that his old man had him workin' while his buddies had the friggin' week off. Christ, when I was his age, I'd be happy as a clam workin'. I was teachin' him how to build stagin'. When this half-bent brace wouldn't fit, he whacked it against the wall and flung it as far as he could, almost decapitatin' two electricians. Then he took another brace, connected it and finished as if nothin' happened. I don't know what was scarier: his initial anger or not acknowledgin' nothin' about it. Anthony laughed it off, sayin' kids have to let off steam now and then."

"What about you and Zachary? You two get along?"

"I never could trust the bastard."

"Christ, you say that about everyone—even me."

"There's the buildin', kid." Walter pointed to a slender, grey-stone, medium-size building in the Seaport District, overlooking the harbor.

Chapter 25

Joanna Turnus

So much of who you are and who you become is determined by others. I became a good swimmer because of a gymnastics class that my father insisted I take—a class, however, that I never attended. It was supposed to make me more agile and athletic—at least that's what he had told everyone—but what better way to explain away increasingly random bruises?

Every Saturday morning my mother dropped me off at the Y, then picked me up at noon. But I never attended class, instead changing into an old bathing suit of my mother's and jumping into the pool.

Saturday mornings were family time, so I judiciously stuck close to everyone (although I'm sure the lifeguards suspected the obvious) watching and learning as parents taught their children how to breath, tread water, float on their stomachs and on their backs. I learned the freestyle, the backstroke, the sidestroke, and the butterfly; but my favorite was swimming backwards, which I taught myself. It wasn't exactly a stroke, perhaps more of a medley: swimming on my back, submerging my ears, caressed by the water blocking the surface noise and the world above, staying afloat with my arms, slightly kicking my legs.

The first Saturday when my mother picked me up, she asked why I had smelled of chlorine. The pool water was just changed, I answered, and its strong smell was everywhere (not exactly a lie). So, every Saturday thereafter, finished with swimming, I made sure to thoroughly wash my body and especially my hair before my mother picked me up. She never asked again.

When my grandfather first invited me to swim with him, the summer before seventh grade, he had no idea how good I really was, so at first, I had to pretend that I knew nothing, (which was difficult since I always thought of myself as a natural swimmer) otherwise even he would have suspected something. He praised me as a fast learner. My grandfather also taught me the frog stroke, which I didn't like because I was super conscious of my big eyes, and the Australian crawl, his favorite and soon to be mine.

He also taught me how to breathe. "You can't focus on breathing *and* technique. Since breathing is natural, forget about it and focus on your technique, which isn't natural, but will become so with practice. With proper breathing and good technique, you can swim all the way to England."

"What if I have to pee?"

He laughed so hard.

Chapter 26

Joanna Turnus

I should tell you something about my grandfather, something that I'm sure you've long suspected, but it's important. That afternoon back in sixth grade, driving home from his birthday celebration at Bubbling Brook, he asked why I didn't shave my legs, but in such a caring way that I could only answer honestly. (It was the first time anyone had asked.) Everything gushed out. Despite our closeness, or maybe because of it, I expected my grandfather to wave his hands in disgust, asking why such a pretty girl would want to become a boy, chastising me for daring to challenge God's plan (as if He had one for me) as so many others would later heartlessly say, as if they were privy to God's inner workings, as if one inelastic exhortation could change me and set me on their pre-conceived self-righteous path, as if they knew who I was. But my grandfather let me speak without interrupting; listening, leaning, handing me an occasional Kleenex, taking my hand (he was driving).

After driving around with no particular place to go, which was fine—it was nice to talk, no matter where, even in his truck, just the two of us, without any distractions—we found ourselves walking along Wollaston Beach in Quincy, comforted by the salt air, Boston's skyline, planes landing at nearby Logan airport, one after another.

My grandfather wrapped his arm around me protecting against a raw breeze snapping off the water, promising to always love me for who I was, and if I wasn't sure, that was OK, there was no rush to find out, he was not going anywhere; that life is rich and diverse and so is identity, so there's no need to pretend based on others' expectations. 'You must become the author of your life, rather than a pawn for others,' he said, 'despite what others have done and what others would like to do. And if so, you *will* find that special someone who will love you for you are and not for who you're supposed to be.' I was surprised by how much my grandfather knew and how much he cared.

He said that my gender uncertainty would give me a third eye, so to speak, a sixth sense, an acumen (I had to ask him what that meant) that no one else had, along with courage, humility, compassion (a special gift from God), a sense of humor, and an empathy that would enable me to go anywhere and do anything; a creative edge that I would use to make the world better.

Of course, back then his words didn't exactly make sense, but I never forgot them: they enabled me to survive the tragedy soon to come, and then graduate top in my high school class and have the courage to go to Columbia Law School, graduating second in my class; eventually finding an occupation that I love and one that I'm able to give back so much.

That evening my grandfather took me to the Old Post Inn, his favorite restaurant, just the two of us, our first of many dinners there. During dinner, my grandfather officially nicknamed me Molasses for being the world's slowest eater, which I was and still am. And if so, he was the world's second slowest eater, so I nicknamed him Molasses Two. My grandfather laughed, promising that my first-born (already nicknamed Molasses Three) would eat even slower and put us both to shame!

Chapter 27

Alexander Morgan

"Welcome to the friggin' penthouse!" Walter beamed, as if the thirty-ninth floor was his and his alone. Stepping out of the elevator, he was immediately accosted by a security guard. "What the hell's this?" demanded Walter. "You know who I am."

"Someone tried to kill Mr. Turnus last week," replied the guard, frisking Walter. "Just after you left."

"He has more enemies than you could shake a stick at," Walter said to me. "And that's just his own friggin' family."

"Everyone has to be checked," the guard apologized to Walter. "Everyone."

"Any idea who it was?" asked Walter.

The security guard shrugged, frisking me. Satisfied, he led us through a metal detector. "His office is at the end of the foyer."

"I know where the hell it is."

If a prize were awarded for the most uselessly expensive foyer, this would win, hands down. The walls were lined with dozens of expensive, museum-looking portraits of people I didn't know, places I'd never seen. And no windows by the way—how can a foyer on the 39th floor overlooking the Harbor not have a friggin' window? About two dozen mustard, oversized royal thrones were spaced about three feet apart. Obviously not for sitting—so why bother with them, as if anyone on their way to see Zachary Turnus would have the luxury of sitting? In the middle of the foyer, hung the biggest chandelier I had ever seen.

"For the life of me I don't understand why he went to Spain for this friggin' thing," said Walter.

Directly below the chandelier was a granite water fountain empty-ing into a shallow pool, guarded by two, six-foot golden urns. Ahead, at the foyer's end, was a three-foot, gold-lettered sign,

GENERAL CONSTRUCTION, INC.
WORLD HEADQUARTERS

"*World headquarters?*" I asked.

"Anthony's turnin' over in his grave. And yes, it's real gold."

The door suddenly opened. "Right on time!" Zachary smiled as the two embraced. "I've always liked that about you."

He was taller than I had thought, almost my height, impeccably dressed in a tailored olive suit; his head shaved, his brown eyes stone cold, as if chiseled out of concrete, with a greyish goatee centering a large nose.

"This is Alex P. Morgan," Walter said. "One of our laborers."

Christ, why couldn't he just introduce me as Alex Morgan?

Zachary shook my hand. "P?"

"Peckerhead," offered Walter; the two sharing a laugh.

Expecting Zachary to follow up and ask, I readied with my tidied, oft-told, standardized explanation that my parents had debated for months on end but couldn't agree on a middle name. For there was no way in hell I was going to tell him or anyone else that my middle name was Pierpont.

Pierpont was my father's idea—and I guess I should be thankful that it's just my middle name and not my first, for then I would've have legally changed it when I turned 16, no matter how much my mother liked it. Yeah, she was actually fond of Pierpont, and still is, perhaps reminding her of happier times. Here's how it happened: My parents were watching TV one night; my mother eight months pregnant with me. That night was one of the few that my father hadn't been out drinking, even promising a new beginning. Channel surfing, he came across a biography of John Pierpont Morgan, which really intrigued him. After the program, he suggested naming me Pierpont. At first my mother thought he was joking, but unfortunately, he was not. She rightfully objected that Pierpont wasn't a first name, but my father persisted. So they struck a deal: my mother could choose my first name, as long as it wasn't too off the wall— as if Pierpont wasn't?—with Pierpont as my middle name.

'Alexander,' my mother immediately said. No particular reason: she was just fond of it.

Later, long after my father had left us, I promised my mother that when I became AFL-CIO president, I'll use my full name: Alexander Pierpont Morgan. Not only does it roll off the tongue reasonably well, but it tells the world that this dude named after one of the richest bastards who ever lived, actually cares about the common laborer.

But Zachary didn't ask, leading us through a small, windowless room, barely large enough for his secretary, who was sitting at her desk, on the phone, typing into her computer. Spotting us, she intensified, her smile disappearing. Zachary whispered something to her. She immediately clicked the phone, then redialed.

"No metal detector in your office?" Walter asked with a touch of sarcasm. "A lot can happen between here and the elevator."

"Some nutcase burst into my office with a handgun. Didn't I tell you? Luckily, I wasn't in. It turned out to be a case of mistaken identity."

"Mistaken identity? He enters the elevator in your friggin' buildin', comes to your friggin' penthouse which needs permission and a friggin' security code, walks a mile down your corridor, past your sign, past your secretary—that's a case of mistaken identity? And what about the video monitors?"

Zachary opened his office door, inviting us in. "They were being repaired."

Floor-to-ceiling glass windows afforded expansive views of Logan airport, the harbor islands, and the Atlantic Ocean straight ahead; to the left, Faneuil Hall and the Government center; and to the back right, the Pru and Hancock towers.

Zachary spotted a smudge on the harbor-facing panel. He tried wiping it off with his handkerchief, but it seemed to be outside. Frustrated, he immediately called the building manager, leaving a short angry message.

Centered in the room was a large oak desk, completely bare. No papers, no phone, not even a memo pad. Against the far wall was a large fireplace centered between a half-filled bookcase and a well-stocked, chestnut-paneled bar. Zachary, inviting us for a drink, pointed out that he had personally selected the wood from a six-hundred-year-old tree. Placing three medium-sized, empty glasses on the shelf, he dropped two ice cubes into one glass, filled it with Coke and handed it to Walter. He removed a half-filled bottle of Balvenie Scotch, poured himself a glass, plopped in two cubes, asking if I wanted the same.

I nodded yes, but to skip the ice, watching Zachary meticulously fill my glass, stopping exactly at quarter-point, examining it, as if looking for something. Smudges perhaps? Satisfied, he presented it to me.

"Balvenie?" noted Walter. "This must be a special occasion."

Above the fireplace hung a large portrait—or was it a photo? —of an older man.

"A portrait of my father," Zachary said, anticipating my question, which, by the way, I had no intention of asking. "It was my mother's idea."

"You defiantly have his nose," Walter said.

Did he just say what I thought he just said?

"I meant definitely," Walter blushed, immediately correcting himself.

"I bet my mother ten bucks that he couldn't sit still."

"That's all?" asked Walter.

Was he just being his usual stupid self, or was he deliberately trying to provoke? If the latter, he was doing a good job, although Zachary seemed oblivious.

Walter leaned into me, "That's him kid: always worryin', smokin', fidgedin'."

"Fidgeting should have been his middle name," Zachary said, staring at the portrait. "You know the last thing he said to me? Just two days before he died, like somehow, he knew. That I'd bankrupt the company, run it into the ground."

"He didn't mean it like that," Walter said.

"Of course he did. He never minced words; you know that." Zachary gulped his Scotch, quickly refilling his glass. "Your father was a mason, is that right?"

"Yes," Walter replied. "And my grandfather and my great-grandfather. I come from a long line of masons."

"What about your sons?"

"They're both in sheet metal. Someday they hope to start their own company."

"That doesn't bother you?"

"Hell no! It's great work."

"I mean that you're the last of the masons?"

Walter laughed. "Of course not. Why would it?"

Zachary sat down at his desk, gesturing for us to sit opposite. "You said this meeting was urgent. You're not retiring?"

"Not for a while." Walter sipped his Coke. "You knew that."

"Then what's on your mind?"

"Phil," Walter answered immediately.

"What about him?"

"He's constantly screwin' up. Always makin' the wrong decisions, reversin' the right ones, forgettin' things, not coordinatin' with subs, jeopardzin' our safety and pissin' people off."

"Pissing everyone off." I added.

"And morale sucks," said Walter.

"I don't care about morale, as long as the job gets done."

"That's the problem," noted Walter. "Half the time I'm doing his work. He can't—"

"He's completely disorganized," I said. "Interrupting jobs, sending me on wild goose chases, sending me back to the shop in the middle of the day."

"Last week he forgot to tell the sheet metal guys about the air conditionin' duct in the vault—it's right on the plans—so he sends the kid in with the friggin' compressor."

"Where'd he put the concrete?"

"In the dumpster? Where else would the kid put it?"

Zachary abruptly excused himself and ducked into his secretary's office. "A super needs to be flexible," he said, when he just as quickly returned. "Things come up; you have to be able to think on your feet."

"Thinkin' on your feet's one thing, not knowin' where your nose is, that's another."

"That's not what I'm hearing. Everyone's praising Phil that we're eight days ahead of schedule."

"Only because of the unusually good weather," I noted.

"If it was just the weather, we'd be on time: we factor good *and* bad weather when we do the bidding." Zachary glanced at his watch. "Anything else?"

Walter took out a small spiral notebook from his shirt pocket.

"Is that my father's?" asked Zachary, peering over the table.

"He started me with this goddamned habit." Walter slipped on his reading glasses, flipping through the pages. "There's been some talk about unionizing. The Teamsters have been snoopin' around. I thought you should know."

How the hell did Walter find out, and why's he bringing this up now?

"Unions just don't snoop around," Zachary retorted.

"No one from General invited them," Walter clarified. "If that's what you're getting at. Obviously they see us growin' faster than no one else, so they want a piece of the action. If your father was alive, he'd—"

"Damn my father!" Zachary stood up, hurling his whiskey glass at Anthony's portrait, splattering ice and glass. Then he poured himself another drink and calmly sat down as if nothing happened. "If my father was still running the company," he said in a disarmingly subdued voice, "it would be bankrupt. Times change and you have to change with them. Anything else?" Zachary sipped his Scotch, glancing at his watch. "I have a conference call in just a few minutes."

Walter rose and I quickly rose with him.

"Why don't you check up on Phil now and then," offered Walter. "See how that moron really operates."

"I check up on *everyone*." Zachary glared at me with his stone-cold eyes. "And I don't have a problem with Phil."

We shook hands and said good-bye.

"What the hell was that all about?" I asked, once inside the elevator.

Walter grabbed my arm, pointing to a camera and microphone directly above us. I waited patiently for the elevator to empty us into the parking garage. "Why'd you say that shit about the Teamsters? And how'd you find out?"

"Relax kid. The woman you was talkin' to the other day when you was returnin' to the vault."

"So why'd you ask me who I was talking to if you already knew the reason? And now Zachary thinks *I* invited the Teamsters."

"Relax kid. By givin' you a little of the disease now, it prevents you from gettin' it later; you understand what I'm sayin'?"

"No, I don't understand what you're saying. I never understand what the hell you're saying."

"Listen kid, Zachary knows about the Teamsters, the Laborers, Steelworkers, the UAW, and every other friggin' union wantin' to organize us. So by tellin' him now clears your name. He'll never assume you're guilty if I mention it now. Trust me, kid."

"I don't trust you." I stepped up into his cab and slammed shut the door. *I've never trusted you.*

"Don't you think it odd that there weren't no papers on his desk?" I asked, as we merged onto the Expressway, surprised that the traffic was so light. "And no filing cabinets or plans?"

"Did you happen to notice that door across the hallway from his secretary?"

"No, I didn't notice no door across from his secretary or anyone else."

"*That's* his office. This afternoon he met us in the Conference room. His office has three overflowing blueprint desks, and the walls plastered with before/after photos of every project General's ever done."

"Did Anthony have any family pictures in his office?"

"Anthony? Yeah, lots. Especially Joanna—two peas in a friggin' pod if you ask me."

"She married?"

Walter laughed.

"Just asking."

"She ain't like you and me, kid; she ain't like no one else: she's weird, unpredictable, and explosive—just like her old man. *And* she ain't in your league."

"Didn't know I was in no league?"

"You know what I mean: rich, smart, a lawyer, drives a Lexus."

I stretched back as far as I could in the passenger seat of Walter's truck, closing my eyes. "I'll have to remember that: not in my league."

Chapter 28

Joanna Turnus

Our first practice after our first game was terribly brutal, as if we had lost big-time, as if we didn't know what we were doing, as if the fans weren't on our side, as if we had bumbled through a lopsided, excruciating loss. Coach nitpicked every little fault that no one else would have noticed, that no one else would have even thought to look for, that probably kept her up all night. But, in retrospect, maybe it was good to get chewed out: bringing us down a notch before we got too arrogant; after all this was the beginning of a long season.

I couldn't imagine how such a long practice could've been any longer or any worse, or even what it would have been like had we lost, but just when we thought it was finally over (already ninety minutes later than usual) Coach said that she had videotaped everyone's game performance and wanted to meet with us individually, immediately; in her office.

Of course, my meeting was last (we went alphabetically), and of course it was the longest (although I had assumed that when she finally got to me, she would have exhausted herself)—and it would have been even longer, had not her husband called.

She handed me my video wrapped in manila paper as if it was a report card. Plastered on the front was my grade (so far, the highest grade was a C- with several Fs):

C+ *SEE ME*

"See me?" I wondered out loud. "But I was a hit with the moms?" Indeed, they had raved about my 'infectious enthusiasm' making everyone want to dance, which I guess was easy when we scored on our first six possessions cruising to a lopsided shutout, in what was supposed to be our biggest test, our closest game all season. With our ebullient fans dancing in the stands, anticipating another undefeated season, it would have been tough to find fault with anything that afternoon.

Except for Coach.

"You have to correct this," Coach said, seeming like she was getting her second wind, or perhaps she never lost her first? She hurriedly unwrapped the paper and injected the tape into the machine. "Sometimes—but not always—you strut like a boy, not in your walk but in your dance—disjointed, discordant; deliberately exaggerating your arms and hips like you have something to prove."

Strut like a boy? deliberately? like I have something to prove?

Coach wasn't exactly angry (perhaps by now she too was tired?), admitting that I had received the most compliments from the moms, but that she was just fixing a 'noticeable problem.' Nevertheless, the meeting was surreal, as if Coach were tiptoeing around a well-guarded secret, knowing full well what it was. I felt like Montag 'hearing something in the silence.'

Coach said that while I was in-sync with the team—more so than anyone else—I was sometimes (thankfully not a lot, otherwise it would have been a major problem) out of sync with myself—more so than anyone else. Her solution was simple, practical, and effective: use my body curves to portray flowing, continuous, feminine motion to preempt any jerky 'masculine' moves. "No need to go overboard," Coach said. "You're a girl, so it should be natural to dance like one."

I practiced night and day, determined to fix my 'noticeable problem.' By the second game, dancing like a girl was almost second nature.

During the first quarter of that game (which, by the way, we also lopsidedly won, although we surrendered a last-minute field goal which angered the defense, even more so than a loss, since they were hoping for back-to-back shutouts), I had an embarrassing mishap. As part of our uniform, we had to wear a skimpy miniskirt and a black outer panty, which was fine, but underneath I wore boys' briefs—I had to: it was the only way I could be myself. It was the only way I could relax and smile in public. It was the only way I could walk (and dance) like a girl. During a jumping routine early in the second quarter, the elastic of my outer panty ripped, sliding down my leg exposing my male briefs. Two cheerleaders, surprised, immediately shielded me from the crowd. Obviously nothing was there that shouldn't have been (except the underwear). Obviously I was a girl.

"My boyfriend's," I said, forcing a laugh. "We got a little carried away."

"So, he's wearing your panties?" snickered one girl.

"If he did, he wouldn't be my boyfriend."

As soon as I said that I wanted to retract every word, preferably all at once, as if never said. Sometimes we're forced to say things we don't really mean, uttering a scripted line, unrehearsed; at the time convincing to everyone but ourselves. Sometimes we say things too quickly—later wishing we never had—to comport with the callous, inelastic expectations of others, as if that's the only barometer, as if that's all that matters.

I was sure Coach was in the stands secretly videotaping, knitting evidence against me. But she had left at the beginning of the game for an urgent family matter and didn't return until half-time. Perhaps she had someone else videotaping me? But I saw no one suspicious, no one pointing their camera at my skirt. Only two cheerleaders witnessed, and everything happened so quickly that even if someone in the stands had happened to see, it wouldn't had been exactly clear what they saw. My friends laughed it off as innocent fun. Nevertheless, I felt the Hound's presence, getting closer, 'like a wind that didn't stir the grass.'

My friends on the cheerleading squad accepted me. Yeah, I was a little weird, a little masculine now and then, but who was 100% feminine, whatever that meant? I also laughed a lot (more than anyone) and was (very) pretty—everyone said so—and I had a major crush on Terry, which made me really fit in. But I was jealous of the other girls, jealous that every morning they'd do their make-up, their hair, slip uncontested into clothes, never thinking twice about being a girl—no self-doubt, no questions asked, no need for discussion.

As I got older, an inner voice warned that this charade couldn't continue, that the longer it lasted, the worse it would become; a threatening, ominous voice, becoming more frequent and more persistent. My body had become a silent battleground; nothing secured, nothing battened down, and it wasn't clear who was going to win.

Chapter 29

Alexander Morgan

"Hey, Walter, is that the Comet?"

"Too bright in the city to see nothin', kid."

"No, the coffee shop? Can you back up?"

"In the middle of traffic?"

"Then drop me off."

"Getting a head start on mornin' coffee, kid?" Walter asked, pulling to the curb.

"My sister-in-law works here. Care to join me?" I only asked because I knew the answer.

"Just lookin' at caffeine at night keeps me up."

"Then have a decaf."

"I don't drink nothin' that don't do nothin' for me. And, besides, I have to get home."

"It ain't even six-thirty."

"It's seven-fifteen, almost my bedtime. Sister-in-law you said? Be careful, kid."

"I'm *just* having coffee."

Walter laughed. "That's how it starts: She makes you a coffee. Extra strong. You like it. She makes another. You're wide awake. You wait for her until she's done work. You both stop at a bar for a drink. Then another. She invites you home. You have a night cap. Then, in the mornin' you come to work with a goddamned twinkle in your eye."

"I'm having *one* coffee, then leaving." I opened the passenger door and stepped out. "And I certainly won't be coming to work with no goddamned twinkle in my eye."

"You have a gate key, kid?"

"What gate? No, I don't."

"How'd you expect to get in without a key?" He handed me his gate key, along with the key to the trailer. "Don't lose them, kid."

The L-shaped Comet's floor-to-ceiling windows afforded a great view of the traffic. Lisa, her hair tied back, was working the espresso machine. "I thought that was you." She smiled seeing me, wiping her hands on her black apron. "What a nice surprise!"

"I think I'm addicted to switchblades?"

She laughed. "I'll make you a just-as-good caramel whipped–creamed decaf that won't keep you up all night."

"Caffeine don't bother me at night."

"A switchblade will. Trust me."

I took a seat next to people sitting alone or sitting alone with someone else, typing into their laptops, writing on their note pads, texting who knows who.

Lisa returned with my coffee and an over-sized brownie.

I took a long sip, nodding my approval.

"Glad you like it!" She sat opposite. Perspiration beaded on her forehead.

"Is this really a decaf?"

"I told you that you couldn't tell the difference! Are you working overtime tonight?"

I explained my visit with Zachary.

"I'm closing tonight," she said. "Someone called in sick, so I'm working a triple shift: opening this morning, a day shift, and closing."

"Maybe you need one of them switchblades."

Lisa's phone vibrated. "Now what does he want?"

"Who?"

"Who do you think? He's called three times in the last hour, accusing me of an affair—I have to get back to work. I've already taken my break, and I can't loiter with customers, no matter how cute." She rose and kissed me on the cheek. "Thanks for stopping by! Are you still coming this weekend?"

"Yes."

She smiled. "We're leaving Friday night right after work. 5.15. And don't be late."

Chapter 30

Joanna Turnus

My grandfather nudged me awake. "We're here, Molasses!"

"Anthony!" my grandmother reprimanded. "She has such a pretty name."

I had been asleep in the warm front seat of my grandfather's truck—quite comfortably I might add—snuggled between my grandparents, on the way to the Lake, three weeks after homecoming. My grandfather's lake: the lake where he swam every Sunday, the lake where he met my grandmother, the lake that he promised to take me swimming (hopefully waiting until summer), the lake that gave me my middle name.

My grandmother helped me down from the truck. I stretched, rubbing my eyes, not sure if I was awake just yet, half-listening to my grandfather excitedly explain that we had parked on a scenic overlook along the southern shore of the Lake, on Highway 11, just east of Sleeper's Point.

"I can see how Sleeper's Point got its name," I said, exaggerating a yawn.

My grandmother laughed.

The Lake sprawled before us: 22 miles end-to-end. I had never seen so many islands in one place; 258, my grandfather boasted. The air was crisp and the sky clear, unusual for New Hampshire in mid-November.

My grandfather wrapped his arm around me. "See the large expanse of open water just east of them two islands? That's where I swim. It's called the Broads because it's so open. Sometimes it's as rough as the ocean—the winds can be so unpredictable—and sometimes it can be smooth as glass—like today."

Too bad it's so cold.

"You should start her off in a cove, Anthony. She's just thirteen."

"She'll be fine; and besides, I'll be right with her."

Seeing the two of them now, you'd never guess that he was the swimmer. My grandfather didn't have much of a swimmer's build, and actually my grandmother was more athletic looking: slender, strong, stern, outwardly dour but inwardly warm. She never swam with him but instead accompaning him in a dinghy to shield him from bigger boats—after all, no one expected a swimmer in the middle of the Lake—and in case he ever got a cramp (which he never did, my grandfather had boasted).

I nestled between my grandparents listening to my grandfather: "That's Rattlesnake Island. Some people say that from the air it looks like a rattlesnake, while others say that years ago the island periodically would become so infested with snakes that the residents would have to burn everything—but they always returned."

"The people or the snakes?" I asked.

My grandmother laughed, clasping my hand.

"Any water snakes?" I asked.

"Not where we swim, Molasses; they don't like people. See the island just to the left of the Broads? That's Bear Island, where your grandmother and I picnic when we're done swimming. When I was younger, sometimes I'd see a bear swimming around the island, but not now, there's too many people."

"Anthony, you're scaring the poor thing with rattlesnakes and bears."

"As long as there isn't a piranha island," I said, half-serious.

Directly across from us was a non-functioning lighthouse perched on a narrow spit.

"If you look north/northeast, Joanna," my grandmother said, pointing. "That's Center Harbor. I grew up just west in a wonderful farmhouse overlooking the Lake."

Beyond Center Harbor, rose steep, cold-grey hills, and further yonder, a range of mountains. Looming majestically in the distance was snow-clad Mount Washington.

"It's unusual to see the Mount," my grandfather boasted, seeming surprised. "Especially in November. On a clear day, you can see it from the Atlantic. It used to have the world's highest wind speed, but someone beat us out in Australia, I think."

"Hard to imagine," I said. "It looks so calm and peaceful."

"That's where all the North American air masses converge. The summit is—"

"I'm sure Joanna's hungry." My grandmother scooted me into the truck. "And I'm getting cold."

We drove down the hill, away from Sleeper's Point, then west along the long wide bay; my grandfather rattling off the names of the towns and villages that dotted the Lake: Meredith, Weirs Beach, Laconia, Gilford, Alton Bay, Moultonborough, Tuftonboro, Center Harbor, Wolfeboro—"

"I'm glad you two didn't meet in Wolfeboro; I couldn't imagine being Joanna Wolfeboro Turnus."

My grandmother laughed.

"The lake's clear as glass today," said my grandfather. "Perfect for swimming, but too bad it's so cold."

Thank God.

We pulled into the parking lot of the Center Restaurant in Meredith at the base of Meredith Bay; the same restaurant where my grandparents had first met. We sat at the same Formica table (looking like it hadn't changed a bit, my grandmother said) that my shy grandfather sat in as a young man (while my future grandmother and her father sat just across the narrow aisle, so narrow in fact, that I couldn't believe it took them three just weeks to talk).

My grandfather and I ordered blueberry pancakes with extra (real) maple syrup; and my grandmother ordered homemade oatmeal with walnuts and locally grown cranberries.

"When I was 18," my grandfather began, eager to explain how he had met my grandmother. "I was training every day for the Olympics." [1968 in Mexico City, which I'll explain shortly]. "Every Sunday, mid-

May through mid-December, I drove the 2½ hours one way to the Lake rain or shine to swim, often donning a wet suit. It was more of a relaxing psychological reward after a long, hard week of training. Surrounded by pine-scented hills with the White Mountains in the distance, the water was—and still is—crystal clear, and so clean that you could—and still can—drink from it.

"I would first breakfast here, loading up on carbohydrates—they make the best blueberry pancakes (with the best maple syrup). One morning I noticed this pretty young lady eating with an older gentleman. At first, I assumed they were a couple, but it soon became obvious they were father and daughter. Finally, after the third Sunday, I was determined to break the ice."

"I never understood why it took you three weeks to say anything," chided my grandmother.

"Having your father sitting next to you glaring at me, didn't exactly help matters."

"Oh, he's harmless; you know that." My grandmother took my hand. "We couldn't believe how your grandfather would meticulously dissect each pancake into quarter-inch squares, then inspect them as if bestowing grace, taking deep breaths like a tightrope walker about to traverse Niagara Falls. And once he started eating, he was so focused he never looked up."

"How many pancakes did grandpa eat?"

"You'll never guess," challenged my grandmother. "And each was as big as a regular plate!"

"Two?"

"Ha!"

"Three. Four? Five?"

"Six?"

My grandmother nodded.

"How could anyone eat six pancakes?"

"I could've eaten twenty," my grandfather boasted.

"And the only reason you didn't, was that it would've been dark by the time you finished and then time for supper."

"To think that I could've been named Joanna Pancakes Turnus?"

My grandmother laughed, such a light, endearing laugh, slightly tilting her head back, displaying a fun, elfish look.

"My plan," my grandfather winked at me, "was to accidentally bump into your grandmother in the register line."

"That was a plan?" laughed my grandmother. "Jacques Clouseau had better-made plans!"

"It worked, didn't it?"

"He was so nervous in line rehearsing what he wanted to say," said my grandmother, "that he hadn't notice me talking to him, taking his arm, laughing that I'd never met anyone who could eat so many pancakes."

"That morning we sat for more coffee while her father did a few errands," my grandfather continued. "And after swimming, her parents invited me for Sunday dinner, which soon became our weekly tradition."

"How many dinners did grandpa eat?"

"Just one. But the portions were huge—my mother was fore-warned."

"Then I had to stop for ice cream not even half-way home."

"I'm surprised that he waited that long," my grandmother said to me, laughing. "And this was after my mother made him a huge doggy bag."

When my grandmother had finished her breakfast—us slowpokes weren't even half-done—she handed me a small package wrapped in purple, my favorite color. "Joanna dear," she said with emotion, "we don't care if you have pierced ears or not, if you wear clip-ons or no earrings at all, or even if you let your holes close; but we thought that if I you choose to wear earrings, you might like these."

I had difficulty opening the package, never mind seeing it. Like my grandfather, I can get quite emotional. My grandmother gladly took over, while my grandfather handed me a Kleenex.

"Diamond earrings?" I exclaimed, wiping my eyes.

My grandmother scooted closer, gently pulling my hair back. "No matter what you wear or don't wear, we love you Joanna Meredith Turnus. We're proud of who you are; always remember that." She slipped one earring in, clasped the backing, then slipped in the other. "There!" She held out her compact for my inspection. I was wowed by how much they prettied my ears and were the perfect size.

The waitress refilled our coffee, complimenting my earrings and how pretty I looked.

While us slowpokes resumed eating, my grandmother asked for the *Lake News*, the bi-weekly paper. She always enjoyed reading Mrs. Mildred's gossip column, 'Roundabouts,' saying it was 'wonderfully entertaining,' although I couldn't tell if she was serious.

As my grandmother read, my grandfather hooted and howled at practically every word, the banality of Mrs. Mildred, although it was chilling how much she knew:

> "Mrs. Collins' younger sister Eleanor just visited from New Jersey—I'm sure you all remember her visit last summer—who can forget? This year's trip was calmer, and thankfully no one caused a scene—exactly why I'm not sure—although last summer's trip had enough scenes to last a lifetime.
>
> This year's trip started similarly, which worried yours truly and everyone else in the Lakes Region, with the two sisters breakfasting at the Center Restaurant, sans husbands. A good idea since they never would have got a word in edgewise. I'm sorry to say that I didn't get to see them. I arrived early (the same time as her last visit) thinking they would want to get a head start on such a beautiful day, but they had overslept (out late the night before at a neighborhood party, which somehow I had missed?) and almost canceled their 10.15 pedicure/manicure (also a tradition) but Eleanor insisted that a weekend visit wouldn't be the same without first breakfasting at the Center. (How about a little flexibility: Maybe Sunday brunch to wrap up the weekend?) So, they called

Lucille and rescheduled for 11.00. Of course, Lucille was super busy (when is she not? especially on a Saturday?) but she happily obliged, only because their husbands graduated together from Inter-Lakes High School, Class of 1977 (along with yours truly).

Then it was on to a late lunch for the ladies, which was more of a social event, since neither could have been hungry after such a big breakfast. Lucille said that the two sisters debated for 'quite some time' where to lunch (as if we have a lot of choices in Meredith) finally deciding on the Turkey Farm (is there a better place for lunch, Saturday mid-afternoon?)

Delores ordered the turkey special with all white meat, but Eleanor couldn't decide between white or dark. The waiter suggested ordering both; a nice young man, one of the Wilkenson boys, rather tall for his age, but unfortunately looks just like his mother (poor boy) but, thankfully, doesn't stir the pot like her. When finished, they discussed desert, although if you ask me, neither needed any. They finally decided on the home-made mincemeat pie..."

Who monitors everyone's whereabouts, what they debated having for lunch, what they said and didn't say? I felt Mrs. Mildred's presence at the Center Restaurant, writing about me, this strange girl from Massachusetts who didn't fit in, who wants to be a boy, yet has a major crush on the team quarterback, whose grandparents just gave her diamond earrings; although I'm sure she would write that they were fake. I smiled, tugging on my ears, knowing that despite all the stuff she was writing about me, at least my diamond earrings were real.

Chapter 31

Alexander Morgan

The parking lot gate was locked—remind me to give Phil a medal for finally doing something right. But my truck was gone. Along with the dumpster. What the fuck? Was my mind playing tricks on me? Did I hitch a ride with Walter to work? But I distinctly remember parking my truck next to the dumpster *this morning*, and *this afternoon* getting a T-shirt—a Pat's T-shirt—the same one I'm wearing now.

I called Walter. If anyone knew anything about anything, it was him, although, to be honest, if he wasn't with me the whole time, he would have been my prime suspect.

Doris answered, surprised that I was calling at 8.45 PM knowing full well that Walter had long been asleep. I told her it was an emergency

"Maybe some kids hot-wired it; it ain't that difficult," Walter said, finally answering. "Same thing once happened to me."

"No shit. But why would they also take the dumpster? And the gate was locked, so whoever took it also took the dumpster *and* had a key."

"You're assumin' that this all happened after the gate was locked, but it could've been taken anytime durin' the day."

"Someone would've noticed."

"Maybe the dumpster guy emptied it and took your truck, pissed that you'd parked so close, like I'm always tellin' you."

"Then he would've gone straight to Phil. Like when Paul parked the bulldozer right in front of the dumpster. And besides, it was just emptied on Friday and he *never* empties a half-full dumpster."

"Maybe Phil noticed your truck when he locked the gate?"

"He couldn't notice his ass from his elbow."

I called the dumpster guy and of course he knew nothing about it. He was just as pissed as I was, and immediately called the police.

I called Phil. He answered on the first ring, that prick.

"Was *my* truck there when you locked the gate?"

"It was."

"And the dumpster?"

"Yes."

"My truck *and* the dumpster were both there?"

"I just said that."

"You noticed both?"

"Yes. Did you call the dumpster guy?"

"He didn't take it."

"Maybe he moved it?"

"He didn't."

"Maybe the graders moved it?"

"They wouldn't have taken it home with them."

"Call the police and report it stolen."

Son-of-a-bitch.

I called Paul. The phone rang six times. No answer. I called again. I knew that bastard was home, sitting on his Lazy-Boy, watching TV; that's all he ever does. I called again. Finally, on the fifth ring he answered. Of course he knew nothing, although he did mention that he saw my truck and the dumpster when he left that afternoon, wondering where the hell I was.

I called the police and reported a stolen truck.

Paul only lived fifteen minutes away but even if he were the last person on earth, I wouldn't have stayed with him. And if I stopped at the Comet or even called Lisa, who knows what would have happened? I thought about taking the T home, but the Orange Line was down, and in the morning the Orange and Red Lines would both be down, meaning that I'd have to take a bus to the Green Line to Government Center, then the Blue Line to Park Street, and then re-connect with the Red Line. Fuck it, it was almost 10.30 and I was tired, so I decided to sleep in the trailer and worry about my friggin' truck in the morning.

The trailer was stuffy and warm, smelling of everything ever used at a construction site: turpentine, diesel, gasoline, asphalt, paint, grease, wooden shingles, cement, weed-killer, fertilizer. I plopped the trailer door open with a couple of bricks, arranged several turpentine-tinged drop cloths into a makeshift bed, and with canvases for pillows, fell fast asleep. It was surprisingly comfortable—almost as comfortable as my friggin' own bed.

During morning coffee, Gary was going on and on about some bastard who had tried to rob a bank under construction on the other side of Harvard Square, as if that was the only news item of the day, as if everyone was interested. "He assumed it would've been a cinch breaking into the vault from the roof," Gary continued. "He's walking along, then steps on nothing but tar paper. Lucky for him, he landed on staging just below, only breaking a leg and some ribs. Now he's suing the contractor."

"Are you kidding me?" asked Abe. "What did he want? A sign? Please pardon the inconvenience; we are renovating to make your robbing experience more pleasurable."

"That's like getting someone pregnant," Paul said. "Then suing the condom maker because it had a hole."

"Speakin' from experience?" asked Walter.

"If there's a hole," I said. "Return the sucker."

"Who inspects a condom before using it?" asked Gary.

"You have to have sex in order to use one," Walter said, laughing.

"Sex without protection?" I said to Gary. "You might as well take a gun and shoot yourself."

"If you were marooned on a desert island," Gary asked, "with a beautiful woman and no condoms, what would you do?"

"First of all, I don't live on no deserted island," I replied, standing up, stretching my arms. "And second, if I was planning on getting marooned—especially with a beautiful woman—I'd make sure to bring along a year's supply of condoms."

"Why just a year?" asked Abe.

"Where you goin' kid?" Walter asked. "Coffee break's just gettin' started."

I crouched next to Walter. "Can you meet me at the Scarlet Pumpernickel for lunch? I need to talk about some shit."

Walter reached in his front pocket, "How much you need kid?"

"I'm good. I just need to talk."

"You know I bring my lunch every day. Why don't you meet me in my truck and save some money for once?"

Just then a white limo pulled into the parking lot, parking at the bank's rear entrance.

"Must be nice," said Abe. "Chauffeured to the bank to count your millions."

Zachary stepped out, impeccably dressed in a brown suit. He was immediately greeted by the bank president, tie-less and short-sleeved. I'm sure I wasn't the only one who noticed—I mean how could you not notice unless you were friggin' blind—but it ain't that often that you see such hairy, thickly matted arms, as if he was wearing a shaggy rug. I always thought that my arms were hairy, but at least you can see skin. I couldn't imagine a woman, or anyone for that matter, finding that attractive. But what's the alternative? Shave your arms? That's almost as bad as a guy shaving his legs.

The two shook hands, chatting and laughing, as if old friends. Then the bank president returned inside. Zachary briskly approached us, removing his jacket and slinging it over his shoulder; his gold cuff links glistening in the morning sunlight.

"Looks like we're finally getting them raises," said Abe.

Zachary shook hands with Walter. "Nice to see you again." He removed his sunglasses, surveying the circle. "I have an announcement."

No shit.

"While my father was alive, we had our disagreements."

"The understatement of the year," muttered Walter.

Zachary wiped his brow with a monogrammed handkerchief.

"Maybe *disagreement* is too strong? Let's say we had our differences. My father—bless his soul—was a product of his time. For one month out of respect, I did nothing different."

"Didn't even wait a day," whispered Walter.

"Then I renamed us General Construction, determined to become the largest construction company in Massachusetts. We succeeded in one year and now we're the largest in New England."

"Size means nothin'," said Walter.

"Depends how you want to spend your Saturday night," I said.

Everyone laughed, except Paul, of course.

"My father was content with a small company," Zachary continued, loosening his tie. "Back then things were different: business was local, and everyone made a good living. But times change and you have to change with them; a lesson my father never learned. In today's global economy, if you're small and unattached, you don't survive. We're thinking big and building global, and to help meet our goals, we will soon be acquired by CCB, a London-based private equity company."

"How can a goddamned construction company be acquired?" Nick asked.

"They'll own us for a month," I whispered to Nick. "Strip our assets, lay everyone off, then shut us down."

I felt the glare of Zachary's cement-cold eyes. "CCB's given us a green light to expand. We'll operate as a fully independent subsidiary. You won't notice much of a difference: we'll keep our name and logo, our vehicles and equipment will remain green, but our official letterhead will change, and your paychecks will look different."

"As long as they ain't smaller," said Abe.

"Of course not," Zachary said, joining the laughter. "And CCB's offering their own health care, much better than ours. They want us to be profitable." He started toward his limo, then turned back, shooting me an icy glare. "And CCB wants nothing done differently. Nothing."

"I can't imagine Joanna on board with this," I said to Walter, as we watched Zachary's limo pull away.

"One way to find out kid, we'll set up a meetin'."

"You and your friggin' meetings."

BOOK TWO

Chapter 1

Joanna Turnus

"Midway on our life's journey, I found myself in dark woods, the right road lost." So begins Dante's *Inferno*. I'm sure a normal person, anxious to experience Dante's Hell, would have skipped the narrator's self-reflection, but for someone like me, who as Ovid said, "hovers between the sexes," I paused, wondering where my right road is, what it looks like, how I would reach it, and if I ever did, how I would I recognize it.

For me there was (and is) no 'right' road. I was forced to make my own where none existed, often obscured by mist and pummeled by fierce storms; hacking away at suffocating underbrush with no guiding lights or markers, sometimes detoured by self-appointed vigilantes—the high priests of society, the self-righteous, anointed with the self-certainty that they alone understood God's order, exhorting me to change, to find the right road—before it's too late—no matter how painful and arduous, as if I could choose, as if I had a choice, as if there was only one road. Sometimes I would see an illusionary path, a clearing. Sometimes I would help those who, like me, stumbled and faltered when forced to travel the 'right' road. Sometimes, seeing others travelling the 'right' road I imagined what that would be like.

I spent a lifetime trying to understand who I am and why 'I found myself in dark woods, the right road lost.' I spent a lifetime trying to understand why I was never given a choice. I spent a lifetime trying to understand why my prison-body announces to the world that I'm a girl, that I'm supposed to wear girl clothes and do girly things but that I always knew I was a boy. I spent a lifetime parrying mean-spirited exhortations to stay on the 'right' road. I spent a lifetime clearing away "rough and tangled" underbrush trying to survive, trying to find my own path, my own road, however non-linear, however 'wrong' it may be.

I used to curse God for my long, sleepless nights, nights that seemed like days, days that seemed like months, not knowing if I was male or female. But now I'm thankful that I never traveled the 'right' road, that I "hover between the sexes," that I'm a transgender person. I marvel at life's wonderful diversity. I listen to the rain. I understand what it means to love and be loved, to empathize, to be accepted and rejected, to be despaired and fulfilled, to be male and female.

Chapter 2

Alexander Morgan

The morning began clear and calm, but by 8.00 the winds were gusting to 50 m.p.h., darkening the sky with so much dust and shit, that it looked like a summer storm rolling in. It should have been a no-brainer to shut the crane down—any unionized place would've done so—but Phil insisted that it wasn't that bad, that the crane was away from the crowded street, shielded from the gusts, and that the wind was blowing away.

Bullshit.

I squirreled up the crane ladder and banged on the operator's window urging him to stop.

"I can handle it," he snipped, wiping his forehead, surprised that anyone would dare question his judgement, especially a lowly laborer like me, and especially in his private space, his inner sanctuary. "If it gets bad, I'll stop." Just then a sharp gust ripped the huge American flag onto the roof of Luke's house.

"If it gets bad? What'd you call this?"

"I've worked in much worse. I'm into to the wind. And besides I've my orders from Zachary," he shouted, closing his window.

Luke's mother, crouched on her knees, was working her garden. I scampered down, yelling for her to go inside. She shook her hoe at me, unfazed by the violent wind, yelling something in Spanish. I had no idea what she was saying and I'm sure likewise, although my English was perfectly fine. Frustrated, I searched the front of the bank for Phil or Zachary or Walter—anyone, but no one was around.

No sooner had I returned when a sharp gust twisted off a terribly large sheet of metal from the old roof, just missing me as I ducked for cover but decapitating Luke's mother.

The OHSA, the City Commission, and the mayor's office, officially ruled the mother's death an accident. Construction is dangerous they said, people slip, get run over, hit over the head, fall off roofs. They even blamed the mother for being outside, working her garden—her fault for growing her own vegetables and living 'too close' to a construction site.

Bullshit.

This was one accident that shouldn't have happened. At the very least, the roof should have been secured with any loose shit covered or removed, *and* the friggin' crane should've been shut down.

Of course Phil refused to allow us to attend the funeral, insisting that we couldn't afford to fall behind schedule. Really? A poor immigrant gets decapitated in front of her soon-to-be demolished home and we couldn't even take an hour off to attend her funeral?

Bullshit.

I told Phil to dock me an hour, two hours, a full day, a week even; I didn't give a shit. And if he fired me, I would have told every Boston TV station what really happened.

At the funeral I sat in the back row, inconspicuous—at least I had thought —dressed in a white shirt, tie, and black jacket. But as the Mass began, people started murmuring, whispering, pointing. Suddenly a middle-aged Spanish dude, sitting in the front row, stood up. Riding a cascading wave of hatred, he scolded me for 'audaciously' attending a funeral that 'my company' caused.

I rose, scared; my voice unsure, saying that I was just as outraged, that I had tried everything in my power to prevent what had happened.

"Yes, that's true," agreed a younger woman standing next to the dude.

"I was in the kitchen," said another. "And I heard him."

"This was an accident that never should've happened," I said, emboldened by the unexpected support, my voice rising in anger. "I am sorry for her death. If you want me to leave, I will."

The dude gestured for me to stay, as did the woman, as did the priest.

As Mass ended and everyone herded outside, a Channel 56 news reporter asked for an interview. I reluctantly agreed and was about to speak when I saw young Alex, confused, crying, arm-in-arm with the angry dude.

I couldn't. Even though it would have been a hell of a story.

Nick was pissed when I returned from the funeral, not so much for attending —for he was glad that at least someone from General attended, although it should've been Zachary or Phil, or both, but for not setting the sidewalk wire before I left—necessary to ensure that the finished sidewalk don't crack. Sure, it will eventually as the earth moves and shifts, but there ain't never been a sidewalk poured without first doing so—which should have been done yesterday, or the day before, or the day before that. But every time I had started, Phil sent me off on one of his wild goose chases—always something more important. So to get it done—today—and to ensure that Nick didn't have a friggin' heart attack, I worked through lunch—on my own time.

It's a breeze with two people—which, by the way, is how it should be done, like jackhammering horizontally, or hanging a door, but it was lunchtime, and no one was around, so to get it done I had to do it myself. First, I rolled out six feet of wire, then holding it in place with four sledgehammers—to prevent it from rolling back—I was about to cut it when someone jerked my shoulder from behind. Assuming it was Phil pissed that I had attended the funeral, I turned ready to smack him—someday I will—accidentally letting the wire go, letting it roll backwards.

Walter was laughing like a bastard. "Why so jumpy, kid? And why you workin' through lunch? You ain't sick?"

I explained.

"I'm glad someone went. I set up a meetin' for us with Joanna right after work."

"I can't."

"Why?"

"I've a basketball game which I can't miss."

"Look kid, if you want to get elected AFL-CIO president, you have to make a friggin' name for yourself and get yourself noticed. You need an issue and this is yours on a silver platter."

"I already have one."

"What? A crane accident? Accidents happen all the time, kid. Not much you can do. This meetin's too important. There'll be other games. Meet me at my house at 5.30."

I hesitated. "I ain't got a truck, remember?"

"Then meet me at my truck at 4.00 and don't be late. And don't eat nothin.' Doris cooked a shitload for dinner. And make sure you clean yourself up; you can't ride with me like that."

We pulled into Walter's garage exactly at 5.00, give or take a few minutes. Doris was in the breezeway struggling with two large, overstuffed, foiled-covered trays. I jumped out immediately to help. Wiping her hands on her apron she smiled and hugged me, smelling of onions and tomatoes.

"We feeding an army?" Walter asked.

Doris frowned, scrunching her overly wrinkled face from one too many afternoons in the sun. "It's my turn to cook for bridge night; and then I'll freeze the rest. It's great for leftovers."

"We'll have enough left over to feed a friggin' army."

"JoJo just called. Her meeting ran late, she's on her way."

"She's always runnin' late."

"Can you two please take these two trays to the backyard picnic table. There's more coming."

"More?"

I followed Walter into his quarter-acre vegetable garden. "JoJo?"

"Doris calls her that."

"And you?"

"Joanna."

"What about everyone else?"

"Joanna."

"And Zachary?"

Walter stopped at the garden's outer two rows. "That's a good question, kid," he said, examining several of the brown, wilted corn stalks, as if searching for gold. "Them two haven't said two words since the will."

"What will?"

"The one I told you about it."

Yeah along with so much other useless shit.

"You never pay attention to nothin' I say. And you expect to be elected AFL-CIO president without learnin' how to listen? Anthony wanted the will to accomplish what even God himself couldn't: reconcile father, son, and granddaughter. But Joanna wanted nothin' to do with her father or the company. She wanted her own law firm, and, of course, Zachary's plans never included Joanna. But the will gave them no friggin' choice. Zachary needed the company for his own ambition and Joanna would never go against her grandfather's wishes. So the will made Zachary president and Joanna legal counsel, with each ownin' half the company. Neither can't do nothin' without the other's consent—and they can't stand each other—how's that for a friggin' family company?"

Walter then led me through two rows of what had been lettuce, peas, and radishes; a row of pumpkins, then two rows of squash, proudly rattling off their names like they were the greatest inventions ever: butternut, pumpkin, spaghetti, acorn, white zucchini, green zucchini. He offered me a butternut and an acorn squash to take home.

"No thanks. I only eat stuff straight from the grocery store; that way I know it's fresh."

Walter shook his head.

The garden's last four rows were tomatoes, with each row seemingly wider than the last.

We placed the trays on a red-cedar picnic table, strategically located right in the garden's center. "A Father's Day present from my two boys," Walter boasted. "Made it themselves."

"What do you do with all these friggin' tomatoes?"

"What we don't eat right away Doris cans. She makes enough salsa and spaghetti sauce to last all winter." He picked a dozen ripe tomatoes and pyramided them next to the trays. He raised one foot onto the table bench, took out a small saltshaker from his pocket, half-bit into one, then generously doused it with salt.

"You always carry a saltshaker?"

"I took it from the garage." He plopped the tomato into his mouth, squirting juice and seeds everywhere. "Nothin' better than a hand-picked tomato. I'll be pickin' the rest this weekend, if you want any."

"Can't stand the suckers."

Walter wiped his mouth with his sleeve.

"You took a saltshaker, but no friggin' napkin?"

"Can't think of everythin' kid. When the weather's good, Doris and I eat out here in the garden. Sometimes durin' warm summer nights, you can even hear the corn growin'."

"Not much privacy with them stalkers! Ha ha!"

"Privacy? *Privacy!* Let me show you somethin'." He quickly led me through the garden's other side, sidestepping over-ripened tomatoes, past the outer rows of his garden, to the edge of his property. "Nothin' makes my blood boil more." He pointed to a video camera resting atop a twelve-foot wooden pole. "At first, I thought it was the County's mosquito program, but then my friggin' neighbor tells me that he erected it, without never sayin' nothin' to me or even askin'."

"It's on his property?"

"That ain't the point kid. He keeps it on all the time pointed at my property."

"How you know it's on? Could just be a decoy?"

"It rotates. You can see it now."

"Then you and Doris should give him some real entertainment."

"Yeah right."

"Caulk it, so he can't see nothing."

"It's on his property."

"Then erect your own camera directly opposite, so he only sees yours."

"He'll move it."

"Then move yours, wheel it on staging."

"Hmmm. Not a bad idea kid."

"Walter?" Doris called from the garage. "I could use your help."

Walter led me back through the rows of tomatoes, the rows of pumpkins and squash, the rows of what had been lettuce, peas, and radishes. At the corn stalks he turned and placed his hand on my shoulder. "Just some advice, kid: If you say somethin' and JoJo don't laugh, don't take it personally. She don't know how to laugh. None of them Turnuses ever did."

"You don't exactly have people rolling in the aisles yourself. And just yesterday you told me to stay away, that she aint' in my league, remember; now, you're offering advice?"

"I'm just sayin' kid."

Doris entered with a stunningly beautiful woman with shoulder-length brown hair and flirting, big brown eyes. Almost my height, she wore a red jacket and black pants. She was talking on her cell phone, waving one hand emphatically. Finished, she smiled at Walter, stuffed her phone into her purse and hugged him.

Doris took my arm. "Isn't she beautiful?"

"Yes." I said, a little louder than intended. *Is this the same woman who was leaning into Walter's truck a while back? It can't be?*

"JoJo, this is Alex Morgan," Walter said. Joanna glanced about, as if searching for something lost. "The next president of the AFL-CIO."

Can't he ever just friggin' introduce me as Alex Morgan?

Joanna smiled, offering her hand, showcasing long, graceful fingers with bright red nails. "Are they all this cute?" she asked Walter.

"A requirement to work at General," I said; then nodding to Walter, "of course, there's always exceptions: *He* was grandfathered in long before he was even a grandfather."

Joanna burst out laughing.

I glanced at Walter who seemed to be busying himself with the silverware.

"JoJo dear," said Doris, "I would've made something more elaborate, but on such short notice—just garden vegetables and a corn frittata, and a lovely dish of sausage, peppers and onions."

"*Lots* of garden vegetables and *lots* of lovely sausage, peppers and onions," added Walter.

Joanna smiled at me, "This is absolutely wonderful."

Doris and Joanna sat next to each other, and Walter and I sat opposite. I poured a Coke on ice for Walter, and three glasses of white wine, while Doris dished the frittata and vegetables. Joanna complimented Doris on the food, particularly the gouda cheese giving the frittata a nice smokiness.

"Were you able to find out anything about my neighbor's friggin' camera?"

"It's legal," Joanna replied. "Anyone can take a picture from their property."

"Then I can erect stagin' on my property to block it?"

"He can legally monitor your property to protect his but if you deliberately obfuscate his right, he can sue."

"For what? Doin' something on my own property?"

"Don't be stupid," Doris sipped her wine. "It ain't worth spending our retirement in jail."

"While he buys up your property," I added.

Joanna laughed.

"Isn't she darling?" Doris exclaimed, clasping Joanna's hand.

"As a lawyer," I asked, "don't that camera make you nervous, along with all them corny stalkers?"

Joanna burst out laughing, coughing, sputtering wine.

"Are you OK?" Doris asked, lightly tapping her back.

"*Corny stalkers!*" Joanna repeated, laughing.

"So your father and PCB?" Walter asked. "He ain't bluffin'?"

"CCB," I reminded Walter. "Thank God we weren't acquired by a PCB company."

Joanna laughed again.

"Alexander, stop making JoJo laugh. She'll never finish her dinner."

"He might be lying, but he's not bluffing," Joanna said, trying to compose herself. "I conference-called PCB this afternoon—Ha! Now you have me saying that! Nothing's definite yet, although it looks like the acquisition is a go. They're still crossing the *T*s and dotting the *I*s, which might take a while, given their reputation for being fastidious."

"Will they break us up?" I asked.

"There's nothing to break up; it's not like we're multi-divisional. We're just one company, but, of course, one of their golden eggs."

"In a meetin' the other day your father said nothin' about no merger. Then the next mornin' he announces to me and the kid and everyone else that it's a done deal. Ain't that right, kid?"

"The kid?" Joanna laughed.

I gritted my teeth. "Only *he* can get away with that."

"So, what happened between the meetin' and today?"

"It isn't a done deal," replied Joanna. "There's a lot that can go wrong (or right) even in this final stage. My father has long known about this merger proposal. And right now, CCB is concerned about the Teamsters."

"How did they find out so quickly?" I asked.

"They're in the business of information *and* it's their business to know everything about us." She glared at Walter. "Everything." Joanna's phone rang. She stood up, excusing herself. It was dark now, but Walter's floodlights on the roof of his house lit up the backyard as if high noon. Talking friggin' non-stop on her cell, Joanna plucked a ripe tomato from an over-extended vine, rubbed it on her jacket and took a bite. She paced the garden's inner sanctity, talking, slurping her tomato.

"JoJo, should I reheat your dinner?" Doris asked when she returned. "It's getting cold?"

She apologized, busying herself with her food; asking for seconds.

"So, JoJo what do you know about CCB?" Walter asked.

"They break up companies, sell the pieces; pretty standard, no surprises."

"Your father said CCB gave us the green light to expand?" I asked.

"I'm sure he did, but he knows full well that's not how CCB operates. They're offering him a very attractive package, which he'll use to start his own construction company." She sipped her wine, staring at Walter. "But I think he already has."

"Why don't you ask him yourself instead of beatin' around the bush?"

"I have. He's denied it."

"Maybe he's tellin' the truth?"

"He never does."

"Your father also said that CCB will increase our profits?" I asked.

"There are good PE companies and bad ones. The good ones pump money in, transmuting them into something better; the bad ones siphon money out, regardless of profitability, expecting to earn even more, assuming their Midas touch can do no wrong. CCB? They acquire super-winners like us, increasing profits by 15-30% before sucking them dry and collapsing the company, destroying in two years what it took generations to build; then moving on to the next profit-making acquisition in a never-ending cycle; in the meantime, making themselves filthy rich." Joanna sipped her wine. "If CCB has their way, in two years General will no longer exist. But I promised my grandfather to keep General private and family owned. And it's a promise I intend to keep."

"Times change and you have to change with them," Walter said.

"You sound just like my father." Joanna rose checking her text messages, apologizing to Doris that she couldn't stay, that she was already late for another meeting.

"You're always having meetins'."

"What do you think we do at foundations?"

"Can't you at least stay for dessert?" Doris asked. "I made apple crisp, your favorite." Joanna's phone rang; she let it go to voicemail.

"Just a second," Doris excused herself to the kitchen. "I'll fix you something to go."

Joanna protested but to no avail.

I suddenly remembered that I was truckless. Before Walter goes to bed, which should be any minute—after all, it was almost seven—I reminded him that I needed a ride to the T.

"I'll take you." Joanna smiled. "It's actually right on my way." She glanced at her watch. "But we have to leave now." Turning to Walter: "CCB and my father want to destroy General, but I won't let that happen."

"What are you proposin'?"

"Just for starters, a publicity campaign about CCB's track record, while gathering evidence for a lawsuit."

"A lawsuit? Over what?"

"Right now, I can't exactly say, but you'll soon find out."

Doris returned with a large piece of apple crisp and a generous slice of frittata. "I'd give you some ice cream, but it would melt before you reached the end of the driveway."

I stood up, eyeing the dessert.

"Alexander, you don't have to leave."

"I'm giving him a ride," noted Joanna.

Doris nudged Walter.

"I'd like to," Joanna insisted, smiling at me.

"Let me get you a piece of apple crisp, Alexander," offered Doris.

"Have Walter bring it in the morning," Joanna said. "I really need to go; I'm already late."

Walter was itching to say something but whatever it was, it was going to have to wait.

Chapter 3

Joanna Turnus

Seeing someone's soul is not the same as falling in love. You might never see a person's soul, yet still fall in love with him; and of course, you can see someone's soul without ever knowing him, but it's rare to fall in love *and* see someone's soul—it's magical, you both know it instantly and there's no turning back. And no, my first time wasn't with Terry; although, yes, of course, I was very much physically attracted to him—who wouldn't be? —but it wasn't until much later that I saw (and liked) who he really was.

I was a junior in high school returning by train from Columbia University. Terry had already accepted a full (academic) scholarship to Princeton to play football, and although I was also accepted to Princeton, I was looking at Columbia for its pre-law program (a strong attractor: a well-known TG Boston attorney whom I admired had graduated from Columbia's law school, and she offered a letter of recommendation).

Outside it was snowing: a quick-moving storm barreling up I-95, as if it knew where to go; inside, I was comfortably warm, dozing off with *The New York Times*, losing my battle to stay awake. Suddenly the train lurched. I sprang up, worried that I had overslept and had missed my stop. I tripped on the leg of the guy next to me, stumbling into the aisle. Embarrassed, I apologized. He smiled, helping me up. In that split second when our eyes met, we connected. Intimately.

He quietly re-assured me that we were only in New Haven. I brushed my hair back, smiled and sat down. He was a freshman at Boston College, returning from a family visit to New York. We talked about everything (well, almost everything). At the 128 Junction—his stop—I rose with him, assuming we would leave together, as if that was the most natural thing in the world. But his expression abruptly changed—like he had peered deep into my soul and saw something terribly wrong. (Maybe I had inadvertently said something? But at least as far as I could recall, my words, gestures, and thoughts were nothing but normal?) He left without saying anything. Without even a goodbye. Without even asking for my phone number. I was stunned. Even as he stepped onto the platform, as the train slowly pulled away, I thought he was testing to me to see my reaction, and that he would quickly return.

I never saw him again.

Of course, afterwards I felt guilty about betraying Terry, even though nothing had happened (although he had nudged his leg against mine)—that's just the person I am. It was a lapse in judgement; a lapse that I promised to eventually confess to Terry. But I never got the chance.

The last thing I expected (or wanted) at Walter's garden was to fall in love, especially with a laborer from my grandfather's construction company. Not that I'm class conscious or anything like that—I honestly could care less—although I guess I never really thought about it. And no, it wasn't because of Alexander's GQ looks—I've dated others in that mold—Terry for one. Nor was it his ambition—Terry was set to begin pre-med at Princeton. But in that split second when our eyes met, in that moment of blurred past, present and future, there was no quizzical look, no damming look of shame, only deep and connected acceptance. Alexander understood and accepted me for who I was. I knew that.

Everyone in New England knew (or assumed) that my father was super rich, and that so was I. Guys wanted to date me just for *his* money, without caring who *I* was. But even though we had intimately connected at the soul, and Alexander was sweeter and more innocent than anyone I had ever met, and unlike most people, didn't initially pull back, I had to be sure.

"What's it like working for my father?" I asked, as we pulled away from Walter's driveway.

"Your father? Since I started at General, I've only seen him twice—both in the last two days."

"That's more than I've seen him."

"I thought you worked with him?"

"We work for the same company—my grandfather's—but I don't work *with* him. We don't get along—we never have."

"Why? I can't imagine a father ever disliking his daughter, even if she was an axe murderer."

"I might be a lot of things," I said, half-laughing. "But not an axe murderer."

"That's good to know."

A red light.

I admired Alexander's deep tan that would linger well into the winter; his soft, playful brown hair that most women would consider a tad too long, combed straight back, pillowed against his ears, loose strands taking a life of their own, sometimes moving in one direction as he talked, sometimes unexpectedly in another.

Alexander's T stop was two blocks ahead.

My phone rang. I answered, promising to call back, then stuffed my phone into my purse.

"Alexander, I have to tell you something. My father...My father and I don't get along. We never have...I legally cut myself off from his will."

"Really?" He smiled at me. "I think that's cool."

"*You think that's cool?*"

"Yes. And after meeting your father, I kind of understand why."

"So that doesn't bother you?"

"Of course not. Why would it? In fact, it makes things a lot easier. So how about skipping your meeting and going for a drink?"

"I'd absolutely love to, but I can't. How about a raincheck? This weekend?"

Alexander frowned. "It's my sister-in-law's 30th birthday and we're all celebrating in New Hampshire, at her parents."

"New Hampshire? Whereabouts?"

"Lake Winnipesaukee."

"*Lake Winnipesaukee?* Really! Where? My grandfather used to take me swimming there when I was a little girl."

Alexander shrugged. "Not exactly sure. All my sister-in-law said was that it's near a lighthouse."

"Spindle Point! I know exactly where that is!"

He reminded me (politely) that I had passed his T stop. I circled back, put my car in neutral, reached over and kissed him. *Delicious!* "I have to go—so, I'll see you Sunday night when you return, for a drink?"

Alexander smiled. "Just one?"

Chapter 4

Alexander Morgan

If Lisa says 5:15, she means 6:15. Throw in an additional fifteen minutes for good measure and you have on-time expected departure of 6.30. No problem if you plan ahead. But as everyone knows, the longer it takes them to do anything—especially packing for an out-of-state trip—although it was just to New Hampshire—still a major ordeal for them, the greater the odds of a major blowout. In fact, I was expecting Lisa to call, upset, apologizing for a major rift, that they weren't speaking to each other—certainly not the first time—and that the friggin' Lake trip was cancelled. But unfortunately, no calls. They picked me up exactly at 6.30, as expected.

Lisa blamed Derek for being late and of course, Derek blamed Lisa; and I'm sure they had earlier blamed me, as if I had anything to do with it.

The first fifteen minutes or so of our drive to the Lake was quiet, although not exactly tranquil—it never is—since at any moment either one, or both, could erupt, over any issue. And sure enough, we were just getting onto 128, when Lisa matter-of-factly said that she had forgotten her makeup bag and had to go back. Granted, that would be enough to start an argument between most couples but Derek, as usual, turned it up a notch, asking why she needed makeup in the middle of the woods, accusing Lisa of an affair, which really pissed her off. Her anger escalated. As did his. The only good thing about that intense, emotional fight was that it quickly burned itself out, although the cinders were never dormant.

I've dated enough women to know that they carry a lot more shit in their makeup bag than just makeup—like birth control pills, which explains why Lisa was so adamant and why we turned back.

Back on the road again, heading north, neither Derek nor Lisa said anything for quite a while. Certainly not because they had exhausted every arguable issue, for there's always a nuance, a new twist to any half-lingering, long-simmering issue. Nevertheless, it was nice to have some relative peace and quiet. I stretched my legs and tried to make myself as comfortable as I could in the backseat of Derek's Jetta. I shut my phone off, leaned against the window and was soon asleep.

"Even the New Hampshire smells better!" Lisa exclaimed lowering her window.

I sat up, assuming we had arrived, but we were only at a toll booth, just over the state line. I suddenly remembered Lily. "Shit!" I said louder than expected. *How could I have forgotten about her?* Especially when I had taped a reminder to my bathroom mirror?

"You forget something?" Lisa asked, practically craning into the back seat, as if she already knew the answer.

I clicked on my cell phone. Four messages from Lily. *Christ!* The first asking where I was, nicely. The last pissed as hell. If I had texted Lily right then and there, she'd assume I didn't have the balls to call, but how could I call with Lisa practically hovering over me?

"I was supposed to meet this union organizer tonight after work," I said, rereading Lily's texts. "And I completely forgot."

"Male or female?" Lisa asked.

"Huh?"

"What difference does that make?" demanded Derek.

Their anger was escalating. So typical.

"Both," I said.

"*Both?*" asked Lisa. "How could he—or she—be both?"

"Probably one of them transgenders," mocked Derek.

"Don't even talk about those weirdos," Lisa said.

"I was supposed to meet *two* Teamsters to talk about organizing General: One female, one male. I completely forgot."

"I can turn around?" Derek offered.

Lisa nudged him hard.

I leaned back, texting Lily, carefully mulling over every word. But how could I tell her the truth? That I met this seductive, intriguing, intelligent woman, with tattoos and piercings, who had the balls to disinherit her father's fortune, and now I'm heading to the Lake with my sister-in-law who desperately wants to fuck me? So instead I texted that I completely forgot about this New Hampshire family reunion. Lame, I know.

"Really????" Lily texted back.

Lisa sighed, stretched back, folding her arms.

Women have a sixth sense: if you lie about work or shit no big deal but if you lie about them or another woman, they know instantly, and usually long before you tell them.

Derek was rambling about some unionization attempt at his workplace; although I wasn't quite sure, staring out the window, mentally replaying everything that had happened the last few days, wondering how I could have forgotten about Lily; and wishing that Derek had indeed turned back.

Derek abruptly slammed the brakes, bringing the Jetta to a complete stop.

"Jesus Derek!" Lisa screamed. "What the hell are you doing?"

"I'm driving, and then all of sudden we're on this cliff?"

"What cliff? This is a road, you idiot! We're on the top of a very steep hill."

Lisa was right, although I could easily see how Derek mistook this for a cliff, especially after driving for almost three hours and now on a road with no streetlights.

"Our cabin's at the bottom of this road, after it winds around a bit," said Lisa.

In front of us, stretched a large lake almost to the horizon, shimmering under the moon-lit sky.

"Where are the streetlights in this God-forsaken place?" Derek snipped.

"There aren't any. This is a remote road, only used by people living here."

"I still don't see why we couldn't stay with your parents," said Derek.

"I told you a thousand times: They're redoing their bathroom and with my nieces and nephews staying, there's no room for us."

Just then Derek hit a big pothole, then swerved to avoid another.

"You idiot!" Lisa screamed. "Watch where you're going!"

"It was in the middle of the road! You want me to drive in the woods?"

At the bottom of the hill, the paved road with potholes curved sharply to the left, giving way to a gravel road with potholes.

Lisa opened her window ushering in pine-scented air. "Look for Number 197; it's on the right."

"Did you grab the bait?" Derek asked Lisa.

"What bait?"

"The bait I had left in the refrigerator."

"You left bait in the refrigerator? Our refrigerator?"

"I assumed you packed it when I saw the refrigerator empty."

"I didn't see any bait and if I did, I would've thrown it out—that's so disgusting."

"You must have taken it, because I put it there when I came home from work. Then I when I went to get it, it was gone, so I assumed that you had packed it."

"I threw out some old Chinese food-looking containers."

"That *was* the bait! I can't believe you threw out sixty dollars of bait."

"Sixty dollars!" Lisa screamed. "You spent sixty dollars on bait! Are you nuts?"

Derek hit the brakes, then reversed. "I'm going into town."

"What! Are you crazy? Nothing's open this time of night!"

"Relax Derek. In the morning I'll help you dig for worms."

"I use leeches."

"Leeches! You put leeches in our refrigerator?—Slow down! Number 197! You just passed it, you idiot. Back up! The driveway's on the right."

If I wasn't so tired, I would've left right then, truck or no truck. "Relax Derek, I'll help you dig for leeches in the morning."

Derek abruptly stopped at a metal chain strewn between two birch trees blocking the driveway. "If this God-forsaken place's so remote, why's it padlocked?"

Lisa turned to me. "The key's next to the birch tree on the right, in a small envelope."

"Brilliant," Derek muttered. "Why even bother?"

I stepped out, stretching my legs, relieved to be out of that tense, uptight, intensifying atmosphere, even if just for a moment. I unlocked the chain and wrapped it around the left birch tree, then waved Derek on.

"Don't get lost," Lisa smiled playfully.

If only I could.

Birch and pine trees crowded both sides of the driveway, steeply descending to the cabin, with the shimmering Lake just beyond. Pinecones mixed with red and yellow leaves blanketed the ground. The night air was still.

The cabin, recently painted a rich chocolate brown, stood about thirty feet from the water's edge. I hesitate to use the word 'painted', since I could've done better blindfolded. Streaks were everywhere, brown paint slapped over green windowsills.

The back door was locked— or was it the front door? I had always assumed that the front door had the street number, except if you live on a lake, I guess, then the lakeside becomes the front? A barely noticeable '197,' was here in back, so this must be front door, although I've seen better back doors that actually looked more like front doors.

I walked around to the 'back' finding the 'back' door on the side of the house, opening to a screened-in porch and then a cramped, living room, faintly smelling of burnt logs and Pine-Sol. A stone fireplace jutted from the knotty pine wall, seemingly the living room's main attraction. Three blue, plastic chairs with a matching loveseat lined the opposite wall, bare except for a 3'×5' painting of two loons. Next to the painting was an old-fashioned dial phone.

"Wonder if it works!" Lisa slowly dialed.

My cell phone rang.

"Hello? Hello?" Lisa repeated. "Voices on the other end? What are they doing on our line? And at this time of night?"

The too-small kitchen barely contained an old-fashioned gas stove, a sink, and the tiniest table ever made, sitting only one and a half people, who had to be really small to sit comfortably. A narrow passageway led to two small bedrooms, each with a set of bunks and a dresser. Sandwiched between the bedrooms was a tiny bathroom.

"Where's the shower?" asked Derek.

"We use the Lake."

"I thought people drink from it?" I asked Lisa.

"It's spring-fed."

They took one bedroom and I the other. I laid down on the short, narrow bed—obviously not made for anyone over six feet. I faintly heard Lisa say goodnight.

I was wide awake at 5:30. Needing a shower, I remembered Lisa saying to use the Lake. Fuck that. I made a pot of coffee, filled my cup, grabbed a pen and paper and headed outside. The eastern sky seemed to be brightening, although perhaps I was only wishing so, so I could do my obligatory fishing with Derek and then get the hell out of here.

Yellow-leaved birch trees arched over the water, their roots tenaciously clinging to boulders along the shore. A wooden rowboat was moored to a long, aluminum dock that protruded like a matchstick into the still, pre-dawn air.

It looked like we were in a large bay. Straight ahead, about 120 yards or so, was a tall black and white marker, and just beyond, a footbridge that connected the mainland to a small island. Gentle hills, ablaze with red and orange, ringed the shore in every direction.

I inched along the aluminum dock, creaking and shifting with every step, worried that one wrong step would inadvertently plunge me and the dock into the water. Finally, making it to the dock's end, I sat down and dipped my feet into the crystal-clear water, surprised by its warmth. A crayfish clutching a minnow darted along the sandy bottom.

I wrote Derek's list for October 12, 2018:

- Wish Lisa Happy Birthday
- Have sex
- Get up
- Take a leak
- Read this friggin' list
- Give Lisa her birthday present
- Pay Alex twenty dollars
- Have coffee with Alex
- Dig for friggin' leeches
- Breakfast
- Take a leak
- Fish
- Lunch
- Take another friggin' leak
- Nap

Still nursing my coffee, I felt the dock squeaking and moaning.

"I'm going into town for some leeches," Derek said, his booming voice echoing across the hills. "You coming?"

"Keep your voice down for Christ's sake. Relax—it's Lisa's birthday. Have some coffee and enjoy the morning with me. When Lisa wakes up, we'll go into town and have breakfast, then get your friggin' leeches. We'll make it a fun morning."

"I'm here to fish."

"The fish can wait."

"Morning is the best time."

"Then fish tomorrow morning."

"The winds are changing with the storm coming in tonight, and then who knows where the fish will be."

"In the water?" I handed Derek his to-do list which he promptly crumpled and tossed in the boat.

"We don't exchange presents."

"Are you shitting me? After spending sixty dollars on bait?"

"Fifty-six dollars."

"Christ almighty!"

"I'm here to fish."

"Then buy her something in town: roses, a gift certificate for dinner, a manicure—anything. Don't come back empty-handed."

"I only have enough cash for the bait."

I handed him my credit card, which Derek snatched storming to the Jetta. He slammed shut the door and sped up the driveway, spewing pebbles and pinecones.

The warm morning promised a hot and hazy day. I stripped to my underwear and dove into the water. It was surprisingly warm—like a bath. I swam past boulders, rocks, pinecones, crayfish, minnows. When I surfaced about thirty yards away, treading water, I noticed Lisa perched on the dock's edge, wearing a red, see-through negligee.

"Come on in!" I said, knowing full well that she doesn't swim. "The water's like a bath."

"Are you kidding?" Lisa glanced at her watch, folding her arms, pacing the end of the dock, while I swam back slowly, dogpaddling, flipping onto my back like a dolphin, swimming backwards, squirting long arcs of fresh water.

On the dock Lisa wrapped a beach towel around me and kissed me.

"Mr. Suspicious," I said, "who suspects you sleeping with everyone, including me, sees you in a see-through negligee as he's leaving for town?"

"It's only see-through if you care what's underneath."

"What makes you so sure he ain't at the top of the driveway waiting?"

"Are you kidding? All he only cares about his stupid bait. That's all he talked about last night." Lisa glanced at her watch, tugging me toward the cabin.

I noticed a fair-sized bruise on her forearm.

"It's not what you think," Lisa said, noticing my concern. "Last night—didn't you hear the commotion? I was sure I woke you? I was going to the bathroom and stepped on a mouse or some disgusting thing. I screamed and must've banged my arm on the bureau." Lisa held the cabin door open, smiling. "But I knew *exactly* what I was doing cleaning out the refrigerator."

"And forgetting your makeup bag?"

"Actually, *that* was an accident." She led me through the living room, past the too-small kitchen, into the narrow hallway. On the wall was a photo of an older man proudly displaying an oversized catfish, or was it a carp? No, it was definitely a catfish—at least two feet long. I didn't know that catfish were that big? Or maybe it was some type of fish that I was not familiar with? Perhaps a river monster? Unique to the Lake? The black and white tiled floor hinted of lemon, as if recently washed. Several tiles were irregular, haphazardly pointing different ways; one was chipped with its jagged edge pointing upwards. "Did you see this?" I knelt down and bent off the jagged edge, doing my best to smooth the remaining piece.

Lisa pulled me into the hot, stuffy bedroom. She opened the window, pointing to a small hole in the screen, "Last night, a chipmunk or a squirrel or something was trying to get in."

"My phone? I must've left it on the dock?"

"What? It'll be fine there."

I pushed back. "I don't want some eagle flying off with it. I've seen eagles carrying fish bigger than my phone."

"They can't eat a phone." Lisa sighed.

The phone was right where I had deliberately left it: underneath the rowboat's middle seat, safely hidden from predators. An older gentleman, fishing—I'm sure using worms like everyone else—from a small, electric-powered dingy chugged by, resembling the man in the hallway photo. I asked if he had any luck. No, he hurriedly replied, and rather rudely I thought, abruptly turning towards the black and white marker.

Returning to the cabin, I noticed about a dozen pinecones pyramided, each with its fat end facing me. I pulled the bottom cone, collapsing the pile. A chipmunk popped from a neighboring hole, then disappeared. I plunged in a long stick, hoping to jab it, but no luck.

"Alexander?" Lisa implored, impatiently holding open the screen door in her red, see-through negligee.

She led me through the narrow hallway, over the chipped tiles, past the photo of the man with the catfish into her bedroom. She pulled me close, kissing me. She ripped off my shorts. I slipped off her negligee, nudging us onto the bed.

"My condoms?"

"Where are they?"

"In my wallet, on my bureau."

Lisa sprang up, and just as quickly returned with a condom and Lily's business card. "Lily? Who's this?"

Are you friggin' kidding me? "One of the Teamsters' organizers that I was supposed to meet last night."

Lisa sighed, gently sliding us onto the mattress. She slid on top of me. Her warm body felt good. She fiddled with the condom, finally slipping it on.

A chipmunk stuck his face in the window, chattering, nudging the screen.

"It *is* a chipmunk," I said.

Lisa giggled, "It's definitely bigger than a chipmunk!"

"No, at the window."

She screamed, throwing a pillow, missing. I hurled another, knocking the chipmunk off. She slid back on top of me. Her warm body felt good. Just then we heard a distant car approaching.

"It can't be him?" Lisa glanced at her watch. "He shouldn't be back for another thirty minutes?" We laid still, certain the car would continue on the graveled road, past the driveway, towards another cabin. But the car slowed, paused at the driveway entrance, then sped down, crunching gravel and sputtering pinecones.

"That asshole!" Lisa yelled, scrambling to get up.

I threw on my shorts, raced down the hallway, through the living room, onto the dock, then into the water. I swam along the sandy bottom as far as I could, surfacing about 40 yards away, surprised that I could swim that far; treading water, catching my breath, staring at the black and white marker looming large, afraid to turn to the cabin, certain that Derek was on the dock with a shotgun.

"Alexander?" Lisa called.

I reluctantly turned. Lisa stood alone on the dock's edge, wearing jean shorts and a gray hoodie. "That wasn't Derek. It was a black Lexus with Massachusetts plates."

My heart stopped. "A black Lexus? Did she stop?"

"She?" Lisa asked suspiciously.

"He/she/they? Did *they* stop?"

"I couldn't make out his face, but he definitely had a beard or moustache or something. He drove down the driveway, slowly as if looking for someone or something, like he was casing the place—but why would a Lexus driver want to rob a rental? I was just about to call the police when he turned abruptly and left."

"Maybe he was a Mafia guy looking for Derek?"

"I wish."

Chapter 5

Joanna Turnus

My grandfather loved old Chris Crafts. Meticulously made, with a powerful engine, they were (and are) the best-looking boat on the Lake. Whenever he saw one—on the water, in a parking lot, at a boat show—he promised to someday buy one, but of course that day never came; something always came up, something always more pressing. When I got accepted into law school, my grandfather offered to pay my entire tuition, that is, until he found out how much it was, but even then, he paid as much as he could and then a little more, which meant that he worked even longer hours, longer than even I thought possible, only taking time off to swim with me.

If I hadn't gone to law school my grandfather would still be alive. I know that. He wouldn't have worked so hard and could have easily afforded a Chris Craft. He would have relaxed more and not had a heart attack at the age of 62. Instead, he'd be riding his beloved boat every weekend on the Lake with me.

"Don't ever think that, Joanna!" snapped my grandmother when I had told her, just after my grandfather died. "Absolutely nothing made him happier. You have no idea how proud he was paying your tuition."

Of course my grandfather insisted that I never had to pay him back. And of course I knew I would. Since we both knew he would never accept cash, I decided on a vintage Chris Craft. Of course. I began saving immediately during law school, which meant that during summer and Christmas vacations I worked even longer hours than my grandfather, which I didn't think possible, only taking time off to swim with him, every Sunday at the Lake (and sometimes a Tuesday or Wednesday night at Carson Beach or Revere Beach—cold water never bothered us).

Buying a (used) Chris Craft isn't like buying a used sofa—the owner had to be just right, my grandfather always said. Not to be snotty, but the owner had to worship the boat almost as much as life itself and have the right reason for selling.

During my second year of law school, late October, I took a rare, spur-of-the-moment weekend off and drove to Meredith, just to get away. That was my favorite time on the Lake: past peak foliage and peak tourist season; the weather calm and uneventful, autumn's last thrust. And no snow, yet. If *Late October* on the Lake had a personality it would be resigned, polite, still, introspective, listening, yet secretly triumphant knowing that despite the soon-to-be changing of the air masses and the upcoming winter harshness, the land would bloom again and life would return, as it has for millennia.

I invited my grandfather along. Even though I knew he probably couldn't come last minute, I still asked, secretly hoping so. Of course, he was disappointed to say no, and of course, if anyone understood, it was me. (He respected my need for solitude, and we would have enjoyed each other's company without even saying a word.)

I rented a cabin on Meredith Bay, with no plans other than studying and swimming (the water temperature was an unexpected 63 degrees: more like early October, significantly above my cold-water threshold of 57), with forecasted daytime highs of 70 degrees and no rain; although, I had secretly wished for rain: nothing more relaxing than Lake-side rainy walks and swimming in the rain, although I'm really fine with any weather.

I left for the Lake after my late-morning class, pulling into the Center Restaurant just in time for an early dinner. It was busy as usual, and I had to park in the overflow lot, coincidentally next to a 1926 Chris Craft on a trailer with Maine plates. It was the most beautiful boat I had ever seen. Unfortunately, it was not for sale (at least from what I could tell). Nevertheless, I was determined to meet and talk to the owner. Inside, I immediately clinked a glass calling for the owners, surprised at my boldness. An elderly couple, about my grandparents' age (the man's moustache was quite similar to my grandfather's) tepidly acknowledged; I'm sure wondering why a young woman with a strong Boston accent was inquiring.

I explained who I was, why I was there, and my interest in the boat, putting them at ease, despite my tattoos and piercings—or maybe because of them? They invited me to join them for dinner. Of course they knew my grandfather (I've yet to meet anyone associated with the Lake—even casually—who did not) and were saddened of his passing, assuming that active swimming would keep him fit until old age. Although they had never met, they had seen him so many times in the water, my grandmother rowing alongside (they lived on Bear Island, so their paths often crossed, and I know my grandfather knew their boat) that my grandparents had become regular features in their lives, always waving to each other like long-lost friends.

They told me that their boat had been in their family for three generations, and with lots of grandchildren it wasn't for sale at any price. Of course, I understood—if I owned such a boat, I would never even think about selling it.

We talked about boating, the islands, and the Lake. Then we ordered dinner. Driving up from New York, I had been craving the Center's *Lake Trout Sandwich*—the best around (although they willingly confess that the fish isn't caught from the Lake, but from northern New Hampshire, but still never frozen and directly shipped early every morning). It is delicious. And the accouterments are either locally grown (lettuce, tomatoes, red onions) or made on site (pickles, Italian bread, and the lemon/garlic aliho sauce—although just a tad is needed since the trout is that good—and of course their spicy curly fries). But that night they also were offering their famous Lobster Roll. The best in New England, and a rare treat during the off season. Made perfect with only two deviations: a homemade brioche bun rather than the traditional hot dog bun—it's visually appealing, and homemade aliho sauce rather than mayonnaise; although of course, there's nothing wrong with deviations. And needless to say, their lobster is delicious, direct from Portland.

Since I had a hard time deciding, the couple suggested ordering both, keeping one for Saturday night so I wouldn't have to cook or go out again and could spend the whole day on the water.

I ordered both.

We talked about their long weekend boat trips exploring every corner of the Lake and just about every island; the beauty of the Lake in winter; and how my grandparents had first met. After a delicious dessert of warmed (freshly made) apple pie with vanilla bean ice cream (also freshly made), I invited them to stay the night with me, but they took a rain check, anxious to return for their granddaughter's 16th birthday the next day.

About a month later they called, excited to tell me of a similar boat for sale (same size, but more horsepower and slightly more expensive), saying that it would sell quickly and that several people were already interested; however, I had first dibs, but only twenty-four hours to decide. The owners sent pictures: it was exactly what I wanted. I depleted my savings (not much), sold my Lexus (brand new) and took out a loan for the remainder (a lot) and the boat was mine. (My banker not only knew my grandfather—who didn't in Massachusetts?—but as a child, when his family home was about to be foreclosed, my grandfather bought it and sold it back to them for one dollar, never asking anything in return, even fixing their roof for free. The banker never forgot that gratuitous act of kindness and was glad to give me a really good interest rate— zero—and forego a co-signor—most likely my father, although I did have other options.)

I re-upholstered the boat, re-varnished the mahogany, and despite contrary advice, replaced the inboard motor with twin inboard-outboard engines (I wanted more stern room for a deck, and I love inboard/outboards even better than inboards, as did my grandfather). But I never had the chance to present the boat to my grandfather—he unexpectedly died of a heart attack one month later, I'm sure from working long hours, seven days a week, never taking time off except to swim with me.

Nevertheless, this was *his* boat which someday I will give to my children (keeping my grandfather's spirit alive) and then someday they will give it to their children. A boat to be cherished in our family for generations, never to be sold.

My grandmother cried when I told her that I had christened the boat, *Molasses I II III.*

Chapter 6

Alexander Morgan

"Let's make breakfast for Lisa." I immediately said to Derek when he returned from town.

"I'm not hungry."

"I am. *And* so is Lisa."

"How would you know?"

Just then Lisa slammed open the porch screen door. "Where're the keys to the Jetta?"

"In the car," said Derek matter-of-factly from the rowboat, not noticing that Lisa had been crying, that she was still fighting back tears, terribly oblivious that this was one of those fork-in-the-road moments.

"I'm meeting my sister in town for breakfast," said Lisa.

"Why don't we all go?" I said, hoping to get the weekend off to a good start, forgetting that it couldn't have begun any shittier, leaving even the most optimistic amongst us—me—with a sinking feeling that we've already seen the best.

Lisa hesitated, pausing on that precarious metaphorical bridge, hoping for an unexpected yes from Derek, but that bridge was about to give—obvious to everyone but Lisa—plunging her into the raging chaos below.

"I'm here to fish, and besides, I thought we were eating here?"

"You think breakfast just cooks itself?" Lisa cried, storming away.

If what was supposed to have happened didn't just happen—although I never should have let it *almost* happen—I would've gone with Lisa and spent the whole morning with her and her sister visiting every friggin' shop in town, or whatever else she wanted to do.

"Why not just *you two* go?" I said loud enough for Lisa to hear, hoping that she'd stop or that Derek, at least, would do as expected and go with her.

"This morning's the only time I can fish," he said without emotion.

How can anyone be so stupid?

"How could you not notice what she was wearing?" I asked, hearing the Jetta start.

"Dirty, stinking sweats? That's all she ever wears."

What?

"You coming?"

As if I had a choice? I stepped into the rowboat, already regretting my decision not to go with Lisa. I locked the oars in place, aligned the bow with the black and white marker, and the stern with the screen porch and began rowing.

"Head to the marker," Derek said.

The bay, or cove, as Lisa called it, was about a half-mile wide, ringed by cabins, some quite small, others too large and out of place. To my left was a public beach and to my right the cove opened to a larger bay. Rising behind our cabin was the long, steep road that we descended last night, although in the daylight it didn't seem that long or that steep.

The sun was rising above the red and yellow hills, transforming the cement-grey water into a translucent blue green. The brooding silence was punctuated by the dip-pull of the oars.

"Did you at least get her something?" I asked.

Derek handed me my credit card. "It didn't go through."

"What?"

"It didn't go through."

"Sonofabitch."

A loon bobbed on the water, laughing, diving; re-surfacing about ten yards away. A lone dog relentlessly barked, echoing through the hills.

"So you didn't get her anything?"

"I got her an IOU for a manicure."

"That should go over well."

I noticed that my texts to Lily had finally gone through. She had read them, only responding to the last: 'DON'T BOTHER!!!!' And three texts from Joanna, all within the last thirty minutes. The first: 'Such a beautiful day! Got up early. Decided to drive to the Lake!' My heart skipped a beat or two. Was that her Lexus? But Lisa said the driver had a beard? The second text: 'Where are you? I'll stop by to say hello if that's OK!' And the third: 'I'm at the Center Restaurant. Stop by if you're out and about.'

"Sorry, just getting your messages," I texted back. "Really bad service. My brother and I are fishing in the cove near the lighthouse."

She immediately texted back a smiley face.

The sturdy black and white marker stood erect, extending several feet below the surface, cabled to cinder blocks heaped on the sandy bottom. I was amazed at the water's clarity: at least thirty feet deep and I could easily see the bottom.

"Black and white means pass to the north and east," Derek said, as if common knowledge.

"I thought it was west and south?"

"Head towards the bridge, slowly. And be on the lookout for two huge boulders. They come out of nowhere."

A slight breeze rippled the otherwise smooth water. The island ahead had three small cabins, partially obscured by birch and maple trees. The birches had lost most of their yellow leaves, but the maples were bright red. Suddenly a huge boulder appeared, just as Derek said, barely beneath the surface. I braced, expecting it to gash our hull, sinking us in thirty feet of water but we passed unscathed. Barely.

"There's another just ahead, starboard."

"Starboard?"

"To the right."

We passed just to the left. We dropped anchor between the two boulders, quickly catching about a dozen walleye. I threw the small ones out, keeping four of the largest, stashing them in the fish basket attached to the stern, exactly where an engine would've been if we had one.

"Let's head to the lighthouse," said Derek.

For once I didn't argue: The quicker we reached the lighthouse, the quicker we'd fill up the fish basket, the quicker we'd return to the cabin and cook breakfast, and the quicker I'd get the hell out of here.

"I'm after big-mouth bass; that's why I got the leeches. And they're near the lighthouse. Pass under the bridge and it's straight ahead."

Easier said than done. We had to limbo low to pass under the railroad-timbered bridge, and still got stuck, having to push up on the bridge and down on the boat to get out.

Ahead loomed a white-stucco lighthouse perched on the tip of a long, narrow spit, with the open lake beyond. I rowed fast. The August-like sun was hot. Sea gulls floated lazily; gentle swells lapped from the open lake. Reaching the spit, I anchored in about two feet of water. Derek immediately cast toward shore and I opposite toward the open lake, trying to forget what just happened with Lisa—or what didn't just happen.

A powerful motorboat roared along the southern shore.

"Wonder how much gas it takes to fill that sucker?" mused Derek.

"Must be nice *just* to have a friggin' motor."

The boat abruptly changed direction, heading straight toward us at full speed.

"Christ, the fuckin' Marine Patrol." Derek scrambled for the bait box, retrieved our fishing license, waving it at me. "This is what they want."

The powerful, cigar-shaped boat leveled off about forty yards away, its twin engines gurgling and sputtering. Derek was muttering something about the boat's horsepower, but I was focused on the shapely, red bikini-clad woman wearing a half-unzipped, white windbreaker. "Since when does the Marine Patrol dress like that?" I asked.

"They dress like that and nab you for every violation."

"She can nab me all she wants."

The woman thrust the engine into reverse, then shut it off. She scrambled to the bow. "Alexander! Hello!"

"Joanna?"

Stunning in her red bikini, she waved us over. "It's a perfect day for a boat ride. The Lake's smooth as glass! Come on!"

"You coming?" I asked Derek, grabbing my cell phone and wallet.

He cast toward the shore. "I'm here to fish."

"Fine. See you back at the cabin." I stepped into the water and waded towards Joanna's boat, gingerly side-stepping rocks and unannounced boulders.

Chapter 7

Joanna Turnus

I greyed my Fu Manchu (for a more sophisticated look), slipped on a white, long-sleeve dress shirt (deliberately one size too big) with a white binder underneath (as uncomfortable as any bra), khaki shorts with brown sandals, and a Red Sox cap. I removed my nail polish but kept in all my earrings.

Perfect!

Perfect, that is, if I was going to Fenway Park or Faneuil Hall or a walk around the city, but I was driving unannounced to surprise-visit Alexander. Paradoxical? No. Self-sabotaging? No, not really. You see, when I'm nervous and unsure of myself (which happens a lot), I dress like a guy, especially now that I'm a lot more passable (except for my high-pitched voice, which I'm working on). But, at the same time, this is not something ephemerally self-gratifying, like dressing up for Halloween, then quickly reverting to my normal self (as if I had only one and knew what it was). I'm male, female, non-binary, transgender, happy and depressed all at the same time. When I feel more female than male, I'll dress like one, and when I feel more male than female I'll dress like one. I like the fluidity. Paradoxical? No not really; only if you don't understand it. This is me. This is who I am, although it took a long time to understand and an even longer time to accept. But, like my grandfather said, it has given me an edge, an empathy. And I wouldn't trade my life for anyone's right now although I wouldn't wish it on anyone either.

As I made coffee that morning, I debated canceling my trip, something that even a normal (God, I hate that word) woman would contemplate. You see, with the forecasted hot weather, I decided to spend the weekend at the Lake (I re-scheduled my appointments and rented a nice townhouse in Laconia, away from the water, so I could work at night and early morning, and boat all day—a half-compromise, the best of both worlds). Then I find out that this guy that I had just met, that I really liked, that I had deeply connected with, was also going to the same Lake the same weekend. Of course, I didn't want him to think I was weird, chasing after every guy I meet. (I don't.)

I did almost cancel but decided last minute to go. After all, the Lake is big enough so that we wouldn't bump into each other (although I knew where he was) and it's one of New England's most popular vacation destinations in any season, so he wouldn't think it odd even if we did see each other. And besides, I knew that if I had stayed home, I wouldn't have got any work done on such a warm, August-like day, even closing the shades and turning the air conditioner to 60 degrees.

On the way to the Lake, I kept thinking about my strange dream, strange because I was a 'normal' woman (at least at the beginning), although an exaggerated normal, more like a Laura Petrie than a Joanna Turnus: wearing a pencil skirt, my hair perfectly poofed, my make-up flawless. My husband and I were walking in the forest, my head softly on his shoulders. Although I couldn't see his face, I knew it was Alexander: tall, strong, tanned arms, but his head was shaved, and his voice was high-pitched like a girl's. We came upon a clearing and saw two snakes with human faces copulating. I snapped a large stick in two, giving one to Alexander. We simultaneously touched each snake. Immediately I was transformed into a male with a penis and a full beard, and my husband into a woman with breasts and a vagina. I was ecstatic, but Alexander, seeing what just happened, angrily slashed at the snakes, as if there was anything he could have done. I pulled him close, kissing him, which apparently calmed him— I guess his female hormones kicked in seeing me naked. We made love in the soft, green grass. Then we dove into a nearby pond. I held his hand diving deep, reaching for the bottom, but there was only endless water. When we surfaced, we had become one, intertwined and interconnected, as if always so; neither male nor female but both. There was no alarm, no wondering, no attempt to dive deep and reverse what had just happened. Just sheer happiness.

Driving to the Lake, sipping coffee, I wondered how I would react if I was 'normal' and my husband suddenly metamorphized into a woman. Accept and embrace him as if nothing had changed, as if nothing was different? Or, like Rachel's wife, excoriate him as a moral and ethical failure? But isn't that like loving a book only for its cover, then jettisoning it after the cover had been made more aesthetically appealing, without ever reading its contents? Sure, everyone is attracted to physical accoutrements (and I'm certainly no different) but you also love someone for what's inside—his soul, his inner being—which is more constant and substantive, and can never be superficially changed.

Just north of Concord, I-93 stretches interminably with only an occasional car sharing the road. I laughed, suddenly remembering Terry and I almost at this very spot, senior year in high school, on our way to the Kangamangus Highway to view the foliage early on a Sunday morning. He was driving and I, playfully bored, was well into oral sex, when he matter-of-factly warned of a van of nuns fast approaching: The Sisterhood of Our Sorrowful Mother.

I laughed, assuming it was another of his jokes (that's what I loved about him: always making me laugh) and mechanically waved hello. Then, Terry squelched my hand, scrambling me toward the window. Inching up, slowly, I saw a long, white van with *The Sisterhood of Our Sorrowful Mother* painted in large, blue letters, just passing.

"You *were* serious. I thought you were joking. Why didn't you say so?"

"You should've seen their faces! Did you know that being seen by nuns in the act is a ticket straight to hell?"

"For both of us?"

"Yes."

"Who said that?"

"A bunch of nuns."

But perhaps not? I silently smiled. Wouldn't God be pleased that my actions finally comported with my birth sex?

It was 7.30 when I arrived in Meredith. A splendid August-like morning. I drove along the Bay looking for Alexander, then north of the lighthouse around the Cove; surprised that not many people were out and about on such a beautiful morning, although it was still early.

I returned empty-handed to the Center Restaurant, the same restaurant where my grandparents had first met. I ordered a pot of coffee and blueberry pancakes with real maple syrup and began reading a book that I had long been anxious to read: about this woman living in Berlin during the last weeks of the Second World War (her husband had never returned from the Eastern Front), who was repeatedly raped by advancing Russian troops as Berlin fell. As the world rejoiced, her nightmare began.

When I finished eating (a little speedier than usual, since I was anxious to see Alexander, which in turn, gave me a slight indigestion) I picked up a stray copy of the *Lake News*—I'm sure Mrs. Mildred insisted that extras are always around. Sure enough she was still writing the same column with the same drivel. I ordered another cup of coffee and began writing my own column; a column about this disturbed and disturbing 'guy' from Massachusetts:

> This Saturday morning—yes, I know many of you were at the flapjack feed— a young man from Massachusetts—a most unusual 'man' and I use that word lightly, pulled into the Center parking lot in a black Lexus with Massachusetts plates. Nothing against our friends south of the border—a warm New Hampshire hello to our good friend Nancy Deshlow! Will you be spending Thanksgiving with us? But a black Lexus in the Center Restaurant parking lot—that's a first!

Now, back to this young man, or perhaps young woman? To be honest, at times I couldn't tell, despite his facial hair, or maybe because of it? (I couldn't get close to see if it was real, but I will his next visit—mark my words.) The young man (for now let's call him that) insisted on waiting for a particular booth—why I have no idea, since they're all the same with the same view—then began reading a book. Who reads a book here? A newspaper, yes, so you can keep up with yours truly, but a book? How rude! I couldn't see the full title since he kept it flat, seldom raising it, although the words 'Woman' and 'Berlin' left little to the imagination. Keep that racy stuff in the bedroom and not at a family restaurant.

He took his time before ordering, hardly saying anything, completely ignoring his waitress—Mary, Mrs. Stanley's niece, such a lovely girl. She seemed interested in this young man; why, I don't know, certainly not my cup of tea. Too many earrings—yes, but I guess that so many young men wear them these days that I'm sure Mary didn't even notice—not like in my day when just one raised a lot of questions. Nowadays, one is OK, like my cousin Russell, and to be honest he doesn't look that bad, although maybe I'm just used to it? But this young man had five piercings in his right ear, and six—yes, six in his left. I don't even like that many earrings on a girl. What was he trying to prove? I have just one in each ear, although my sister Margaret has two and keeps pestering me to get another, which I suppose I will someday, just to keep her happy.

The young man eventually ordered blueberry pancakes— if he had waited any longer, it would've been lunchtime. Mary suggested that he also order the homemade bacon or sausage—everyone does—that's what the Center's known for— but he abruptly refused, and rather rudely

I thought. She tried so hard to start a conversation, obviously liking him—sometimes I just don't understand this younger generation. He asked for real maple syrup—really? Everyone knows that the Center restaurant only serves the real stuff.

He didn't talk to anyone, just kept to himself. How rude! But when he did, sometimes it was high-pitched, like he was deliberately trying to talk like a girl. Maybe something to do with all those earrings?

I've never seen such effeminate hands on a man: slender like a female pianist's—not exactly a compliment. He was obviously rich, driving a Lexus—I'm sure he probably never had to work a day in his life. And from what I could tell, no calluses either—a safe bet that he's never chopped a cord of wood.

The young man used his right hand for everything, while hiding his left on his lap. I assumed his hands were manicured but sorry to disappoint, they were not, which is good because you don't see that around here, although sometimes in Manchester I'll see a young man with black polish, or an older gentleman with clear.

He had lots of tattoos—way too many—and that's just what I could see. His sleeves were rolled up just above the wrist—yes, it was warm outside but inside it was chilly as always. On each wrist was a scar about four inches long. At first, I thought it was part of the design, but the more I looked, the more I realized what it was and why it was there.

He finished his breakfast (it took him forever) without talking, then asked for coffee to go. (How can anyone drink that much coffee and not use the bathroom?) He wanted to pay with an American Express Gold Card. Really? Everyone knows that the Center doesn't accept credit cards. Then he gave the waitress a fifty-dollar bill insisting that she keep the change! Mary immediately smiled, tried to talk with him, but he hurried away, a tad off-balance, exaggerating a low step in his walk as if compensating for one leg being shorter or something. But at least he held the door open for two young ladies, who looked related, like they were sisters, even chatting briefly.

I signed the letter Mrs. Mildred.

At my boathouse (in Paugus Bay near Weirs Beach) I removed my Fu Manchu, changed out of my male clothes into a red bikini and put on a pretty red nail polish. I high-ponied my hair and dashed on mascara (waterproof, of course) and lip gloss. I slipped on a white windbreaker, suddenly realizing that while searching for Alexander, earlier that morning, just before breakfast, I was wearing a Fu Manchu. Imagine the awkwardness had I run into him?

It was a splendid morning. The air was warm and the water smooth as glass, the sky cloudless. I sped past Governors Island with its large houses and well-manicured lawns stretching to the water's edge, each with a boat house larger than most homes, thinking about the woman in the book that I was reading at the Center. Beautiful and passionate—at least that's how I imagined her at the beginning. I wanted to meet this woman and talk to her. Was she able to love again? Did she lead a normal life after being so brutalized? (How could she?) How did she begin every day? Did she remarry? Was day or night more agonizing? Did she work? Have children? Was she able to listen again to the rain? Could she remember her past, long ago? How did she survive?

I sped past Timber Island, Welch Island, circled the Broads, then headed toward the Lighthouse. I floored it at 40 RPMs; the smooth water making it seem even faster. To the north, snow-clad and majestic Mount Washington was clearly visible. (My grandfather used to say that snow on the Mount by Columbus Day meant a long winter.

But there was no truth to that old wives' tale; indeed, the opposite was often true.)

I spotted Alexander in a rowboat just off Spindle Point (who wouldn't!) casting his line, reeling it in, casting again, not giving the fish a chance to bite; flexing his strong arms as if prepping for a body-building contest, as if the whole world was watching.

But who was that with him? Didn't Alexander say that he was fishing with his brother? But this person was older, looking nothing like Alexander: short, pudgy, bushy black hair, an unkempt beard; dressed as if it was 50 degrees, in jeans and a red/black plaid shirt. Perhaps Alexander misspoke and that was his father?

I reversed the engine in plenty of time to avoid the lighthouse shoals, then shut it off. I waved to Alexander like I was a normal woman in a normal relationship, happy to see my boyfriend. I dropped the back anchor and lowered the ladder between the engines, inviting Alexander and 'his brother' for a boat ride. His brother refused, and rather rudely I thought.

Helping Alexander into the boat, I had to steady myself, grasping his strong, masculine hands. My legs turning to jelly, imagining us walking in the rain, on the beach, my head softly on his shoulder.

"We thought you were the Marine Patrol," Alexander said, laughing.

"Really, Alexander? In a red bikini?"

"My brother insisted—"

"*That's* your brother?"

"We always said that he was adopted."

I took the driver's seat and flipped the engine blower on. "Alexander, I had every intention of boating today, long before I met you. In fact, when you said that you'd be on the Lake, I almost canceled...I didn't want to give the wrong impression."

Alexander smiled. "The wrong impression?"

"That I chase after every guy I meet."

Alexander started to speak, then paused, as if searching for unconnected words, or perhaps a long-lost thought?

"Alexander, you wanted to say something?"

"Oh. Nothing."

I lifted the anchor, then started the engines, rifling like clapped thunder.

"Christ almighty!"

"Sorry, Alexander, I should've warned you. They're twin inboard/outboards, 550 horsepower each." I backed up slowly, adjusting the rearview mirror, glancing at the depth-meter. In twenty feet of water, I reversed the boat and slowly chugged south, toward Weirs Beach.

Alexander nestled against me. "Where should I stand? Or should I sit?"

I smiled. "This is just fine!" I explained the significance of my boat's name after Alexander had asked, then opened the throttle. The bow steeply rose as the RPMs increased: 10,15, 20, 22, 30, finally settling at 35. The wind rushed past billowing my windbreaker. Then we turned west and raced along Meredith Bay.

Approaching town, I slowed the boat almost to a complete stop, pointing out the Center Restaurant, explaining how my grandparents met and the significance of my middle name.

"Do you think we can park this thing and get something to eat?" Alexander asked impatiently. "I'm starving."

I assumed that he had eaten already, but apparently not. I told him that I had packed a picnic lunch, which could easily become a picnic brunch, and had the perfect spot in mind. From the glove compartment I pulled out a map showing Alexander the broad expanse of the Lake, Meredith Bay, Weirs Beach, the Lighthouse, the many islands, and where my grandfather and I used to swim. Heading east toward the Broads, I offered Alexander the wheel. "Just like driving a bulldozer, except a little faster."

Alexander laughed trading places. "You can drive a bulldozer?"

"You should see me with a backhoe."

Alexander looked at me incredulously.

"And, I have a Class One license."

"Now, that I don't believe."

I reached for the glove compartment, fumbled through my purse and proudly displayed my Class One Massachusetts Driving License. "My grandfather said that someday I might have to drive a trailer."

"Good advice for a granddaughter." Alexander opened the throttle, racing past the Lighthouse, Stonedam Island, Pitchwood Island, Governors Island. Passing Bear Island, I pointed out Mount Washington, then retook the wheel, slowing down as we circled the Broads, explaining to Alexander the significance of the Lake's different markers and flashing buoys.

We stopped in the middle of the Broads, far from land. Even though it was dead calm I dropped anchor: the winds on the Lake can change abruptly, often without warning. Alexander helped me set a tablecloth over the engines, accidentally tripping over life preservers neatly tucked against the back-engine hood. Mid-morning and it already was hot. Alexander helped me raised the back canopy.

I pulled Alexander close. He wrapped his arms around me. We kissed. I'm not sure how or I why stopped (although his stomach growling was getting louder, and I knew he was hungry) but it was so delicious that we both knew that we'd soon pick up right where we left off. Right after lunch. Right here in the middle of the open Lake.

From my cooler I took out an old-fashioned picnic basket, its interwoven slats still intact after so much use. It was my grandmother's. When my grandfather died, she gave it to me laced with so many fun memories. She would always pack a picnic lunch for us swimmers: cold meatloaf sandwiches with homemade German potato salad was my grandfather's favorite; sometimes meatball sandwiches, which was mine (always good cold); and sometimes cold roast beef sandwiches.

Opening my picnic basket unleashed a wonderful aroma of southern fried chicken, coleslaw, collards, baked beans, and biscuits.

"KFC?" asked Alexander approvingly.

"JMT." I dished him a plate. "I made everything—even the honey for the biscuits."

He started eating right away, tepidly apologizing for not waiting for me to sit down, although I probably would've done the same if my stomach had been growling so loud.

"Absolutely delicious," he said, as I dished my plate. "The best fried chicken I've ever had. Hands down."

I grabbed two bottled beers from my cooler, offering Alexander one, taking one for myself.

"Narragansett?" asked Alexander, examining the label.

"My grandfather's favorite. And sometimes my grandmother would even have one, but only if the day was hot."

"Like today?"

I smiled. "Yes. And perhaps today, even two!"

A delicious smell of lake water laced with spent gasoline and fried chicken intoxicated me. The engine vents gurgled. Seagulls cried overhead.

I confessed that the fried chicken recipe wasn't mine, that it was a good friend's from Georgia. I was tempted (almost) to tell Alexander that he (Eliot) was a female-male TG whom I had met by chance (so typical of everything in my life), who taught me so much; without mentioning anything about me, to test the waters so to speak, knowing that eventually I would have to confess. But not today—I wasn't ready, so I assumed the 'normal' woman persona meeting a normal guy whom she really liked: "Someday you'll meet him," I said blandly, "he's such a dear friend."

"Dear?"

"Alexander, you're jealous," I said, laughing. "We're cooking friends, nothing more." I sipped my beer, explaining how we met. "Two years ago, I was in Atlanta for a conference. Bored, I rented a car and drove alone to Savannah; a city that I'd always wanted to visit. I was relaxed, listening to music." [I didn't mention that I was dressed as a guy.] "About an hour later, I noticed the sky quickly darkening into an eerie green. Sirens went off. The radio warned of a tornado on Highway 341 heading southeast, exactly where I was and where I was going. Alone on the road (I guess everyone else had heeded the warning) in the rearview mirror I could see dust, dirt, and debris from the fast-gaining tornado. I pulled to the side of the road, jumped out and laid flat in a culvert, covering my head just as the tornado roared past. It was the most frightening thing. I was OK, other than some minor scratches but my rental was gone. The next day a farmer found it—almost intact—in his peanut field about a hundred yards away. A state trooper gave me a lift to the nearest town, telling me that just as the tornado passed, it abruptly lifted into the sky, sparing the town from catastrophic damage."

"God must've been watching over you that day."

I started to laugh, but was arrested by Alexander's endearing innocence, a child-like naivete that most women would find charming. I took a long drink of Narragansett. "In town, I came upon this restaurant boasting the world's best fried chicken, but even if boasting the worst, I would've stopped in, I was so hungry. And yes, it was the best: Greasy, oily outside, perfectly seasoned, super moist inside—just how it should be. In fact, I was so impressed, I went to the kitchen and asked for the chef. We hit it off instantly." [I didn't tell Alexander why.] "He gave me his fried chicken recipe, along with his recipe for pecan pie and sweet potato pie, which, by the way, I made for dessert. I visited him in Georgia last New Year's for three wonderful days of cooking and eating, and invited him to Massachusetts for this New Year's. I'd love for you to meet him; he's such a wonderful cook who's taught me so much."

Alexander looked at me suspiciously.

"There's nothing between us. And besides, he's not my type— really." I blushed, dishing more chicken, collards, and baked beans. "We're good friends, nothing more. We love cooking together, trying out new recipes."

"You make cooking sound so fun."

"Cooking *is* fun, Alexander."

"I wouldn't know where to start."

"Are you serious? You live alone and don't know how to cook? How do you eat? *What* do you eat?"

"Fast food, usually. Sometimes Chinese, or KFC."

"That gets expensive, not to mention that it isn't good for you."

"I'm always working and I'm too tired to cook when I get home."

"Cooking really doesn't take that much time and effort. Start off by keeping your refrigerator well-stocked. You do have a refrigerator?"

"Yes," he answered, laughing.

"Stock it with eggs, vegetables, cheese, bread so you can make yourself a quick omelet. Then with some already-boiled potatoes, fry them, and with any leftover meat, you can make a skillet; throw in some peppers and onions and you have a—"

"You two need help?" a male voice called, startling us, from a thirty-foot sailboat passing just off our bow; its two sails down, powered by a small engine. "Just checking if everyone's OK? Severe storms this afternoon. Cold front moving through." Two women and another man were with him and said hello.

I assured him that we were fine, offering them fried chicken.

"No thanks," a woman said. "But it does smell good."

They bid us goodbye.

Alexander stretched his legs, watching the sailboat chug north toward Moultonborough. "Your grandfather was a good swimmer?" he asked, as the boat became a distant speck.

"Yes." I handed Alexander another Narragansett and took one for myself. "Swimming was his passion... Senior year in high school, already owning two school records, and with high expectations to break a few more, he expected to be team captain. But the coach had it in for him, not so much for his results, since he always placed at least third, but for living off his God-given talent (Coach's words) never surpassing his self-imposed limits, which wasn't true at all. In fact, the opposite was. But the coach was old school—once he formed an opinion he never deviated, no matter how erroneous.

"Part of it was not having a swimmer's build, despite spending so much time in the water. His coach constantly exhorted my grandfather to lose weight, saying that looking like a linebacker handed his opponents a psychological edge: like watching a basketball team that you're about to play get off the bus with no one over 5'8". In swimming, that edge might only be a tenth of a second, but often, that's enough to separate first from third.

"My grandfather didn't even make the team his senior year. He was stunned along with everyone else. His teammates pleaded with the Coach, but to no avail. My grandfather was so angry that he decided to try out for the 1968 Olympics in Mexico City—two years off—to prove to himself (and everyone else)."

"I would've transferred schools."

"He almost did but couldn't for logistical reasons. But my grandfather knew enough about swimming that in order to make the team, he needed to train full-time with a special coach. But he didn't have the money, nor could he have raised it, and he couldn't afford not to work which irked him, because he knew that everyone else trying out for the Olympics had been training since grade school. But he couldn't let his family down since they really needed his income, which only made him more determined.

"So, after graduation, he worked full-time, training for two years before and after work. Despite having two strikes against him, my grandfather had cut almost two seconds off his time, which in swimming is an awful lot; and knowing the times of practically everyone, he was confident that he would make the team, and perhaps even win a bronze medal in Mexico."

"And?" Alexander impatiently asked.

"He missed the qualifying heat by one-tenth of a second."

"*One-tenth of a second?*"

"That's a lot in swimming. In that heat, one-tenth of a second separated the top four, and my grandfather placed fourth. He said that maybe if he had done something wrong, made a mistake or something, he would've tried again four years later, but everything was perfect; his race was flawless—besting his own personal record by six-tenths of a second; there was nothing he could have done better. It was his best race."

"One-tenth of a second? I couldn't imagine going through life losing by one-tenth of a second."

"He didn't lose. It just wasn't good enough. That race made him realize how good he actually was—performing at the outer limits of his capability—but that his opponents were just a tad better. I know he was disappointed that lack of money prevented him from training professionally (although he later said to me that even with training, he couldn't have raced any better). I think that's why he's since worked so hard: so that money would never again be an issue, especially for me."

I took a long drink of Narragansett, savoring the warm morning sunshine. We smiled at each other. "Alexander, I hardly know anything about you—other than that you can drive a bulldozer and that your brother looks nothing like you—surely someone as cute as you must be dating someone?"

"Me? I broke up with this girl about six months ago."

"Why?"

"She never laughed."

I burst out laughing, not because I wanted to impress, but because I laugh easy—everyone knows that. "What do you mean she never laughed? How can someone *never* laugh?"

"I don't know." Alexander helped himself to another piece of chicken. "She just never laughed. Not even once."

I glanced toward the Belknap Mountains along the southern shore, thinking about my mother (I'm not sure why at that particular moment, although her melancholy sometimes intrudes like an unwelcomed guest) wondering if she once laughed as much as my grandfather claimed, and if so, was it genuine, or a pretense for something else?

"And you?" Alexander asked.

"Huh? Me? I laugh a lot. I like to laugh."

"I noticed. I mean someone as pretty as you; you must be dating someone?"

"No. I'm not. I...I haven't been in a serious relationship for a while." Tears welled up unexpectedly.

"I'm sorry if I struck a nerve. We can talk about something else?"

"That's OK. It might be good to finally talk about it. I *should* talk about it...I haven't talked about it—yes maybe it's good to finally talk—he... he was captain of the football team. Star quarterback, lots of scholarship offers, and chose Princeton. I really wanted to go to Princeton with him but decided on Colombia...Senior year in high school we were undefeated and won the state championship for the third year in a row. I was cheerleader captain. The next night, everyone was going out to celebrate, but I was grounded for some stupid idiotic reason, which even if I told you, you'd never, never understand... Terry was hit by a drunk driver, killed instantly along with another player." I wiped my eyes with my index finger. "If...if I was with him, we wouldn't have got into that accident. I know that...That night was supposed to have been very special. And not just to celebrate our championship...During warmups before the game, I wrote Terry a note, sealed it in an envelope and gave it to an assistant coach to give to Terry. He initially thought it was a court summons, then recognizing my handwriting, assumed that I wanted to break up with him. He debated opening it; quickly deciding yes, thinking that if I were, nothing would have incentivized him more.

"He was always pressuring me to have sex—always—and I was the reluctant one, only because I wanted to wait until we were married— call me old-fashioned." *Did I really just say that?* "But that day I'm not sure what changed my mind. In my note I promised that afterwards, during our victory celebration party (I knew we'd win, as did everyone else) to sneak away (even for just a brief moment) and celebrate our new life together—temporarily apart but forever one. After the opening coin toss, he skipped to the sidelines and kissed me with that wonderful twinkle in his eye. He threw four touchdown passes and ran for two more."

"Did you win?"

"But we never got the chance," I said, my voice cracking. "The next day I was grounded. If I was with Terry that night, he'd still be alive. We would have left earlier and would've missed that drunk driver."

Alexander apologized, holding me, letting me cry.

"Is that why you became a lawyer?" he asked after a silence. "To do something about drunk drivers?"

I took a small helping of collards, tempted to tell Alexander the truth, tempted to explain who I really was and the real reason I decided to become a lawyer, tempted to be honest with myself, tempted to stop pretending that I was a normal person with a normal, ordinary reason for attending law school. I slipped on my sunglasses and looked away toward the southern horizon. No. Not today. I wasn't ready to go down that road with Alexander. I glanced over the water, tightening my windbreaker. A sailboat was marooned in the distance. A motorboat chugged by. "I did so to help the less fortunate," was all that I could muster, which by the way, was the essence of the truth.

"Is your brother older?" I asked, desperate to change the subject.

"Younger. By two years."

"Really? He looks much older."

"Everyone says that." Alexander grabbed another piece of chicken. "And if he didn't dye his hair, he'd look even older. He was completely grey at twenty-five."

"And you?"

"If I went grey or bald, so what? That's me. I hate people pretending to be someone else."

I crossed my legs, shifting my weight. "Hate's a pretty strong word."

"People should accept who they are."

"So grey hair (or baldness) defines you?"

"Yes."

I took two Narragansetts from the cooler, handing one to Alexander. "Are you close to your parents." I assumed so. After all, isn't everyone?

"My father left us when I was four."

"I'm sorry Alexander."

"No need to be sorry. He met someone younger, someone without four kids."

"That must've been really hard on your mother?"

"Yes."

"Have you seen him since? Does he keep in touch?"

"No."

"How do you know if he's still alive?"

"My mother knows for legal purposes. She'll tell me if I ever asked."

"And?"

"I've never asked."

"Why?"

"Why would I want to meet someone who ran out on my mother?"

"Curiosity? If nothing else?"

Alexander pointed to the distant sailboat. "Like asking that guy where he lives."

"That's not the same, Alexander."

"I did run into him once. I knew it was him. And he knew it was me." He took a long drink of beer, finishing it. I handed him another. "A couple of years ago Paul and I were at Gillette for a Pats game. I had to take a leak and saw this guy coming out of the men's room as I was going in: the spitting image of my brother. Without never seeing his picture, I knew it was him and he knew it was me—I look just like my mother."

"She must be really pretty."

"We both stopped for a split-second, then went our separate ways."

"Really, Alexander? That's it? Your own father?"

"He's not my father. And besides I had to take a leak. But I knew it was him—"

"That's even worse, how could you let that moment slip?"

"A guy who walked out on my mother with four young kids?"

"Did you at least turn around to see if he had turned around?"

"Never even crossed my mind."

I dished Alexander more collards. "Has your mother remarried?"

"She just met someone, and they set a date for June. I actually like the bastard. He's taking me to the Miami game next weekend; just the two of us, to get better acquainted."

"In Miami?"

"I wish. He's nice to her. Treats her like a queen. Has a nice house and money."

"Money's important?"

"Not for me, but I want someone who can support my mother financially. She deserves that after all these years, sacrificing everything for us, working two jobs."

"You must have a picture of her?"

Alexander took out his cellphone and showed me a family photo. "That's my mother in the middle."

"*That's* your mother? She's beautiful. And you do look just like her."

"Everyone says that. My sisters always wanted to borrow some of my mother's looks, saying that it wasn't fair to waste them all on me. Unfortunately, they both look like my father, especially my older sister Elaine. She's next to me on my right. She lives in Providence and is an editor at the *Journal*, recently divorced. That's my younger sister Jeanne on my mother's other side; we're only eleven months apart but we look nothing alike—she lives at home with my Mom, works at a bank, taking night classes, studying to be a beautician."

"I'd like to meet your family, Alexander, soon; especially your mother." I smiled stretching my legs. "Walter says you'll be the youngest AFL-CIO president. And certainly the cutest. Gompers, Meany, Lewis, Kirkland—come on! Although Trumka could give you a run for your money."

"I was raised by a single mom working two jobs. People like her need a voice, someone to go to bat for them. Trumka worked in the field for five years, getting a bachelor's degree *and* a law degree; and I'll be following in his footsteps, except for the law degree. This winter I'm starting on my bachelor's in political science at Northeastern, taking online and night classes. My mother was thrilled when I told her."

"So if you want to get elected, why'd you ask Walter to be your campaign manager?"

"I didn't. And he isn't my manager, at least not yet."

"He lost every election he ever ran in. Three locals, and a district, I think it was?"

"He says he knows what *not* to do and the mistakes to avoid. He does have a point; and besides, it's in his best interest to get me elected, so at least I'll listen."

"My grandfather never could trust him."

"Neither can I."

"You have to take everything he says with a grain of salt."

"How about a saltshaker. Like telling me your grandfather collapsed in his arms, right on the staging?"

"He told you that? My grandfather slipped and fell from the icy staging, which Walter was supposed to have cleared but either forgot or did it his usual half-way. They ruled his death a heart attack. But no one knows if he had the heart attack first, then slipped, or fell first, then had the heart attack."

"He didn't die in Walter's arms?"

"He's the last one my grandfather would've chosen. Whatever Walter says, the opposite is true; at least he's dependable."

"Like saying you and your grandfather never laughed."

"What? He said that? I *always* laugh and we always laughed together. Everyone knows that, especially Walter."

"He also said that you have a temper and that you're always on the edge."

"On the edge of what?"

Alexander shrugged. "So what? Everyone does."

I frowned, brushing away a tear. "Yes, I can be on the edge. And yes, I have my father's temper." I stared at snow-clad Mount Washington, peacefully looming over the distant cold-grey mountains. "Things fester with him and unfortunately, the same with me. I've tried walking away, not walking away, holding my breath, not holding my breath, counting to a million."

"A million?"

"Even that doesn't even work. The only thing that does work is leaving. Immediately. Whereas my father stays put, his anger gestating, coalescing into a firestorm, scorching guilty and innocent alike—"

Just then I remembered something from a long time ago, something that I thought I had forever banished from my memory, something that I had no intention of telling Alexander or anyone else for that matter, but the untethered words gushed out: "One of his worst outbursts was during a sleepover in eighth grade, in front of my friends. (I'm not sure what I was thinking inviting them over?) I had been pestering my mother to let me get my ears pierced but she adamantly refused."

"Why?" Alexander innocently asked.

"You'll never understand. No one ever will. So, a week before my sleepover I pierced them myself. I had to in order to remain on the cheerleading squad." I told Alexander about Coach buying us these purple ball earrings, then continued, "The first night of the sleepover, my friends and I were in the kitchen making hot chocolate, talking, laughing, having fun; just being girls. The night was warm, and I had innocently tied my hair back. My mother happened to come into the kitchen for something and froze when she saw me, like she had seen a ghost. She left and returned immediately with my father, who stood glaring at me, like a bull ready to charge, arms folded like I had committed some egregious crime."

"I can picture him," said Alexander.

" 'I'll count to ten,' my father snorted. 'If they're not out, *I'll* take them out.' "

"My friends stood shocked. 'Everyone has pierced ears,' I heard one say."

"My mother flinched."

" 'Four ...Five...Six.' "

"I never felt so humiliated. My body was numb."

" 'Don't cause a scene,' " my mother whispered.

"*I'm causing a scene?*"

" 'Seven...Eight.' "

"My mother hovered next to me. For a moment I thought she was going to protect her daughter, but she forcibly removed the studs, ripping the right earring against the hole, causing it to bleed...I slumped over, crying. My father said something, but I was a million miles away."

I pointed to my expensive diamond earrings, "A gift from my grandparents when they found out." I took a long drink of beer, then looking into Alexander's eyes continued, "Senior year in high school, two weeks before our championship game, I got another piercing in each ear (everyone on the cheerleading squad did—at least those who hadn't already—so we could wear the same purple and white double earrings for the game; celebrating four years without a loss). That's why I was grounded. I could only go to the game (I was surprised they even allowed that) and to school. I was forbidden to see Terry."

"Why? I don't get it?"

"No one does." I brushed away a tear. "No one ever will. The night of our celebration Terry stopped over pleading with my father to let me go. 'A once-in-a-lifetime celebration,' he said, even offering to double the punishment if I could just go this one night. Terry hated my father; hated how he treated me. If he had said yes or if I wasn't grounded in the first place, we would've missed that drunk driver. I know that. But my father didn't budge...One of my friends riding in the back said that just before the accident Terry's phone rang. That was me, just wanting to hear his voice. He struggled finding his phone, and then the accident happened. Perhaps I distracted him enough that he didn't see the oncoming car?"

Alexander hugged me. "You can't think shit like that, Joanna."

I was sweating in the warm sun. "I didn't choose this family I was born into." I slipped off my windbreaker, inadvertently revealing my tattooed wrists: A man on my left and a woman on my right, smiling at each other.

"You and your high school boyfriend?"

I wanted to explain that each tattoo represented a part of who I was: male and female but couldn't put the words together. "I'd never tattoo myself. I'm not that narcissistic and I'd never tattoo my boyfriend, dead or alive—I'm sorry, Alexander, what a terrible thing to say." I rose and perched on the stern's edge. I could sense Alexander staring at my back, at my large tattoo; I mean everyone asks, so why wouldn't Alexander? "It's the Pyramid of the Sun," I said without looking at him. "In Teotihuacan. Just north of Mexico City." My father says I got that (and others) for attention, which shows how little he knows me. "It's a national symbol of Mexico. I got it in Mexico City to honor my grandfather...He never approved of any my tattoos and always talked me out of getting more. But he understood." I dove over the engines deep into the water. The deeper I swam, the more the murky green sunlight played tricks on me. Was that a submerged log? A shipwreck? A large fish?

Chapter 8

Alexander Morgan

"How deep is it?" I called out to Joanna, spotting her some thirty yards away.

With one hand holding her nose, and the other straight up like an arrow, she lowered herself, standing in what appeared to be five feet of water.

I dog-paddled toward her, while she swam towards me with fast, powerful strokes.

"Where'd you learn to swim so well?" Joanna asked, laughing when she reached me, not exactly halfway.

I treaded water, trying to catch my breath. "I can dog-paddle with the best of them."

Joanna wrapped her arms and legs around me. "This is the deepest part of the lake, two hundred and fifty-two feet."

"I thought you were just standing?"

She laughed, slipping off my trunks. I unstrapped her bikini, pressing her close to me, cushioning her with my arm, trying to stay afloat, trying to keep us both afloat, trying to keep her body from turning; water streaming into my nose. Her warm body felt good. She treaded water, holding me tight, kissing me, submerging us; I wanted to apologize that I came too quickly, wanting to keep going, wanting to say that I had enough gas for seconds and even thirds, but a strong breeze picked up pushing the boat away.

"I hope that's just a prelude," she said, kissing me.

The breeze was strengthening. Joanna swam steadfastly toward the boat. By the time I reached the ladder she had secured the anchor, which indeed was loose, or perhaps as Joanna said it was never secure, given that we were in the deepest part of the lake. She smiled seeing me, helping me up the ladder. She wrapped a large beach towel around us, pulling me closer, smiling with her flirting brown eyes.

If there is anything that I ever said in my life that I wished I could've taken back before I said it, it was what I was about to say. I'm still not sure why I said *anything*, when nothing would have been best. Perhaps deep inside I was afraid of Joanna, although exactly why I wasn't sure? Perhaps everything that Walter had said about her was true, even the stuff I didn't want to believe? Even still, I thought I said it in innocent fun, but that's not how Joanna took it. "Doesn't *The Godfather* end when Michael, alone at the lake, kills his brother?"

"What?" She pushed herself away. "What are you saying? Are you implying that I would do something like that? What on earth made you say that? Of all the things to say to me!"

Before I could even think of apologizing, she strapped on her bikini and dove over the engines, swimming fast toward the lighthouse. I expected her any minute to turn around, swim back and embrace me as if nothing had happened, but her speed seemed to be increasing. OK, that was a stupid thing for me to say and now she's pissed. I get it. But what was she trying to prove?

A phone was ringing. In the glove compartment. In Joanna's purse. I picked up. The line clicked. A voice message. Someone named Rachel.

I sifted through keys, lipstick, mascara, nail polish, loose change, not sure if I should be going through a woman's purse, not even sure what I was looking for. Perhaps a hint, a clue, why she left so abruptly and where she could have possibly gone. I found a reservation for the Laconia 401 for this evening. A man's wallet—what was she doing with a man's wallet?—but with her license and credit cards and one hundred fifty dollars in cash. A pair of boxers folded tightly. What the hell? Is she seeing someone else? Then a small package, wrapped in newspaper: a leather pouch sealed with wax. Inside, was a razor-sharp, never-used knife. I shivered. Now everything made sense. That's why she exploded when I asked about *The Godfather*. That's why she took me to the deepest part of the lake. She's toying with me. She's clever, giving me a chance to say no, to back out. Maybe she hates men, only pretending to like them, has sex, kills them, then keeps their underwear as a souvenir?

I took a Narragansett from the cooler and tried to figure out what the hell had just happened and what the hell I should do. Maybe I was overreacting? Maybe this was her way of letting off steam? I decided to give her a few moments to get everything out of her system and if she didn't come back, I'd go after her. The strong breeze had subsided. It was hot even in the shade. Gentle swells rocked the boat.

A loud, thunder-like clap jolted me awake. Joanna starting the engine? But the boat was empty and no sign of her. A menacing thunderstorm was billowing to the north. Scanning the Lake, I called the Marine Patrol, describing Joanna, asking if anyone had seen her. Nothing. They promised to search for her, warning of an approaching severe storm and to seek shelter immediately.

No shit.

I turned the ignition key. The engines clapped loudly—Christ almighty. Inching the throttle forward, I noticed laminated instructions taped just beneath the ignition:

> Open engine hood. Turn on blower and keep on at least
> two minutes. Press Choke. Turn key to start both engines.
> If not, repeat.

Too friggin' late.

Another loud thunderclap. I chugged the boat in a broad circle now assuming the worst. Maybe she hit her head on a rock? Maybe she was eaten by a deep-water fish, or run over by a boat? No sign of Joanna or anyone else for that matter. Then I spotted something bobbing off to the right. Joanna gasping for air? But it turned out to be a huge log. What the hell was *that* doing in the middle of the Lake? Suddenly the boat lurched to a halt, the motor chattering like a muffled Skil-Saw. Another log? I checked the depth-meter—three feet. What the fuck? I was just in the deepest part of the Lake—Joanna had said so herself and now I'm in three feet of water? Rocks were everywhere, some with barely exposed tops. The left engine had become wedged between two rocks, its propeller gashed, and the right propeller was chipped. Another loud thunderclap. I stepped into the water and was surprised that without my weight, the propeller immediately became unstuck. I pushed the boat toward deeper water, then climbed in. I lifted the engine hood, expecting the worst, but the floorboards seemed to be intact with no apparent structural damage other than the propeller.

I started the boat, this time following the laminated instructions. Checking the depth-meter and the rearview mirror while searching the water ahead, I guided the boat slowly, toward the lighthouse, wishing I was heading in the opposite friggin' direction, toward the open blue sky.

Chapter 9

Joanna Turnus

Locked in my Australian crawl, I could have beaten anyone, even my grandfather (although surprisingly we had never raced). If the Olympic trials were held that morning, I would have easily made the team; and if I hadn't strayed off course, scraping my knee on the rocks just north of Governors Island, I would've reached the Center Restaurant at the tip of Meredith Bay in record time, although not exactly a record to be proud of.

I stumbled over the rocks, my legs like jelly, my heart sinking, distraught that I had actually swam this far.

"Are you OK?" called a male voice in a southern drawl. I assumed it was Alexander's brother, but it was an older, smaller-framed man, with thin-wired glasses, squinting from the mid-day sun, approaching in a small dinghy powered by an electric motor; I'm sure wondering why a tattooed, bikini-clad woman was struggling on the shoals.

I forced a smile as the old man helped me into his boat. My left knee was bleeding; thankfully not deep, just a lot of blood. While he dressed and bandaged it, I introduced myself, explaining what had happened. He asked if I was related to Anthony Turnus. Of course, he knew my grandfather—who didn't? And it seems that they were good friends (he smiled when I explained the significance of my middle name) although it was strange that I never heard my grandfather talk about him. The man was a retired pilot for the *Sophie C* and sometimes for the *Doris C* (mailboat for the Lake islands and tourist boat, respectively) and often spotted my grandfather swimming, sometimes veering slightly off course so its steep wake wouldn't swamp my grandparents' boat.

The old man told me that since retiring, he had been fishing full-time professionally, often entering fishing contests (which he usually won), and working as a fishing guide, spending the ice-free months on the Lake, then fishing Louisiana's bayous. He showed me several catfish that he had caught earlier that morning, just off Stonedam Island, inviting me to his home (on the mainland of Sally's Gut) that evening for a wonderful-sounding jambalaya and catfish pie that his Louisiana-born wife would soon be making. I told him my affection for southern cooking; about my good friend Eliot; and what I had made for Alexander. His wife would especially enjoy meeting me, the old man said.

The sky was darkening, the thunderclaps becoming louder. The old man warned of the impending storm, with wind gusts approaching hurricane strength. I reluctantly declined his dinner offer, gave him my cell phone number, and promised a rain check. Soon. Before Christmas.

Just then we heard a loud engine roar, sounding like my boat. Indeed it was Alexander, slowly chugging toward us.

"Is that yours?" asked the old man. "It seems to be listing?"

Yes, the boat was listing to the right, the engines gurgling, fluming water in a high arc. Another loud thunderclap. Alexander killed the engines. The old man hurriedly pulled alongside the stern.

"Where the hell were you?" demanded Alexander, unfazed by the old man's presence. "I've been looking everywhere."

"Will you be OK?" the old man asked, as Alexander helped me up the ladder.

"Yes. Thank you." I bid him goodbye, then curtly apologized to Alexander.

"Are you going to explain what the hell just happened?"

"Once I get this boat to safety."

It would have been easiest to dock my boat on an island or even the mainland, but I feared that the gusts and high waves from the rapidly approaching storm would do more damage. The safest place would be in my boathouse, a good ten minutes away even at top speed.

I lifted the engine hood, asking Alexander what had happened.

"I thought I was in the deepest part of the Lake—you said so yourself. And then I'm in three feet of water."

"You must've gone through the shoals."

"What shoals? I was looking for you! How the hell was I supposed to know about any friggin' shoals?"

The engine and floorboards appeared to be fine—thank God. The right propellor seemed to be OK. But the left propellor was completely broken off.

A huge lightning bolt lit the sky, followed by an instantaneous clap of thunder. Alexander made the sign of the cross. "I didn't know you were religious?" I asked.

"Neither did I," responded Alexander, crouching low.

I turned the boat toward the southern shore, toward the blue sky and opened the throttle. The engines gurgled, listing the boat to the right. I shut the left engine off. It wasn't until we passed under the Route 3 Bridge into Paugus Bay that I slowed down. (I'm sure the Marine Patrol would have forgiven my disregarding the *No Wake* sign.) We parked at a gas station. The water was calm. The sky overhead was blue. The fierce storm was raging to the north.

I felt faint and needed to eat. I took a piece of fried chicken from the cooler and sat on the engine cover. The storm seemed to be gliding eastward.

"What are you doing with men's underwear." Alexander demanded.

"You went through my purse?"

"Your phone was ringing. I thought you were calling."

"From the water?"

"How the hell was I supposed to know *where* you were? Do you seduce guys, kill them, then take their underwear? Is that why you carry a knife? Is that why you freaked out when I asked about *The Godfather*?"

"I can explain all that."

"Please do."

I fumbled for words—any words—knowing that whatever I said

would be terribly inadequate. I wanted to confess that the underwear was mine, that I had worn it that very morning looking for him, along with my Fu Manchu and my baseball cap. I wanted to confess that I was transgender, and to finally be honest with myself and with Alexander. But I couldn't find the words. "People get tattooed for all sorts of reasons," I began.

"What the hell does *that* have to do with anything?"

I showed Alexander my wrists, feeling disconnected to myself and to Alexander, as if I were a normal person listening to someone else. "Each tattoo covers a scar. That knife in my purse...that...that was from my first suicide attempt. I carry it with me. Always. And the underwear. As a talisman."

"What? I don't understand? *The first time?* What the hell are you saying!"

"I'm glad you don't understand, Alexander." I glanced at the raging storm, wanting to explain, but the words were nowhere to be found, instead asking for his help in covering the boat, which I didn't really need, for I could do it in my sleep (and I'm sure I probably have), then offering him a lift to his sister-in-law's, which he abruptly refused.

"Why don't you stay the night me?" I found myself asking. "I rented a townhouse in Laconia."

"I'm going back to Boston."

My eyes watered, realizing that this relationship was over. There was nothing I could say or do. In a way I was glad, for Alexander deserved someone better, someone at least halfway normal. I offered him a ride to the bus station, but he said no, insisting on an Uber; his ride arriving soon.

Chapter 10

Alexander Morgan

"OK, which one of you bastards started this friggin' rumor?" I asked, distributing the morning coffee.

"Three guesses," Abe nodded to Walter, "he spreads them before they even start."

Walter removed the lid to his coffee cup, taking a sip. "All I said was that you had a nice weekend; ain't that right, kid?"

"Whatever gave you *that* idea?" I took my seat next to Nick.

"You had that twinkle in your eye this mornin'."

"Twinkle in my eye? I was just happy that this wasn't a friggin' three-day weekend."

"Well?" Nick asked, lighting a cigarette. "You going to keep us in suspense all morning?"

"There are nice weekends and *really* nice weekends," I began. "And there are *shitty* weekends and *really* shitty weekends, and mine couldn't have been any *shittier*. We got caught in a bad storm, my sister-in-law tried to seduce me, I forgot about this woman I was supposed to meet for dinner in Worcester Friday night, I ran this other woman's yacht aground and will probably spend the rest of my life paying for it, I almost got hit by friggin' lightning, and this other woman, who I really liked, jumped overboard and swam away. I took a four-hour bus ride home. Christ, I was surprised that the bus didn't explode or that I wasn't abducted by friggin' aliens. Last Friday I was involved—if that's the right word—with three women, now today, each wants to kill me."

"Hopefully one will succeed," said Abe.

"My advice," offered Nick. "If you date more than one woman, then date the same one, so it don't matter if one finds out about the other."

"Well, well, look at this," Walter pointed to Gary, running—or rather, waddling towards us.

"One of nature's rare sights," said Abe.

"Just because...I...don't...sweat like you animals," Gary said, catching his breath, entering the coffee circle. "Don't...don't mean that I ain't working."

"The master speaks," Abe said.

Gary sat on what had appeared to be a full bucket of drywall cement, but it split in two, throwing him backwards. "Son-of-a-bitch." He pushed himself up, wiping his forehead with a handkerchief. "While you guys were slaving away in this miserable heat, I was inside vacuuming the executive offices; the ceiling guys had made quite a mess."

"Sounds like another week-long project," Nick said.

"Or at least until the weather cools," added Abe.

"Then suddenly I had to take a crap," Gary said. "But the men's room was locked, so I ran outside to the shithouse."

"You mean my office," I said.

"I saw you coming and ran like hell out the back door," Nick said to Gary.

"There's a back door?" I said to Paul.

"I just made it," Gary said. "And man did it stink; it must have been a hundred and ten degrees in there. I held my breath, afraid to sit, hovering just above that stinkin' mess, when this bird starts swooping at my pecker."

"A hummingbird, no doubt," Abe said. "Looking for its frickin' mate."

"Too small," I said.

Walter's phone rang. "It's Phil."

"Don't answer it," I said.

"He knows we're here," Walter said.

"All the better reason," I insisted.

Walter handed me the phone. "He's pissed. He wants to speak to you."

"When is he *not* pissed?" I put the phone on speaker so everyone could hear: "I want you to go back to the shop and paint all of our staging, you lazy-ass bastard."

"Now?" I asked. "In the middle of the day? This should be done first thing in the morning or at the end of the day."

"Zachary wants it done immediately, you goddammed son-of-a-bitch."

"At least he got the name right," said Abe.

"Last night someone stole our staging from another job. Paint it so everyone knows it's ours. And get going! We need it ASAP."

Click.

I finished my coffee, stood up, and flung the empty cup at Nick. "So when you guys are wondering where the hell I am all friggin' afternoon."

"I won't be giving it a second thought," Abe said.

A squad car pulled into the parking lot. "Finally, they're arresting that bastard." I muttered. But the officers asked for me. They had found my truck abandoned along the Merrimack River on the New Hampshire border, with the keys still in the ignition. No suspects. Not a scratch anywhere and nothing was missing, not even the loose change on the dash. But the dumpster was never found. It didn't make no sense—in fact the whole thing didn't make sense: stealing a truck *and* a dumpster, leaving one intact but taking the other?

Stuck in stop-and-go traffic—this is why you don't send someone back to the shop in the middle of the day—I kept replaying yesterday's events, especially my spur-of-the-moment decision to return to Laconia. We had stopped in Manchester to switch buses. I was about to board, and I'm not sure why or even how it happened—I hadn't given it any thought at all—and instead hopped on the return bus to Laconia, telling the bus driver that I had forgotten something.

Maybe I had overreacted? Perhaps if my girlfriend had died tragically, I would have kept her underwear? And who knows, maybe I would have been suicidal, especially at such a young age, and especially if I was supposed to have been with her that very night and that my presence could have prevented the whole thing? Maybe I had judged her a little too harshly?

At the Laconia station I asked a bus driver on break if he knew where the 401 townhouse was.

"Straight ahead. Can't miss it."

The quite ordinary 401 was sandwiched between a flower shop and a somewhat upscale hair salon. Its wide-open French windows, intricately latticed with oak, and its second-floor balcony latticed with almost real gold-looking bricks, hinted of undeserved pretentiousness.

The townhouse door was locked. I pressed the intercom asking for Joanna Turnus.

"She checked out."

"*Checked out? When?*"

"About ninety minutes ago."

"Where?"

"I don't know and even I did, I wouldn't tell you."

Returning to the bus station, I was glad that she had gone, relieved that this relationship—if that's the right word—was finally over.

The only good thing about being stuck in stop-and-go traffic—unusually heavy for mid-afternoon, even by Boston standards; perhaps due to construction or an accident?—was that I had time to think about my design for the friggin' staging. I sketched out the essentials:

- It had to be our colors, green and white.
- Paint only one small part of each piece of staging, and not the whole piece.
- Visible from a distance so no bastard in his right mind would even think of stealing it.

- Spray paint it, which would be quicker and much cheaper.

Surprisingly, the design came quickly: A five-inch stripe with alternating green, white, and yellow fluorescent bands on two of the four upper rungs (alternating diagonally) of each piece of staging; and the same stripe on each brace. Simple, cost effective, elegant, cheap, and most importantly, friggin' theft-proof.

At the hardware store, I explained my design to the clerk, who, as it turns out, was able to pinpoint with surprising accuracy my needed supplies, without even using a scratchpad. And yeah, it felt good to legitimately charge everything to General and then sign my name in big bold letters.

At the shop I decided to save time and money by constructing a prototype that I could slip onto each piece. No need for taping, and I would only have to measure everything once. I welded several pieces of small pipe together, leaving enough space for the stripes, using clamps to sleeve the pipe into place, then built another thinner piece with tighter clamps for the braces and was ready to go. I lined the staging and braces against the shed's outside wall, covered it with a shitload of canvases, strapped on my headphones—fuck Phil's no-music rule—and spray-painted like a bastard.

I finished exactly at 1:04, give or take a few minutes.

I stepped back admiring my work: precision-cut and ready-dry, noticing that I had inadvertently skipped two pieces in the middle. No problem. Only took a minute. Satisfied, I threw a sample into the back of my truck for Phil's inevitable, fault-finding inspection when I noticed Joanna approaching from the office, dressed in a shapely brown skirt and jacket, and a black, half-unbuttoned blouse.

"Here to do some real work for once?" I asked.

She smiled. "I had a meeting with my father and noticed this cute guy out back. Alexander, that was sweet of you to come back to the 401."

"How'd you know it was me?"

"I don't know too many people fitting your description." Joanna said, then apologizing; as I did, after all, it was really my fault for saying such a stupid thing.

"What brings you back to the shop in the middle of the afternoon?" Joanna asked.

I explained Phil's call during coffee break, her father's demand, then my visit to the hardware store when she burst out laughing; a wonderful, contagious laugh. I know she laughs easily, but friggin' hardware stores?

"You'd think my grandfather being a construction guy," she said, still laughing, "would've been right at home in a hardware store; after all, what's there not to like: Musty oak floors with creaky clerks who could find anything in their sleep? But he absolutely hated them."

"Hate's a pretty strong word."

"No other word does it justice, believe me. Whenever he needed something from the hardware store, he *always* sent someone else, usually Walter. And sometimes even me. But this one Sunday afternoon, he was working on his deck—alone—and needed a box of eight penny nails. He had asked everyone—even a neighbor—but no one was around, so he had no choice but to go himself. At the store he was fidgety, nervous, visibly agitated; I'm sure impressing everyone that he was going to rob the place. Wasting no time, he plopped his nails at the register, telling the clerk to charge it to A.J. Turnus."

" 'Who are you?' " the clerk demanded. " 'I know all of A.J. Turnus' workers, even the granddaughter but I ain't never seen you.' "

"My grandfather took out his driver's license, displayed it to the clerk, saying with a wonderful twinkle in his voice, 'I'm A.J. Turnus.' "

Joanna laughed at me with her fun, flirting eyes. "Alexander, I'd like to take you to dinner, to apologize *and* so you won't have to pay for the propeller."

"I'm the one who broke it. And besides, propellers are expensive."

"So's the place I'm taking you. Does tonight work?"

"Tonight? I have a basketball game that I can't miss."

"Saturday night?"

"My sister Jeanne invited me for a long overdue dinner. I've already cancelled twice and if I cancel again, she'll disown me. Hey, maybe Sunday? Brunch? Downtown?"

"No...I have...there's this harbor cruise...that I...it's more of an obligation—I have to go. It leaves at noon."

"A high noon cruise on Boston Harbor? Must be important."

"Maybe dinner afterwards?"

"I'm meeting with Walter in the afternoon; it's the only time we can meet. How about Friday night?"

Joanna checked her cell phone calendar. "That actually might work. I've a meeting practically next door to the Old Post Inn; it ends at 5.30, so how about 6.00? At the Old Post Inn."

"Make it 6.05. Walter says you're always runnin' late to meetins'."

"It's my meetin', so I'll make sure we end on time. But I'll have to meet you there, if that's OK. You know where it is?"

I nodded.

"You'll have to wear a jacket and tie."

"How will you recognize me?"

She smiled. "I don't think that will be a problem." She pulled me close and kissed me, longer than either of us had anticipated.

Leaving the shop, I noticed Zachary glaring from an upstairs window.

BOOK THREE

Chapter 1

Alexander Morgan

Despite my misgivings, despite every internal alarm bell going off, Sunday mid-morning I found myself getting ready for a high-noon cruise on Boston harbor. Don't ask why. One of the great unsolvable mysteries of our time, that Einstein himself couldn't have solved even if he lived to be 100.

I had no idea if this cruise was formal or informal, and no idea what to wear, and since I've never been on one before, I called my sisters for advice. 'Cruise casual' was the consensus, 'you can't go wrong.'

Since it was too hot for anything but shorts, and autumn ruled out anything but brown, I decided on a brown casual jacket with olive green shorts, and a white T-shirt. If it was informal, I could roll up my sleeves, untuck my shirt and wrap the jacket around my waist, and if formal I'd keep the long-sleeves and tuck in my shirt. Either way, I decided on shorts: who'd be looking at my legs?

At the last moment I dashed on a little Armani, which I hadn't worn in a long time.

Chapter 2

Joanna Turnus

I wore a Red Sox cap, windbreaker, black jeans, sneakers, my grandparents' diamond earrings, and of course my Fu Manchu. Standing atop the gangplank I was the boat's unofficial greeter: a comforting beacon, welcoming old friends and new acquaintances drawn by the hypnotic beat of the band; some already dancing, shuffling up the steel gangplank; the band muffling the jetliners overhead, one after another, landing at Logan Airport just across the harbor. With a warm sun and a cool ocean breeze it was a splendid afternoon for a cruise on Boston Harbor.

Suddenly I realized that I was still wearing my nose rings (three pink diamond studs) which I usually remove when I dress as a guy, unless I forget, which happens a lot. Like this one time, not yet comfortable going out in public, worried that I wasn't passable and that someone would easily recognize me, but still anxious to present myself as a male, I decided to go solo to the movies, where I could linger alone with others in a tapestry of darkness. The movie queue snaked out the door, then doubled back, so that everyone had to pass each other. A woman holding hands with another woman approached, wearing a pretty brown sundress exposing exquisite tattoos on her back and shoulders. About to compliment her, she snickered to her tattoo-less, earring-less companion, "He has a nose ring!" Apparently, earrings *and* nose rings were too much. Sometimes you find intolerance where least expected.

Everyone arrived with so much pent-up energy, they went straight to the dance floor. Guys with guys, girls with girls, girls with guys, not really caring, just having fun. Rachel was touching up in the ladies' room, and this, after spending the whole morning getting ready! I was about to text her that the band had started, that there were lots of people I wanted her to meet, when my heart stopped: Was that Alexander in the parking lot? The last person on earth I expected? What made him decide to come? Yes, it was him, stepping down from his truck—although he didn't dress up? How could he not have known that everyone dresses up on this cruise?

He walked briskly toward the gangplank, as if worried about being spotted. He quickly ascended, brushing past me, annoyed that this guy (me) was smiling at him.

"Alexander!" I called in my Joanna voice.

He turned, looking past me.

"It's me. Joanna." I reached out, but he stepped backed, as if I had the plague.

"Joanna?" Alexander asked, with a tinge of contempt.

I removed my Fu Manchu and took off my baseball cap, carefully ignoring his contorted look of unsure superiority that something was wrong, that something was amiss. "Alexander, it's me. I guess I forgot to tell you that everyone on this cruise dresses up—I really wasn't expecting you."

"Obviously."

The whistle blew. It was five minutes before noon. The gangplank was about to be raised and the boat would soon depart on its four-hour cruise of Boston Harbor.

Sensing his agitation, I led him to the bar, hoping that a drink would loosen him up. We snaked through the outer edge of the dance floor, carefully avoiding being sucked in by the centrifugal, hypnotic beat.

"Why's everyone staring at me?" he asked, after I bought him a glass of champagne and took one for myself.

"Because you perfectly nailed it: being a guy."

"That's because I am a guy."

"Everyone here has an idealized picture of how others see them, each striving for that elusive, imaginary ideal, but most fall short."

Alexander took a long sip. "So you mean the guys are actually girls pretending to be guys?"

"No one here pretends, this is who we are. When we leave, we have to pretend. Sure, this is fun while it lasts but it's artificial and ephemeral, like an electric light in the Arctic. We want to bathe in real sunlight but for most of us that's unattainable, so we have this artificial, make-believe fantasy world for four hours—where no one criticizes or disparages. And for many of us, that's just enough to keep us going—then back to reality: living in two worlds, rejected by both, accepted by neither. The high priests of society, the self-righteous, the self-anointed judges of humankind, say we'll burn in hell for daring to challenge God's plan."

"So, everyone thinks I'm a girl dressed as a guy?"

"They assume you *are* a guy."

"OK, that's fine: I'm a guy dressed as a guy. As long as everyone knows that."

Alexander still didn't get it. He drained his glass, wiped his mouth with the back of his hand, and handed it to me.

"Do I look like a butler?"

"As a matter of fact, yes, you do."

I set our champagne glasses on a mushroom-looking table. "If you feel uncomfortable about this cruise or about me, you don't have to stay. No one's forcing you. But this is who I am, and these are friends." I slipped on my Fu Manchu and put on my baseball cap and headed to the dance floor, trying to find some space, not expecting him to follow. Squeezing into a small but quickly collapsing niche, I was pleasantly surprised to see Alexander close behind. I bumped into two old friends—literally. I'm sure Alexander assumed they were lesbians—which they were, but I didn't say that each was born male, had fully transitioned and had happily found each other. They shared their good news of adopting their second child, who like her older brother was severely mentally and physically handicapped; inviting us to celebrate later, after the cruise.

No sooner had we separated, than Hope, a fourteen-year-old girl, rushed to me, seeming quite agitated, saying that she was so glad to finally be here—but I couldn't tell if she was laughing or crying—then darted away before I could respond.

"Looking for her parents?" Alexander asked innocently.

"She's here despite her parents. She was born male but always knew she was female, something that her religiously conservative parents couldn't tolerate. Frankly, I was surprised to see her today— her first cruise—surprised that her parents allowed her."

"Wow, this really is a hall of mirrors."

"The outside world is a hall of mirrors where we have to dissemble to fit society's preconceptions."

We danced a few more songs. Alexander seemed to enjoy the dancing, and for a big guy was pretty smooth and agile.

Chapter 3

Alexander Morgan

At least on the dance floor I could be myself with no one staring like they've never seen a real male before. Of course I asked Joanna several times to remove her false beard—not an unreasonable request, as any real male would—but she refused. "I'm here for my friends," she insisted, without missing a beat. Not exactly sure where that left me.

Then just halfway through the third song she asked for a break.

I asked to keep dancing.

Looking tipsy and nauseous, like she was about to faint, she didn't even wait for the song to end and headed straight for the bar asking for aspirin and a glass of water. I ordered two beers, quickly downed one and followed her to the deck.

She was leaning over the railing. "The fresh air feels good," she said, straightening up. "I couldn't breathe inside."

Maybe if you had removed your false beard, we both could have breathed easier?

An attractive, tall, well-proportioned woman approached us—at least I thought she was a woman, although I had no reason to suspect otherwise, but then again, no one on this fucked-up cruise seemed to be who they were supposed to be. But she was too pretty not to be a woman? Long brown hair flowed to her shoulders, a few strands drooping over her right eye—kind of sexy—wearing a low-cut black dress that accentuated a large friggin' rack.

"Blake! Where've you been?" the woman asked in a low, somewhat husky voice. Her lips were full and rich. She had a mole just above the left corner of her mouth, with three large freckles triangled in the middle of her right cheek.

I assumed that she had mistaken me for this Blake dude, but she was smiling at Joanna, as if long-lost friends. She pushed her sunglasses back over her hair and kissed Joanna on her cheek, just above her Fu Manchu. What the fuck?

"I've been looking *everywhere* for you," she said. "I thought you had fallen overboard."

Perhaps in normal circumstances I wouldn't have assumed anything, other than that she was a pretty woman with a husky voice, but these were definitely not normal circumstances.

"Blake?" I reluctantly asked Joanna.

"My male name."

"And this is?" the woman asked with a brooding indifference.

"Rachel, this is Alexander."

She smiled, extending her hand with fingernails painted bright red. "It's nice to meet you. I've heard lots about you."

I glanced at Joanna, or Blake, or whoever the hell she was trying to be.

"Good things!" added Rachel.

"Alexander, this is Rachel, my best friend and soul-sister."

If everyone was dressed up, then she had to be a man dressed as a woman? But if so, how could they be best friends? And how did she develop such large breasts? I felt dizzy.

"Everyone calls him Alex, except me," Joanna said.

"My mother and my sisters call me Alexander. But either's fine—I've been called a lot worse, especially by my mother and my sisters."

Was that stubble on her chin, or just a shadow? Her rack looked genuine, her skin soft, her long legs pretty.

Rachel took Joanna's hand. "Come on, let's dance! I've been waiting all week."

"Not right now sweetie...I feel a little nauseous."

"You're not pregnant?" asked Rachel with a hint of a smile.

"Alexander dear, why don't you two dance for a bit? I need to sit down."

I quickly looked away, definitely not wanting to dance with her, or him, no matter how pretty. "Not right now—my legs are tired."

"You just asked to keep dancing?"

"That's OK." Rachel tersely said and abruptly left.

"Alexander, what was that all about? Just two minutes ago you wanted to keep dancing?"

"With you and not some—"

"Some freak?"

"I didn't say that."

"You didn't have to. You should've seen yourself inspecting her up and—"

"Forgive me for having no idea who's a man and who's a woman. Forgive me for not wanting to dance with her. It's bad enough that I—"

"Bad enough? *Bad enough!* I'm sorry I forced you here. I'm sorry that I even mentioned it. Just go back to your normal natural-born world where no one stares and no one judges, where what you wear doesn't matter, where people aren't afraid to smile back, where people fall in love and live happily ever." She ripped off her Fu Manchu, tossed it overboard and stormed inside.

If I was a friggin' smoker, I probably would've gone through at least a pack, staring at the green, seaweed infested water trying to figure what the hell just happened. But no real male would have danced with her or him, or whoever Rachel was pretending to be? Right? That's like confessing to the whole world that you're gay.

The boat had just passed Boston Light for the second time; apparently, I was on the deck longer than I had thought. Inside the band was just breaking. No sign of Joanna—or Blake, or whoever she was. I spotted Rachel sitting alone on a wooden bench at the far end of the dance floor, elbows on her legs, resting her head in her palms, and walked over to apologize.

"Don't patronize me," she snipped, wiping her eyelids with her index finger.

"I'm not patronizing you or anyone else. I *am* sorry."

"Then leave, you made your point."

"What is with you people?"

"You people!! You people?" She started to cry. I tried sitting next to her, but she schussed me away. "Just go. Haven't you done enough damage? You think you're so perfect, saying whatever you want, treating us like dirt."

"I *am* sorry. Listen, I acted like a jerk, but it wasn't deliberate. Everything's happening so fast. I just met Joanna last weekend and never felt like this about anyone, then she invites me on this friggin' cruise—I had no that she was going to wear a false beard and no idea that I was supposed to dress up; then everyone's staring at me, inspecting me like a new species at the zoo."

"Join the club," Rachel said ruefully.

"It's like every day seeing the sun rise in the east—never really thinking about it or even noticing—then one day it rises in the west."

"So why didn't you dress up?"

"I had no idea I was supposed to *dress up*."

"If you *had* known, would you have?"

"Of course not!"

"Why do you say that so sardonically? For us, *this* isn't dressing up. When we leave and return to so-called reality, then we must dress to please everyone; everyone, that is, except ourselves."

"I'm not gay."

"This has nothing to with being gay–that's a separate issue–this is about expressing who you really are."

"I need a beer."

"Get me a Diet Pepsi. Lots of ice."

When I returned, Rachel had stretched her back against the wall; barefoot, her long legs extended.

"Here's your Regular Coke," I said. "No friggin' ice, right?"

A faint smile.

I took a long sip of beer. "So, you're a man?"

"I was born into a male's body if that's what you're asking."

"And Joanna?"

Rachel sipped her drink. "What do you think?"

"Just asking."

"She was born female. She likes being female. She's very much attracted to guys but also has a male identity."

"What the hell does that mean?"

"You're are a male, right?"

"What do you think?"

"You identify as a male?"

"Never even thought about it. I was born a male. I've always been a male, so why would I identify as something else?"

Rachel chewed on an ice cube. "I think I get what you're saying. Now think of a woman, say your mother, who identifies as a woman; then throw in a male identity in the same body and mix the two together. That's how it is with us. Some of us are lucky enough to know one way or the other, but many struggle our whole lives, not knowing how or even why we were given this ambiguity."

"Most of us don't like ambiguity; if we order steak, that's what we expect."

"We're human beings, not cuts of beef."

"I know that."

"Maybe someday they'll check before birth to see if the inside matches the outside, and if not, change the outside while still in the womb—it's a lot easier."

A short silence.

"You two have an argument?" Rachel asked.

"I guess I'd call it that. Have you seen her?"

"She's OK."

"So you've seen her?"

"No."

"So you've talked to her? Texted her?"

"No. But she's OK. She's probably in the men's room, or on the deck having a cigarette."

"She doesn't smoke. How do you know she's OK if you haven't seen her?"

Rachel took a long drink of Coke. "Did Joanna mention anything about how we met or how we became best friends?"

I shook my head, not exactly sure I wanted to know.

The boat abruptly stopped, as if hitting something. "Probably a crosscurrent," Rachel said unconcerned. "Or even a rogue wave. Happens now and then." She chewed on an ice cube, crossing her legs. "We met six months ago in a hospital. A mental hospital. We were the lucky ones, I guess. Suicide survivors. If that's the right phrase. My second day there I heard this sweet innocent laugh; such sweetness in such a god-forsaken place. We hit it off instantly."

"Were you dressed like this?"

"If you're asking if she's attracted to me as a male and I to her, no. We're both women. We're best friends, soul sisters. In the hospital we talked about everything. We made a pact to always be there for each other—to never let that happen again. That's why *I know* she's OK. She would've called me."

"Her phone could've fallen in the water? She could've fallen overboard, or been kidnapped?"

"Kidnapped? Off this boat? And if she fell overboard, she's fine; she's a good swimmer."

I sighed. "I know."

Rachel chuckled. "Don't take it personally; you wouldn't want to be around her when she's angry."

"It's hard *not* to take that personally."

"I'd be worried if she called, or worse, left a message."

"I'd feel a lot better if we at least looked for her."

Rachel got up, stretching her long arms. "If that makes you happy."

She searched the restrooms; and I the upper and lower decks.

"Let's talk to the Captain," Rachel suggested, returning empty handed.

"You just said that she's OK; now you want to see the Captain?"

"She *is* OK. I just don't know where she is right now. Maybe the Captain knows."

As we snaked through the edge of the dance floor, this guy asked me to dance. With most people on this fucked-up cruise, I honestly couldn't tell the difference but not him— smeared lipstick and overdone mascara—as if he wanted the whole world to know that he was a guy haphazardly dressed as a girl. Of course I said no, which surprised the hell out of him, as if he had really expected me to say yes?

"Wow, if looks could kill," Rachel muttered, tossing back her long brown hair. I followed her past the bar, past the restrooms and up a narrow, spiral staircase. Halfway, she turned to me, "Let me do the talking. Just play dumb— ha! that should be easy."

On the upper deck, Rachel rapped on the first door past the stairway.

"How do you know this is the Captain's?"

She pointed just above the door frame. "Remember, let me do the talking."

A female—at least she seemed to be, but then again no one was who they were supposed to be—slightly overweight with short, jet-black hair, opened the door. "Yes?" she answered in a high-pitched, feminine voice, I'm sure wondering who we were, or who we were supposed to be. Or perhaps she assumed that everyone was pretending to be someone else? Makes it easier, no second guessing.

"Are you the captain, mam?" Rachel asked.

"I am."

She has to be a woman. Soft face, high-pitched voice? No male mannerisms, no sign of maleness, no trace of a beard.

"We might have an emergency," said Rachel.

"What is it?" the Captain inquired in an unconcerned voice, giving the impression that emergencies on this cruise were not that uncommon.

"A friend of ours is missing," Rachel said. "We think she might be in trouble."

"Did she jump overboard?"

"Maybe."

"Call the police."

Rachel displayed an ID badge from her purse. "I *am* a police officer."

The captain examined the badge. "OK. I just let her off at Long Wharf. We happened to be very close by. She was agitated, and nauseous."

"Can you also let us off?" Rachel asked. "We need to find her."

"I can't be letting people off every five minutes."

"She needs our help."

"We're close to Hull," the Captain said, checking her watch. "I can stop in eleven minutes."

"Hull?" I objected. "I'm parked at the Pier. Can you stop there?"

"That's forty-one minutes. I thought *you* said this was an emergency? This isn't a speed boat. Do you want an air lift?"

"We'll wait," sighed Rachel.

"Be at the gangplank in forty minutes." The captain closed her door.

We returned downstairs. Rachel took a seat on the long, wooden bench, while I bought us another round of drinks.

"Great stuff about being a cop," I said, delivering her Diet Pepsi with lots of ice. She had removed her shoes, stretching her long legs. She tossed back her long hair, reached into her purse and showed me her cop ID.

"You *are* a cop? Robert McNair?" I held the ID up to her face. "Really? This is you? A moustache? It doesn't look anything like you."

"That was five years ago when I first joined the force."

"How do you...how do you hide everything?"

"It ain't easy."

"Let's call Joanna," I suggested breaking a short, awkward silence.

"That's not necessary."

"Why not?"

"It would freak her out."

"So it's better to let *us* freak out?"

"No one's freaking out. She's on her way home."

"How do you know?"

"Where else would she be?"

"A bar, a club?"

"She doesn't drink."

"Where does she live?" I asked.

"In Concord, with me."

I glanced at her with alarm.

"It's not what you think—although who knows what you're thinking. Actually, *I* live in Concord with Joanna. She invited me in after my wife kicked me out and I had nowhere to go."

"You were married?"

"Why so surprised?"

I shrugged.

"Almost three years."

"So what happened?"

"Why so interested?"

"We have forty minutes."

"Thirty-four," Rachel sighed, glancing at my watch. "Even that might not be enough... Six months ago, my wife left for a week-long business trip—our first time apart. I had been counting down the weeks, the days, the hours, planning and replanning what I would wear and what I would do, down to the smallest little detail. The second she left, something came over me that I had absolutely no control over, like another person had taken over my body. I shaved my legs, despite this inner voice warning that she'd return in five days and that I'd have a lot of explaining to do. But the five days seemed like a lifetime. I pierced my ears with a thumbtack and slipped in a pair of my wife's earrings—nothing ever felt so good. Again, that warning voice, but I wasn't listening—the first time in my life I felt alive. I spent a whole afternoon just listening to the rain. That night I took a long walk, hearing things that I had never heard before. But I should've known that God was already laughing. He toys with us, offering a modicum of hope, only to cruelly dash it away.

"The third night, I was relaxing in my living room with a glass of wine, when suddenly my wife burst through the front door, unexpectedly home four days early. (She later told my parents that, having long suspected me of an affair she wanted to catch me in the act.) At first, she thought *I* was the other woman, angrily demanding my whereabouts. Then, inching closer, she recoiled with a look that I'll never forget: anger, shock, surprise, disgust, horror, all seamlessly rolled together. 'Oh my God!' she screamed. 'You pierced your ears! Oh my God! You shaved your legs! Oh my God! You're wearing a bra? Oh my Gooodddd!'

"And yes, God was definitely on her side. Part of me was relieved—strange as it may seem—that I no longer had to pretend, and that somehow this revelation might even bring us closer and we could once again be intimate. How naïve was that? I tried apologizing but she pushed me away. 'Don't touch me!' she screamed hysterically. 'How could you do this to me? How could you destroy our marriage like this? I want you out immediately and if not, I'll tell everyone how I found you, down to the last *disgusting* detail.'

"She slammed the door, yelling for all to hear that she was getting a lawyer. That was the last time I talked with my wife; that is, if you call that talking. The next day I awoke in the hospital, thinking it was a bad dream, until I saw my bare legs and felt my sore earlobes. (Later I learned that my wife had returned to the house for something and found me slumped over—I guess I had taken a lot of sleeping pills—and called 911.) In the hospital my parents were yelling at me for stupidly giving up the wealth and power of her well-established New England family, condemning for me for something I had no control over, chastising for me for finding out who I really was.

"That hospital was like a prison. No pens or pencils allowed. No alone time. No privacy. No jewelry, knives, electrical sockets, wires, or even sheets. One communal TV chained high on a shelf—even taking a shower they kept a watchful eye, only allowing one electric razor tied to the bathroom door... I asked this really pretty nurse, who had taken a liking to me and respected me for who I was—at least I had thought—her reaction if her husband started wearing lip gloss and mascara. Her silent look of disgust betrayed her real thoughts. I felt so incredibly alone. I withdrew and didn't speak to anyone.

"They put me on high suicide alert for two weeks—I was already in a high suicide ward—until *they* were sure I was no longer suicidal, that I could be sent home intact, good to go; as if they somehow magically could have known, as if they could just tap into a formula and repackage me. Everyone at the hospital said that this was a new beginning, that doors were opening, but that was bullshit. My doors, the doors that I was familiar with, the doors that I loved, the doors that I thought would be forever open were now closed. Permanently.

"The ride home from the hospital was surreal. My whole world had come crashing down, but my father—in between reprimanding my stupidity—was rambling about some stupid 1980s airline merger, as if I was interested, as if I cared, as if that really mattered; while my mother was ranting about the hospital food."

"Everyone has their own way of dealing with shit."

Rachel wiped her eyes with a napkin. "Later my wife later asked why I had deceived her, why I hadn't said anything. But I honestly wanted nothing more than a normal relationship with a normal woman, as-suming that *this* would go away, that marriage would somehow make me normal, that marriage would stifle these feelings once and for all. How naïve was that?" From her purse, Rachel displayed a wedding photo, slightly worn at the edges: the couple silhouetted against a dark background; she emotionless, staring at a clutched bouquet and he—masculine, mustached, strikingly handsome—looking past her, brooding, distantly effusive. "My tuxedo was suffocating me, I longed to wear the bridesmaids' soft lavender, cool bare-shouldered dresses."

"You wanted to wear the bridesmaids' dresses? What guy thinks that on his wedding day?"

The boat abruptly slowed. Forty minutes had passed. Rachel stood up and slipped on her shoes. "I need some fresh air."

I apologized for being so abrupt, following her to the gangplank.

No sooner had we descended, the gangplank was raised, the boat surged backwards and resumed its boisterous tour of Boston Harbor.

In the parking lot Rachel showed me the only empty slot. "That's where we parked this morning. She's home by now."

We walked in silence.

"A brand-new Silverado?" Rachel asked when we reached my truck. "Yours?"

"No, I stole it."

"Not the smartest thing to say to a cop."

"Then don't ask such stupid questions."

She snatched my keys, helping herself into the driver's seat. "You've had too much to drink and that's just from what I saw. If you get pulled over—and you will, this is quota day—you'll get a ticket."

"This is a standard, you know," I said, watching Rachel familiarize herself with the dashboard.

"What's a standard?" Rachel fumbled—gently and deliberately as it turned out—through first gear. "How do you shift into third? Or can I shift right into fourth? Ooops, I forgot to shift into second, how about if I go right into fifth?"

"Pull over."

"Relax, Alexander. I have a standard." She rested her hand on the gear shaft. "But where's your shifter?" She laughed—an endearing, feminine laugh—shifting into first, then seamlessly into second, then third and fourth, putting me at ease.

We drove north on Atlantic Boulevard, then onto Route 93. "Wouldn't it be easier taking the Pike to Route 2." I asked.

"I know my way home. Where's your air conditioner? I'm roasting."

I flipped on the AC. "Earlier you had said your wife suspected you of an affair? Did you?"

Rachel sighed. "If it was just an affair, we'd still be married. I know that. But then again, if the shoes were reversed, I would've suspected her. There were lots of telltale signs: Lipstick on a wine glass, panties in the dryer, an artificial nail under the bed, nail polish remover. She asked point blank if I was having an affair. Of course, I denied everything. But with each lie I was suffocating myself."

"You're all set to grill a nice sirloin, then realize it's a cheap cut and angrily demand your money back. But if you bought the cheap cut first, knowing what it was, that's different."

Rachel wiped a tear from her eye. "It's not that easy."

I handed her a Kleenex.

"Early in our marriage, I decided to tell my wife, although I knew that she'd never understand, and that whatever I said and however I said it, would probably end our marriage. Still, I had to say something. It would've been easier confessing I was gay—she probably would've accepted that, and we'd still be friends, going shopping and stuff. But to tell your wife that you're a woman inside and have always been, what could possibly be worse? I mean realistically what was I expecting her to say?"

Rachel dabbed her eyes with a Kleenex. "That night I made her favorite dinner—shrimp linguine with garlic, bacon, salami and parsley—hoping to put her in a receptive mood. But during dinner I was nervous, agitated. My wife kept asking what was wrong. I said something at work. I tried to confess but couldn't get the words out no matter how much wine I drank. We made love that night after dinner. But I was a million miles away."

Traffic had slowed to a crawl.

"This is why we should've taken the Pike," I said, matter-of-factly, although it was hard to see ahead, squinting directly into the sun.

"Accidents can happen anywhere."

A cop was waving traffic onto the breakdown lane, forcing us almost to a complete stop.

"I know him," Rachel said. "He's from my precinct."

"Then let's stop and say hello."

"Dressed like this?" Rachel responded with a touch of fear. "No one at work has seen me—yet. And they're not exactly tolerant."

Passing the cop, I noticed that Rachel had caught his eye as one male glancing at an attractive woman. Traffic quickly eased and returned to normal—normal that is for Sunday afternoon in suburban

Boston. As we drove west, I wondered if Rachel's rack made her think like a woman or if she still thought like a man. But if she thought like a male before, then wouldn't she still do so now, even though she dresses like a woman? And what did she think about driving with her wife on a Sunday afternoon, perhaps on this very road? What did they talk about? What were her thoughts while making love to her wife? Was there any indication in her mannerisms or her talk, back then, of how she really felt, of who she really was?

"When you dress like a man at work," I asked Rachel. "Do you think like a friggin' man or a woman?"

"I've *always* been a woman. I don't know what it means to think like a woman *or* a man."

"You know what I mean: If a beautiful half-naked girl passed you right now, what would you be thinking?"

"If you're asking if I'd be attracted to her, no. Not at all. I'd probably just glance at what she was wearing, that is if I noticed her at all."

"But you married your wife? You must have found her attractive?"

"Yes. And I still do ... When I got released from the hospital I went straight to her parents' house—I knew she was there. I wore the same tailor-made herringbone suit that my wife had bought for our rehearsal dinner. I thought that seeing me as a man—the same man that she had once fallen in love with—might trigger something. My father-in-law answered the door, insisting that my wife wasn't home and that she never wanted to see me again, then slammed the door in my face. I rang the bell again and kept ringing—this was my marriage, and I was determined to get my wife back. My father-in-law opened the door waving a gun demanding that I leave at once. That's when I called Joanna. She invited me to live with her. I ripped up that suit and threw it in the dumpster. God toys with us, giving us a modicum of hope, only to cruelly dash it away."

Traffic was thinning. Rachel had picked up speed.

"Have you seen your ex-wife since?" I asked.

"Briefly in court, during the divorce hearing, although she refused to speak to me, not even looking at me, as if I wasn't there...Then about a month ago—it was really weird—I had stopped at a red light in my old neighborhood. I was dressed as a male, except for artificial nails. I was admiring them on the steering wheel, when suddenly this woman in the car ahead began snapping pictures of me with her cell phone. It happened so quickly, as if she had expected me to be there, at that light, wearing artificial nails."

"Was it your ex-wife?"

"It wasn't her car, but it looked like her, although with the glazing sun I wasn't exactly sure. But she had a passenger who resembled one of my friends, which I dismissed as coincidental, since the two never really liked each other—at least that's what I had thought...Deep down I knew that my wife nor my parents would ever accept me for who I really was. But I always assumed that my friends would, that—"

"Don't you have that ass-backwards? Friends come and go, but parents love you unconditionally?"

"I'm not sure what unconditional even means," Rachel muttered. "The Fab Five we called ourselves. We did everything together, although now I realize how superficial our friendship really was. My first night at the hospital I received a letter from them, written by the least-well liked, even by their own standards, whose wife had a well-known affair with her doctor:

Dear Robert— (No one ever calls me Robert.)

We can no longer be friends and must curtail all meetings and correspondence. You violated our trust and failed to honor the bounds of friendship. You deceived us. And your recent abhorrent and inexplicable behavior has been deplorably embarrassing. Like that one Saturday morning having coffee after biking (I'm sure you remember; we all do, my wife still can't stop talking about it) when all of a sudden and without reason, in the middle of our conversation, you started crying. How embarrassing. Everyone was staring at us. You tried to brush it off as allergies, but we all knew better. Your ill-timed jokes also embarrassed us, and your failure to laugh at ours and avidly participate in our conversations underscored what everyone already knew. We can especially no longer trust you to our children, setting such a poor example of what it means to be a man, and going against God-given precepts. While all this was definitely a factor in rendering our decision, in our view we would have terminated the friendship anyway; it had run its course.'

"Are you friggin' shitting me?" I asked.

"They assumed that I'd be chagrined for being kicked out of their monied group; that losing their friendship, money, and self-inflated status would self-reform me. They can cheat on their wives, exploit and use people, then run for school board to make themselves feel good, congratulating themselves for their compassion, but actual human beings—people with thoughts, feelings and real fears—they manipulate and discard; their money cocooning them into a self-righteousness arrogance.

"So I wrote my own letter in response:

Dear 'friends':

I never expected complete acceptance, especially from people who have weaved a self-delusional, deceptive cocoon shutting out life's travails, although perhaps a little understanding and support. Obviously, I was the one who was self-delusional.

Friendship is not just a connivance for sunny days, cookouts, and ballgames. It also requires a commitment to be there in times of darkness and despair; to reach out, listen and support.

I pray you never have to experience life's tragedies—you wouldn't know how to deal with them. Your money has insulated you. You manipulate people to suit your needs and then summarily discard anyone no longer useful, like an old dishrag.

While you are free to say whatever you want, however callous and ill-conceived, please don't invoke God, for this underscores how far you have strayed from the true message of the Gospels and your willful ignorance. The God I know is kind, loving and caring of all his Creation, not just the pious few who think they know who God is. And your children can see right through you. They silently call you a hypocrite, as you diligently read your Bible early in the evening where everyone can see, ostensibly incurring favor with God, nodding and underlying and jotting notes as if you understood, and then impugning and debasing His words with your actions.

Please forgive me for thinking that our friendship meant something, that you would have at least listened. I assumed we'd always be there for each other. How naïve was that?'

"I mailed, emailed, texted, and even delivered the letter, but never got a response. Then two weeks later I had read in the paper that my mother-in-law had died of a stroke—no doubt stressed by the divorce. No one had contacted me. The head asshole, the Fab Five's self-anointed spokesman, said that I was no longer on their radar. Really? My mother-in-law for Christ's sake. I can still picture them in their secluded enclaves overlooking the water, dispensing their self-suffocating edicts.

"Last Saturday I happened to be at the same Mug-N-Muffin we used to frequent after biking Saturday mornings. I was dressed as a complete guy for once—not sure what happened—except that I had forgotten to take my earrings out. Stuff like that happens now and then. They strutted in like they owned the place—which I'm sure they probably do—expecting everyone to bow and acquiesce. Noticing me, they decided to leave, I guess, so I wouldn't disturb their perfectly cocooned existence. On the way out, the head asshole, referring to my triple-pierced ears, snickered, 'When's it going to end? How many more?'"

"Did that bother you?"

"People notice your pierced ears and their brain re-configures. Some overly compensate and become super friendly—more so than if you didn't have them—they don't want to seem uncool, a relic from another age; some pretend not to notice; and some get angry (I never understood why) as if you had betrayed the male race."

"No, I mean your friends? That they could've used that opportunity to reach out?"

"Reach out?" Rachel sneered. "Four people without any worries in the world calculating the utilitarian costs and benefits of friendship on the back of a napkin, judging everyone by how much money they make, by their usefulness, and then summarily discarding a person just like a used dishrag."

"Real friends don't abandon someone in need. *They* weren't your friends."

"God invented us to uplift others. Seeing us, they hold each other tight, thanking God they're normal. They don't—"

Rachel's phone rang. "My phone! In my purse. Underneath your seat!"

As soon as I took it out it, Rachel grabbed it. "Joanna? Joanna! Joanna?"

"Rachel!" I yelled, as she swerved avoiding an oncoming car. "You just went through a red light!" No sooner said then a police cruiser, flashing its blue and red lights, pulled directly behind us. A female cop got out and slowly approached. Rachel slumped back, opening the window. "Of all the times to be pulled over."

"Since when do cops give other cops tickets?"

"She's never seen me like this."

"Then let me do the talking."

"Then she'll really be suspicious. Stuff my purse under the seat. I'd rather be fined for not having a license than have to explain everything to this bitch—of all the people to pull me over."

"You know her?"

"She's from my precinct."

The female cop slowly approached. "Mam, do you know why you were pulled over?" she asked, leaning almost into the open window.

"I'm sorry, officer," Rachel responded in a feminine voice. "I just got my period. I didn't have any tampons—I was looking for a drugstore."

"Maybe if you *were* going the speed limit, you would've noticed a CVS two blocks back. License and registration, please."

"It's in the glove compartment," I said.

"Remove it, slowly." The lady cop pointed a gun towards me. "And keep your hands where I can see them."

"What's going on?" Rachel asked.

"Mam, I need your license and registration."

"This is my truck, officer," I said, handing the cop everything she had asked for. "I had too much to drink."

"Have you been drinking?" the cop asked Rachel.

"I don't drink."

"I need you both to step out of the vehicle."

"Why?" Rachel asked.

"The male passenger was seen stuffing something under the seat. We have to search the vehicle." The cop helped Rachel dismount; then finding Rachel's purse, emptied its contents onto the hood of my truck. "What's this? An officer's badge? Robert McNair? What are you doing with Bobby's badge?"

Rachel sighed, explaining in a male voice, "Mary, it's me, Bob."

"What?" The lady cop fondled Rachel's dangle earrings. "Bobby? It *is* you? You got your ears pierced? I must say of all people I never would've guessed. Hmmmm...Nice legs! Who's your friend?"

"He's a friend of a friend's."

"We were at a Halloween Party on the harbor," I said.

"And you're dressed as?"

"John Havilchek."

The lady copy chuckled, returning to her squad car.

"Christ. By now, everyone at the station knows," Rachel muttered.

The lady cop took her time in the squad car. Returning, she handed Rachel a few tampons, laughing, "Keep these in your glove compartment, you never know when you might need them." Then she tore up the ticket, laughing as the pieces floated to the ground.

"Mary, can you *please* keep this confidential? Just between us?"

"Hmmm. Ok. But I have to mention the tampons, and let's see, nice legs, pretty dress but the wrong earrings." Turning to me she asked if I was a girl dressed as a guy. Can you imagine? I quickly pulled down my shorts and underwear leaving no room for doubt.

Smirking, she left us.

"That was stupid," Rachel said, climbing into the driver's seat. "She could've ticketed you for solicitation or obstruction or indecent exposure—I would have."

Rachel slowly eased back into traffic. "By now the whole station knows. And the precinct. And every precinct in Massachusetts. But the captain, a woman, whom you think would understand, has absolutely no toleration for deviation."

"I'd like to see you as a male," I said, after a short silence.

"Why?"

"No particular reason."

Rachel sighed. "There's nothing to see. There's really nothing left. Back then, I had a moustache, now I don't even have facial hair— That was a pretty impressive package you showed back there." Rachel smiled playfully. "I mean not that I was interested. Just happened to notice."

"Just happened to notice?"

"You flung it out for the whole world to see."

"Where do you buy false beards?" I asked, quickly changing the subject.

"I wouldn't wear one if you'd paid me a million bucks."

"The world doesn't revolve around you."

"You'd look good in one!"

"I can grow my own, thank-you."

"For Joanna?" Rachel smiled. "That's so sweet! There's a store near Faneuil Hall and let's see, another near your work, in Harvard Square."

"How do you know where I work?"

"How do you think I know where you work?" Rachel slowed down, exiting the main road. "You ask a lot of stupid questions."

We took a right, another right, then a quick left onto a winding hilly road without any streetlights.

"How much longer?" I asked.

"This is her driveway."

"Christ, it's longer than my friggin' street. So, about another half hour or so?"

Rachel laughed.

Suddenly the well-lit house appeared out of the darkness: mid-19th century, fully restored, granite and a brownish brick; a sprawling mansion with a steep roof and several widow's peaks, surrounded by thick pine trees.

"Christ, how many people live here?"

Rachel opened the automatic garage door. "Just us."

"So you need an eight-car garage for two people?"

"It's just a five car garage." She pointed to Joanna's Lexus next to a BMW. "Joanna's home, just like I said."

"She has a Lexus *and* a BMW?"

"The BMW's mine."

I opened the door and scrambled out.

"Where do you think you're going? You're the last person she wants to see. Stay put. I won't be long."

Chapter 4

Joanna Turnus

"Rachel?" I sat up. Is that you?"

She was sitting on the edge of my bed, damping my forehead with a warm bath towel. "I made you some tea."

I wrapped my hands around the teacup, savoring its warmth. "Is Alexander here? I thought I heard his voice?"

Rachel propped my back with two pillows. "He's waiting in the driveway. You were quite restless. It seems like you had a bad dream or something."

"So it was a dream?"

"Joanna, why'd you get off the boat? What happened?"

"Were there any birds? Inside the house?"

"Birds? What're you talking about?"

I loosened my blouse, turning as best as I could to feel a long fresh scratch on my upper shoulder. "So it *did* happen? It wasn't a dream?"

"What're you talking about?" Rachel asked, taking a closer look. "Joanna what happened!" Did you get scratched trying to get off the boat?"

I straightened up against the pillows. "I was in the woods when suddenly this huge bird swooshed at me, clawing my hair and my back. And then another—or was it the same bird? No, there *were* two...When I came home, I wanted a hot bath—but then I found myself walking toward the woods. Everything was so green. That's why I thought it was a dream—how could everything be so green when everything was so brown? Two teenage boys passed me, laughing. Cars floated by like bubbles, as if on water. Everything seemed so big, with colorful razor-sharp edges. Then, deep in the woods I found myself in this strange, most awful place: trees: long rows with frightfully crooked branches, stretching, reaching—like dead limbs. I was leaning against the only live one when—"

"Joanna, why didn't you call! We had a pact. We were trying to call you. Why didn't you pick up?"

"Everything happened so quickly. On the boat, I felt nauseous, wobbly. My head was spinning, like I'd been drinking all day, but all I had was water. I asked the Captain to be let off. Luckily, we were close to the Wharf. Once outside, I felt a lot better and was able to drive home." I took Rachel's hand, apologizing, asking for forgiveness. "I remember looking for my phone, then realizing I had forgotten it. And just then these two birds started attacking me."

Alexander was texting me. I handed Rachel my phone. "I can't talk right now. Sweetie, can you stay with me tonight? Please?"

"Of course. I'll be right back; I left my purse in Alexander's truck. You'll be OK?"

Yes, I nodded, yawning.

Chapter 5

Alexander Morgan

I was tempted to steal away for something to eat—I was starving and hadn't eaten anything since breakfast—although with my luck, Rachel would call inviting me in, or Joanna would come down, smiling as if nothing had happened. So instead, I decided to call for delivery: pizza, Chinese, fast food—anything, as long as they could deliver fast. Scrolling my phone, the neighborhood silence was interrupted by yelling from next door; the anger quickly escalating. I cut through thick dense pine trees—some with gnarled and twisted branches, and steep, overgrown brush, onto the neighbor's freshly cut grass.

The argument was intensifying.

"Who are you?" demanded the neighbor; his friggin' wife, I presumed, beside him.

"A friend of Joanna's, I heard the commotion. What's going on?"

"None of your goddamned business," shouted the neighbor.

"This prick ordered a pizza and now refuses to pay for it," retorted the pizza delivery guy.

"Why didn't you call back to check? Any moron would have."

"I did. It was ordered by someone in this house at your residence."

"No one here ordered any pizza. And I refuse to pay for it." The neighbor stormed inside slamming his door.

"Son-of-bitch." The delivery guy was looking for a place to trash the shit, when I took out my wallet, asking what he had and how much.

"A large pepperoni," he quickly answered, relieved and surprised. "A small sausage, a liter of Coke, and two orders of breadsticks. Fifty bucks."

I emptied my wallet: two bucks short. I offered a check for the difference, but he waved me off, happy as a bastard just to get that much.

Back at Joanna's driveway, I called inviting myself in, bearing Coke, breadsticks, and pizza.

"Joanna's fine," Rachel answered, after I had asked. "She's sleeping." She then explained what happened. "I'll be down shortly; I left my purse in your truck."

I lowered my tailgate and set places for two, minus the plates, silverware, and glasses.

"You *were* serious about the pizza!" Rachel exclaimed from the garage. "I thought you were joking."

"I never joke about food, especially when I'm hungry." I helped her onto my tailgate, then gave her several slices of pizza, taking one for myself, explaining my encounter with the neighbor.

"He'd do such a thing—he thinks we're lesbians—Ha! If he only knew!"

My mouth full, I gestured for the Coke bottle.

"You're not worried about my germs?" Rachel asked laughing. "That you might start wearing women's clothes or something?"

"I'll take my chances."

Rachel swished a breadstick in the marinara sauce. "You know when I first met you— just this afternoon—God it seems like ages ago—I thought you were just a dumb-ass construction worker."

"What? You yelled at me for generalizing—that's what started this whole thing, remember?"

"I didn't say that you *were*, just that *I thought* you were. You know what I mean: Whistling, googling at women like you've been living on a deserted island your whole life."

"You've been whistled at? You should take that as a friggin' compliment; we have our standards, you know."

"Standards?"

"Not everyone gets whistled at."

"It's demeaning, treating us like we're pieces of meat."

"It's all in fun." I offered her another piece of pepperoni. She quickly devoured it, asking for another.

"Christ, Rachel, I almost got lost in your backyard without a map and my friggin' compass."

"That's what you get in Concord. Somehow it's supposed to compensate for not being able to talk with your neighbors."

"I'll take my city neighborhood any day. I noticed a basketball court—full court. I didn't know Joanna played?"

"She doesn't." Rachel answered in between bites. "I do."

"You?" I asked, laughing.

"What's so funny?"

"You don't look like the type."

"I played in high school."

"So did I."

"And in college."

"Really?"

"BC."

"*Boston College*? That's big time."

"As the sixth man—Ha! Did I just say that? That's funny. Everyone said I was the next Danny Ainge with his same scrappy, in-your-face defense, and I even looked like him. In high school I got several scholarship offers, but chose BC since I thought it offered my best chance to go pro *and* it was close to home, so my family could watch me play—that was really important."

"You were that good?"

Rachel nodded. "My junior year during the off season I had a knee injury, which turned into a really weird infection—I almost lost my leg. After that I was just never the same. I was still good enough to help us win most of our games, but a step below what I used to be and two steps below what I needed to be, no matter how hard I practiced. The top two guys on our team both got drafted. I didn't, although deep inside, I knew that I had lost it and could never get it back." Rachel wiped the base of her eyes and blew her nose.

"It must've been tough giving up your dreams," I said, handing her a Kleenex.

She shook her head. "It's not that. I had my criminal justice degree to fall back on. I wanted to be a cop almost as much as I wanted to play basketball. I got into the Academy and never looked back." She wiped her eyes and then blew her nose. "I was thinking of my high school coach. I do that a lot nowadays."

"You had a crush on him?" I blurted without thinking.

Rachel wiped her eyes, looking toward the woods behind the basketball court. "My senior year in high school, I was in the gym practicing free throws before practice when Coach entered from a cold, mid-December rain. He came over right away, happy to see me, as always. I immediately noticed his mascara-smudged eyes. Acting in my unscripted role as the silent inquisitor, I must have given him that same twisted, distorted look that I'd received so often—that you had given me. An automatic cursory look that must be hard-wired into everyone's DNA, even ours. Coach instantly recognized that look—we all do. He abruptly left and quickly returned, vigorously toweling his hair, practically in my face, apologizing that it wasn't a good day to get his hair dyed; even asking me if he had removed all the dye from his forehead. Then several week later, just before Christmas, I was in Coach's office, sitting opposite at his desk, about to watch films preparing for our upcoming tournament, when he wheeled himself to the file cabinet, accidentally backing his leg up in front of me. I was shocked to see Coach wearing black nylons. He followed my unscripted gaze, realizing immediately what I had just seen. Then he retrieved the film, talking as if nothing had happened, as if I hadn't seen anything.

"Then...then, the next day—two days before Christmas Eve—Coach took his own life. His wife found him hanging from a tree in the backyard... I was the last non-family member to see him. At the funeral, I wanted to say something to his wife, but I was scared that someone would find out about me and my own secret that I was desperately trying to hide. If I had said something to Coach, alone in his office that afternoon, or in the gym—if I'd reached out, he'd be alive today.

I know that. But I was scared and confused. I didn't have a handle on it and neither did Coach—that's why we could've helped each other."

"You can't lay all that shit on yourself."

"I just couldn't put the words together. And even if I could, I wasn't exactly sure what to say. But how could I say anything when I was trying to hide *it* from myself?"

I offered Rachel a breadstick, taking one for myself. "Earlier, you said that you always knew you were a woman. So you were always like this? When did you first know?"

"*Like this?* This is *me*, Alexander. This is who I am. I was always me—there wasn't a switch that one day went off—although sometimes I wished it happened that way." Rachel took a long drink of Coke and looked at me sort of wistfully, like we were long lost friends relating a mutual childhood story. "I always knew that I was different from my two brothers, not just as the oldest, but as night differs from day. They worshipped my father, emulating everything he did, dressing like him, wanting to be just like him. And I ...I wanted to be like just like my mother. I remember this one Easter Sunday, a beautiful spring day with a warm breeze blowing through the open windows. I was seven years old. Through my mother's half-opened bathroom door, I watched her ready for Mass, imitating everything she did: brushing my hair one way then another, putting on foundation, dabbing mascara, eye liner, eye shadow, lipstick, slipping in earrings, then whisking a wonderfully sweet, strawberry-lavender perfume; confident at who I was, confident at who I had become.

"Suddenly my father yelled from my bedroom, wanting to know where I was, why I wasn't dressed like my younger brothers. I tepidly approached, feeling like a sheep about to be slaughtered. My father impatiently looked at his watch, reminding me that as the oldest I had set an example, and that because of me we were going to be late. He nodded at my already-dressed brothers, then turning me around, stood behind me with necktie in hand. 'You hold the long end like this; wrap the short-end up, then loop it over and through;' weaving his hairy, aftershave-infused hands like a spider spinning its web. So many times my father had shown me how to tie a tie and so many times I had forgotten.

"My father then led us to the garage, reminding everyone that we were going to be late because of me, although we really weren't. As everyone piled into the van, I excused myself, saying that I had to pee really bad. I heard my father mutter something, my two brothers chiming in. In the bathroom, I closed the door and whisked my mother's strawberry-lavender perfume on my wrist, just enough to hide my father's aftershave, then a little mascara; too little to get noticed but enough to know I was wearing it.

"Driving to Church, my mother caught me several times looking at her flowery, lavender-perfumed dress, free-flowing in the breeze, as if part of her body. She must have smelled my perfumed wrist. She must have noticed my slightly mascaraed lashes. She must have noticed my longing to be a girl, just like her. But she smiled back as if to say that she was glad to be my mother and glad that I was her son; a smile, however, warning that I could never be like her, that I could never wear the same clothes, whisk the same strawberry-lavender perfume, that I could never get my ears pierced; a smile warning to never shatter her happiness, to never admit that I wanted to be a girl."

Rachel wiped away a tear. "We are born like this; we were never asked. Some of us, like Coach, live in limbo, in two separate worlds, shunned from both, surviving in neither. It's when we question ourselves, when others do, when others unexpectedly find us before we're ready to tell ourselves, that we break down and can't cope and can't survive.

"It wasn't until much later—after I had done something similar— that I realized that Coach sticking his leg out in his office might have been an attempt to provoke the issue, hoping that someone else would find out, someone who empathized, someone who had the same ambiguity—for we are experts at sniffing and spotting ambiguity, even though I had long buried it deep within my soul—or at least I had thought—although sometimes I guess it's just there, no matter how much I try to hide it, for others to see. Having been found out is a lot less painful than confessing, which made me even more resentful that I let that moment slip by.

"The last year of my marriage, just before everything began unraveling, we were at the family cabin in Maine, raking leaves, readying it for winter, reveling in the camaraderie. I camouflaged myself in the giddy expectations of others, forgetting who I really was, trying to fit in, even laughing at my brother-in-law's ribald jokes. But as the day wore on, I became increasingly agitated, watching my life incrementally slip away. I decided to make a statement to myself of who I really was. And what better statement than shaving my legs? Sometimes we do things to our body without knowing why, without realizing, without being in control.

"I excused myself to the bathroom. I was nervously calm, as if on autopilot, immersed in the smell of turkey, buoyed by the alcohol, the smell of burning leaves. I stepped into the shower and lathered my legs thick with soap, fondling the razor with anticipation. Suddenly my wife banged on the door asking what I was doing, yelling that the septic tank was overflowing. I hurriedly rinsed off my still-hairy, unshaven legs, opened the door, apologizing that I had fallen asleep in the shower, blaming it on the beer."

Rachel and I reached for the breadsticks simultaneously. Our hands touched. I inched away. Rachel blushed, withdrawing, "Was the pizza guy wearing a uniform?"

"What? Huh? No—I mean yes, not a uniform; a badge."

Rachel stared off toward the woods. "Alexander ...There's something—there's something you should know about Joanna."

"Christ, I thought I knew all her friggin' secrets?"

"Maybe I shouldn't even be telling you this?"

"Tell me what?"

"Joanna needs to lay out all her cards on the table before she can be intimate."

"What does that mean?"

Rachel shook her head. "I can't tell you. Only she can."

"Tell me what? And if *she* has to tell me, why are *you* telling me?"

"So that when she *does* start talking about it, you won't leave."

"I'm not the one who leaves. How do you expect me to know when she starts talking about *it* when I have no idea what the hell you're talking about now?"

"Trust me, you'll know." Rachel's phone vibrated. "It's Joanna... She's awake. She's feeling better." Rachel hopped down from my tailgate. "I have to get ready for Mass."

"Mass? On a Sunday night?"

"The six o'clock mass. Want to come along?"

I shook my head. "Joanna's OK?"

"I wouldn't go otherwise, and besides, I'll only be gone for an hour."

"And you? How are you?"

"I'm fine." Rachel smiled, hugging me. "Thanks for asking. And thanks for the pizza."

I watched her enter the garage, then imagined her entering her bathroom, nonchalantly flipping on the light switch, readying for Mass, staring at her once-masculine, handsomely stubbled face—a face that women used to find attractive; cautiously applying foundation, gaining confidence, then mascara, eye shadow, lipstick; whisking strawberry lavender perfume just like her mother. I imagined her stepping back, admiring who she was and who she had become.

She'll be fine. At least for today.

Chapter 6

Joanna Turnus

I assumed my phone vibrating was Rachel checking in (again), inviting me down once again for pizza—she's so sweet—but it was CCB's VP of human resources texting my father, copying me,

> 'Effective immediately, every subsidiary must make redundant any employee who no longer comports with our long-term interests and long-term financial security, including and especially union supporters. To be efficacious, it need not be more than one, unless, of course, the situation calls otherwise; in fact, extirpating one to make an example is highly recommended *and* highly efficacious.'

Extirpate? If someone's not performing, he's fired, not extirpated, and if someone's unionizing, extirpate the threat, not the person (without a paper trail), unless you either want a lawsuit (which I'm sure they don't) or they're trapping someone (which has to be me).
My father immediately responded:

> 'I have several individuals in mind. In fact, it would've been done anyway. Necessary spring cleaning.'

I thought of Alexander and immediately texted back:

> 'As General's legal counsel, for the record, I state categorically that we will not fire anyone singularly based on union activities. This is, as you know, illegal, but even if not, I fail to see its necessity: Our long-standing, non-union modus operandi is well-known and will not change.

So why deliberately draw attention to something palpably illegal? We have *always* strictly complied with the law (and its spirit) and will continue to do so. I oppose this illegal action and do not endorse it.'

My father immediately called, of course, which I let go to voicemail.

Chapter 7

Alexander Morgan

Just minutes from the bank's parking lot, my phone rang. It was 7:10. Phil's usual calling time to head back to the shop for something that he had forgotten or that he should've brought yesterday. Sometimes he forgets that I'm supposed to start work promptly at 7.30 and not 8.30, and that my job description is a laborer and not a Phil gopher.

But it was Joanna, chattering incomprehensibly.

"Did something happen to Rachel?" I asked, alarmed. "Are you OK?"

"Rachel's fine," she answered, in a calmer and more deliberate tone. "Actually not, but nothing new there. Listen, after everything, I've no right to even ask, but I need your help. Someone's been leaking confidential stuff to CCB, although I've a pretty good idea."

"Walter?"

"How'd you know?"

"I'm good at guessing."

"But I need to be absolutely sure. If you could indiscreetly, surreptitiously, accidentally let it slip that you overheard me talking to a lawyer—um, say Judy Brown—about taking General public. (And no, we're not going public, at least if I can help it.) He'll pester you for more information. And if he's the leak, which I suspect, he'll go immediately to CCB."

"So what? They own us. Why can't he talk to the—"

"They don't own us just yet, and not if I can help it."

Phil was calling me. Fuck him. This was my time. He'll have to call back at 7.30.

"By starting his own company and destroying General," Joanna continued, "my father rids me *and* extirpates my grandfather's legacy, finally getting out from his shadow, which has always bothered him—killing two birds with one stone, so to speak. And what better way than a lawsuit after an accident? My father's not trying to hide it, like he wants to be found out. And CCB has the resources to enable him to do whatever he wants."

"His name will be shit."

"Not necessarily. Depends who's blamed. That's why I intend to stop him. I have dozens of photos of my father and Walter in his garden, laughing, shaking hands, exchanging money with inspectors. Alexander, do you still have that piece of concrete from the vault?"

"Yes. In the trailer, and the last time I checked, the trailer's still there."

"Does anyone else know?"

"No."

"Not even Walter?"

"Especially."

"Good. I'll stop by this morning and get it analyzed. Thanks Alexander."

No sooner had I clicked my phone and pulled into the parking lot, then Phil was barking in my window. "Have I got a job for you! You're going to wish you'd—" His phone rang. It was Zachary. Phil listened, nodding occasionally, arms at his side, saying only 'goodbye.' "Change of plans," Phil said to me, clicking his phone. "Zachary wants the concrete scraped from all the first-floor windows. The bank president's been complaining that he can't see nothing out of them. Pick up some razor blades and Windex at the hardware store."

"I've been saving some in the trailer just for this purpose." I almost added that I would've have done this job myself more than two weeks ago, had it not been for all his shit jobs and wild goose chases.

"Bullshit."

I led him into the trailer, wishing I had bet that bastard money—twenty, ten, five bucks—anything—and promptly showed him a Styrofoam cup magic-markered with my initials on the desk, directly underneath where the fire extinguisher should had been, half-filled with used razor blades. He grunted and left. Translated: good thinking.

I spotted Walter in his truck, finishing his coffee. I hurried over. "You have a few minutes?"

"You need more money, kid?" Walter dug into his pocket. "You're always needin' cash."

I shook my head, climbing into the passenger seat. "Can you shut your window?"

"It *is* shut."

I opened the door. "Nah, I can't say nothing."

"You can't say shit like that, then not say nothin'. What's eatin' you? What happened in the trailer?"

This guy misses nothing. I shut the door, tightly closing the window, even though it was already tightly closed. "It's about Joanna."

"I warned you kid to stay away, but you didn't listen. You never listen to nothin' I say."

"It ain't about that. I overheard her talking to a lawyer about taking General public."

"Takin' us public? Which lawyer? When did she say this?"

"Wendy Brown, no Judy—Judy Brown? Just the other day. So what does this mean? Are we going public?"

"She told you this directly?"

"I just said that I overheard her talking on the phone. She didn't know I was there."

Walter shrugged. "I think I would've heard something, kid. Did she say anything else?"

"No." I opened the door and stepped down from his cab. "Don't say nothing about this to Joanna. She don't know that I know."

"Don't worry kid; your secret's safe with me."

"You coming? We have a bank to build."

"Just a second. I have to call Doris."

Lisa texted me. "Can we talk?"

"Working." I clicked my phone and stuffed it into my back pocket.

Walter quickly caught up to me, chatting about what needed to do be done today, when this effeminate guy in baggy green pants and a brown baggy shirt, approached.

"You know him kid?" Walter sneered. "He seems to be smiling at you."

Walter was right. He was smiling at me. I feigned ignorance, recognizing Rachel haphazardly dressed as a male.

"Ask him what he wants, then get him the hell out of here before he gets the shit kicked out of him."

"Alexander!" Rachel said, watching Walter return to the front of the bank. "You asked to see me as a male, so voila!"

"Males don't wear dangle earrings and lipstick."

"It's just lip gloss."

"Couldn't you have done a little better?"

She handed me two small, wrapped packages.

"What's this?"

"The Fu Manchus that you'd asked for."

"I didn't ask for any."

"I was at the store. It's only a couple of blocks away."

"I only need one."

"The other is for you."

"I can grow my own facial hair, thank you."

"Joanna would really appreciate it. And besides, you might have some fun."

If someone had told me just a month ago that I'd be having fun with my girlfriend wearing a false beard and enjoying it, I would've accused the person of insane madness.

"What do I owe you?" I asked, taking out my wallet.

"It's on me. I mean, ha ha—I'd never wear such a thing. That's OK. Don't worry about it, Alexander."

"Rachel—or should I call you Bobby?"

"Rachel."

"Rachel, can you put these in a bag or something and stick them in the back of my truck: it's the black Silverado next to the dumpster."

"Oh, I almost forget." She handed me an already opened letter. "From Joanna."

"You read it?"

"She knew I would, so she gave it to me already opened. I can seal it if you'd like."

I stuffed the letter into my back pocket.

Rachel reached over, giggling and in an exaggerated feminine motion, snatched it and handed it to me. "Joanna wants an immediate answer. It only takes a second to read."

"Fine." I started reading:

> 'Dearest Alexander:
>
> I am sooooo sorry. I don't know where to begin or what to say. I understand if you want nothing to do with me. After all, in just the short time that we have known each other, I've disappeared twice, if that's the right word. However, I would like to invite you to dinner at my house, tomorrow night, around six. I would like it very much if you came, although I understand if you said no.
>
> Joanna
>
> P.S. I miss you!
>
> P.S.S. There's no water around so you don't have to worry about me jumping overboard!'

"Well?" Rachel asked.

I found myself saying yes, not exactly sure why.

"She'll love you for this!" Rachel reached out to kiss me, but I quickly stepped back, hoping that whoever was watching didn't see what almost happened.

Rachel said good-bye, skipping across the parking lot toward the front of the bank. I imagined her without nail polish, without earrings, and with a full stubble. But there was no masculinity left—she even walked like a woman, gracefully exaggerating hand and wrist movements; her baggy clothes barely concealing her curves.

"Loafing again?" Phil asked, staring with disgust at Rachel.

"That customer was a little lost."

"I should say. If it's OK with you—if I'm not interrupting anything, and if you have nothing else to do, I need you to chip two holes for the electricians."

"Why can't they ever do their own shit?"

"Because they actually do some work, unlike some people around here. The holes are on the first floor where the new addition intersects the old building. I already chalked them: two-inch square. No need for a ladder or staging, just get it done, you goddamned son-of-a-bitch."

"What about them windows you said was so urgent?"

"This will only take ten minutes."

"Ten minutes here, ten minutes there. No wonder I never get my friggin' work done."

"Work?" Phil hurriedly left to who knows where.

Joanna texted that she just received an angry call from CCB's North American president asking what the hell was going on, followed by an angry voice mail from her father. "Mission accomplished," she said, thanking me for my help.

Just as I finished shit job #1, Phil approached with the bank president. Christ, now what? Were the holes too big? Not big enough? Too square or too round? Did my drilling disturb the bank customers?

"Who were you were just talking to?" the bank president asked with a worried look.

"Me? Why? What happened? Is she OK?"

"*She?* the bank president asked.

I shrugged. "She's transitioning to a woman."

"That still makes him a he," Phil said, "and a sorry one at that."

"Watch it Phil," warned the bank president; then to me, "Who is she? What was she doing here?"

"She's a cop, and a friend of Joanna's."

"*A cop?*" They both asked.

"Yes. Why? Is she OK? What happened?"

"No she's not OK. She's at the hospital. I was upstairs in the conference room wrapping up a meeting," explained the bank president, "when I saw this guy with dangle earrings putting on lipstick. You just don't see that out in the open. Then two teenagers jumped out of a white Oldsmobile coming around the rotary and started whaling the crap out of him. I called the police and ran out. It all happened so fast. She's at Brigham and Women's. The hospital said that she's lucky—it could've been a lot worse."

I left for the hospital at exactly 4.00. Rachel was sleeping on her back with tubes sticking from her nose, mouth, and wrists. She had two black eyes, a broken nose, stitches on her lower lip, and two broken ribs. A nurse was taking her blood pressure, saying that it could have been a lot worse, that she was lucky that none of her internal organs were damaged.

I sat on the edge of her bed and took Rachel's hand. She smiled, closing her eyes. Concerned, the nurse explained to me all the blips and oscillations and her vital signs, which were all good. "She's sleeping. If the oscillating stops, then we worry."

Joanna arrived with the bank president carrying a big-ass bouquet of flowers; in fact, so big that the nurse had to place it on a special table. I gave Joanna my spot on the bed, while the bank president and I each pulled up a chair. Rachel was still. Her breathing regular, her heartbeat echoing on the monitor, the blips blipping, the oscillations oscillating.

We sat for quite some time, motionless, alone in our thoughts.

Chapter 8

Joanna Turnus

I had Rachel transferred to a top-floor suite, which for the next two weeks became my temporary office. She slept a lot, especially during the day, enabling me to get a lot of work done. She gradually improved and seemed physically stronger with each passing day. While physical recovery was easy (or relatively so), psychological recovery was another story. Discharged after two weeks, she rested at my house for another week, sleeping on the sofa bed in my office.

At week's end I re-invited Alexander for dinner—three weeks late; an invitation, which, by the way, he had previously accepted. For dinner I wanted comfort food, and nothing more comforting than my marinated flank steak. Yes, that sounds quite ordinary, but isn't that the essence of comfort food? A basic dish cooked with flair? Here's how I made it; nothing intricate by any means:

- First marinate the steak in soy sauce, dry mustard, and apple cider.
- Grill it medium rare, basting it with a soy/ginger/ketchup mix.
- Slice it very thin.
- Serve it with grilled baby bok choy (large is too chewy), Japanese noodles splashed with red pepper flakes and sweet cider, and roasted red potatoes in olive oil and sea salt.

And for dessert: Martha Stewart's homemade tarts filled with sour cream and blackberries, topped with fresh basil—Rachel's favorite, although lately she's been so fixated with her weight that she refuses to even look at one.

It was five minutes before six. I removed my apron and smoothed my full-sleeved, black dress. Noticing a few wrinkles, I slipped it off and hurriedly ironed it. The doorbell rang. I breathed deep. Stan, Rachel's dog, was barking. (The cutest thing: a five-pound Mekei toy poodle, with big droopy ears. When Rachel moved in, Stan was part of the package, which was fine; I have two cats myself, and despite an occasional hissing moment, everyone gets along.) I dabbed on some lip gloss and opened the door. Alexander was stunning in a gray herringbone jacket and black tee-shirt, coincidentally matching my black dress.

I led him through my seldom used dining room into my kitchen—about four times larger than most kitchens, which is why I bought the house. Rachel jokes that I should have just bought a kitchen and an office instead of such a large house; that I could live anywhere as long as I had a kitchen. But I can't just live anywhere. I love my house and especially my kitchen, with its southern-exposed French windows (overlooking my pool) warming my house on even the coldest winter days; my two ovens each with a fully functional copper hood; and my small, semi-closed greenhouse with a retractable roof, where year-round I grow herbs and vegetables, fruits (lemons and limes) suffusing my kitchen with an ever-present farmers market aroma.

"Most people only need one," Alexander teased, spotting my two ovens.

"This from a man who never cooks?"

"My mother cooked for five people and a shitload more on holidays. She survived on just one."

"With all the cooking I do, even two's not enough."

A non-traditional wall rose behind my ovens: the lower half, half-finished with Tuscany stone (matching my Tuscany-stone kitchen table with non-matching chestnut, tall-back chairs, that didn't re-ally match the table, nor anything else in the kitchen). I suppose I could've gotten a chestnut table, or stone chairs (really?) but the chairs and the table are fully functional, and I use them a lot. (That doesn't justify incongruity, but a little now and then is good for the soul.) And the upper half: traditional red brick extending to the wood-raftered, twelve-foot ceiling. (I love the contrasting look of wood, brick, stone, and copper.) Between my ovens was a 3'x 6' bookcase, made of stone-washed elm, stocked with Cuban, Chinese, Creole, French, Indian, Mexican, Russian, Spanish, and of course, Martha Stewart cookbooks. On either side of my ovens were matching stone-washed, elm armoires. Fifty-five copper pots of every possible size draped the sides.

"And yes, I use all fifty-five," I said, anticipating Alexander's question.

"At once?"

I laughed. "Eight's my record, although I'm looking for a recipe that uses all 55."

"We all have goals."

I offered Alexander my grilled peppered pineapple appetizer: A narrow pineapple triangular wedge, inserted with peppercorns, grilled on both sides, and dashed with red pepper flakes.

"It won't bite," I said, laughing, watching him discreetly nibble the edges. "You have to eat the whole thing to get the total effect."

So doing, he smiled his approval; then took another. And another.

I invited him to sit opposite me. (I thought about moving the place mats so we could sit next to each other but decided to keep it as is.)

Alexander, noticing a third place mat, asked if I was expecting Rachel.

"For dessert." I poured us each a glass of wine. "Here's to a nice dinner," I said, hoping it wouldn't be our last.

Alexander handed me a small package wrapped with Thanksgiving (turkey) paper.

"For me?"

"It's not what you think it is."

"And what would that be?"

"Whatever you think it is."

I nervously fondled it. *A ring? But that would be absolutely insane? (as if the rest of my life isn't insane?) We just met and barely know each other.* I shook the package. "An armoire?"

Alexander laughed. "That's about the size I could afford." He took out an identical package from his inside jacket pocket. "Hint: they're matching."

I shook the package. "Swimsuits? Matching swimsuits!"

"Hmmmm. Not a bad idea. Maybe for Christmas?"

"Ah ha! Panties? You bought us matching panties?"

"Are you serious?"

"Just for the record, Alexander Morgan, I don't care if you wear men's underwear, women's underwear, or even if—heaven forbid— you don't wear *any* underwear."

"What if I told you right now that I was wearing women's under- wear?"

I inched closer, giggling, "Are you, Alexander Morgan?"

"Of course not!"

"It wouldn't bother me in the least and I'm not just saying that, and you can take back that smirk." I cautiously and slowly unwrapped the paper. "A Fu Manchu?" I exclaimed, surprised and somewhat relieved. I stretched long across the table and kissed him. Delicious! "This is so sweet." Off balance, I quickly scooted back, otherwise I would have collapsed in his arms—not a bad idea—but I was starving, and so was Alexander.

"You *will* take it off before you kiss me?"

"If that's what you want, Alexander. Although sometimes it's easy to forget, like just last week, I was at the mall and had to pee really bad. Heading toward the ladies' room, this woman practically tackled me, blocking my entrance, saying it was for women only. I forced my way past, insisting that I was a woman, not sure why she was so upset. I locked the stall door and sat down, suddenly realizing that I was wearing my Fu Manchu. I heard her outside complaining to a security guard, so I slipped it off and stuck it under the backside of my bra. I opened the stall door, unloosened my blouse, exposing my breasts, spread my legs and was inserting a tampon when they

296

entered.

"'Do you mind!' I screamed, shutting the door."

"The guard profusely apologized—it was quite obvious that I was a woman."

"'But she—she had a beard', the lady insisted. 'I saw it!'"

"The security guard apologized, closed my door and ushered her outside."

"Did that make you feel good?" Alexander asked. "Deceiving her?"

"I didn't deceive her—I honestly forgot. If I *had* remembered, I would have removed it. But you should have seen the look on her face, like I was a child molester or something. For what? Peeing in the *wrong* bathroom?"

Alexander refilled our wine glasses. "The same thing happened to me at the bank a while back: I went to take a leak in what I thought was the men's room—I had to go so bad that I guess I wasn't paying attention. Inside, I was looking for a urinal with my friggin' dick in my hand, surprising the hell out of this woman doing her make-up."

"I should say! And how'd you know she was a woman?"

"I know a woman when I see one. She demanded to know what I was doing, threatening to call security. I still thought it was the men's room and that *she* was intruding, but not seeing any urinals, I slowly realized that *I* had made the mistake. I apologized for being an idiot, said I couldn't wait and entered the stall."

"Did you sit down?"

"Of course not."

"If the shoes were reversed and you were in the men's room and this woman entered, how would you react?"

"Depends on her objective."

"What objective could there possibly be other than peeing? What was yours entering the ladies' room?"

"That was an honest mistake."

"When you realized, what did you do?"

"I went about my business. Urgently. Then left I as soon as I could, embarrassed as hell."

"So why would a woman's motive be any different?" I asked, rising. "I'm a woman and the last place on earth I'd want to meet a guy is the men's room."

"I can think of worse places."

From the refrigerator I retrieved the food and quickly microwaved it. I dished us each a plate, while Alexander refilled our wine glasses. We sat down, opposite; smiling at each other. I extended my legs and straightened my dress, admiring how beautiful everything was and how perfect everything smelled. "Here's to a nice dinner." I said, clinking Alexander's glass.

After just a few bites of steak, his smile abruptly disappeared.

"I cooked it rare. I can cook it more if you'd like."

Alexander shook his head, placing his silverware alongside his plate. "Rachel told me what happened," he said calmly, looking into my eyes. "Sunday, after you returned home."

My heart sank. "Exactly what did she say?"

"That you got attacked by wild birds and two teenage boys rescued you. God must have been watching over you."

"What do you mean?"

"Those two boys didn't just happen to be there. God must have a plan for you."

I cut my steak into minute pieces. "Alexander, do you remember that young girl that you met on the cruise?"

"I met a lot of *girls* on that cruise."

"She came up to us on the dance floor. Remember? You asked if she was looking for her parents. Two days later she took her own life. So where was God? Was that in his plan?"

"God didn't take her life."

"Of course he did. It's like giving someone a loaded gun hoping she doesn't shoot herself; or leading someone blindfolded to a precipice, hoping she doesn't fall. Our lives aren't fully scripted, there's no master plan, no one's watching over us. Sometimes chance can alter one's life for the better and sometimes for the worse."

"She was a coward."

"Really, Alexander. That's all you can say? A coward? Someone who had the courage to stand up to the whole world, while everyone else was against her?"

"She was born a male—how did you expect people to treat her?"

"Sometimes God makes mistakes."

I switched subjects. It had been a long day, a long week, and I wanted to talk about something else—anything.

Chapter 9

Alexander Morgan

The front door suddenly swung open. It was Rachel, looking haggard and tired, as if she had been crying. We rose immediately; Joanna rushing to embrace Rachel. "What's the matter sweetie? What happened?"

"The Captain just texted me," Rachel said, as Joanna wrapped her arm around her, leading her to the table.

"And?"

"She rescheduled my end-of-the year meeting for next Tuesday."

"Why?"

"Why do you think?"

"I don't know, sweetie; I'm asking you."

"She wants to resolve things sooner rather than later."

"What do you mean, resolve?"

"Isn't it obvious? They'll be discussing my review, which is already written. And I know it's negative. The Captain could have written a very different evaluation, much more positive but she's using all this TG stuff to fire me."

"That's illegal, sweetie."

"She has the evidence to back it up. And I'm giving it to her on a silver platter." Rachel tossed back her long, brown hair. "She's never liked me. Even before all this. She's jealous, sees me as a threat rather than as a colleague. I also heard—and someday I'll find out if it's true—that she slept with someone at the Academy in order to pass."

"Sweetie, you can't stake your future on rumors."

"Last November, a group of us—seven to be exact—complained to the Chief about her poor management, lack of empathy, intolerance—

all longstanding simmering issues. At first, I wasn't going to go, knowing the Captain's vindictiveness if she were to find out—and I knew she would. We all did. But they were my friends whom I socialized with, sat next to at meetings and roll call, played basketball with, had a beer with after work. I decided to vote my conscience with my friends. The Chief promised to keep our meeting confidential, but the Captain found out that same afternoon: One of my friends happened to look out the window and saw them arguing back and forth; and like watching an Italian opera, everything unfolded clear as day. The next day, another friend overheard the Captain saying that she'll be firing all of us; it's just a matter of time. Since then, three have transferred, two resigned, one was fired, and now I'm the only one left."

"Why didn't you transfer with the other three?" I asked.

Rachel shrugged. "Hindsight's always perfect."

"I'll be with you Tuesday, sweetie; we'll fight this."

"It's not open to public."

"I'm not the public. I'll be your lawyer representing you, suing for gender harassment and discrimination. You won't lose your job. I'll make sure of that."

"TG isn't mentioned anywhere in the Captain's Review, as if I was completely normal, no different from any other cop. I'm sure that every point is legitimate."

"Sweetie, how do you know this?"

"I just do. Every screw-up, every complaint, was caused by my TG stuff clouding my judgement, constricting my thoughts. And yet the Captain has interwoven everything into one seamless, unassailable story. I'm a much better cop than how she's portraying me."

"I know that. That's why I'll be at the meeting."

"Will you be dressing as Rachel?" I asked.

"I'm supposed to be a male cop."

"You can't constrict your identity just to please others, sweetie. You have to accept yourself. If you don't, it doesn't matter if the whole world does. You have to feel good about yourself, about who you are."

"How would you react if someone at work suddenly dressed as the opposite sex?" Rachel asked.

"You know my answer, sweetie."

"How about you Alexander?" Rachel asked.

"Me? Construction's different."

"Why's it different?" asked Joanna.

"I don't know?" I shrugged. "You're asking my friggin' opinion. It depends how he looks, I guess. Rachel, you look like a woman, a very pretty woman."

"She *is* a woman."

"OK, OK. But if, say Walter, came to work in high heels and a dress, people would laugh and not take him seriously."

"*That* would not be a pretty sight," Joanna agreed.

"Some might even be offended," added Rachel. "Seeing a little of themselves, worried that once inhibitions are let down, they might start dressing like that. They're scared, so they attack first."

Rachel started laughing mischievously.

"I know that laugh, sweetie. What's going on in that Rachel mind of yours?"

"I was thinking of wearing a bikini for my meeting with the Captain."

"Rachel! Be serious! Your job is on the line."

"I *am* serious. You've always said that I have to show the world who I really am. So what better way, especially when I have the body?"

"Having the body is not the issue. This is your job we're talking about. Dress as a woman, if you'd like by all means, but do it conservatively."

"Conservatively? What does that even mean? Clothes hide a lot, and you don't have to worry about being flat-chested."

"I wouldn't exactly say you're flat-chested," Joanna noted.

"With a bikini everything has to gel: Makeup, hair, sunglasses, earrings. You can't walk too fast or too slow but with a purpose, like you're actually going someplace, even if you're not."

"So, everyone stares at you like you're a piece of meat?" Joanna asked.

"How's that different from my life now? People stare no matter what I wear or what I don't wear. So why can't I wear something that I'll look good in?"

"Sweetie, you're not making any sense!"

"My whole life doesn't make any sense! Why criticize me for wanting to dress like a woman? And what woman doesn't want to look good in a bikini?"

"I'm a woman and that's never topped my list. If you were on a deserted island, alone, naked with no clothes, how would you classify yourself?"

"Lonely," I said.

"Classify? Like some sort of specimen?"

"How would you feel?"

"What do you think?"

"*That's* what really matters. The rest is just superficial accouterments. Sweetie, no one's more supportive of you wearing whatever you like than me—you know that—but jewelry and makeup and clothes don't define you."

"I express myself with clothes and makeup. It makes me feel good about who I am. And besides if the Captain saw me in a bikini, she might finally realize that I *am* a woman, and stop accusing me of being a man who wants to dress as a woman."

"You can still show her who you are by dressing conservatively, while not succumbing to the male idealization of female beauty."

"That's nonsense. I am who I am, and I should be able to wear what I want when I want."

"Alexander," Joanna asked. "What's your opinion on all this? You've been unusually quiet."

"Joanna's right, Rachel. You should dress conservatively, after all these are cops we're talking about. But at the same time, I like your in-your-face attitude. Like *Animal House* when the Dean is about to expel them, they decide to throw a toga party."

Rachel nodded. "I'll be fired no matter what I wear or don't wear, what I say or don't say. At least I'll feel good about myself."

Joanna annoyed and flustered, dished Rachel a plate. "You must be hungry?"

She nodded. "Alexander can you please get me a beer."

"Rachel!"

"One beer won't kill me. Can you put it into a tall glass with lots of ice?"

Joanna reluctantly nodded approval. I took this moment to slip on my Fu Manchu while grabbing a beer for myself.

Rachel burst out laughing, while Joanna slipped hers on.

Rachel took a long drink, laughing. Then her smile abruptly disappeared.

"What is it sweetie?" Joanna asked, glancing at me as if to say what the fuck?

"Just when I thought my screwed-up life couldn't get any more screwed up...I met someone. A man."

"A man? Who? When? Why didn't you say anything to me?"

"Sunday night, at the six-o-clock mass. You were asleep when I came home."

"Why didn't you wake me?"

"I wasn't exactly sure what to say."

"This is wonderful!" Joanna held Rachel's arm, smiling.

Rachel brushed away a tear. I handed her a Kleenex. "I still love my wife, but now I'm attracted to men. I mean really attracted."

I looked away, avoiding Rachel's eyes.

"These feelings didn't just appear overnight sweetie; they were always there. You're finally listening to yourself. How'd it happen? How'd you two meet?"

I was afraid to look directly at Rachel, afraid that even a casual glance might send the wrong message.

"He was sitting directly in front of me. During the Sign of Peace, he turned around and that was that. It was totally unexpected."

"Alone I presume?" Joanna asked.

"Yes. He's divorced. An airline pilot...He invited me to Amsterdam with him next month. He's really sweet. After Mass we went for sushi."

"Wow Rachel, this is serious!" said Joanna. "You hate sushi."

"He could have invited me for chopped liver and I would've gone. I don't understand this? How could this have happened so suddenly? And how come I never had these feelings before? I just went to Mass, alone, minding my own business, and now I'm in love with a man whom I can't stop thinking about."

"You're sorting things out, sweetie," Joanna said, taking Rachel's hand. "So what happened next?"

"What do you mean?"

"Do I have to ask?"

"We kissed. That's all."

I imagined meeting someone, kissing 'her,' then finding out she was a guy or used to be, I would have gone berserk, no matter how pretty.

"How was it, sweetie? Your first time?"

"It was wonderful, except at first, I was scared of his moustache."

"*Scared of his moustache?*" Joanna asked, half-laughing.

Rachel sipped her beer. "When I had my moustache I practically apologized before kissing my wife because she absolutely hated it. But this guy never even asked, assuming that I'd like it just because I'm a woman."

"Sweetie, we gob ourselves with makeup expecting guys to kiss us."

I handed Rachel my Fu Manchu. "Wear this if his moustache still bothers you. The two will offset as if you're wearing nothing."

"Then he'll really think I'm screwed up. I'm fine now with it."

"When are you seeing him again, sweetie?"

"Wednesday night. He's taking to me to dinner."

"Wonderful! Sushi?"

Rachel laughed.

"I'll help you pick something to wear."

I helped myself to more flank steak and dished more for Joanna.

"Sweetie, would you wear a bikini to Sunday Night Mass?"

"No."

"Why?"

"I just wouldn't."

"Next Tuesday, you might think wearing a bikini is a good idea, but it will backfire. Trust me. I'm a lawyer, I know these things. You can still express who you are, just do it conservatively. You have the rest of the life to wear bikinis, but just this once, when your job is on the line, dress conservatively. You don't want to burn bridges, at least not yet. You're a wonderful, lovely person: My best friend, my soulmate, who's also a cop and a very good one." Joanna hugged Rachel. "Go to the meeting confident as Rachel McNair. And just be yourself."

"*Just be myself?*" Rachel cried.

Joanna glanced at me with alarm. "That's the whole point sweetie—you decide who you are. Let no one else constrict you into a predetermined—"

"*Just be yourself?* What the hell does that even mean? Maybe '*Be yourself*' I could understand, but '*Just be yourself*'? Why is 'just' even necessary? Only a "normal" person needs reminding to *Just be yourself* as if that's the most natural thing in the world, like finding a pair of socks to wear for the day, and as if she only had one self. So much of this world is not for us. I can't live my life today by a simple adage, for I might be different later today, and then tomorrow. And I don't have pregnant expectations to compel anyone else to do something."

"What the heck does that even mean? There's no compulsion, sweetie. You're with the two people who love you more than anything else."

"Damn friggin' right," I said.

Rachel rose and excused herself for the bathroom.

"This is so typical," Joanna said, exchanging glances with me, practically in tears. "She's sky high one minute and then the next, rock bottom. And often both at once. No advance warning."

I helped Joanna clear the dishes, worried, asking what can be done.

"What more can I do?" Joanna threw up her hands in exasperation, then hurriedly set the table for dessert: Martha Stewart's basil blackberry tarts and a glass of port; both of us hoping that Rachel would return relaxed and positive.

Chapter 10

Joanna Turnus

Rachel seemed more relaxed when she returned, although her countenance often betrays the opposite of her real feelings. But she did seem genuinely happy to be joining us. Perhaps it was the basil blackberry tarts (her favorite) or confessing that she likes men (I've known all along) or Alexander joining us for dinner and staying for dessert (I've long noticed how she looks at him) but whatever the reason (I'm sure it was all three) it was good to see her smiling and laughing.

Finished with dessert (Rachel had two tarts despite her weight protestations), I suggested a story-telling contest: something that had happened to us which was embarrassing at the time, but now (quite) laughable.

"Funny *and* embarrassing don't usually go together," quipped Rachel.

I placed three one-hundred-dollar bills on the table.

"How come everyone has friggin' C-notes except for me," muttered Alexander.

"That's the whole point sweetie. Now we can and should be able to laugh about it. Whoever tells the best story wins. Keep it under 15 minutes. We each have one vote and can't vote for ourselves. It must be something that happened to you and it must be true."

"Why make it so difficult?" asked Alexander. "I can't tell a story in less than fifteen minutes, especially if it's true."

"What about a tie?" Rachel asked.

"A lie?" Alexander asked. "Now we're talking. A lie would make it easier to tell the truth."

"*A tie!*" said Rachel and I.

"Just one story?" asked Rachel. "I could write a book: Caught in the wrong bathroom, going through a drive-through with my wig half off."

"That's a wig?" Alexander asked.

Rachel smiled tossing back her long, brown hair. "Alexander, did you ever absent-mindedly answer the door half-dressed in the clothes of the opposite sex, or get caught wearing makeup when you shouldn't have?"

"Can't say that I have. But once my ex-girlfriend caught me putting on women's deodorant."

"Women's deodorant?" I asked, laughing. "What possessed you to do such a terrible thing?"

"Did the sky blacken?" Rachel asked. "Did your bedroom curtain rip asunder?"

"I was at my girlfriend's—my ex-girlfriend's."

"The one who never laughed?"

"I had just showered when I realized that I'd forgotten my deodorant; then I saw a women's travel-size deodorant in my girlfriend's makeup bag, right on the counter."

"A life altering decision," I said.

"That's how I started," Rachel added, "first women's deodorant, then a woman's razor."

"The same with me, sweetie, except it was men's deodorant, then a man's razor."

We shared a laugh.

"Let me guess," Rachel said. "You forgot to put it back. Shame on you Alexander, that's the first lesson we learn: if you use something always return it *exactly* as you found it."

"Worse: She opened the door and caught me red-handed, asking what else I had tried on."

"Women's deodorant?" I exclaimed. "Are you serious?"

"You *should* have tried on eye shadow or mascara or something," said Rachel.

"So that's your story?" I asked Alexander. "Great! You're up, sweetie."

"Hell no, I'm just warming up, building rapport with the audience." Alexander grinned. "I think I might have something."

"Remember, it must be something that actually happened."

"To me?"

"Yes," I answered, laughing.

"OK, OK. I think I might be in the Guinness Book of Records for the shortest blind date ever. After my girlfriend and I broke up—"

"Because of the deodorant?" Rachel asked.

"What'd she look like? Any pictures?"

"Can I please tell my story? After we broke up everyone was setting me up on blind dates—even Paul, that bastard. At first, I wasn't interested, because he doesn't exactly have the best taste in women."

"Taste in women?" I hinted a smile.

"But he kept pestering me. So I agreed to meet this woman for dinner at a local restaurant. That afternoon, *coincidentally*, I had just got friggin' contact lenses, which—"

"I thought you didn't believe in coincidences?" I said.

"Coincidences are never coincidental. They always happen for good reason and there was a good reason why this coincidence happened and not another one."

"Were they male or female lenses?" Rachel asked.

"Can I please tell my story? At the doctor's, I should have kept the lenses in, but I had to drive home and needed my tinted sunglasses. At home, I assumed putting them in would be a cinch. But I really struggled, frustrated that it was so difficult. Then I remembered the nurse saying to fold each lens like a friggin' taco but I don't eat Mexican food, so I had no idea what a friggin' taco looked like."

"Are you serious?" I asked.

"Maybe that's the problem," Rachel said, laughing. "Everyone knows what a taco looks like, but a *friggin'* taco—what the hell's that?"

"I was wondering that myself."

"A taco's just a taco—it could even be something else—but a friggin' taco has no ambiguity—everyone knows exactly what it is. It always was and always will be a taco."

"How can a taco be anything but a taco?" asked Rachel.

"Alexander has a wonderful way with words," I laughed to Rachel.

"I noticed."

"Actually, Alexander your problem was *folding* the lens instead of shaping it into a bowl on your finger and then inserting it."

"Bowl? Why didn't someone say that? That would've been a lot easier: everyone knows what a friggin' bowl looks like."

Rachel laughed. "I can't picture a *friggin'* bowl?"

"Alexander, at the doctor's office, why didn't you ask the nurse what a taco looks like if you had no idea?"

He shrugged. "I didn't want to sound like an friggin' idiot. At home, it took me forever to get one lens in, and then when I did, I couldn't get the other one in. So not wanting to be late, I tried getting the out one in and the in one out but couldn't do either. So I drove to the restaurant with one in and one out. No problem driving, but once I sat down, I couldn't see her or read the menu. I kept rocking back and forth trying to focus. My date was scared—at least from what I could see—asking if I was on drugs. I almost told her the truth but didn't want her to think I was a friggin' idiot. She got up and left without ordering. She didn't even say good-bye. Then Paul—that bastard—told me that a couple of weeks later she met someone else, and they got engaged."

"So you're only here because you had no idea what a taco looked like?" I asked.

"A *friggin'* taco," added Rachel.

"I still don't." Alexander winked at me. "See, there's a reason why I never ate tacos. And it ain't no coincidence."

I chuckled. "Ok Rachel, your turn, that is, if you're finally finished Alexander."

He gestured for Rachel to begin.

"What if I tell two stories and you vote for the best?"

"Only one, sweetie; I'm sure you can think of something."

Rachel sighed. "That's not the problem, it's deciding *which* one."
Rachel thought for a moment, then smiled at Alexander. "Remember
when I told you about my wife coming home unexpectedly?"

"Go with it."

"I've something even better (or worse). About a week earlier, I
went to Victoria's Secret to buy a bra. My first. I was nervous and
giddy with anticipation. I must have walked past the store entrance
at least a half dozen times before I summoned the courage to enter.
And once inside I lost myself in every display trying to relax and stop
my fast-beating heart, which I assumed the whole store could see
and hear. After what seemed like an eternity, I approached the most
sympathetic-looking clerk, telling her that I was transitioning and
that this was my first bra. She was so sweet and helpful. She asked if
I had been fitted. 'Yes,' I answered confidently, '36 B.'"

"Thirty-six? B? Rachel!"

"I guess I had idealized myself into a 36. They were so much
prettier than the larger ones. I found a blue polka dot, a lacy purple,
and this really pretty peach, but wasn't sure which, if any, would fit.
The clerk suggested trying them all on in the dressing room, saying
that the store wasn't that busy. I was in the most feminine of stores,
surrounded by women happy to be women, confident in their gender
and sexuality; trying on different bras in the fitting room just like
every other woman; giddy, except that the 36s were too tight—"

"I should say," I added.

"Great! That's your story?" asked Alexander, eyeing the prize
money.

"Unfortunately, I'm just getting started. Pretty sad, though, looking for affirmation from a store clerk."

"Sweetie, you envisioned her seeing you as a full-fledged woman,
and even though she might have wanted to, she can't help but see
you as a man trying to be a woman."

"But even that did wonders, although I should have realized that
God was laughing at me, that he was already planning his revenge,
that my short-lived euphoria was about to abruptly end. I decided

to go with the peach, even though it didn't exactly fit, but it was the most elastic. I opened the fitting room door, clutching the three bras, and was startled, surprised, and practically speechless to see my next-door neighbor with her twelve-year-old daughter, patiently waiting to enter. I was caught red-handed, nothing I could do or say. The mother smirked, suspecting the obvious, 'Bobby, this is a surprise; buying a bra for that special someone?' Absolutely nothing I could say. 'Go with the polka dots,' she said, laughing, 'they're in right now.' She guided her daughter into the fitting room, asking her mother why I was trying on a bra. 'To make sure it fits!' I heard her say.'"

"Did she rat on you?" Alexander asked.

"Surprisingly no. Although after my wife left, I'm sure they had a field day."

With Rachel wrapping up I was thinking about my own story. (She was right: the problem was not finding *a* story but deciding which one.) I suddenly remembered something from my childhood, a long time ago; something that I thought I had banished from memory: the only time that my grandfather had ever yelled at me.

"We don't have all night." Alexander said.

I began: "I was ten years old and rather tall for my age."

"OK!" said Alexander. "That's your story? Time to vote."

"Alexander, sometimes you can be so annoying. When I was ten years old, my grandparents visited some friends on the Lake, taking me along. They had this wooden, three-level diving board: one-meter, four meters, and ten meters. Almost immediately my grandfather and his friend took to the top, while the rest of us watched from the dock.

"'It's a piece of cake,' my grandfather kept repeating, constantly eyeing me. 'A piece of cake.' My grandmother said to ignore him, that he's acting like a spoiled child. Not exactly easy with him prancing up and down, repeating 'it's a piece of cake.' Then just before lunch— when no one was looking—I found myself climbing the ladder, my heart pounding, determined to jump from the top, determined to make my grandfather proud. 'A piece of cake,' I kept hearing my grandfather say, or was it just my imagination? At the top level, I was stunned how high I was and how small everything looked. Inching along, the board became narrower. The cold-grey water was hard as slate.

"My grandfather had gathered everyone on the dock, waving me forward, proud as a peacock that his ten-year-old granddaughter was about to jump off the ten-meter board. 'It's a piece of cake,' he kept repeating, 'a piece of cake.'"

"How deep was the water?" Rachel asked.

"Twenty-five feet. The height was deeper than the depth. And my height made the board seem that much taller. I tried so hard to jump but couldn't. Then I sat on the edge of the board, my feet dangling, thinking that sitting would make the height less formidable and I could inch myself off, but that was worse: how do you jump from a sitting position? My grandmother said to climb down, reprimanding my grandfather that I was just a ten-year-old girl and that he should be thankful that I love the water just like him. But my grandfather insisted that since I climbed up, I had to jump off. 'No one climbs *down* a diving board.'

"I stood up, determined but couldn't budge, so I sat down again. Then I stood up and closed my eyes trying to inch forward but couldn't do that either. My grandfather stormed away waving his hands, yelling, 'I can't believe this; I just can't believe this.'"

"What's the record for sitting on a diving board?" Alexander asked.

"I had to pee, and I was getting sunburnt, so I inched backwards—I was never so humiliated. I scampered down the ladder, went inside and cried. My grandmother reamed him out; I never saw her so mad. Of all the stupid things I did in my life, of all the times I had really embarrassed him, that was the only time he had ever criticized me—and in front of others. It was so unlike him."

I handed everyone an index card. "I'm done. Time to vote. Remember: One vote and you can't vote for yourself."

Alexander folded his card several times, then handed it to me.

"Everyone knows which one is yours," I said.

"Not necessarily."

Rachel scribbled, crossed out, rewrote, then handed her card to me.

I glanced at Rachel, then Alexander, then back to Rachel, raising her arm. "Rachel two, Joanna one, Alexander zero."

"I demand a recount," said Alexander.

"Rachel two, Joanna one, Alexander zero." I handed Rachel the prize money.

"I can't take this from you," said Rachel, yawning.

"You won it sweetie, fair and square."

"So Rachel ol' buddy, ol' pal; what you going to do with your friggin' winnings?"

"Buy some new clothes after all this *friggin'* dessert." Rachel yawned, stretching her arms, rousing Stan. "I'm tired, I have to go to bed." Rachel hugged us good night, then slumbered up the stairs, seeming like she could fall asleep any minute, on any step.

"She's in a funk," I said to Alexander. "She needs to find herself and not look for herself in others."

"Sounds rather harsh."

"She's looking everywhere for right answers, everywhere but herself."

Alexander, yawning, glanced at his watch. "Did she really win?"

"Yes."

"So why didn't you vote for me?"

"Rachel's story was better, and besides I wanted her to win. She needs something to feel good about, even something trifling like this."

"Three hundred dollars ain't exactly trifling."

"In the bigger scheme of things, it is."

"Then why didn't you just give her the money?"

"You're missing the point, Alexander. I wanted her to feel good about herself."

"So the contest was rigged?"

"Of course not. I just wanted her to win."

"Did that diving board stuff really happen?"

"Of course it did. And something else that also happened: Last summer I returned to the same cottage (something that I had long wanted to do). Just myself. The new owners had completely rebuilt the dock and the diving board, replacing the wood with no-slip aluminum. They also added a fourth level—two meters higher! Four aluminum diving boards, alternating left and right, just like the Olympics. I introduced myself to the owners, explaining my purpose. They were really sweet, offering to take pictures. I climbed like a monkey to the highest board. I imagined my grandfather pacing the dock, looking at his watch, yelling, embarrassing me. Although my initial fear returned, I wasn't going to let it defeat me. The secret was taking a running start and not looking down."

"Did you jump or dive?"

"What difference does that make?"

"It's called a diving board, not a jumping board."

"You sound like my grandfather. You could do a triple summersault, reverse double-axle (which I think I did accidentally) and it's still a diving board and not a triple summersault, reverse double-axle board."

"Did you tell anyone?"

"No."

"So what's the point? Like a tree falling in the forest, if no one's around, no one knows."

"I was around. That's all that matters. Although I did wish that my grandfather was there, but then again if so, maybe the old fears would've returned?"

Alexander yawned.

"Why don't you stay the night?"

"Actually, I would, except I have to work tomorrow."

"Tomorrow? Saturday?"

"Yeah, Saturday *and* Sunday, landscaping at the bank."

"You, gardening?"

"It's pretty easy; everything's spelled out in the friggin' plans."

"I've some gardening to do around here, perhaps you can stop over some time after work?"

"Nah, I never take my work home with me."

I laughed at his playful eyes. "Why don't you leave from here in the morning? I'm up super early."

"I would but I have stop at my apartment to get my gardening shit, and it's easier if I go back now."

"Gardening shit?"

"Tools."

I offered him the last tart, wishing that he'd reconsider.

"What if Rachel gets up in the middle of the night, hungry?"

"Are you kidding? She'll starve herself for two weeks trying to squeeze into a size sixteen."

"How many calories in this sucker?" Alexander asked.

"Since when do you count calories?" I laughed, wiping his mouth with a napkin.

We hugged goodnight. I held the door open. He took one step out, then turned back. "Rachel? She'll be OK?"

"Yes."

"Has she ever thought of doing something else?"

"Being a cop is all she's ever wanted to do. Why do you ask?"

"She's missing that confidence, that edge, that cockiness that all female cops have."

"What makes you such an expert?"

Alexander smiled. "I was pulled over for speeding three times in one month by the same lady cop."

"How many tickets did you actually get?"

"The third time I was driving Paul's souped-up car, doing seventy in a thirty-five. But Paul, that bastard—I don't know why I even listened to him, said to ask when her radar was last calibrated."

"That's like asking me when my law school degree was re-examined. And?"

"She gave me a ticket."

"You sound surprised?"
"I thought we had something."
"Are you serious?"
"We did date for a while, though."
"Spare me the details."
"Is Rachel really a woman?"
"What do you think?"
"Do I have to ask the obvious?"
"She's a human being, just like you and I."
"You know what I mean."
"She hasn't fully transitioned yet, if that's what you're asking."
Alexander brushed my hair back over my forehead.
"I should get a sticker," I said, smiling at his playful green eyes.
"I know. The food was delicious."
"No, I mean this is our third date and I'm still here." I pulled Alexander close. "It's supposed to be warm tomorrow, maybe the last warm day before the weather changes. I have a swimming pool…Why don't you stop by after work? I'm making Chinese food."
"I'm not good with chlorine."
"Neither am I. That's why I have salt water. And, if I jump overboard, there's nowhere for me to go."
"How can I say no to that?" Alexander smiled, kissing me.

Chapter 11

Joanna Turnus

It was well after midnight and I couldn't sleep, upset that Alexander was about to become the first non-family causality of my father's ambition. Determined to not let that happen, I sprang out of bed, flung on a pair of sweats and drove to my parents. Even though their house in Newton was only a twenty-minute drive, it could have been on Mars for all the times that I've visited (and them likewise).

No sooner had I parked in the driveway when an upstairs hall light flickered on. The three-story house loomed smaller than I remembered and the surrounding oak trees more menacing, with long-stretching branches threatening to envelop the house.

I rang the doorbell. The outside light clicked on.

"What do you want?" demanded my father through the intercom.

"We need to talk."

"About what?"

"I know about the concrete."

My father opened the door.

"Is the whole bank like that," I asked, "or just the vault?"

"What the hell are you talking about?"

"I can sample every inch of the bank if you'd like. I also know about the cash to Walter, and to the building inspector and to the concrete inspector."

"Who's there?" my mother asked, tepidly descending the stairs. "Joanna? Is that you? Have you been drinking?"

"It's amazing how little you know about what's really going on," I said to my mother. "Ask him some night during dinner; it'll give you two something to talk about." Then to my father, "I want Walter fired immediately."

"What?" my mother cried. "You can't do that."

"Just watch me."

My father schussed her quiet. "I've no reason to fire him," he said, gritting his teeth.

Rachel called. I let it go to voicemail.

"Don't listen to her," my mother said, clutching my father's arm. "She *has* been drinking."

"You can listen to me or not listen to me, but if he isn't fired immediately, I will take this public, starting with CCB." I started to leave, then returned. "And if anything happens to Alexander, I'll—"

"So *that's* what this is about?"

"If he falls off a roof, gets hit over the head with a two-by-six, steps on a nail, gets struck by lightning—if his mother gets hit by lightning—you'll have a major lawsuit. I'm not going to stand idle while you destroy my grandfather's company." I stormed away without a goodbye.

Rachel called. I picked up on the first ring.

"Where are you?" she asked, alarmed.

"I had to see my father, sweetie. Urgent business."

"At this hour?"

"Alexander's about to be fired and I'm not going to let that happen. You OK?"

"I'm in your bed. I can't sleep. You'll be home soon?"

"Yes. I'm on my way."

Chapter 12

Alexander Morgan

During coffee break the next morning Paul was boasting of his newest invention: A cigarette, that once lit, never goes out. "So you don't waste time lighting up every hour. Think of the money saved."

"That's the most ridiculous thing I've ever heard," Nick said, lighting a cigarette as if on cue. "It's when you light one up—that self-satisfied split second, when the world could be on fire, but you're calm as hell—that's when you actually think of shit. All the world's great inventions started like that. Like the Wright brothers. One Sunday afternoon, they was taking a break outside their garage, pissed that they hadn't had a day off in months. Wilbur lit a cigarette and exhaled toward the sky and that's when he got the bright idea of inventing the goddamned airplane. With an airplane under their belts, he says convincingly to his brother, they could finally afford to take off weekends and get out of the bike business once and for all. And Henry Ford, whose wife, as everyone knew, wouldn't allow smoking in the house, so one evening, he was outside stewing in his garden in the middle of all his tomato plants. He lit one up and right then and there got the bright idea of inventing the Model T. And Da Vinci, was pissed that he had to work four weekends in a row and couldn't go fishing with his buddies. On coffee break one Sunday afternoon, he was laying on his back on the goddamned grass, staring at the clouds; he lit one up and decided to paint the goddamned chapel ceiling instead of the foyer walls like he was supposed to."

"That was Michelangelo, you moron," Abe said.

"Maybe you should start smoking," I said to Paul. "So you can think of shit people actually need."

Nick offered Paul a cigarette.

"Give him the whole pack," I said. "Whatever happened to that snapper of yours?"

"It's almost done."

"*Almost done?* It takes two minutes to weld it together."

"I'm fine-tuning it."

"*Fine-tuning it?*"

Suddenly Phil slammed open his trailer door, heading straight toward us. He abruptly stopped, getting a telephone call.

"Must be Zachary," Walter said, watching Phil scribble notes on a scratch pad. "He ain't flappin' his arms up and down like a friggin' windmill, objectin' and complainin'."

"He better be careful with that envelope," Gary said, pointing to a green and white envelope, usually reserved to pay subcontractors, dangling from his front pocket.

"Ha!" Abe said. "Remember when Phil accidentally paid the wrong sub—in cash—before he'd done any work, and then he denied everything?"

"That'd be enough to get any of us fired," I said.

"And then telling Zachary that a gust of wind blew it away." Nick added, laughing.

Phil had barely clicked his phone, when he was approached by someone, looking like a subcontractor.

"Now there's a rare sight," Nick said. "A sub looking for money."

"And an even rarer sight," added Abe. "A sub not waving his arms up and down in anger."

"How about a Phil robot for your next invention," Abe said to Paul. "So we can pay the goddamned bills on time."

"His next invention?" I objected. "How can there be a next invention when there ain't never been a first?"

"So why ain't Phil payin' him?" said Walter. "And why ain't the sub pissed as hell?"

"That's how he is," I said. "Never taking the blame for nothing."

"Maybe he's laying one of us off," Gary said, looking directly at me.

"Not a good time to be layin' anyone off," said Walter. "Especially the kid. Two months before the holidays?"

"Companies do it all the time," Nick said, lighting another cigarette.

"So they don't have to pay no Christmas bonus," Paul added.

"When was the last time *we* got a goddamned bonus of any kind?" Nick asked.

"Phil's here to lay the kid off," said Gary. "Mark my words."

"Why would anyone mark your words?" Abe asked. "You've never been right about nothing."

"Are you kidding?" I said. "If he was laying me off, he'd be grinning from one end of his face to the other, jumping up and down like a friggin' baboon. He would've been here at six o'clock this morning. This would've been the highlight of his friggin' career."

"The kid's right," Walter admitted.

"Maybe *he's* being laid off and he has to give the envelope to himself?" Abe suggested.

"He'd even screw that up," I said.

"You don't lay someone off in the middle of the day," said Walter. "Unless he fucked up then and there."

I suddenly remembered my encounter with Mr. Hudson, my lunch at *The Edge*, and signing Paul's name for the compactor.

"Maybe he's giving us a bonus checks for all the times we saved his ass?" said Abe.

"Ain't no envelope big enough," Walter said.

The sub, or whoever he was, bid goodbye. The two shook hands. Phil approached us slowly, the envelope dangling in his pocket even more precariously; his eyes riveted on Walter. My phone vibrated. I didn't dare answer. It went to voicemail. Phil, hands shaking, handed Walter the envelope.

"What's this?" Walter asked. With a razor knife from his pocket, he slit open the envelope. "A check? Last week's overtime?"

"Two weeks' pay," Phil said, his voice cracking.

"*Two weeks' pay?* So why's my name on it?"

"It wasn't my decision," Phil said in a slightly stronger voice.

"Then *whose* decision was it?" Walter asked, finally realizing what was happening.

"Zachary's."

"Zachary's?" Walter whipped out his cell phone: "Zachary! What the fuck's goin' on! Call me!" Walter tore the check into pieces.

"That was stupid," said Phil.

"I'm goin' back to work until Zachary clears this up."

"You've been fired," retorted Phil, seemingly more confident. "By Zachary. And if you don't vacate the premise, you'll be arrested for trespassing. Zachary's orders. Is that what you want?" Phil asked reaching for his cell phone.

No answer.

Chapter 13

Joanna Turnus

I started the main course, Peking Duck, the day before (it needs 24 hours). Then Sunday morning I made the rest of the dinner: potstickers (with my own dough); egg rolls; shrimp fried rice (I didn't catch the shrimp nor grow the rice); and my grandmother's shark fin soup (I substituted swordfish for shark, which she wouldn't have approved, but times have changed). The soup was one of my favorite dishes growing up (my Scottish grandmother could best any native Chinese chef); and today, I'll often eat it as a meal itself, made with green chiles, cilantro, jalapenos, a spicy fish oil, bean sprouts, lemongrass, shitake mushrooms (although I absolutely love portabellas, only shitakes work) and of course, freshly caught swordfish.

I made my sweet and sour sauce slightly sweeter to compensate for the extra spicy shark fin soup (i.e., swordfish soup minus the fin). Every now and then I like a little symmetry in my life. Ha!

I didn't intend for all this food, but I like to cook, and Alexander likes to eat, and so does Rachel, although lately she's been eating like a bird.

Speaking of Rachel, she eagerly helped me set the table, smiling and singing as she brought the dishes poolside. She looked pretty in her khaki shorts and pink tank top, barely concealing her purple two-piece; giddy with excitement, her first time wearing a bikini (I gave it to her Memorial Day, hoping that she'd wear it during the summer, but here it was late-October).

I decided to have our dinner poolside underneath my A-frame canopy. (After remodeling the house shortly after I had moved in, I had enough leftover Tuscany stone—actually, a lot—to build a five-foot base on the long sides, keeping the other two sides open for the A-frame, which I then extended three feet with oak and topped with a retractable canopy. The oak matches the front exterior of my house and the stone matches my kitchen. I also built a small, but well-stocked bar.) And, needless to say, given the warm night with no rain in sight, I retracted the canopy.

Stan barked at Alexander's truck pulling into the driveway.

"He's not used to him," I said to Rachel.

"Neither am I," Rachel smiled. "Ha! I'm glad I'm not barking."

Alexander galloped toward us in dirty, sweaty work clothes. He hugged Rachel, then kissed me.

"You came straight from work?" Rachel giggled, plugging her nose.

"Why don't you take a quick dip before dinner?" I suggested. "But shower first. It's behind the A-frame."

Alexander sheepishly confessed that he forgot his swimsuit. "OK if I jump in with my underwear?"

"As opposed to?" I asked, hearing Rachel's heart skip a beat or two.

Alexander showered and then perched at the pool's edge. "How deep's the deep end?"

If I wasn't so hungry, I would've joined him, dinner or no dinner. "It's twelve feet everywhere," I said as he hit the water; "there's no deep end."

"The water's really warm?" he said when he surfaced, more as a statement than a question.

"Eighty-two degrees. I keep it open year-round."

"Even in winter?"

"That's what year-round means."

"Your third date with Alexander on the water," said Rachel, watching him alternate between dogpaddling and swimming on his back. "How's this going to end?" she asked with a touch of sarcasm.

"Don't worry sweetie, I'm not going anywhere."

Rachel's pleasant countenance suddenly disappeared. So typical. Her volatile moods were becoming more unpredictable and tougher to tolerate. Was it something I said? Did I trigger a long-harbored memory? Or perhaps she was jealous of Alexander and I?

But before I could ask what was bothering her, she began. "Last night I stopped for dinner at this nice restaurant," Rachel brushed away a tear. "Behind me sat this family celebrating a young woman introducing her new boyfriend. Everyone was happy, asking him all sorts of questions. I saw my wife someday doing the same, fully confident in his masculinity, nodding as he rubbed his stubbled chin at just the right moment, mulling each question, perfectly orchestrating hand movements, carefully enunciating the right syllable; everyone admiring his self-assuredness."

I waved Alexander in. I was hungry and the food was getting cold. "Sweetie, you have to get over her. She's moved on. And so must you."

Alexander flipped over, gulped water and squirted a long arc of saltwater. He helped himself up the ladder. On the deck, I handed him an oversized towel and an over-sized men's bathrobe (I'm sure he was relieved) and walked him to the A-Frame table. Rachel was sitting with her legs crossed, smiling.

"You should get a video camera like Walter's," Alexander said, kissing me. "Especially being out here alone at night."

"I can take of myself. But I do have a high-resolution camera on the house."

"So we have to behave?"

"Not necessarily!" I invited Alexander to sit next to me and Rachel across, while dishing everyone a plate.

"Joanna made everything," Rachel boasted. "Except the soy sauce and the sweet and sour sauce."

"I made the sweet and sour sauce, sweetie; like I always do."

Alexander wolfed down an egg roll and helped himself to a pot sticker, then another. "This is delicious. As good as any Chinese restaurant. How'd you learn to cook Chinese? From your mother? Is your mother Chinese?"

"*My mother?*" I asked, surprised at the question, surprised that anyone would insinuate that I had learned anything from my mother, especially about cooking.

"No, certainly not, although she wasn't exactly a bad cook—I've certainly had worse." I tried recalling a good meal that stood out, that was fondly ensconced in my memory, but there was nothing except foggy snippets of store-bought chicken pot pies, shake and bake, overdone steak, hamburger helper, soggy tuna casserole, and canned vegetables. "For my mother cooking was a chore—no different from vacuuming or dusting. She never had fun cooking or eating. And she never sang while she cooked."

"Like you always do," added Rachel cheerfully.

"My mother always sings while she cooks," Alexander said matter-of-factly, dipping what was left of his egg roll in the sweet and sour sauce.

"I like her already." I smiled at Alexander. "That says a lot about her."

"Then there's me," laughed Alexander. "Who can barely flip on a stove."

"You'll be easy to teach," I said, dishing the main course for Alexander and Rachel; pleasantly surprised that she was eating so much. "Cooking should be fun and enjoyable." I then told Alexander about my good friend Maria, a cooking aficionado if there ever was one. An inspiration, who taught me (at an early age) that cooking can be fun, a creative art, something to be enjoyed.

The word 'aficionado' perplexed Alexander, so I explained: "An aficionado teaches and inspires by example, mastering each dish's subtle nuances, infusing it with her own imprimatur. In another life she might have been a great novelist—a Márquez, Tolstoy, Hemingway, a Fitzgerald; a master chef with words... I met Maria freshman year in college during Christmas break, when I was hospitalized."

When Alexander asked why, I brushed him off, not exactly eager to tell him that I was in the psychological floor (after a suicide attempt), but Rachel abruptly informed him, not maliciously of course, but matter-of-factly, like everyone should have known, as I'm sure everyone does; and I guess that's OK for I just remembered that I had told Alexander about my talisman in my grandfather's boat. On the Lake. When we were alone. Although it's not something that I'm proud of.

"Maria was a second-generation Cuban immigrant," I continued, enjoying watching Alexander gobble seconds; "completing her nursing internship at Brigham and Women's. She really took a liking to me, at first not understanding why such a pretty girl (her words, not mine) would want to take her own life. After I explained, she opened up about her brother: a TG who was murdered in Havana. We became very close and every day she would share her homemade lunch with me, always bringing extra portions, relating in wonderful detail the intricate steps of Cuban cooking, weaving enthralling snippets of her grandmother, her mother, and especially her aunt 'the improviser', who would never follow a recipe exactly, tweaking and twisting, but only to a certain degree and always making it better, improving the dish and inspiring others to improvise. But only an aficionado can improvise to create something just as good or even better than the original.

"Maria's oxtail soup, always made with the freshest ingredients, can solve the meanest tempest. She also introduced me to Russian cooking. Her borscht is delicious, and you'd never know it was made with beets."

"Can't stand the suckers," said Alexander.

"Russian?" asked Rachel.

"Maria's grandfather was an engineer from Moscow, came to Havana for work, met a woman and settled in the capital. They passed their recipes down to Maria. One of her favorites, so simple but immensely satisfying, which I often make for dinner: fried eggs topped with salmon, caviar, fresh dill; served with a side dish of parsnips and sliced oranges.

"Maria inspired me to cook. She was my muse. My first year in law school I started cooking for friends. At first just a few, but as word quickly spread, more people came, so I always cooked for more, never knowing exactly how many people would show up. Every Sunday afternoon at two o'clock—a tradition, by the way, still going strong. I soon became one of the most popular women on campus. The school paper interviewed me. My weekly menu (along with the recipes) becoming a regular feature; and the University Press published my recipes as a book. The dinners were fabulous—often ethnic, lasting well into the evening; everyone eating, talking, laughing, and drinking, as if my kitchen was the only place in the world.

"I always experimented but I also had my requested standbys: Carbonaro, borscht, beef stroganoff, Peking Duck; always using fresh herbs and spices—basil, parsley, lemongrass, mint, tarragon—whatever the dish called for, making it visually and aromatically appealing. And on a cold snowy afternoon nothing was (and is) more comforting than my roasted lemon and garlic chicken, with mashed potatoes and tarragon butter, cornbread blueberry stuffing, and Brussels sprouts stuffed with nutmeg and halibut, which amazed everyone because no one knew that Brussel sprouts could be so good.

"Once a month I made Cuban, always adding a twist, a slight deviation, just like Maria's aunt, but always ending with Tres Leches, perfectly made with no deviations. It's one of my favorite desserts on the planet, and the main reason I jog every morning. There's nothing worse than a bad Tres Leches—it's not even edible—but nothing beats a really good one. And mine was the best—everyone said so, and as good as Maria's—she said so herself.

"Maria helped me to survive. She taught me that it's OK to be in the middle, that life doesn't always have to be black and white, that binary opposites suffocate and constrict, forcing people into predetermined delusions. And I inspired her to follow her real passion: cooking. After she finished her internship and got her nursing degree, she enrolled in Johnson & Wales and never looked back. (So because of me there's one less nurse in the world.) She was a great nurse, but a much better cook.

"Maria worked her way up in kitchens in Saugus and Medford, quickly becoming sous chef. Last year she opened her own restaurant in the Seaport District to great reviews. Every Wednesday I make it a point to work late in the city and stop at her restaurant, right at closing. She whips up something—usually seafood, usually scrod, one of her restaurant's specialties, selecting the fish herself—first thing every morning right from local fishermen—that's what makes her food so good: fresh ingredients locally bought, and locally grown vegetables. Everything made in-house, even the sauces and breads."

"You ain't no slouch yourself," noted Alexander.

I sighed. "She's one step above me. And she keeps getting better. I love watching her transform even an ordinary dish like meatloaf into a work of art."

"Your pot roast can give her a run for her money," added Rachel.

Alexander shook his head. "Never been one of my favorites."

"You've never had Joanna's," Rachel said. "It's absolutely out of this world."

"My mother was a pretty decent cook," Alexander said. "But her pot roast was always dry and bland—she said so herself."

"People lower their expectations because it's so ordinary. Since not much is expected, cooking *and* eating becomes a letdown instead of an invitation to be creative without losing sight of the dish's simplicity. I add several Cuban ingredients that give it a verve which it might not otherwise have (and some might even say, doesn't deserve). And a blueberry mango sauce that makes the meat melt in your mouth."

"You haven't made it in a while?" Rachel noted. "I've been craving it."

"You're right sweetie. And tomorrow's one of those rare Sundays without any guests. It'll be just Rachel and I."

"*Just Rachel?*" she teased.

"How about tomorrow afternoon then? A Sunday dinner: Cuban pot roast—oh I forgot, Alexander, you have to work?"

"Actually, we got a lot done today. Phil gave us tomorrow off."

"Wonderful! Dinner, tomorrow afternoon, two o'clock?"

Alexander dipped his half-eaten eggroll into the sauce gulping it in one bite. "So why didn't you become a chef like Maria and follow your friggin' passion? Perhaps open a restaurant together? I could see you two doing that."

"Someday I will. Someday when my foundation work is no longer needed."

"Don't stand on one leg waiting for that to happen," Rachel muttered.

"We've actually talked about it. We cook well together; our styles complement each other very well. We even decided on a name: *Dangling in the Moment*."

"I like that," Rachel nodded; "I like that a lot."

"What about a part-time catering business right now? Just make a little more during Sunday dinners. It'd be great for tailgating and shit."

"I can't take time away from my foundation. Not now." I got up, slipped off my black dress revealing my red bikini; the same one I had worn at the Lake.

"You know what happened the last time you wore that," said Alexander, a little worried.

I pulled him close and kissed him. "The farthest I'll swim is the edge of the pool. And only with you."

Rachel slipped off her blouse, folding it several times before placing it on the table. Then slowly and methodically removed her shorts. (If I didn't know any better, I would've suspected her of strip-teasing Alexander.) "No need to feel embarrassed, sweetie." I said, silently urging Alexander to shoot her a compliment.

Alexander kissed her forehead. "You're fuckin' beautiful." Then he skipped to the pool's edge. "Where's the friggin' diving board?"

"Too much of a *friggin'* liability."

"So how do you practice your jumping?"

I pretended a laugh, then followed Alexander into the water. When I surfaced Rachel was gradually easing in off the ladder steps. Then she dogpaddled toward me, keeping her head well above water.

"Rachel, if you want to be a woman you have to learn to live with wet hair."

"I am a woman."

"You know what I mean."

"I don't want to wash it tonight."

"My grandfather always said that water isn't refreshing until you completely dunk and swim along the bottom."

"I'm not a fish," she said, as Alexander surfaced between us, catching his breath.

"Is this a dream come true?" I asked. "Two women, at night, in bikinis, alone in a swimming pool?"

"Where were you two when I was in high school?" asked Alexander.

"Studying," I said.

"Chasing girls," Rachel replied.

We watched Alexander swim to the far end of the pool bobbing up and down like a loon on steroids.

"Joanna, I quit my job."

"What! Why? I thought we were going to fight this?"

"The writing's on the wall. Resigning on my own terms will make it easier to get another job, but if I'm fired, who would hire me, especially now? Maybe the Captain's right? Maybe I should do something else?"

"Sweetie, being a cop is what you've always wanted! You said so yourself so many times. Why are you giving up like this?"

"I'm not giving up. I'm just being realistic...This morning I asked the Captain if we could talk, away from the station, at a local coffeeshop. She wanted to wait until Tuesday, but I said no, that it was urgent. When she saw me, or, more accurately, when she saw who I really was, that I wasn't Bobby McNair—that I was Rachel—she gave me that same horrified look that my wife did. Maybe I should've warned her? At first, she wouldn't sit down, but I insisted on talking. She still wouldn't sit, so I stood up. I asked for a six-month unpaid leave of absence so I could fully transition and return to the force as Rachel McNair. I was surprised at my bluntness, at how calm I was. She scoffed, calling me a freak, working herself into a frenzy, saying that none of my colleagues would want to work with me, that they'd be too afraid that I wouldn't have their back, that my presence would sully our ongoing community involvement program. 'Find another precinct,' she said. 'And your Review will make that happen.'"

"She actually said that? Really? In public? Perhaps we can get some of the customers to corroborate?"

"I did one step better. I taped the whole conversation on my phone."

"You did what? What possessed you?"

"I knew that no matter what I said, the meeting on Tuesday wouldn't go my way. I just knew. I wanted some evidence."

"Wonderful sweetie."

Rachel yawned. "I have to go to bed."

"Can we talk about this? Now? It's important."

"I can barely keep my eyes open."

"Then, first thing in the morning?"

Rachel nodded.

"Why don't you sleep out here on a chaise lounge? That's why I bought them."

Rachel yawned again. "I need my bed tonight."

I kissed her on the cheek.

Rachel pulled herself up on the ladder and dried herself with an oversized towel; wrapped it around her and headed inside.

"What happened?" Alexander asked, swimming toward me. "You two have an argument?"

Alexander wasn't surprised at all when I told him what happened. "Maybe she should take a stab at something else? Perhaps HR?"

"General doesn't have an HR department."

"Yeah, no shit. And that's why we have Phil. What about your friggin' foundation?"

"It's just me and I don't earn a paycheck, so how could I pay someone else?"

"How about CCB?"

"No experience."

"She has lots of people experience. That's what really matters."

"I'll see what I can do."

Stan started barking.

"I thought I heard a car door." Alexander asked. "You expecting someone?"

I smiled at Alexander. "Just you."

Stan continued barking.

"There's lots of animals out here at night: deer, raccoons, skunks, foxes," I said. "They drive Stan nuts."

"Anything bigger than us that we should worry about?"

I laughed. "They're all harmless."

Alexander kissed me, loosening my bikini string. Rachel's bedroom light flipped on. I waited for it to flicker off, hoping that she'd sleep peacefully, hoping that tomorrow will be a new beginning. But it never did.

Chapter 14

Joanna Turnus

Rachel must have slipped into my office while I was on the phone, catching up on my emails, like I do every Sunday morning. She sat on the edge of my much-used (and unfortunately, worn-out sofa bed; a vestige from my law school days, which I can't seem to part with) painting her nails, plum red—not her best color.

It was 7.00 AM, terribly early for Rachel, especially on a Sunday.

She smiled when I got off the phone, chatting incessantly about her impromptu trip—her lively staccato voice exuding long-lost confidence—later that morning to Faneuil Hall to shop, buy some earrings, walk along the harborside in the rain, the Seaport District, then the North End for espresso. She invited me along, forgetting that I work every Sunday, finishing stuff from the week before and the week before that.

Rachel suddenly stood up and opened the French doors overlooking my pool, ushering in a warm breeze hinting of rain. "Did Alexander leave for work?" she asked. "I wanted to chat with him this morning and noticed his truck was gone."

"Chat about what?"

"Nothing really. Just wanted to thank him for all his support; it's been so unexpected."

"He really cares about you, sweetie; almost as much as I do." I then explained that his mother invited us to the 8.00 mass and then to brunch.

"So why didn't you go?" she asked in a tone of voice suggesting I had committed an egregious crime for letting Alexander go alone, that nothing was more important than meeting his mother. Indeed, Alexander had invited me, but I politely declined because of my work backlog; and to be honest, because I was worried about Rachel, more so than usual.

"And leave all this?" I said, throwing up my arms.

"You can take off a Sunday now and then."

"Actually, I can't, sweetie." I was surprised at the temerity of her tone, especially her knowing full well that I have to work every Sunday just to catch up. "And besides, I've already met his mother," I said, typing into my computer. "We've had lunch several times, and we get along quite well."

Rachel glanced at my oak bookshelves filled with rows and rows of books. "You've read all these?"

"Most," I quickly replied, glancing at her, pleasantly surprised by her question; the first time she had ever asked about my books. "And the rest I'm sure I will someday."

She pushed my bookcase ladder to the left, as far it would go, pulling out a book. "*Half of a Yellow Sun?*"

"It's wonderful."

"There's a movie?" Rachel asked, flipping through the pages.

"I haven't seen it."

While Rachel sat on the edge of my sofa bed reading, I escaped to the kitchen to make an impromptu breakfast of cantaloupe, strawberries, blueberries, fresh cut parmesan, and coffee. When I returned, Rachel was thoroughly engrossed in *Half of a Yellow Sun*; the first time I had ever seen her reading a book.

I placed the breakfast tray between us and sat next to her.

"The author has a lot to say," Rachel said.

"It's about a civil war. In Nigeria."

"I'm not reading it that way."

"Yes, I suppose you can read it on several levels. Why don't you take it with you, sweetie, stick it in your purse?"

"That's Ok. I'll read it later."

"My office door is always open. It's never locked. You're always welcome to come in and read, even when I'm working."

"I *have* snuck in a couple of times. It's the coziest room with your fireplace and the bright sunlight. One afternoon I started reading *Women in Love* and couldn't put it down. Ha! If ever there was a title for me: A woman still in love with her ex-wife and falling in love with a man."

I was anxious to chat about *Women in Love* and about D.H. Lawrence, one of my favorite authors, who was always comfortably ahead of his time, when she abruptly rose, kissed me goodbye, excited (and anxious) to be meeting her newfound boyfriend James in Faneuil Hall briefly before he headed into Logan.

She left for Faneuil Hall joyous—the happiest she had been in a long time.

Ideally, I like to cook my pot roast the night before, first letting it marinate in Maria's mojo (adding a touch of blueberries, although Maria adamantly insisted that blueberries weren't necessary, that they would be subdued by the sour oranges, but I disagreed: the blueberries give it a sweetness that it might not otherwise have; and they can hold their own vis-a-vis the garlic. By the way, I think that was our only disagreement regarding cooking although Maria did compliment me that her aunt probably would have done so) but with so much happening yesterday, I just couldn't. So I was a tad dismayed that my first-time pot roast for Alexander was not going to be as good. I thought about making barbequed meatloaf instead or perhaps lemon garlic chicken, which I hadn't made in a while (and perfect for such a gloomy, misty day) but decided to go with the roast, welcoming the same-day challenge.

But instead of oxtail soup, I made portabella mushroom soup, not because it was easier (I always like a challenge) or because I had a bevy of portabellas in the bough of maple trees behind my basketball court that I was anxious to use, but that I had suddenly remembered Alexander raving about the portabella mushroom soup at the Old Post Inn, that it was the best he ever had, the night of my confession and I was determined to best it. And besides, with the spotty rain steadying, it was perfect weather for mushroom soup. (My secret is to add an eighth of a sour orange, an eighth of a granny smith apple, and a splash of blueberries. Although it sounds overpowering, it really isn't: somehow it brings out the flavor of the portabella mushrooms like nothing else can. And Maria approved!)

I was in a girlish mood—excited that this would be Alexander's first of many Sunday dinners (hopefully), although today it would be just the two of us, with Rachel promising to arrive for coffee and Tres Leches. I wore a puffy-sleeved, white blouse, and a red plaid skirt with a pretty, matching scarf. Flirty and playful, yes, although most women would laugh that I looked like a priggish schoolgirl. But so what?

At two o'clock the doorbell rang. It was Alexander, exactly on time, looking really cute in jeans, a black causal jacket, and a black tee-shirt. A cool, heavy rain was falling. I led him through my kitchen and then into the A-frame for a poolside, before-dinner Scotch (another inheritance from my grandfather, although it took a while before I had actually acquired a taste for it. 'Genes,' my grandfather always teased, whenever we would enjoy a Scotch together, 'it's all in the jeans').

A distant splash of thunder.

I made us each a Scotch listening to Alexander update on his sisters, his mother, his mother's fiancé, his mother's wedding plans; nodding occasionally, thinking about Rachel, wondering if she was OK, if she was still at Faneuil Hall having coffee with James, if she had found any earrings, if her mood was still good, if it was raining in Boston.

Suddenly my phone rang. I immediately answered anticipating Rachel. But it was work. I promised to call back after dinner. Alexander and I clinked our glasses, excited for an afternoon together. But I was becoming increasingly worried about Rachel. I decided to call her, before dinner, just to hear her voice.

"How are you sweetie?" I asked, putting the phone on speaker, knowing that Alexander wouldn't mind.

"I'm at Faneuil Hall," she answered ebulliently, somewhat putting me at ease. "I bought a pretty pair of turquoise dangle earrings!"

"How was coffee with James?"

"Absolutely wonderful! I can't wait for you to meet him."

"Send some pictures!"

"He invited me to Amsterdam with him next month! And we're meeting for dinner when he flies home Wednesday night."

"Why don't you take him to Maria's; it's the best in town."

"Hold on. My mother's calling. I suppose I have to answer."

"Just let it go to voicemail and enjoy your afternoon, sweetie."

"If I don't answer, she'll keep bugging me all day."

"Let it go to voicemail."

"Gotta go! Give Alexander a hug for me and save me a *big* piece of Tres Leches!"

"She sounds great?" said Alexander.

I tersely nodded.

My phone rang. Rachel calling back? Perhaps her mother? But it was work. Too important to ignore and too important to let go to voicemail, I excused myself to take it in my office, worried that it might take longer than either of us wanted.

Alexander popped in once. Then again.

Finally finished, I took Alexander's hand and led him into the kitchen, asking him to open a bottle of red wine: Ménage à Trois Merlot 2008, while I placed the food on the table and dished our plates.

"It has a lush bouquet with an unsuspecting loftiness," Alex said. "A tad conceited but well-deserved. Unabashedly deceitful, delectably hinting of berries fully ripened, tantalizing with a peppery seductiveness."

"You didn't even taste it yet!"

"That way I'm not biased in making my review."

"Maria's looking for a good wine steward."

"I only do red," Alexander said pouring me a glass. "If that works for her. Although I suppose I could say the same stuff for white wine?"

"It's delicious," I said, sipping the wine, as I knew it would be. And there's nothing peppery."

"Berries?"

I shook my head. My phone rang. A short yes/no answer. And then again. This time I let it go to voice mail, apologizing to Alexander that this is why I work on Sundays.

"You need a friggin' secretary."

"How about a *friggin'* deal: No friggin' phones during friggin' dinner?"

"Does that include friggin' dessert?"

"If you'd friggin' like."

"You OK?" he asked, feeling my forehead.

I shut my phone off, handing it to Alexander. "Hide it in the kitchen drawer."

"What good is that? You know where it is."

"I promise I won't use it until Rachel's home."

"Can I get that in writing?"

Alexander devoured his portabella mushroom room. "This is the best I've ever had!"

"You said that about the Inn's."

"I hadn't had yours."

"I added a touch of chili sauce and a touch of Cuban sour orange, not enough to overpower the mushrooms; in fact, you hardly notice it, and only if you're looking."

Alexander also praised my pot roast. When I apologized that it would've been a lot better had I started cooking the night before, he was befuddled how such a delicious dish could have been any better. He loved my black beans (I made them myself), my Cuban bread (which I also made); and couldn't get enough of the fried plantains (his first time), eating them like candy, and of course Maria's mojo, which was quite exceptional even by her standards. But he didn't like the taste or the texture of the Cassava—which admittedly takes some getting used to—especially after I explained that eaten raw it's lethal, so it has to be thoroughly cooked.

"Then why bother?" Alexander asked. "Especially with so much other shit available?"

I explained that Cassava has always been one of my favorites, and like so many things in life, has to be transformed to be palatable, but then again it was and always will be Cassava.

We talked about the much-needed rain, his work, my work, and practically everything else except Rachel. To be honest, I was glad to have a break from her, and I'm sure Rachel was delighted that I hadn't called her in 1 hour and nineteen and a half minutes.

With Alexander having thirds of everything (except the Cassava) and me eating at my usual snail's pace, we finished at about the same time.

"How about a walk?" I suggested, pushing my dish aside.

"In the rain?"

"It'll be fun." I stood up and took his hand. "Come on! We'll have dessert later. And no cell phones. Just you and me and an umbrella."

"Stan?"

"He doesn't like the rain."

"What's your record for being without a cell phone?"

"I just bested it halfway through dinner."

"You having withdrawals? I noticed your hands shaking."

I kissed him and led him outside into the cool, soothing rain, past my pool, the basketball court, past the mushrooms ready for picking, into the woods behind my house; listening to the flickering rain, the rhythmic crunching of the fallen leaves; the canopied trees, ablaze with bright red and yellow, shielding us, brightening our path as if the day were clear and the sun bright, my head softly on his shoulder.

Perhaps indeed my hands were shaking during dinner? For I was nervous about what I was about to say, nervous about Alexander's reaction—nervous about my own reaction. I had postponed this as long as possible (although I almost confessed this at the Inn, and perhaps would've had not I left so early.) If we are to be married (which we will someday—I know that) he needs to hear this, and to hear it from me. For if the shoes were reversed, I would like to know, although I can honestly say it wouldn't make any difference.

"Joanna, most couples discuss this sooner or later," Alexander said unexpectedly, just as I was about to confess, but with such tenderness, that I squeezed his hand, pleasantly surprised to hear us referred to as a couple. We continued walking, listening to the rain. "It's natural to ask," Alexander said. "Every couple discusses this at some time—have you ever had sex with anyone? I mean before me?"

I laughed, not at the question—just that it was unexpected, although Alexander was right: every couple discusses this sooner or later; and to be honest, I was wondering the same about him. "I've only had sex with you, Alexander Morgan. Something I don't intend changing."

"Really? Why?"

"*Why?*" I stopped and looked at him. "I don't know *why*. Maybe I've been working too hard or not hard enough—I never sat down to figure it out—it's not something I brag about, it's just me right now—how many women have you slept with Alexander Morgan?"

"Guess?"

"If it's that many, I don't want to know."

"Before I met you. One."

"And since?"

"People assume I sleep with every woman I meet."

"Do you?"

"No."

"Then why would they assume that?"

Alexander shrugged. "Looks, I guess."

"Who was she? The one who never laughed?"

"We were engaged."

"What? You never told me that."

"I broke it off."

"Why?"

"She had absolutely no emotions. At her grandfather's funeral, *I* was crying, and I hardly knew the bastard, but she was cold as cement. I told her it's OK to cry and show emotion—I just couldn't go through life married to someone like that."

"And then you met me!"

He pulled me close; my head nestled on his shoulder. We walked in silence. I was tempted to never mention what I needed to say (after all, the effects would barely be noticeable and he would never know otherwise), to keep walking in the cool, peaceful rain, my head softly on his shoulder. But I couldn't live with myself if I wasn't completely honest—that's just who I am.

"Alexander, there's something I have to tell you. Something you must know about me."

"Christ, I thought I knew all your secrets?"

"There's no secrets Alexander. Everything's out in the open." *Or soon will be.* "I can't be intimate unless I'm completely honest. You have to accept me for who I am, warts and all. And, unfortunately, I've a lot more warts than most. I can't pretend I'm someone else and then have you love me for someone I can never be."

"What are you trying to say? Are you seeing someone else?"

"No. And I've no intention."

"Then what is it?"

I looked away, so tempted to never mention this again. "Alexander...I'm talking a very slight estrogen blocker...and an extremely light dosage of testosterone."

"What? What did you just say?"

Perhaps I had gone too far? Perhaps there really wasn't a need to mention this, especially with the effects barely noticeable. But if I hadn't said anything, I couldn't live with myself, knowing full well that he loves me for someone I'm not. I felt relieved when I told him, even more so than after my confession at the Old Post Inn. "It's called survival, Alexander. If I hadn't said anything, you'd never notice; it's such a light dosage. The effects are barely noticeable."

"Dosage? Effects? *What* effects? What're you talking about!"

"A very slight decrease in breast size. Slightly more body hair which I can shave off. My skin won't be as smooth, but I can use lotion. More energy. Lower blood pressure. It's not enough to affect libido, or even getting pregnant."

"I can't believe this!"

"If I hadn't told you wouldn't have noticed anything. I can only be intimate with you if I'm completely honest." I looked Alexander directly in his eyes. "And I do want to be honest with you."

"So this is supposed to make *me* want to be intimate with you?"

My eyes started watering. "No one's forcing you to be intimate. No one's forcing you to stay. I've told you everything about me without sugar coating. If that's not acceptable, if that's not good enough, then leave and go find your normal woman."

"Fine," he said, briskly walking away. "Maybe I'll just do that."

Chapter 15

Alexander Morgan

I wasn't gone that long—twenty minutes, a half hour at most—when it dawned on me that perhaps this was what Rachel was trying to warn me about? But if so, why didn't she tell me directly, instead of beating around the bush? But even if I had known, my reaction would have been exactly the same. Did she really expect me to jump up and down for joy? If the shoes were reversed, I couldn't imagine telling Joanna, or any woman for that matter, that I was taking female hormones, growing my breasts and expect her to joyously embrace me.

Almost to her house I turned back. Call it a guilty conscience, for I've never left a woman crying. I hurried, tripping over an extended branch. She was clumped on the ground, in the same spot; although by now, I had assumed she would have walked, or ran, all the way to Lexington. I helped her up. She was rain-soaked and cold. We embraced. I'm not sure how or why, but we kissed, falling to the ground. The crumpled leaves, the naked tree branches, shiny and oily, vibrant with moss. The heavy, steady rain. Wrapped in each other's arms. Warm water streaming off her forehead. The hard ground softened by the rain.

We fell asleep in each other's arms. It was dusk when we awoke. Still together. The rain seemed to be intensifying and the thunder seemed to be louder. I kissed her forehead. We smiled at each other, as if meeting for the first time.

"Rachel!" Joanna exclaimed, suddenly springing up. "I'm sure she's back by now."

We dressed and ran to the house, finding the door unlocked.

"Rachel? Rachel?" Joanna called going room to room; our concern escalating with each non-answer.

Returning to the kitchen empty-handed, I handed Joanna her phone.

"Oh my god! Oh my god! Oh my god!!" Joanna screamed listening to her messages. "Oh my God! I can't believe this!" She took my hand and raced to the garage. Before I could ask, we were racing up the driveway in Joanna's Lexus; she speed-dialing Rachel: "Answer the phone, Rachel! Rachel! Answer! Damn it!"

Not even a mile away—or maybe it was longer?—Joanna pulled alongside a heavily wooded area, calling for Rachel, running deep into the thick, slippery mist, with me following, trying my best to keep up. She anticipated every boulder, every fallen tree, every unexpected twist and turn, as if she knew where to go, slipping occasionally on the rain-soaked leaves, quickly righting herself, not stopping until we had entered a clearing bordered by bare oak trees, their naked branches bowing and pointing towards each other.

Joanna screamed when she found Rachel slumped against a tree, her wrists cut, her clothes bloodied; crying hysterically, wrapping herself around Rachel, slumping to the ground.

Chapter 16

Joanna Turnus

Some letters try to exonerate, but let's face it, there's nothing you can say to exonerate. Some letters beg forgiveness, although the letter isn't about forgiveness. Some letters blame, as if you could pinpoint a cause, as if you knew, as if there was only one, but the exact cause is often unknown, the reasons diffuse. Some letters try to take control, the first opportunity to say what you want, to even presume consequentiality. Thoughts flow quickly and lucidly, or so you think, but it's a false seduction. Time stands still, becomes obtuse, tantalizing you with an inflated sense of self-worth. For both author and reader, the letter gestates a tyranny of guilt and self-doubt, rendering each more susceptible and determined. The letter unites and separates, diminishes and strengthens, simplifies and complicates.

Initially, I wasn't going to read it. After all, I knew what it said. In fact, I knew every word. Even so, I was struck by its temerity, its self-assuredness, its self-satisfying finality, its almost-convincing self-worth, its exoneration:

> Forcing me to be a man was like asking someone to be a nuclear engineer who knew nothing of the subject, only because society needed one, and only to please others. No one asked me before I was born, no one asked when I was young. Everyone assumed that just because I was born a male, I would be happy and content, as if I had a choice.
>
> I don't care if there's an afterlife, but if so or if I'm born again or some stupid thing like that, then I ask God that

since He screwed me up in this life, that in the next I'm *either* male or female but not both and with no desire to be the other.

And for everyone who never could accept me—my very existence disrupting your peace, your normalcy, embarrassing you, causing discomfort and loathing, blurring your God-given distinction between male and female—I'm glad that you are finally released from me, that you never have to see me again, that you can go on with your lives, as if I never existed.

I don't want any ceremony. I don't want anyone to know about me. I don't want anyone to know that I cried or listened or sang or laughed.

Joanna and Alexander, I am sorry. That sounds so terribly stupid. Doesn't it? But I hope one day you can forgive me and that we meet again in a peaceful, happy place. I pray for forgiveness and acceptance.

And please don't feel sad. I'm finally happy now. I know that.

Why did I find happiness and Rachel didn't? Why does this wonderful man love me for who I am? Why did everyone who really mattered to Rachel—wife, friends, family, reject her, leaving her without anything to hold onto, without a life raft, without any hope?

Chapter 17

Alexander Morgan

I'm sure it was the raw, abrasive finality, but initially, Joanna thought that *she* had slit Rachel's wrists. That *she* had cut her hair. Obviously, I was with her the whole time, save for 20 minutes or so, and even if not, Joanna's the last person on Earth that anyone would have suspected, never mind accused. But if you ask me, Rachel's death was pre-ordained, like watching a chess match unfold; early moves made later moves inevitable. Go back and change any one and Rachel would still be alive.

The doctors insisted that Joanna spend three weeks in a psychiatric ward—yeah, she was that bad: grief, remorse, anger, guilt, despair, all knitted together. I visited Joanna every night after work, and by the end of the first week, she was talking, recognizing me, happy to see me; slowly becoming aware (and accepting) of what had happened, although she still blamed herself. Of course, I insisted otherwise— that she did everything possible and then more.

Sure, I could've brought food in from the market, or had it catered from Maria's restaurant, but I decided to cook for Joanna every night, knowing that she'd appreciate that more.

Easier said than done.

At first it was hard, and to be honest not enjoyable (like learning how to play golf). I spent the first weekend in Joanna's kitchen teaching myself (a crash course if there ever was one) throwing away my mistakes yet learning from them (mostly what not to do). I began with easy shit like barbecued pork chops and chicken, shake and bake, and sloppy joes. Then, after some early bombs, cooking actually became enjoyable, and the disasters fewer and farther between. Like following a set of blueprints (so much so that there's no excuse for a bad cook, other than not following directions, using the wrong proportions, skimping on the ingredients or trying to show off by improvising). Of course, having every appliance imaginable at my disposal in Joanna's kitchen, and every friggin' cookbook ever written certainly made it easier.

My first attempt at something more innovative (and creative) was a relative success, at least according to Joanna: grilled meatloaf with homemade barbecue sauce, garlic mashed potatoes, and carrots (no friggin' dessert; I haven't mastered baking yet, and probably won't for a while). I also made mushroom soup. (I always assumed that making soup was easy, but I found it more intricate and time-consuming since all the ingredients must blend just right.)

Joanna loved everything, especially my homemade sauce, saying that the smaller details are just as important, if not more so than the bigger stuff—although I think she liked the effort more than the end result—bragging to everyone who'd listen what a good cook her boyfriend was, although I insisted otherwise. And no this wasn't just false modesty: The meatloaf, although a big step for me, was a mundane recipe meticulously followed, but in the hands of a friggin' aficionado like Joanna, it would've been brilliant.

During dinner, I decided to buy Joanna an engagement ring. I snapped a selfie of us, then brought it to a local jeweler, who was able to correctly guess Joanna's ring size. (I had to sell my truck to pay for it—but no big deal, I've already started saving for a down payment on another, although this time I'll probably buy used.) Sure, there'll be future tantrums, she'll swim away again (it has to be in her blood)—perhaps on the alter we should pledge to stay away from the water, and perhaps move to Phoenix—and yeah, there'll be fights and arguments where we'll want to kill each other (hopefully not literally) but I refuse to let the inevitable determine the present.

After we had finished dessert, Joanna told me of a strange and disconcerting (her words) visit that afternoon from Rachel's mother. Strange, because it was her first visit, and the first time that Joanna had met her, despite countless invitations and a standing invitation for Sunday dinner (although once she had met Rachel's father accidentally while she and Rachel were out for breakfast). Rachel's mother refused to accept Rachel as a woman and absolutely detested Joanna for criminally enabling her (the mother's words). Joanna was amazed by how much Rachel (as a woman) looked like her mother—maybe that was the real reason for the mother's anger?

And disconcerting because this time the mother was contrite, for once not dishing out blame. Apparently suffering from a guilty conscience, she wanted to atone by setting the record straight; at least that's what she said.

Joanna began explaining: "The mother had called Rachel just before we sat down for dinner Sunday. She said that Rachel was initially giddy, talking non-stop just like a schoolgirl about some stupid earrings that she had bought."

"*Why did she call?*"

"I don't know. She didn't say and I didn't ask."

Joanna, quite emotional, then repeated the conversation verbatim:

"I met someone," Rachel said, excitedly.

"Really? That's great! She'll be just what you need. Maybe she'll snap you out of—"

"I met a man."

Silence.

"I'd like to bring him home to meet—"

"A man?" the mother screamed. "What do you mean you met a man? And bring him home—Do you think *that* would make me happy?"

"You've been in denial for a long time about—"

"I'm in denial? What about my needs? I raised a son and did a damn good job at it."

"Denial doesn't change who I am."

"If you want to dress like a woman and live the gay lifestyle, wait until after I'm gone. It would kill me to see you in a dress, or worse, with another man. Is that what you really want?"

"Is Dad there?"

"You think he wants to speak with you? He's even more heartbroken than me. You've aged us beyond our years. You can call yourself Rachel or whoever the hell you want, but that will never change who you are. I want my son back." The mother sobbing clicked the phone.

Joanna was surprised at the mother's honesty, not glossing over any detail no matter how brutal. But it was too little and too late. "The effect's the same. Perhaps worse," was all Joanna could say.

"I think you're too hard on her. If I were her and my son was growing boobs and began to look like me, I'd be shocked and angry."

Joanna had that same look on her face as that afternoon on the Lake, just before she strapped on her swimsuit and jumped into the water, except that this time, thankfully, she couldn't go anywhere. "If the mother had taken the time to find out who she really was instead of who she wanted her to be, she wouldn't have been so surprised."

I decided to officially propose the last night of Joanna's hospital stay. Sure, I could've proposed at the Old Post Inn, Faneuil Hall, or even Carson Beach, but I wanted to make a statement and what better place to make a friggin' statement than a high 'suicide-watch', psychiatric ward. That night I had made Joanna's Cuban pot roast, along with her Mojo (the week before I did a trial run for my mother and sisters and they raved about it) but it was several steps below Joanna's, we both knew that—although she insisted otherwise.

When we finished dinner, I presented her with an over-sized box, wrapped in Christmas paper.

"Why'd you even bother wrapping it?" she asked, laughing at my not exactly stellar performance. She shook the box. "Ahha! I know what it is!"

"How could you possibly know by just shaking it?"

"Because if the shoes were reversed and I was giving you what I think you're giving me, I'd wrap it exactly the same, then tape it to the inside of an oversized box, so you'd think it was something else. But once I put it on, Alexander Morgan, I will never, ever take it off. But first, I must tell you something."

What now? She wants a sex change? She fell in love with another woman? She wants me to become a woman?

Joanna laughed, noticing my alarm. "No worries. Actually, it's mostly good news with a tad of bad news. First, the bad news, although after hearing, you might reconsider giving me what's in the box?"

"Then, give me the good news first."

"I prefer bad news first; get it over with. Alexander, I've never lied to anyone, but I did lie to you—once. I had to."

"Is this the good news or the bad news?"

"The bad news, although it's really not that bad. Yes, I lied to you, but I promise that I will never, ever lie again." She took my hand. "Do you remember what I said about my father's will?"

"That you disinherited yourself or something?"

"I lied."

"Huh?"

"When I'd first met you, I had feelings that I hadn't had in a long time, despite not expecting anything; I mean after all the stuff Walter had said."

"What stuff?"

"It doesn't matter."

"You can't say that and then not talk about it."

"None of it's true, and I refuse to sanction his lies. Obviously, he doesn't know you. So many guys chase after my money—my father's money—like *I* don't even exist."

"Is that what you lied about?"

"I resigned as General's attorney. I quit the company—I would have a long time ago if it wasn't for my grandfather. My father can keep General and do whatever he wants, as long as he doesn't touch the will. That means there's no conflict of interest when you run for AFL-CIO president. I'll get an annual stipend, twice my salary."

"You never talked about this—at least with me? So how could you have lied about it?"

"Alexander, I didn't cut myself off from my father's will: That's what I lied about."

"What? I don't understand?"

"There's nothing to understand. I might be an honest friggin' bastard—but not a stupid one."

"I don't get it.

"I will explain, but first, why'd you come back that Sunday afternoon?" she asked, with flirting big brown eyes. "In the rain, in the woods?"

"The house was locked."

Joanna laughed, unwrapping the box and immediately slipped on the ring. "This is absolutely beautiful!! And it fits perfectly! How'd you know my ring size?"

"I'm good at guessing."

"Like I said, Alexander, once I put it on, I'll never take it off."

I apologized that the ring wasn't as big as I had wanted, that it was all I could afford, that I had been saving, and hopefully I'll (soon) be able to upgrade. (I didn't tell about selling my truck, although I guess I will have to eventually.)

"I absolutely love it. It's perfect Alexander, just as it is. And please don't ever upgrade." She stretched her long, graceful fingers in admiration. "Alexander, I didn't disinherit myself. Everything's in a trust fund accessible in five years, just when you're elected AFL-CIO president. I'm sorry I lied to you—my first and last time—but I needed to be sure that you're interested in me for who I am, warts and all."

"You do have a lot of warts."

"You're about to marry a very rich broad Alexander; can you handle that?"

"Even if you were the poorest woman on Earth, I'd still marry you."

"Yes, I know that. Woman, though, right? You did say woman?"

"As a matter of fact, yes."

"Good. Now about our wedding date."

"Just out of curiosity—what do you anticipate wearing to our wedding?"

"This neat tuxedo with subtle grey pinstripes," she giggled. "With a long, classy tail. Do you think I should wear a top hat? I'll take it off during mass." She knelt down beside me. "Please!"

I frowned.

"Just kidding." She kissed me. "What would you like me to wear, Alexander Morgan?"

"I was thinking a dress. A wedding dress? White? Traditional?"

"Traditional? Me?"

"It *is* our wedding."

"OK, OK. And for the rehearsal dinner I have this beautiful, high-cut, black lacey dress—prim and proper."

"And the bridesmaids? *They* will be bridesmaids?"

"Of course, I wouldn't have it any other way."

"Joanna, I'd like my mother to be my best man."

"You can't. First of all, this is a traditional wedding, and the groom—that's you—has a best *man*; that's what best *man* means: a man. And besides, I already asked your mother to be my maid of honor."

"What? You barely know her? And how'd you know I was going to propose?"

"I'm good at guessing...I do have one small favor?"

I frowned. "You want me to wear a wedding dress?"

"If that's what you want, Alexander Morgan." She giggled. "But would it be white?"

"I'm going with a tuxedo. And you can't technically wear a white dress?"

"I've only had sex with my husband, so I can wear whatever color I want; and besides, that's an old wives' tale."

"So what's your favor?"

"Alexander, can we have the wedding as soon as possible?"

"Why?"

She smiled, kissing me. "Why do you think?"

About the Author

When I was younger, I cursed God for my long, sleepless nights, nights that seemed like days, days that seemed like months, not knowing if I was male or female. But now I'm thankful to be non-binary, for it has given me a creative edge, a humility, a sense of humor, the willingness to listen to the rain, and a desire to help the marginalized. My previous (nonfiction) book *Rebuild: The Economy, Leadership, and You: A Toolkit for Builders of a Better World*, offers a hopeful recipe for tackling our interconnected crises by reimagining ourselves, our organizations, and our economies. Just like being male and female has enabled me to become a more compassionate human being, writing both fiction and nonfiction has enabled me to become a better writer, teacher, listener, and parent. I live in Eau Claire, Wisconsin, with my son Patrick, two cats, and a dog, where I teach economics at the University of Wisconsin-Eau Claire.

Acknowledgements

To my children, Elizabeth, and Patrick: our lives are forever interconnected. Your zest for life vitalizes me and inspires me to make the world better for you and your children. You have taught me so much. I love your curiosity, humor, and compassion for diversity. My novel, that you were forever (or at least so it seemed) inquiring when I would finish, is finally in print!

Charles Wilber, Larry Marsh, and Chuck Craypo of the University of Notre Dame, for believing in my fiction writing when no one else did.

The 'lunch bunch' at the University of Notre Dame: Carol Wambeke, Augusto de la Torre, Marie and Scott Vander Linde. We came from different parts of the world, connected, and became life-long friends.

Tim Crain, the first of my close friends to whom I confessed. We remain close. Thanks!

Jeanne Charbonnet. We met by chance on a flight from Paris; two saucy rebels who became spiritual soulmates. Thanks for being you! I'm glad we're on the same journey!

Sharon Heinz: your counseling, wisdom, and belief in Jack Reardon gave me hope during my darkest days.

My good friend and *Rebuild* co-author Graham Boyd. A chance meeting in London developed into a great friendship. I'm happy to say that our second book is in the works.

And finally, the gang at Evolutesix, especially Jhonny who did the typesetting, and Niki who designed the cover. Thanks!